SWORD
OF
FIRE

SWORD
OF
FIRE

Book One of The Justice War

Katharine Kerr

DAW BOOKS, INC.
DONALD A. WOLLHEIM, FOUNDER
1745 Broadway, New York, NY 10019
ELIZABETH R. WOLLHEIM
SHEILA E. GILBERT
PUBLISHERS
www.dawbooks.com

For Alis Rasmussen

acknowledgments

Many thanks to St Michael's Salle des Armes for their excellent demos of rapier technique when the goal is mayhem, not sport.

And many thanks to Steve Gordon for all his help with computer matters!

PART 1

ELDIDD AND THE WESTLANDS
1428

Never loose an arrow with your eyes shut.

—*Westfolk proverb*

CHAPTER 1

UP IN A HIGH tower chamber, Alyssa vairc Sirra stood at a lectern and studied a massive book of ancient chronicles. A shaft of sunlight, pale from the encroaching fog, fell through the window onto the page. Now and then she looked away from the passage she was memorizing and glanced out at the view. She could see down to Aberwyn's fine new harbor and the Southern Sea beyond, dark blue water, just flecked with white caps in the last light of the day. Soon, she realized, it would be too dark to read.

"Lyss! Lyss!" Gasping for breath, Mavva flung herself into the chamber. "You've got to come. Now!"

Alyssa looked up from the book. Mavva's long dark hair had slipped from its clasp. It hung in tendrils around her face, normally so pale, now flushed and red.

"Why?" Alyssa said. "What's so wrong? And you shouldn't run up the stairs like that. No wonder you're all out of breath."

"You don't understand. He's dying. Cradoc the bard."

Alyssa slammed the chronicle-book shut.

"Let me just get my surcoat. I'll come with you!"

With their red students' surcoats flapping over their skirts and tunics, the two women hurried down the long spiral staircase. They ran out into the main courtyard of the United Scholars' Collegia in

Aberwyn, where they were studying in residence. The news had spread as Mavva had passed by, it seemed, because some thirty other students, men and women both, were milling about on the grassy lawn near the front gates of the scholars' preserve. A pair of chaperones, older women dressed in black, fluttered at the mob's edge and called out cautions. A dark-haired lad with the pale orange surcoat of Wmm's Scribal Collegium over his breeches and shirt hurried to join them.

"Here's Alys!" Rhys, Mavva's betrothed, called out. "What shall we do, go up to the dun?"

"That's where I'm bound," Alyssa called back. "If we want to see him fairly treated, we'd best all go."

The pack followed her out of the gates into the streets of Aberwyn, dim with the early twilight of a damp spring day. Already the lamplighters were out working, one to steady a ladder while the other climbed up to light the wicks of the oil lanterns from his coil of smoking fuse. Shopkeepers stood yawning at their doors; townsfolk hurried home with baskets of food from the marketplace or trotted out on one last errand. Every now and then a fine coach and four clattered down the narrow streets and made the students jump back against the shopfronts.

As they panted up the last steep hill, other students and the merely curious joined them from taverns or public squares, calling out the news to those still behind them. No one could believe it, that Gwerbret Ladoic would go so far as this, to let a true bard starve himself to death before his gates.

"Every bard in Eldidd will be singing his shame in a fortnight," Mavva said.

"If it takes that long," Alyssa said. "The news will go out with the mail coaches, I'll wager."

The grand dun of the gwerbrets of Aberwyn stood on the highest hill in town, as befitted the dwelling of one of the most important noblemen in the land. A wall of worked tan stone set it off from the city, but its cluster of towers and brochs stood so tall that you could see them, pointing up like hands, over the wall. Some of the towers bore a conical roof, covered in slate tiles, in the new courtly style, and glass caught the setting sun in every window. A fortune, that dun had cost the Western Fox clan, and townsfolk grumbled that bribes from the gwerbret's law courts had paid for it all.

Just outside the main gates huddled a crowd of some hundred persons, but they kept a respectful distance from Cradoc, who was sitting cross-legged on the ground and slumped against the wall. Under his dirty gray breeches and a shirt as loose as a shroud, he was so ghastly thin, all bone and skull's grimace, his skeletal fingers clutched round his harp, that Alyssa wondered how he managed to hold his head upright. Kneeling beside him were his two young apprentices, both in tears, and the grim-faced journeyman who'd sworn to take his place when the end came.

"Not one sign of the gwerbret and his wretched heir," Rhys muttered. "May the gods curse them!"

"Hush!" Alyssa snapped. "You'll get yourself transported to the Desolation for saying things like that."

Behind them the crowd swelled steadily. It filled the street, spilled out into the long carriage drive round the dun walls, but everyone kept silent, barely breathing, it seemed. Alyssa felt them as a huge hand pressing at her back, driving her forward. She moved close enough to see Cradoc clearly—the pale gray hair, plastered to the all-too-prominent skull; the eyes, pools of unseeing shadow. One of the apprentices dipped a linen napkin into a jug of water, then held it to his master's lips. For some days now Cradoc had been too weak to drink from a cup. The bard's mouth stayed shut. With a wail, the 'prentice burst out keening and flung the napkin to the cobbles.

"He's gone!" the journeyman shouted. "Look you at Aberwyn's justice!"

The crowd roared. The keening began, high and musical, sobbing and wailing as everyone began to sway, back and forth, back and forth. Alyssa keened with them; she linked her arms with Mavva on one side and Rhys on the other as they rocked, bound by grief. Their leader was dead, their leader had fallen in a battle as real as any fought with swords and crossbows. In a time of change all over the far-flung kingdom of Deverry, the gwerbret of Aberwyn had held firm for the past and its outmoded ways, even while the most famous bard in the province of Eldidd starved himself at his door in protest.

Cutting over the keening and the sobs came the call of a silver horn.

With the grinding of a winch and the grumble of timbers on stone the great gates swung slowly open. Through the widening view Alyssa caught sight of men in red and brown tartan trousers and vests over their loose shirts mounting horses. Cavalry sabers flashed as the horn sounded again. The men were sheathing the sabers and taking some other weapon out of their belts. Alyssa stood on tiptoe to see: horse-whips!

"Run!" Alyssa screamed. She let go of Mavva and Rhys's arms. "When the crowd breaks we'll be trampled!"

But although the crowd swirled as the prudent slipped away, it refused to break. When the cavalrymen edged their horses out, they carried not sabers but horsewhips—after all, it was their own fellow citizens they were facing, there in the darkening streets. For a moment utter silence and utter stalemate held. The troop leader, the gwerbret's younger son, Lord Gwarl, urged his bay horse forward.

"Disperse!" he called out. "In the name of Aberwyn I command you! Clear this street immediately!"

The keening continued. The crowd swayed but never moved to leave.

"Rabble, all of you!" Gwarl stood high in his stirrups and yelled. "Scum! Disperse!"

A rock sailed through the air and smacked Lord Gwarl's horse in the chest. With a whinny it reared, nearly unseating its rider. The crowd laughed and howled. Gwarl settled his horse down and began screaming at the top of his lungs, but his words died in the screech from the mob, laughter and rage all mingled into one hideous noise. Another rock, another—the troop swung horsewhips up and charged full toward the crowd.

Alyssa heard herself shriek with the others. She tried to run, found herself caught in a press of bodies, looked round frantically but saw no sign of Mavva and Rhys. Apparently they'd taken her good advice even if she'd been too stupid to follow it herself. All round her people were screaming, staggering, flailing out at one another as they tried to get free enough to run. Horses neighed and reared; the cavalrymen were swearing and yelling as the whips snapped and swung. As people scrambled to get away from the whips, the crowd turned porous. The horsemen pressed forward into the gaps. Horses kicked and bit. People screamed and bled. Moving back toward town became impossible.

Alyssa worked her way between two burly young men, then darted forward toward the wall just as a whip cracked the air beside her ear. Her mouth framed a soundless scream as she looked up into the sweaty face of a young cavalryman, leaning from his saddle. He was weeping, cursing a steady stream as duty drove him past her into the helpless crowd. The men behind her saw that she was heading for the clear space at the wall so that she could run round the dun and find safety that way. Yelling to one another they surged forward behind her just as another horseman swung his mount round to their direction. Alyssa nearly fell, steadied herself barely in time, kept moving, half-running, half-carried forward as the men behind her pressed forward toward the wall.

The screams turned horrible as agony and terror lashed the crowd. Cries and shouts told Alyssa that people were falling, being trampled. She bent her will to staying upright, staying on her feet. Someone slammed into her from the side as he tried to evade the oncoming horseman. Someone else screamed, slipped, clutched at her arm. She shook him off before he could take her down with him, then staggered forward only to stumble over something hard—she never did see what it was—and nearly fall. Strong hands grabbed her arm from behind and swung her around, hauled her back onto her feet. She found herself staring up at the dead-pale face of a young man. Nothing else about him registered, but that he was as frightened as she was.

"Hold on!" he yelled at her. "We'll get out of this better as two."

She linked her arm with his and pushed forward again. Buoyed up by his strength she could keep walking, keep her head up, too, and see where they were going. From the screams behind her she knew that she didn't want to turn and see where she had been. At last they gained the wall, could sidle along it, could ease themselves in position for one last burst of speed and rush forward. They gained an alley at the beginning of the town proper and trotted down it, turned out into the Street of the Silversmiths and into a pool of lamplight.

Safe.

"Thank every god they hang those street lamps so high," her rescuer said. "If one of them fell into the thatch . . ."

Alyssa felt suddenly sick and oddly cold. He caught her elbow and steadied her. For a few minutes they stood listening to the sounds—the screaming, the weeping, the neighing of frightened horses, and over it all the cracking of the whips and the cursing of troopers.

"This night will light a fire of a different kind," Alyssa said at last. "His Grace will feel its heat soon enough."

"Oho! So you're one of the rabble-rousers, are you?"

"Is that how you see us? Rabble?" She pulled her arm free. "My thanks for your aid, but I've naught more to say to you."

Alyssa turned on her heel and stalked off.

"Wait!" He was calling out, trotting after her. "I meant no insult, fair maid. Just a jest of sorts. Here, look, if anyone's rabble, it's me."

Alyssa stopped in the next pool of lamplight. She could still hear the screaming and the horses, but faintly now, as if the noise had both lessened and moved far away. Was the troop following the mob down to the collegium? If so, she'd best wait to go back, but here she was, a woman alone on a darkening street. And what of Rhys and Mavva? Were they safe? Her rescuer hurried up and made her a bow.

"Forgive me?" he said. "I'm afeared I know naught of your town's politics. I'm from Lughcarn."

For the first time she looked at him with some attention. A tall man, broad in the shoulders and well-built, he had a tousled mane of sandy-brown hair and, as far as she could tell in the flickering light, his eyes were blue. He wore ordinary clothes, a pair of breeches and tall boots, a linen shirt with flowing sleeves and over it a leather waistcoat. At his belt he carried an elven finesword at one side and at the other, a knife with a silver handle. A silver dagger. She recognized the three little spheres on the dagger's pommel. No wonder he'd called himself rabble.

"So, you guard the coach roads, do you?" she said.

"I do, and I've ridden a few barges, too."

When he flashed her a smile, she realized that he was a handsome man in a rough sort of way.

"Cavan of Lughcarn's my name." He made her a bow. "At your service, my lady. May I escort you to the safety of your home?"

Alyssa hesitated, but he at least seemed gallant enough. Who knew what sort of man might be lurking in the riot-torn streets?

"My thanks to you, good sir. My name's Alyssa vairc Sirra, and I'd be grateful for your company. I'm in residence at the collegium. At Lady Rhodda's Hall."

"Ah! One of our new lady scholars, then. And as beautiful as learning itself, from what I can see in this wretched lamplight, anyway."

"You, sir, have a tongue as silver as your dagger, but I'm not the sort to be cut to the heart. Shall we go, then, before the gwerbret's riders come back?"

Together they hurried downhill through the twisting streets of the city. Townsfolk stood, watching the streets, in the doorways of shops and houses, at the gates of an inn here, a tavern there. Some held lanterns, which they raised high to peer at Alyssa and her escort. They called out hopeful names but shrank back disappointed as Alyssa and Cavan passed them by.

"A fair many people came up to the gates," Cavan remarked. "I was having a pint in a tavern when I heard the excitement brewing, so I drifted up to take a look. Too much excitement, but meeting you, I had a silver dagger's luck."

"Let's hope it's not evil luck. Silver daggers have been thrown out of Aberwyn for far less than consorting with rabble."

"Oh, now, here! Don't keep holding that against me! I'm a stranger, and I knew not what I was saying."

"Well, true spoken. You're forgiven."

In the next pool of lamplight, he grinned at her, and despite herself, she returned the smile.

"Lughcarn, is it?" she said. "I hear they call it the City of Black Air."

"The smelter smoke is bad, truly, but we prefer to call it the City of Iron Men. But I don't mean the noble-born by that. The iron trade and the guilds hold the real power there."

"Good for them! So, what brings you to Aberwyn?"

"The trouble up on your northern border. Some of the lesser lords might be wanting to add a man to their warband."

"Oh, now, here! Do you truly think that silly feud will turn into a war? From what I understand, it's over some hundred acres of land and one village."

"It's not the land." Cavan shook his head. "It's the honor of the thing. Gwerbret Standyc of the Bears wants land that one of Aberwyn's allies claims. I don't know which ally. No one farther east seemed to know. But anyway, the ally has appealed to your gwerbret. I did hear that. So now you've got two gwerbretion bellowing at each other like bulls in adjoining pastures. Neither's going to back down."

Alyssa felt like screaming in useless rage. The noble-born fought among themselves all the time, here on the western border of the kingdom. The common folk paid for those bloody battles with their taxes and the lives of their young men.

"If we had true courts of justice," she said, "mayhap we could do summat about these stupid squabbles. Settle them by laws, not the sword. Bulls, are they? Cocks squawking in the barnyard, more like, over the juiciest worms!"

Cavan laughed. "You'd best not say that where Gwerbret Ladoic's men can hear you."

"No doubt you're right, good sir. Shall we go, then?"

When he offered her his arm, she took it, and they headed downhill.

The Scholars' Collegia compound stood behind walls down near Aberwyn's harbor. In the midst of narrow lawns and old oaks rose three separate broch complexes, each a tall tower joined round its edges by smaller towers like the petals of a daisy. Men students occupied the two tallest hives, as the students termed them, while the women's college sat some distance away, caught between the kitchen garden and the back wall. Lady Rhodda Hall had grown from a small seed. Some three hundred years earlier, Lady Rhodda Maelwaedd had provided a bequest to a tutor charged with teaching women to read and write at Dun Cannobaen. The priests of Wmm at the nearby island shrines had taken up the idea and started a course of study based on Lady Rhodda's library. Some ten women a year had finished the course and gone out to teach others, lasses and lads both. Slowly the knowledge of letters and learning had spread through Eldidd from the west.

Thanks to a much larger gift from Carramaena of the Westlands, the queen of the kingdom to the west of Deverry, plus endowments from various guilds, this scattered group had turned into a proper collegium some years back. Compared to the men's collegia, which had noble patronage, it was still small and shabby, but Alyssa loved it all the same. She was always conscious of the great honor afforded her, that she'd been allowed to study the history of Aberwyn and Eldidd, as well as the philosophy of Prince Mael the Seer. Although her father served as master of the Bakers' Guild for all Eldidd, her clan were commoners through and through.

As she and Cavan turned the last corner, they saw a crowd of men and horses standing around outside the collegium grounds. By the light of the lanterns that hung by the gates, Alyssa could just pick out the red and brown colors of the Fox clan's livery.

"Gwerbret's men," Alyssa said. "I wonder if they're waiting to arrest anyone who was part of the mob."

"Not a bad guess, alas." Cavan glanced around and pointed to the deep doorway of a nearby house. "Wait here."

Alyssa stepped into the doorway and watched him from the shadows. Cavan strolled down the street and made a great show of looking around as if he were lost. Off to one side of the pack at the gates stood a fellow holding the reins of a pair of horses. Cavan stopped beside him with a friendly wave. Although Alyssa could hear nothing of their talk, she did pick up a pleasant burst of laughter. With another wave, Cavan strolled back to her.

"They've come to take the gwerbret's daughter back to the dun," Cavan said. "She doesn't want to go with them. That lad with the horses told me that the vixen's found a nice deep den."

"Vixen?" Alyssa snorted in disgust. "It's obvious he knows naught about Lady Dovina. Very well, then, I'd best go round the back way."

Cavan escorted her as she hurried the long way round the collegium wall. At the back, not far from the women's hive, the settling of the ground had caused a section of the stone wall to sink some few feet lower than the rest and bow inward a bit as well. Loose stones made a precarious series of steps up and over. Alyssa started to tuck her skirts into her kirtle, but Cavan was watching the display of ankle with entirely too much interest.

"My thanks for your aid," Alyssa said to him. "No doubt you'll be wanting to get back to your inn and a nice tankard of ale."

In the light from the nearby oil lamps she could see him grin. She had to admit that she found his smile charming—but a silver dagger? Like every lass in Deverry, she'd been warned against the men of that band from the time she could toddle. Mothers pointed them out and made sure their daughters could recognize the dagger they carried. Dishonored men, all of them, who wandered the roads looking for paid employment rather than serving in a proper warband—and they all have the morals of street dogs, Alyssa's mother had always said, when it comes to lasses. Cavan, Alyssa figured, would be no better than the rest of them, despite his smile and the elegant way he bowed to her.

"I know a dismissal when I hear one," Cavan said. "But may I see you again, on the morrow perhaps?"

"At noon on the morrow come down to the old marketplace. Not the new one up by the gwerbret's dun, but the old one near the smaller harbor. If all goes well, you just might find me there."

"I'll pray I do." Cavan made her a deep bow, then turned and walked away.

Alyssa finished tucking up her skirts, then climbed the wall with the ease of long practice. Getting down again required grabbing the branch of the old oak that grew near the wall, swinging herself out and over, then slowly lowering herself to the ground. She managed and dropped lightly into safe territory. She hurried around the women's hive and found the two chaperones standing guard by lantern light. Lady Werra clutched a stout walking stick in both hands, and Lady Graella, an iron poker.

"Ye gods!" Alyssa said. "Are we under siege?"

"We might well be. The porters are supposed to be guarding the front gate. If they weaken and let that yapping warband in, we're ready." Werra hefted the stick. "No men allowed in here after the last bell sounds. They'll have to follow the rules like everyone else in Aberwyn."

"And speaking of such matters," Graella put in, "where have you been, young Alyssa?"

"Oh, come now, my ladies, you saw me leave. Things got a bit more difficult in town than I'd been expecting. I came back the long way round."

"Difficult? You might call it that." Werra turned grim. "All of our lasses are here and safe, now that you've turned up, but two of the men from King's are dead."

"Dead?" Alyssa caught her breath with a gasp.

"And one of them noble-born, at that," Graella said. "Young Lord

Grif, and him but fifteen summers old. The other was the Dyers' Guild Own Scholar, Procyr of Abernaudd. Their fathers will have a few harsh words for the gwerbret once they get the news, and the guildmaster will, too."

"More than words, my lady. Griffydd of the Bear is Gwerbret Standyc's son. I doubt me if he'll settle his feud with our Ladoic all peaceful-like now."

The two chaperones nodded their agreement. Graella sighed with a shake of her head.

"Some of the townsfolk were badly hurt," Werra said "And there's another man dead among them. They say one woman lost an eye from being whipped. She'll be suing in the court for that, I wager!"

"Huh!" Alyssa said. "As if His Grace will listen! They can take a suit to the law court, but who's going to be judging it? His cousin by right of birth! He won't be able to dismiss Standyc's complaint so easily, though."

Werra was about to speak when distant noises reached them— angry shouts, a scream of rage, and then the clang of the iron gates slamming shut. Alyssa heard a strange low pitched throb and finally identified it.

"Someone's shaking the gates," she said, "but those locks are made of dwarven steel. They'll not break so easily."

The two older women agreed with small smiles. Alyssa curtsied to them both, then followed them inside to the women's great hall. In the big round room a scatter of old, scarred tables and benches stood on the floor, covered with woven rush mats for want of money for carpets. Opposite the door stood the stone hearth where a peat fire smoldered against the springtime damp. At intervals around the stone walls hung candle lanterns, flickering in the drafts with the rot-touched smell of tallow. Off to both sides rose spiral iron staircases, splendid examples of dwarven blacksmith work and a gift from the rulers of Dwarveholt, that led to the upper floor and the access doors to the side brochs of the hive.

The head of the collegium, gray-haired Lady Taclynniva, or Lady Tay as she preferred to be known, sat in the chair of honor at the one new table. As always, she sat bolt upright, her head held high, her slender hands at rest together in her lap. The two chaperones took their chairs on either side of her. Both Werra and Graella kept their improvised weapons in their laps, just in case, Alyssa supposed, some enemy rushed in. They were sisters, who years before had fled unsuitable marriages and taken refuge with Lady Tay. Both of them had strong jaws, wide foreheads, and dark hair just beginning to show gray.

All around them the young women, with their loose red scholars' surcoats over their tunics and long skirts, stood or sat on the floor, some weeping, some narrow-eyed with fury, all of them with their hair down and disheveled as a sign of mourning for Cradoc, their teacher of rhetoric. As Alyssa approached, Mavva hurried over to greet her. She had one hand on her tunic and clutched her silver betrothal brooch as if she feared it might be torn off. In the riot, of course, it might have been.

"There you are!" Mavva said. "Thanks be to the Goddess! Rhys and I are both safe, but I've feared the worst ever since I lost you in the mob."

"I was lucky to get out of it, truly. Ah, ye gods, what a horrible day this is for Aberwyn, to lose Cradoc so!"

Mavva nodded, finally let go of the brooch, and wiped tears from her eyes. Alyssa turned to Lady Tay's chair and curtsied.

"Good, you're the last of our strays," Lady Tay said.

"I lingered in town till the streets were clear, my lady." Alyssa decided it would be politic to shift the conversation before she was forced to mention Cavan. "That mob at our gates? I overheard someone mention Dovina."

"No doubt you did, because she's the prey they're after. We all suspect that the gwerbret wants her back in his dun so he can marry her off. The riot tonight will be his excuse, or so Dovina thinks." She nodded at the woman who sat at the far end of the honor table.

Alyssa turned to Lady Dovina, who gave her a sickly sort of smile. "I fear me our lady is right," Dovina said. "I wonder what starveling courtier he's found for me this time?"

With a sigh Alyssa sat down on the bench. As usual, Dovina had an open book in front of her and a candle lantern set nearby. A pretty lass, some twenty summers old, the same age as Alyssa, Dovina had thick pale hair that all the scholars envied and large blue eyes, which, however beautiful, tended to water. She held a reading-glass in one hand—a rectangular lens in a silver frame with a handle like a small mirror. Beauty and her high estate hadn't prevented her from having weak eyesight.

"Perhaps," Lady Tay said, "it will be a worthy man this time."

Dovina made a most unladylike snorting sound. "I don't care, my lady," she said. "We all know that I was born for the scholar's life. All I want is what I have already, tending our bookhoard."

"Nicely put," Lady Tay said. "If only you can convince your father."

"Indeed." Dovina turned to Alyssa. "Lyss, it gladdens my heart to see you safe. I was truly worried. And I need to ask you summat. I've been hearing reports that my father gave that order, when the riders charged the crowd, I mean. I can't believe it of him."

"He didn't. It was your brother, the younger one, at the head of his men. Not that he exactly gave an order."

"Gwarl?"

"It was. He called us all rabble and ordered us to disperse. Someone—I couldn't see who—threw a rock and hit his horse." She paused to get the images clear in her mind. "He didn't give any sort of order. The warband broke on their own. I'd guess it's the honor of the thing, someone attacking their lord."

"No doubt it was just that. My thanks. That's a great relief. My father can be difficult, the gods all know, when he blusters and yells at everyone, but I've never known him to do anything vicious. Gwarl, on the other hand, is a dolt. Always swaggering around and sneering. Rabble. Huh!"

Alyssa listened in sincere admiration. Dovina held the highest rank of any scholar in Lady Rhodda Hall. Her father, Ladoic, ruled Aberwyn and the surrounding territory as gwerbret, the highest rank of nobility in the kingdom, just barely below the royal princes. Dovina said exactly what she wanted about her exalted clan and kin, words that none of the rest of them would have dared voice. Her brothers in particular—to Dovina, the "lout" was the gwerbretal heir, and the "dolt" the younger son. Rank or not, however, Dovina recognized Lady Tay as the leader of their collegium. She rose from her chair.

"My lady." Dovina paused to curtsy. "Has there been a message from the dun yet? About returning Cradoc's body to us? Mavva saw some servants carry it inside the dun."

"No message yet," Lady Tay said. "The Bardic Consortium also has a claim. I did send them a message straightaway when I heard that he was gone."

Dovina curtsied again and sat back down. She turned to Alyssa and smiled, a bitter little twist of her mouth.

"So, what's our next move in this game of carnoic?" Dovina said. "Will you still be speaking on the morrow?"

"I will indeed. There's more need for it than ever." Alyssa felt tears rising behind her eyes. "With Cradoc gone."

The listening women keened, a soft moan, a whispered wail, and swayed. In the candlelight their scarlet surcoats seemed to flicker like the flames.

"It's a hard thing to bear," Dovina said. "But we mustn't let him die in vain. Our cause is just, and even a stubborn dog like Father will see that sooner or later."

Alyssa could only hope so. For some years now the people of El-didd had been begging for a change in the law codes. As things stood, the judges in the law courts all came from the hereditary no-bility. Fathers handed the positions down to sons, and some of the sons barely knew one law from another. The best anyone could hope for was a judge who'd listen to the advice of the priests of Bel. Not all priests, however, were more interested in deciding lawsuits fairly and criminal cases justly than in getting land and favors for their tem-ples. More often than not, if a commoner brought a grievance against one of the noble-born, the commoner would get short shrift in court.

The kingdom's one free city had already forced through changes thanks to obscure legal precedents. In Cerrmor, the heads of the various guilds had equal say with the mayor when it came to picking judges. They'd banded together to found a collegium for the study-ing of law after the model of the Bardekian law schools across the Southern Sea. Advocates and judges both had to complete the course of study in order to appear in a Cerrmor court. The fairness of the city's justice system had become known and admired all across Deverry.

The news of these and other doings reached Aberwyn by barge and mail coach, but His Grace Ladoic, Gwerbret Aberwyn, would have none of these new ways. He was prone to announce—or bellow, as Dovina put it—that he stood firm on and for tradition. The old ways, he often said, were good enough for him.

"And what's good enough for him," Dovina said, "is supposedly good enough for all of us." She snorted again.

"There are other precedents," Alyssa said. "The Justiciars of the Northern Border are the best one. They've been handling the courts in Cerrgonney for what? About three hundred years now."

"Too recent for my dear father, or so he says."

"It's too bad that there isn't some older precedent we could refer to. His councillors talk about tradition all the time, but what if things weren't so traditional? That would take a few of their stones off the game board."

"If his councillors have any stones." Dovina flashed a wicked smile. "Of the other sort."

Everyone with earshot laughed, even Lady Tay, though she cut her laugh short.

"Now hush!" Lady Tay said. "Such coarse words are most unbecoming! I'm sure all of you have studies to attend to. I suggest you go do so."

Whispering together, the scholars rose from where they'd been sitting, grabbed lanterns, and headed for the staircases. Clutching her book and reading-glass, Dovina fell into step beside Alyssa and Mavva.

"You know, Alyssa," Dovina said. "Your thought was a fine one, about the older precedent, I mean. I remember summat about such a thing in a book I read. It's too late now, but tomorrow when the sun's up, I'll look for it."

"My thanks," Alyssa said. "It would be splendid to have a citation."

"Will you be able to stay here long enough to find it?" Mavva said to Dovina. "Or will your father drag you away?"

"If he comes and throws a direct order into my face, I shall have to obey him. Unless of course I can work him round." Dovina considered briefly. "It would be best that I never hear that he's at the gates. If he does come, tell everyone that I've got such a terrible pain in my head that I simply can't be disturbed." She laid a pale hand on her forehead and grinned. "My weak eyes, you know. Such a trial!"

"I'll spread the word," Mavva said. "Lyss, you're not really going to go speak in the marketplace, are you? I know we planned it, but things have gotten so dangerous."

"Curse the danger!" Alyssa said. "I said I'd speak, and I will, because now it'll be a praise piece for Cradoc." She forced her voice steady. "And for Lord Grif and Procyr, too. Do you know the name of the dead townsman?"

"I don't." Mavva thought for a moment. "But I'll find it out for you."

Alyssa spent most of that night in the hive's bookchamber. With her good eyesight, she could read by candlelight. She had a reading candle as thick as her wrist and a good two feet high. The priests of Wmm had gifted the hive with a wooden crate of these candles when the scholars had visited the Holy Island to view the bookhoard owned by the temples. Alyssa read gwerchanau, the famous death-songs of the past, and stored up fragments of poetry in her mind to add to her speech. All of the scholars depended on memory far more than writing. While Bardekian pabrus had become far more common than parchment, and most certainly much cheaper, wasting even scraps of it upon notes and rough drafts lay beyond the women's collegium's finances.

Finally, when the hourglass on her lectern ran dry from the fifth turnover, she closed her books and stumbled off to bed in the sleeping room she shared with six other women. As senior students, each of them had a narrow cot of her own, rather than sharing a mattress as the first-year lasses did. Moving carefully in the dark, Alyssa took off her skirt and tunic, folded them on top of the carved chest that sat at the foot of her cot, then lay down in her underdress and fell straight asleep.

She dreamed of Cradoc, not the skeletal person she'd seen at the end, but as he'd looked in the prime of life, tall and slender, with a mane of silvery hair that he wore combed straight back from his high forehead. They stood together in a landscape of mist and old stone walls, the collegium, perhaps, when the winter fogs rolled thick over Aberwyn.

"Mourn me," Cradoc said, "but don't wallow in grief. You have work to be done. You were my best student, and the work will be yours to do."

"Am I truly worthy?" Alyssa said. "I wish you were still here with us."

"So do I." He smiled with a wry twist of his mouth. "I deem you worthy. Take risks, Alyssa, but judge them carefully. Don't throw yourself away by starving like I did. You have a wyrd to fulfill."

"What is that wyrd?"

"Now that I can't tell you. No one can know another man's wyrd, nor a woman's either. Farewell." He took a step away into the mist, then turned back. "Oh, and do remember to breathe deeply and evenly while you speak."

Overhead a raven cried out. She saw three of the carrion birds circling in the misty sky. When she looked for Cradoc, he'd disappeared, but another glance skyward showed her four ravens where three had been before.

Alyssa sat up in bed, awake and shivering in the morning light streaming through the windows near her bed. Had he come from the Otherlands one last time to speak with her? That bit of advice about breathing—it was so like him! She sometimes did run out of breath when she reached the peroration of a speech. She shivered again, but not from cold.

CHAPTER 2

SILVER DAGGERS OCCUPIED AN odd position in Deverry. They were all proven fighters who'd made one bad mistake, either broken a law or incurred some sort of dishonor that had gotten them kicked out of a warband or exiled by their kinfolk. Although they were outright mercenary soldiers, they had more honor than most men of that sort and a name to protect as well. To become a silver dagger, a man had to find a member of the band, ride with him a while, and prove himself. Only then could they visit one of the rare silversmiths that knew the secrets to forging the alloy in the silver dagger itself. Thus merchants and lords alike trusted them more than your ordinary hired guard. Even so, they had a cold welcome everywhere they went in the kingdom.

Cavan of Lughcarn had found shelter of a sort down near the main harbor. He and his horse shared a smelly shed at the back of the sagging building that housed the tavern, the innkeep, his thin shrew of a wife, and their one servant, a potman of advanced age who moved more slowly than anyone Cavan had ever seen. Just crossing the round room to fetch a tankard of ale took him enough time for a man to die of thirst, as customers often remarked. It was, however, one of the few places in Aberwyn that would take a silver dagger's coin. Blood money, most people called a mercenary's hire.

The tavernman himself, Iolan by name, was as fat as his wife was bony. Unlike wife and potman, he enjoyed talking with his customers while he swilled down his own ale. That morning, while Cavan ate a bowl of cold porridge, Iolan sat himself down on the bench opposite.

"So you had some excitement last night, did you now? I heard the noise of it, and that was enough for me."

"Too much for me, almost," Cavan said. "When the gwerbret's riders charged into the crowd, I thought we were all done for."

Iolan sucked his few remaining teeth and nodded.

"Tell me summat," Cavan continued, "are the courts here as bad as all that? A cause worth dying for, I mean."

"Not to me, but there's some like Cradoc, a good man he was, too, the voice of the people, just like they say a bard should be. The courts? Well, some are rotten, but not so much in Aberwyn. Abernaudd, now—the things you hear! But Aberwyn's got its troubles, sure enough. A potter here in town, a man I know, some bastard-born servant of a lord cheated him out of a week's work. Took the bowls away, never came back to pay. The lord refused to pay. The gwerbret told the lordling, you have the potter's merchandise, so pay the man. But he never did come across with the coin. Nothing more Ladoic could do about it, either, without starting a war with his vassal. Potter had his day at the hearing. No way to make the noble-born pay after." Iolan paused to spit into the straw on the floor beside him. "Noble as my fat arse."

"Sounds like it, truly."

"Other towns, from what I've heard, they wouldn't even have let a poor man into the chamber of justice." He spat again. "If you have the coin, you can buy off priest and lord both."

"And the bards have been speaking out about it?"

"They have, for all the good it did that poor bastard last night."

Cavan scraped the last spoonful of oats out of his bowl, laid the spoon down, and got up. He swung himself clear of the bench.

"Which way is the old harbor?"

"Just follow the street outside downhill."

Cavan found his way to the marketplace just as the sun was reaching zenith. A rough square some hundred yards on a side, too small now to handle all the trade of the growing city, it lay close to Aberwyn's Old Harbor, where the local fishing boats docked. Once that area had been a tribute to the power of new ideas. In the early 1300s, the fashion for square and rectangular houses and shops had arrived from Bardek. The last gwerbret of the Maelwaedd dynasty had given coin to lay the square out among the rows of the then brand-new buildings, which stood in solid rows like walls around the square. Two narrow alleys, one at the northwest corner, one opposite it at the southeast, gave access to the markets and to the houses themselves.

By Cavan's time, the dwellings had decayed a fair bit. The stonework had turned black from years of cooking fires. The wooden buildings drooped and leaned against one another thanks to the settling of the ground. In back of each row of buildings, privies and chicken coops had replaced the once-elegant gardens. When Cavan walked along, looking for the entrance, he even passed the occasional milk cow, tethered out at her hay behind a house. The pungent atmosphere thickened further when he came into the square and realized without having to look that at least half the market stalls sold fish.

Still, he decided, a chance to see Alyssa again made the smell bearable. She was lovely, true, but also he'd never known a lass given to such clever ways of speaking. The combination intrigued him. The square was so crowded with marketers, servants, and town wives that he searched for some time before he spotted Alyssa standing on the south side of the square. She wore her flame-red surcoat over a plain linen tunic and a pair of brown skirts cut in an outmoded fashion, narrow around her slender hips, flaring at the knees to fall in folds at her ankles. She'd put her thick brown hair back in a silver clasp, her only real ornament. Her face was ornament enough, he decided, with her wide dark eyes and slender features.

A half-dozen of her fellow women students stood with her. Around them stood young men with orange surcoats and, in the outer ring, men wearing woad blue. Since Lughcarn had a King's Collegium of its own, Cavan knew that the blue surcoats ranged from the dark color of the first years to the honorably faded light blue of those about to finish their course of studies. Over one shoulder the noble-born among them had pinned scarves in the tartan of their clans. Most of their surcoats bunched at the hip over half-hidden swords. *Things could become exciting fast,* Cavan thought. He took a quick look around and saw four town marshals, conspicuous in their red and brown vests and striped breeches, standing in the entrance to the southeast alley. They carried quarterstaffs, and one had a horsewhip tucked into his belt as well. Cavan glanced over his shoulder, and sure enough, more marshals arrived to stand in the mouth of the northwest entrance.

The men with the orange surcoats dragged over wooden crates from a nearby vegetable stand and stacked them into a rough platform. Two of the men in the blue helped Alyssa climb onto them. The patrons and stall owners paid little attention at first, but when her clear voice rang out, those nearest all turned to listen. Her voice carried a good distance over the buzz and hum of the busy market.

"My fellow townsfolk!" Alyssa called out. "Spare me a moment to share my mourning! Three good men died yesterday under the hooves of the gwerbret's horses, all because of a bard who starved at his gates."

She'd been well-trained, Cavan realized, and he was shocked to find a woman who'd been given a bardic education. Not even in Dun Deverry did you find such a thing! Noble-born women sometimes studied other subjects at the collegia there, but never public speaking. He made his way closer and fetched up next to a skinny fellow in a pair of striped breeches and a red and brown vest over a linen shirt. The man had his thumbs hooked into his belt and a sneer on his face.

"Come to listen to the students?" Cavan said.

"Students, hah!" the fellow said. "Bunch of whores, more like, paid to keep the lads out of trouble. What would females want with books and suchlike?"

Cavan crossed his arms over his chest to keep his hands confined. His temper had gotten him into too much trouble already in his young life for him to want to indulge it again. Besides, he barely knew the young woman who spoke so eloquently. Why should he care about what some mangy dog of a stinking townsman thought of her?

"You all know our cause," Alyssa was saying, "justice in the law courts! What we want would be such a small concession for the gwerbret to make. After all, is he not a busy man with many a serious undertaking weighing down his mind, many a burden that he alone can lift? Why should he not delegate some of the mundane tasks to others, such as the judgments in Aberwyn's law courts?"

Here and there her listeners murmured a thoughtful agreement. Very clever of her, Cavan thought, to make the change seem to the gwerbret's advantage.

"And to us, it would mean so much, a chance at justice and fair dealing. The laws of the land would still hold. The priests of Bel would still be the true arbiters of what is law and what mere tradition. A small thing, truly, is what we ask, and yet Cradoc was willing to die for it! Where is the justice for the likes of us, if a great man dies in vain?"

Most of the townsfolk were nodding in approval. A few called out, "That's right, lass!"

A pair of town marshals pried themselves off the guildhall wall and made their slow way toward the front of the crowd. Two of the noble-born students twitched their blue surcoats back and laid hands on their sword hilts. They stepped in front of the marshals and smiled.

"I would mourn Cradoc ap Varyn with tears, but the tears of a woman come too easily to honor a great man." Alyssa paused to take a deep breath. "A bard deserves the words of a true bard to mark his passing. I would remind you of the words of Gweran Henvardd, that the wild wind of wyrd blows where it wills, cold and bitter at times. A bitter wind has swept away not merely Cradoc, but Lord Grif of the Bear clan, Procyr of Abernaudd, and Scomyr the butcher's son."

At the mention of Scomyr, a woman cried out in a high-pitched wail of grief. Cavan glanced around and saw a stout market-wife who'd thrown her apron over her face. Her shoulders shook with sobs. He found the news of Lord Grif's death more interesting—oil poured on the fire of feud smoldering up in Northern Eldidd.

"If there was no justice for Cradoc," Alyssa continued, "if there was no justice for these three good men, what may we expect, should we need the courts for some redress?" She paused and peered into the crowd as if she looked each and every one of them full in the face. "What? Naught! That's all, nothing at all!"

This time voices in the crowd called out. "That's the truth, she peaks true!" Almost everyone else murmured in agreement. The ?ering fellow cupped his hands around his mouth and shouted, . stop your tongue, you cackling hen! You're naught yourself, vopenny whore!"

Cavan turned and without one thought swung straight for his face. His right fist collided with the fellow's chin with a painful but satisfying blow. His left darted forward of its own accord and sank itself in the fellow's stomach. With a grunt and a spew of vomit the heckler folded over himself and fell forward onto the cobbles.

Yelling for order, the marshals rushed into the crowd, only to be met by a solid block of the blue-coated students. Townsfolk yelled, the crowd swirled, the marshals began swinging their long staves. Up on her pile of wooden crates Alyssa screamed for order, but no one listened. In all the confusion it took Cavan a moment to realize that he was the man the marshals were trying to reach.

"Here!" a young voice shouted from behind him. "We've got to get you and Lyss out of here!"

"Cursed right!" Cavan turned and saw a dark-haired lad who wore an orange surcoat but no sword.

"The men from King's will handle the marshals," the lad went on. "Come on!"

They forced their way through the rapidly thinning crowd. Behind them shouts broke out. Cavan glanced back to see the noble-born men from King's surrounding the marshals, who could do nothing but swear and threaten with their staffs. Whacking some powerful lord's son in the head would cost them dear in the long run. As the threat of trouble eased, the stall holders stayed to guard their merchandise. Some of the bolder shoppers paused their flight and stood looking back at the square, as if deciding whether or not to return. There'd be no riot after all.

By the time her would-be rescuers reached her, Alyssa had already jumped down from her improvised rostrum. Men in orange surcoats surrounded her.

"This is the fellow who felled the gwerbret's spy," the dark-haired lad said to her. "The marshals saw him do it."

Cavan's stomach twisted. Gwerbret's spy? He'd done it, all right, gotten himself into deep trouble without thinking twice.

"We'll hide you in Wmm's," the lad continued. "They won't dare come into our hive."

Alyssa turned and gave Cavan a glowing smile. "You felled him good and proper," she said. "My thanks! I do wish I'd gotten to finish my speech, though."

"And an excellent beginning it was," Cavan said. "I wish I'd gotten to hear it all."

Cavan started to bow to her, but she reached up, laid her hands on either side of his face, and kissed him. The students around them whooped aloud and laughed. Cavan felt that kiss run through his body, as hot as a sword thrust. He would have taken another, but she stepped back into the safety of her knot of women friends.

"There's your hire, silver dagger," the dark-haired lad said, grinning, "but ye gods, we've got to get out of here!"

Cavan glanced over his shoulder and saw more marshals shoving their way into the square from the southeast alley.

"They've blocked the cursed way out of the square," Cavan said. "Where can we—"

"Into the baker's," Alyssa said. "There's a back way out between the ovens."

In the midst of a mob of students, Cavan followed Alyssa. She yelled orders, gathered her troops like a captain, and led them on the run to the downhill side of the marketplace. Farmers swore and grabbed hens and produce out of their way. Hogs squealed in excitement as they passed, dodging through the rough wooden stalls. Ahead lay a row of proper shops. Alyssa waved and pointed. Her troop poured into the doorway of a bakery.

The smell of fresh bread perfumed the warm, moist air. To one side of the dimly lit room stood a long wooden table, piled with loaves. The young baker, draped in a flour-dusted apron over his shirt and breeches, looked so much like Alyssa that Cavan knew he had to be close kin, a brother, most likely, from the way he spoke to her. She was common-born, he realized to his surprise. Somehow he'd thought that a women of her sharp wits must come from a noble clan.

"You've done it this time!" the baker snapped. "Don't you ever learn?"

"Oh, hold your tongue, Alwen! We're just passing through."

"Very well, but hurry! I don't want the wretched marshals in here!"

She laughed, blew him a kiss, and led the way round the table to an open door. The door led to a short stairway, which in turn led to a huge room, as hot as a blazing summer day. Four big brick ovens stood like beehives on one side, while firewood lay piled up on the other. Between them stood a wooden door, guarded by a lad of perhaps ten years. He too looked much like Alyssa.

"Arwy," Alyssa snapped, "shut the door after us!"

"I will." He scrambled out of the way. "But Da's going to be so mad. He told you last time—"

"That was last time. This is different."

Alyssa lifted the bar and shoved the door open to sunlight and the over-ripe stink of Aberwyn's fishing-boat harbor. The mob of students and one silver dagger rushed out into the sunlight. Cavan could see the stone towers of the Collegium rising over the alleyways and stone houses no more than half a mile away. Distantly from the market square he heard shouts of rage mixed with taunting laughter.

"No sign of the marshals," the dark-haired lad said. "No doubt the men from King's are keeping them busy. My name's Rhys, by the by."

"And mine's Cavan. My thanks for your aid."

"You'd best come back with us. The Collegia have immunity, you see, and they won't dare follow you inside."

"Splendid! But I've got a horse stabled at my lodgings."

"We'll fetch him after dark. Now let's hurry!"

Once they reached the safety of the collegia grounds, Alyssa had a moment to think. Not only had she gotten into trouble with the town marshals, she'd kissed a silver dagger right out in a public square. Her usual taste for such wild adventures disappeared when she considered what Lady Tay might say about both dangerous missteps. At the door to Wmm's Scribal's hive, everyone paused to catch their breath. Rhys ducked inside and came out again with an orange surcoat, which he handed to Cavan.

"For a day or two you'd best be one of us," Rhys said.

"My thanks!" Cavan put the surcoat on and pulled it round to cover his silver dagger. "I hope the marshals have short memories."

"I'll hope and pray," Alyssa said, "that the men from King's will fill their memories with less than pleasant thoughts." She dropped Cavan a curtsy. "My thanks again!"

He bowed to her. "It would gladden my heart to see you again."

"If you're in residence here, no doubt you will."

With Cavan safely hidden in Rhys's collegium, Alyssa hurried back to her own hive. She walked into the women's great hall to find Lady Tay standing by the cold hearth in a state of sheer fury. She was talking with the two chaperones, and she punctuated her words by slapping the tiny roll of pabrus she held in her right hand against her left palm. Alyssa stepped toward the wall to stay out of the lady's line of sight, but Tay saw her before she could sneak upstairs.

"Alyssa!" Lady Tay called out. "I have unpleasant news for you."

Alyssa was so sure that she was about to be sent away that she felt sick to her stomach. In the spirit of a hound who's stolen meat from the table, she slunk over to the three ladies and curtsied to all of them.

"We've heard about Cradoc's remains," Lady Tay said. "The gwerbret's refusing to give them over to anyone but his kin and clan."

"What?" Outrage mingled with relief, both so profound that Alyssa had to gulp for breath before she could continue. "Forgive my discourtesy, my lady! But Cradoc has no living kin or clan."

"Precisely! And I'd wager high that our ever-so-noble lord knows that as well as we do." Lady Tay shook the pabrus roll vaguely in the direction of the gwerbretal dun. "This message came from Malyc Penvardd but a few moments ago. He's composing a flyting song, he tells me. His journeymen will make sure it goes out with the mail coaches for the entire kingdom to hear."

"Will that matter to Gwerbret Ladoic?" Werra put in.

"I doubt it, but what else can we do? His Grace says that he'll have the body 'disposed of properly.' Disposed of!" Lady Tay's voice shook and snarled. "As if he were a dead horse! Here!" She held out the roll. "You'll find Lady Dovina in our bookchamber. Take this to her! Well, my apologies. Would you please—"

"Of course, my lady." Alyssa curtsied again and took the message.

As she hurried up the staircase, Alyssa reminded herself that far more important matters burdened Lady Tay's mind than one of her students kissing a silver dagger. With luck, the lady would never hear of the incident at all. The heckler in the market square, of course, was a rather more serious thing. She should have realized, she told herself, that trouble might erupt. A gwerbretal spy—a dropped lantern in a pile of straw. You've really done it this time. When she remembered her brother Alwen's remark, she felt half-sick with fear.

The hive's bookchamber occupied the very top floor of the main broch. A circular room, some fifty feet across, it had windows all round. Wooden shutters covered in oxhides stood ready to keep out the rain. Every spring, the women moved a lectern under each window to catch the best light, and every winter they moved them back to the center of the room away from the damp. Unlike the men's collegia, they had no money to pay for glass windows. Bookshelves stood around in profusion, each a few feet away from the stone walls

On this sunny afternoon all the shutters stood open. Lady Dovina sat at a table near a view of the harbor far below and peered at an open book through her reading-glass. When Alyssa held out the pabrus message, Dovina looked up and took it.

"Have you heard about Cradoc's body?" Alyssa said.

"I have, and it's just like Father to be so stubborn." Dovina paused to unroll the pabrus and read the message. "Good for the Penvardd!"

"Well, a noble lord is supposed to be stubborn."

"According to our beloved Mael the Seer, truly, but in other places he does praise moderation in all things. Stubbornness is only one of the noble qualities, after all. And last time I looked, greed in the law courts wasn't one of them."

"True spoken indeed." Alyssa looked over her shoulder at the open book. "Is this the one you were remembering?"

"Indeed it is, Dwvoryc's Annals of the Dawntime." Dovina rubbed her hands together and cackled like a witch. "It says here, very clearly, that in the olden days, gwerbretion were called vergobretes. They didn't inherit their position, they were elected."

"Elected! Ye gods!"

"All the free men of a tribe would come together and say yea or nay as each candidate was presented to them. The one with the loudest number of yeas got the job."

"That must have changed a thousand years ago."

"Mostly, but why do you think there's a Council of Electors? That's how my clan got the gwerbretrhyn, isn't it, when the Maelwaedds died out? The Council met and voted and chose us over the Bears. The Electors are the last remnant of this tradition." Dovina gave the book a wicked grin. "And how will Father like that ancient folkway, I wonder?"

Dovina got her chance to find out only a few moments later, when Mavva came hurrying up the stairs to join them.

"My lady!" Mavva appeared in the doorway. "Your father's at the gates. Lady Werra told him you lay abed with a headache, but he didn't believe her. He used such coarse language that she's quite upset. He's demanding to speak with you."

"Does he have armed men with him?" Dovina said.

"A few, and a councillor."

Dovina rolled her eyes. "I want to show the stubborn old dog this book, so I suppose I can pretend to surrender. Mavva, if I may trouble you, would you go tell His Grace that I'm rising at his command and will be down once I'm decently dressed? Lyss, will you accompany me?"

"Gladly," Alyssa said. "I want to see what happens."

As a sop to Dovina's rank, Alyssa insisted on carrying the book. Since it had been written onto Bardek pabrus it weighed far less than one of their old parchment volumes, but it still made a tidy armful. They arrived at the closed and locked iron gates to find the gwerbret pacing irritably outside them while his attendants huddled off to one side.

Gwerbret Ladoic was a tall man, heavily muscled if somewhat bow-legged from all the years he'd spent on horseback. He wore his gray hair cropped close to his skull, though he sported a thick, drooping mustache as if in compensation. Although his brown breeches were as plain as a commoner's, his waistcoat was made of the Fox tartan and fastened with big silver knots for buttons. His shirt sported the Fox blazon at the yokes and on the sleeves.

"Ah, there you are," he said. "So you deigned to come down? I want to talk with you. Call a servant, please, and have him open these gates."

"All the servants are busy with the noon meal," Dovina said. "We can see each other well enough through the bars. What did you want to talk about?"

"This rebellion of yours. There are men dead over it, and I want it stopped."

"It's a bit late for that, Father. Cradoc's death can't be taken back. How could you have done it, just let him starve like that?"

Ladoic started to speak but said nothing.

"You thought he'd give in, didn't you?" Dovina continued. "Break his fast, and you'd win. The honor of the thing, not giving in, lords should be stubborn and all the rest of it. Well, wasn't it?"

"What's done is done." But he looked away as he said it.

"And then Gwarl went and made things worse."

Ladoic started to snarl an answer, calmed himself, and began again. "I've spoken to your brother. And that's all I'm going to say about it."

"But—"

"I said, that's all! It's between him and me. Not you."

Alyssa caught her breath, but Dovina dropped him a curtsy, and he nodded in satisfaction.

"Very well, Father. But it's not a rebellion. We're basing our requests on our ancient traditions as the People of Bel."

"Indeed?"

"I'll show you summat."

Alyssa stepped forward, and Dovina took the book. Ladoic snorted, but before he could speak further, Dovina thrust the book at him through the bars.

"I've marked the spot with that bit of pabrus," she said. "Do read what he says about the origin of the gwerbretion. You say you'll stand on old traditions, Father. Well, here's what the oldest tradition says about the law courts."

Ladoic took the heavy volume, but he snapped his fingers at an elderly man, dressed in the long black robe that marked him as a councillor. "Nallyc! Read this aloud."

Nallyc took the book, opened it, and glanced at the marked passage. For a moment he read silently. His eyebrows shot up, and Dovina smirked at him.

"Surprising, innit?" she said. "It makes standing on tradition rather less attractive."

"Indeed, my lady." His voice quavered more with fear than age. "Er, Your Grace, mayhap we should read this in private—"

"Read it now!"

"Very well, Your Grace." Councillor Nallyc cleared his throat and began. "The language is very old and contorted, so I shall summarize. It says here that in the Dawntime, when our ancestors did wish to choose a man to judge them and administer their laws, they held an assembly of all free men. Their rhix—" Nallyc looked up from the text. "That would be their warleader, Your Grace, the man we call the cadvridoc. At any rate, he would put forth several candidates, and the tribal assembly would choose the one they thought fit." He swallowed heavily. "It goes on to say that the laws expressly prohibited a vergobrex from passing the office on to his son."

"Just think!" Dovina put in. "So much for a clan's position!"

Ladoic's face went stone-still. When he held out a hand, Nallyc handed him the book, then drew his robe tightly around him, as if for protection. Ladoic stared at the passage, then shut the book with a snap and a puff of dust. He looked at Dovina with cold blue eyes.

"How do I know you didn't just write this book, eh?" the gwerbret snorted. "Or put this bit in, like."

"Father, be reasonable! It takes months to write out a book this size."

"And you've had months, haven't you?" Ladoic grinned as if he'd just won a game of carnoic. "This thing looks cursed new to me. Nice clean pages. Naught faded or worn."

Dovina reached through the gate and grabbed the book back from his indifferent hands.

"My dear lady!" Nallyc sounded so angry he nearly sputtered. "How can you be so discourteous? He may be your father, but he's also your gwerbret and overlord!"

"And you are common-born no matter how high you've risen! Don't you speak to me like that!"

"Enough!" Ladoic threw both hands in the air. "Silence, the pair of you!"

Dovina took a pace back. Nallyc took several.

"That's better." Ladoic lowered his hands. "No matter what or why, we know what the outcome's been. Riots. Fighting in the market square. I intend to put an end to this rebellion any way I can."

"It's not a rebellion!" Dovina said. "We merely stand on the ancient traditions you claim to honor. If you'd but listen to our legal arguments—"

Ladoic's patience snapped.

"You listen to me!" Ladoic set his hands on his hips. "You're coming with me right now, back to the dun."

"I'm not." Dovina clutched the book to her chest. "And you can't come in to seize me, either, unless I invite you. That's the terms of our charter."

"You stubborn little wench!"

"I'm stubborn? Huh! Why do you want me so badly? Have you found some new landless suitor who's desperate for a wife? Some gouty old widower who's gambled his inheritance away?"

"I have, but he happens to be a decent young man." Ladoic considered her with a small smile. "And a man of advanced ideas, or so I hear, the younger son of Lord Tarryc of Daiver. The gwerbret's nephew. Hah! That made you think!"

Dovina wrinkled her nose in a sneer but said nothing. Alyssa raised an eyebrow. A connection with Daiver? Worth considering, certainly.

The gwerbretion of Daiver occupied an odd position in the nobility. Once, hundreds of years ago, they'd ruled Cerrmor, in the usual manner. Some complicated political intrigue and a brief rebellion back in the 1200s had lost them everything. Since the common people had held for the king, they were rewarded with the charter that made Cerrmor a free city. To prevent further bloodshed, the gwerbretal clan had been fobbed off with scant land and a title derived from an old village near the city itself. In Dovina's time, their connections to the High King kept them prosperous but dependent upon serving the royalty as court officials.

"Besides," Ladoic continued, "the Prince Regent is making a royal progress. We'll be meeting him in Cerrmor."

"So you'd best make a decent appearance." Dovina smiled in the simpery way that meant she'd spotted a weapon. "There's bound to be all sorts of ceremonies around his visit."

"Indeed. The city itself will be holding a feast in his honor. Convenient all round. This man I'm betrothing you to—Merryc, his name is—will be greeting him. So you're cursed well coming with me to Cerrmor whether you want to go or not."

"Cerrmor, is it?" Dovina glanced Alyssa's way. "How awfully interesting."

"Very, my lady." Alyssa curtsied to her and to the gwerbret. Cerrmor, of course, was the home of the new Collegium of Advocates, allies to their cause.

"Well then, Father," Dovina said. "I'll make you a bargain. Give us back Cradoc's body, and I'll come with you willingly."

"I can just go to my law court and order this tower of madwomen to hand you over. Why should I bargain with you?"

"Because if you don't, I'll scream and howl and make such a horrid display of myself in front of the Prince Regent that you'll be shamed in the eyes of every man in the kingdom. Such as Gwerbret Standyc, for instance. And won't old Tewdyr love to repeat the tale?"

Gwerbret Ladoic's face turned so bright a shade of red that Alyssa feared he was about to suffer an elf-stroke. Dovina smirked at him until he cleared his throat and took a deep breath or two. Slowly his color returned to its usual weather-beaten tan.

"You wouldn't!"

"Oh, come now, Father. You know me well enough to know that I would."

He scowled; she smiled. "Oh, very well!" he said at last. "I'll have the servants bring your cursed bard back with all due ceremony. And you'd best be ready to leave when they do!"

"After the funeral, of course. To do otherwise would be unseemly."

"Oh, very well! After the funeral. Besides, I want you home for another thing. Your lout of a brother, as you call him, is visiting. Adonyc's brought good news. You can be decent and help us celebrate."

"What? Has that moo-cow of a wife of his squeezed out a male heir?"

"Just that, and don't call her a cow." Yet he was fighting a smile. "Placid, that's the word we want."

"Placid and fertile, and I'll bet she gives lots and lots of milk."

Ladoic suppressed his smile and turned away with a gesture to Nallyc to follow. He barked out a few orders to the men accompanying him and strode off. Dovina said nothing until they'd all mounted their horses and ridden away.

"Summat's upset Father," Dovina said. "He's not usually as bad as this."

"I'd suppose that the fathers of those dead lads have sent him messages by now."

"That's most likely it. Though he's fond of saying that a daughter like me would drive most men mad." She paused for a grin. "I'll admit the justice of that."

Alyssa kept a tactful silence.

"Let's go back to the bookchamber," Dovina said. "I have a plan, but we've got to find out where the old copy of this book may be. Everything depends on that."

"The old copy?"

"The source manuscript, the crumbling smelly old thing that's in our bookhoard. I've found notes about it from the priests of Wmm. They called it the 'no one' book because it had 'nevyn' written on the first page. I've got no idea what that means, but the notes said some scholars think the book's hundreds and hundreds of years old. If we can get that one into the hands of the guild, Father shan't be able to pretend we've forged it."

"You can smuggle it with you when you go."

"Assuming it's here in the collegium. I have the awful feeling that we're not going to have that kind of luck."

As was so often the case when the subject was books, Dovina was right. According to the notes she found in the journal of the book-hoard, the "Nevyn Copy" of Dwvoryc's Annals of the Dawntime had been given over on loan to Haen Marn so that the Scribal Guild there could produce copies.

"Ye gods," Dovina said. "Haen Marn's over the border. Near the Bear clan."

"Right in the middle of the feud," Alyssa said.

They shared a sigh and sat down together on the wooden bench. The Bear clan of northern Eldidd had once owed fealty to Aberwyn, but years of intrigue had finally brought them some independence and a gwerbret of their own for their widespread holdings, which included a good stretch of southern Pyrdon. They had thus become hated by the gwerbretion to either side of them. To call them "sensitive" about their delicate position lay beyond mere overstatement. For ancient reasons they had hated the Maelwaedds of Aberwyn for hundreds of years, and when the Electors handed the rhan to the Fox, the spurned Bears transferred their hatred right over.

"The roads and canals to Haen Marn," Dovina said, "run right through their territory. I can't send an Aberwyn courier to fetch the book. He'd be arrested and detained if they saw him."

"I know. At least Haen Marn's a separate rhan, sacred and all that. They wouldn't dare interfere with it."

For some long moments Dovina merely stared, thinking hard, at the opposite wall. Alyssa idly studied the framed map of the ancient Westfolk city of Rinbaladelan that hung on the same wall and waited for her superior in rank to speak. Eventually Dovina sighed again.

"I meant to ask you," Dovina said. "How did the speech in the market square go?"

"I barely got started when the marshals marched in."

"What?" Dovina turned on the bench to stare at her.

While Alyssa gave her report, Dovina continued staring, her mouth slack with surprise and, eventually, fear. "My apologies," Dovina said when Alyssa had finished. "I never should have asked you to come to the gates with me. Ye gods! Good thing you carried the book for me! Father probably thought you were a servant or suchlike. He never truly looked at you."

"Are they going to blame me?" Alyssa could only wonder at herself, that she'd not seen this obvious question before. The sunlight in the room seemed to have become very bright and very cold. She clasped her hands to keep them from shaking. "That heckler—I did try to ignore him."

"It was just like Father to put a hound among the hares! And the fellow who hit him—do you know him or suchlike?"

"I only met him the night past. He was caught in the riot at the dun gates like I was."

"I suppose my wretched father will put the blame on him. Silver daggers have that awful reputation, troublemakers and violent and all of that. Father will find some way to charge him with summat bad."

"That's horribly unfair!"

"Of course it is. That's why we're working to change the courts, innit?"

"Well, true spoken. And ye gods, what about me?"

"I sincerely think that my father has too much honor to hang a woman, but I'm sure he'd levy a huge fine on your family. Any chance at a guildmaster's coin, he'll take it. Worse yet, if he nabs this poor fellow, it's the gallows for sure, to make an example of him."

"Here! I can't allow—I mean, I don't want—"

Dovina leaned forward to peer into Alyssa's face. "You're rather sweet on this fellow, aren't you?"

Alyssa blushed.

"Then we simply can't let him hang." Dovina heaved a melancholy sigh. "I do wish Father had bothered to develop his rational faculties. I don't suppose he's ever read Prince Mael's book about Ristolyn. But let me see, what can we do about the silver dagger?"

"Could we hire him to go to Haen Marn and fetch the book?"

"Now there's a thought! It would get him safely out of town as well, and the Bears aren't going to growl at a silver dagger running an errand. But I doubt me if the healers on the island would hand the book over to a silver dagger, even with a letter from me. It's a very rare book."

"Well, I don't suppose giving it to the Advocates would mean much, anyway. It would be a splendid gesture, but just a gesture. Though, curse it all! I want to honor Cradoc's memory with more than a speech! A gesture would have been better than naught."

"Wait!" Dovina paused to think something through. "Would it really be just a gesture? The Advocates could cite it as yet another legal precedent, and this one has teeth. But if we can't fetch the book, truly, it matters very little. You heard Father. It's too easy to claim the new copies as forgeries."

"Would the Lady of Haen Marn refuse to give it up, do you think?"

"We have the loan note." Dovina held up the piece of pabrus. "They have to give it over to someone from the collegium who brings this to them. It's too bad that we don't know someone who's been there, someone they know and would trust."

Alyssa's idea struck her as immensely dangerous, immensely foolish. Had it not been for Cradoc's death, and her desire to do some grand thing to make that death worthwhile, she would never have spoken it aloud.

"What's so wrong?" Dovina said.

"I've been there." Alyssa breathed deeply and forced her voice under control. "They know me, my lady."

"Ye gods! Were you desperately ill, then?"

"I wasn't. Before I came to the collegium, my father fell ill. My mother had to stay and run the bakery, and so I traveled with him when he went to consult the healers." Alyssa paused, remembering. "It's such an amazing place! And the healers! You really start to believe they can work dwimmer."

"Well, if such a thing truly exists. Though you do hear strange stories that make me wonder."

"Indeed. I was sitting with my father when one of the healers came in. Perra of Cannobaen's her name. When she was done helping him, she took a moment to chat with me. Da was sleeping thanks to the anodyne she'd given him. She asked me what I liked to do when I had time to myself. I like to read, I told her." Alyssa smiled, remembering the shock on the healer's face. "I asked her if they had books, and she said yes, but they were all about healing and medicinals. I told her about the guildhall's little bookhoard and how I'd put it all in order and made a list of them and such. Very well, she said, you should be a scholar. She got me my place here at the collegium."

"Ai!" Dovina's eyes widened. "I've heard much about her."

"She's in charge of all the healers there, now, from what I've heard."

"She's a grand patroness to have, truly! This could work out splendidly if we could get you to Haen Marn. We could hire the silver dagger to accompany—er, wait, not such a good idea. Everyone would think you were eloping with him, and you'd be dishonored."

"Better than seeing my family driven into poverty. Or watching him hang."

"Well, I shall do my best to keep that from happening." Yet Dovina sounded doubtful, a rare thing for her.

"You've already got one huge concession out of your father. You shan't be able to get another."

"Most likely that's true, alas. He'll bend a bit when I force things, but he doesn't give in twice over the same matter. Having you go to Haen Marn on your own would be far too dangerous, a woman alone on the roads. And we've got to get the silver dagger out of town— what is his name?"

"Cavan of Lughcarn, my lady."

"Ah, my thanks." Dovina considered this for a few moments. "Hmm. That's oddly familiar. It makes me wonder, but anyway, we've got to get Cavan away quickly. And I certainly don't want my wretched father's wrath descending upon your family, either. Would you be safe on the road with your silver dagger, do you think?"

"I do, especially if we told him he'd not get paid for the job if he gave me any trouble."

"Good thought! What I can do is give you a note, a draft, they call them, to my father's banker up in Haen Marn. Father's got a fair bit of coin in the treasury there. A lot of lords keep treasure there for safety's sake. Only you can draw out the money, not Cavan, not anyone else. So if you don't want him to have one copper penny of it, he'll not get it."

"But what will your father say when he finds out the coin's been taken?"

"I shall tell him I need new dresses to impress this wretched suitor he's dug up." Dovina shrugged the problem away. "My name wouldn't be on the draft if he didn't expect me to draw coin out now and then."

"Very well, if you think taking the money's safe."

"If I didn't, I wouldn't suggest it. That should work splendidly. No matter what they were before, silver daggers always think of the coin."

"I suppose they have to, out on the long road like that."

"Oh, no doubt. Where is he now, in some tavern in town?"

"He's not, but in Wmm's Scribal. Rhys is hiding him there."

"Good for Rhys!" Dovina rubbed her hands together. "Let's go downstairs and find Mavva. You'd best stay inside out of sight, but no doubt she'll not mind taking a message to her betrothed."

"**O**ne thing I don't understand," Cavan said. "Why would the noble-born men in King's join your cause?"

"They're all younger sons," Rhys said. "They've got good reason to want to stick it to their first-born brothers."

"Makes sense." Cavan could understand that motive all too well.

"Besides, they're at the collegium because they're going to end up as councillors or even running the law courts in their fathers' rhannau, and very few of them want to. What complaints come before most small lords out here in the west, anyway? Some farmer claiming a witch cursed his cow or stole his chickens, or neighbors hauling in a townsman who won't clean up his dungheap in the summer. The truly big cases, a guild bringing action against a lord to make him pay his debts, for instance, always go before the gwerbret himself. And you can guess, I'm sure, how such a case is settled."

"Always in the lord's favor." Cavan paused for a sip of ale. "The same thing happens to silver daggers, if some miser refuses to pay your hire."

Rhys nodded in sympathy. They were sitting at one of the polished oak tables in Wmm's Scribal's great hall. These priests-to-be did themselves well, Cavan thought. Bardekian carpets in bright patterns covered the floor, and silver sconces hung between the glazed windows. The long tables and benches shone from polishing. He and Rhys had just shared a trencher of roast meats and fresh bread, washed down with a decent dark ale.

"Not a bad life you lead," Cavan said. "Good ale, anyway."

"We might as well drink now. Once we take the vows of Wmm's priesthood, it's no more ale for us."

"What? Bardek wine, then?"

"None of that, either. Boiled water. On special feast days, spiced milk."

Cavan made a sour face, and Rhys laughed at him. "At least we can marry," Rhys said. "I'd hate to be part of Bel's priesthood."

"So would I." A pleasantly dark voice spoke behind them.

Cavan turned on the bench and saw a tall, slender young man, smiling at them. He wore his moonbeam-pale hair long to cover his ears, but his eyes gave him away: purple, and slit vertically like a cat's. One of the fabled Westfolk, then, even though he wore a shirt and breeches like an ordinary man and the orange surcoat of the collegium.

"Come join us, Trav," Rhys said. "Cavan, this is Travaberiel ap Maelaber, an adjunct scholar here."

With a brief smile Travaberiel sat down on the bench opposite them. He glanced Cavan's way, still smiling, still pleasant, but for a moment Cavan felt as if he'd been skewered by that glance. He had the odd but definite sensation that Travaberiel was looking deep into his soul. The moment passed. *Dwimmer,* he thought. *This man has it.* To break the moment he picked up his silver dagger and began cleaning the meat juice off the blade with his napkin.

"How very odd," Travaberiel said. "Those old tales, the ones about silver daggers glowing when they were close to a man like me—they must not be true."

"Old folk tales, I'm sure." Cavan held the dagger up. No mysterious light shone on it or from it. "I never believed them, but this is the first chance I've ever had to test them."

"And you're the first silver dagger I've ever met. I've not been in Eldidd long."

"You're a, what was that? An adjunct scholar?"

"I'm here to study the Deverry laws and customs that pertain to heralds. That's what I am back home, a herald." Trav signaled a passing servant, who handed him a tankard.

"Some of us," Rhys put in, "go on to join the College of Heralds over in Deverry. That's a bit too much adventure for my taste, going back and forth twixt warring lords."

"No doubt you won't have to," Cavan said. "You'll have an important position at one court or another once you've finished here."

"I can hope, truly. Scribes are always in demand. By the by —" this to Travaberiel "— if any outsiders ask about Cavan, just tell them he's my cousin, come to visit."

"Right. I saw that bit of trouble in the marketplace. I'm tempted to say good for you, dropping that foul-mouthed bastard, but it's doubtless made things difficult."

"Difficult?" Cavan said. "You've got a herald's tact, sure enough."

The three of them laughed, but ruefully.

"Speaking of difficult things," Cavan continued, "will the master of your collegium object to my staying here?"

"I'm a senior student, and we're allowed occasional guests. Besides—" Rhys paused for a knowing wink. "Master Paedyr will be pleased to have you once he finds out why we had to hide you. We've got a hawk flying in this hunt."

"Hunt? You've got to mean changing the law courts."

"Just that. Look, the priests of Bel, they control the laws, don't they? The old laws, anyway, and that's well over half of all the laws— the priests are the only ones that know them. They have them in memory, but somewhere there have got to be books. No one else is allowed to read those. No one else is allowed to study them."

"And that must gripe the very soul of your god," Travaberiel put in. "To say naught of all your priestly souls."

"Just that. All that ancient lore shut away from us! It also makes the laws very—" Rhys waggled a hand in the air. "Very flexible, let us say. If the priests want a bit of land or some coin for a temple building."

"Ye gods!" Cavan said. "Are you saying they take bribes?"

"We don't know if they take bribes. How can we if we don't know the actual laws? They can say anything they like when it comes to most disputes."

All three of them had a long thoughtful swallow of ale.

"I've walked into the middle of a holy brawl, you mean," Cavan said.

"And taken a side before you even knew it. We're going to need to smuggle you out of town some way or the other," Rhys said. "Do you have a hire somewhere?"

"Naught. I came to Aberwyn because I heard of a feud brewing up on the border twixt your gwerbret and the Bear clan. Work for my blade, I thought."

Across the table, Trav set down his tankard and leaned closer. "That situation's a fair bit nastier than you might think. You might want to look in some other direction."

"Indeed?" Cavan said. "I'd be grateful if you'd tell me more."

"I don't know much more, is the difficulty." Trav frowned at his tankard. "But last I heard, it might involve some of my people as well as the village your two lords are squabbling over. You don't want to end up spitted like a chicken."

"I see. My thanks for the warning. Huh, that explains why the word went out. That the lords involved would want silver daggers. They'll put us right in front so the archers can take aim at us, not their sworn men."

Travaberiel winced.

"Just my luck!" Cavan said. "To hear about trouble that turns out to be twice trouble."

The silence hung for a moment between them.

"You're a lucky man in one way, though." Rhys apparently had decided to lighten the mood. "Gaining Alyssa's favor like that. None of the other lads have had so much as a kind look from her."

Cavan allowed himself a grin and had a long drink of ale.

"I—" Rhys paused and turned on the bench. "What is it, lad?"

A servant trotted over and made him a sketchy bow. "A message from your betrothed. She needs to speak with you and your guest."

"Well and good, then. We'll go out directly." He glanced Cavan's way. "The lasses can't come in here, and we can't go into their hall, either, except on certain festival days."

Mavva was waiting for them on the lawn not far from the door into Wmm's hall. With her stood a blonde young woman who wore her red surcoat over a brown dress of Bardekian silk. As the two men approached, the blonde lass raised a reading-glass and peered at Cavan through it.

"That's Lady Dovina," Rhys murmured. "The gwerbret's daughter."

"My lady." Cavan bowed to her.

When she extended her hand, he caught it and brushed his lips across the back of it in a courtesy kiss.

"Hah!" Dovina said. "You are noble-born. I wondered about that."

Cavan winced and cursed himself. Quite without thinking he'd given himself away. Rhys shot him a startled glance.

"Don't worry," Dovina went on. "Whatever you did to earn that dagger is none of my affair. In fact, your birth eases my mind a fair bit. Alyssa needs an escort to Haen Marn. We're going to hire you to escort her. But I expect you to treat her as delicately as you'd treat the queen herself. If you do, there's a good bit of silver in the hire for you."

"Splendid idea!" Rhys put in. "If we can get the pair of you out of the town gates safely."

"During Cradoc's funeral." Dovina took a folded bit of pabrus out of her kirtle and handed it to Rhys. "Father just sent me this message. Tomorrow our teacher's body comes back to us. The Bardic Guild will be joining Lady Rhodda Hall for a grand procession out to the sacred grove." Dovina frowned as she thought something through. "We'll have to get a horse for Alyssa. The pair of them can ride in the procession and then just keep riding when the procession turns aside to go into the grove."

"Excellent!" Rhys said. "We can get together provisions and the like from the collegia. And saddlebags. Alyssa can tell anyone who asks that they're carrying offerings for the grave."

"Good idea!" Dovina gave him an approving smile. "Now listen closely, Cavan. Only Alyssa can draw the coin that will pay your hire. The money will be waiting at Haen Marn itself. If you give her the least bit of trouble, you won't get paid."

"Here!" Cavan snapped. "I've not agreed yet."

"Do you want to stay in town and hang?" Dovina smiled brightly at him. "Sooner or later, Father will puzzle out where you're hiding and get the court to force Wmm's men to hand you over. He is the court, you know. Which means he gets to pass the sentence, too."

Cavan sighed and rubbed his neck with one hand.

"Ah, you understand me," Dovina went on. "Well?"

"My thanks, my lady. I'll take your hire gladly."

And, he reminded himself, the hire offered compensations. Although he had every intention of treating Alyssa as honorably as he'd treat the queen, even queens were known to take a fancy to a man now and then. No doubt a common-born lass would care less for her delicate honor than a high-born woman. Never would he give Alyssa "trouble," as her ladyship had termed it, but it would hardly be trouble if she were willing. The memory of that kiss in the market square made him smile, until he realized that Dovina was watching him with her lips set tight, as if she knew what he was thinking.

"I'm going to tell Alyssa that you're noble-born," Dovina said. "That way she'll know better than to believe a honeyed word you say."

With that she turned and marched off back to the women's hive. Cavan bowed out of habit, but he would rather have snarled. As he walked back to Wmm's with Rhys, he noticed Travaberiel standing in the doorway, watching them with a polite little smile. Smile or not, Cavan felt his suspicions catch fire. What was this fellow, a spy? People always said you couldn't trust the Westfolk if their interests crossed yours. *They're not truly human*, he reminded himself. *Let's just stay on guard.*

Yet what if Travaberiel had dwimmer? The ancient magic—dweomer, they called it in the old days; so many people said it was only an old wives' tale, a silly superstition, or maybe at most a debased witchery. Cavan, however, had seen and felt things that had convinced him it was real and true, perhaps the only truth that mattered. Or was it just that he so badly wanted the dwimmer to be real? He could never be sure, but one thing he did know. The wanting was real enough.

The first difficulty in making their escape, Alyssa soon realized, lay in hiding the preparations from Lady Tay. Fortunately, Malyc Penvardd, who was allowed into the women's great hall because of his advanced age, arrived to dine with Lady Tay and plan Cradoc's funeral. An average-looking fellow, neither tall nor short, with gray hair that barely covered his head, he had a face as wrinkled as the sea. Yet he strode into the collegium grounds as vigorously as a young man. As Alyssa escorted him across the lawn, he told her in his trained and booming voice that he himself, as the chief bard, would deliver the gwerchan in tribute.

"That will be splendid, honored one," Alyssa said.

"So I'll hope. I wanted a private word with you. Let's pause here a moment."

They found a little bit of privacy in the shelter of a pair of young trees near the women's hive.

"I know Cradoc favored you as if you were his daughter," Malyc said. "Your heart must be heavy."

"It is, sir, heavy and near breaking. At moments I remember that I'll never see him again." She paused to wipe her eyes on her sleeve. "I'll honor his memory always."

"As I will, myself. It vexes me, that he died for so little. All we asked of the gwerbret was a fair hearing on this matter of the law courts and the nobility. The bard is the voice of his people under the laws, is he not? That voice has the legal right to be heard."

"True spoken. But it's not a small thing, that right. If the bards are silenced, the people have no voice, and the lords may do as they please with no one to shame them."

Malyc smiled and nodded. "Good answer," he said. "You do understand. Their precious honor tarnishes more easily than silver for all that they value it higher than gold. At any rate, you may rest assured that I shan't let this matter end here."

"That gladdens my heart."

"I thought it would. Huh, it's getting chilly out here. Let's not keep Lady Tay waiting."

They walked on in silence. When they entered the hive, Lady Tay was standing near the door to greet the Penvardd and escort him to the head table. Alyssa took her place with the other senior students. A servant brought the head table wine, and another brought the students boiled water with a bit of wine in it for flavor.

Up at the front of the hall, Malyc announced, in his ringing voice that carried through half the hive, that he had ordered Cradoc's apprentice to abandon the starvation siege at the gwerbretal gates.

"We've lost one of our best men already," Malyc said. "No use in losing two. Ladoic has made it clear that he won't give in, for all his talk about respecting custom and law. I am both shocked and heartsick over Cradoc's death, my lady. I should have stopped this deadly ritual. Had I only known how far the gwerbret would go—" He paused to make one sharp sob. "I never dreamed it would end this way."

Lady Tay made a reply that Alyssa couldn't quite hear. She did catch the words "dreadful shock."

"His note about Cradoc's body was that last drop of water that ruins the ale," Malyc continued. "I intend to make him pay for that."

And how can you? Alyssa thought. Apparently Lady Tay asked something similar, because Malyc said, "I have a weapon that will make His Grace tremble, were I to use it, but by the gods, I'll pray it doesn't come to that! Too many innocent persons would suffer."

"Ye gods!" In her surprise Lady Tay spoke almost as loudly as the chief bard.

Malyc merely smiled and speared a fragment of pork with his table dagger. After that he spoke somewhat more quietly, and only of the funereal details.

Alyssa left the table as soon as she could. She needed to pack supplies for her journey north. Dovina took charge of wheedling provisions out of the hive's cook. Mavva gathered bits of spare clothing from those women who could afford to give it. One of the other senior students handed over a pair of fine leather saddlebags.

"You'd best take as much clothing as you can in the saddlebags," Dovina said. "You'll have to make a decent appearance in Cerrmor, you see. I've scrounged up what coin I can for the first part of your journey. Once you get to Haen Marn and use the draft, you'll be able to buy what you need."

"We'd best travel as fast as possible, anyway," Alyssa said. "If we can get over the border into the Bear clan's demesne, we'll be out of your father's reach."

"True, but you'll have to get the book to Cerrmor. I wish you could go by ship, but you won't dare return to Eldidd. Best go overland to Dun Trebyc and down from there, though ye gods, it'll take so long!"

"Better a long journey than one that ends too soon, In your father's jail."

Later that night, before the chaperones locked the doors into the women's hall, Dovina, Mavva, and Alyssa met Cavan and Rhys out on the lawn. Travaberiel joined them at Rhys's invitation. By the light of candle lanterns they all walked down to the back wall where they were less likely to be overheard.

"Be cursed careful once you reach the Bear lands," Travaberiel said. "If this feud turns into a war, Standyc's likely to arrest anyone from Eldidd. Lie if you have to. He's a suspicious man, Standyc, sure that he has hidden enemies somewhere."

"Is he right about that?" Alyssa said.

"Not to my knowledge. He's got plenty of enemies right out in the open among my folk. You'd think that would be enough for him."

"My thanks." Cavan made him a half-bow. "I'll remember that."

Alyssa felt the night air turn cold around her. Dovina held up her punched-tin lantern and cast spangles of gold light over the silver dagger.

"Will you keep her safe?" The cold in her voice made Alyssa shiver again. "If I find out you haven't, I'll turn you in to my father."

"On my honor, my lady." Cavan made her a full bow. "I swear it on my silver dagger, and that's the truest oath a man like me can swear."

Rhys glanced at Travaberiel, who murmured, "I believe him."

"Done, then," Rhys said. "But you might remember that Wmm's priesthood is like a net cast over the kingdom. Messages do travel."

"I know it well." Cavan laid a hand on the pommel of his dagger. "Fear not. I swore I'd guard the lady, and I cursed well will! I may be a silver dagger and scum of the road, but I've still got some sense of honor."

Dovina and Rhys nodded in satisfaction.

"Lyss, I've got summat for you." Rhys reached into his shirt and brought out some sheets of pabrus, folded into a square in the Bardekian fashion. "If you find yourself needing help, show these around at the nearest temple of Wmm." He dropped his voice to whisper. "Two copies, both signed by a couple of the masters here. Not a word of their names to anyone outside the priesthood, mind. And a third one only for the Advocates Guild."

"A thousand thanks!" Alyssa took the packet. "Please tell those men who don't exist that I'm truly grateful, not that they've done anything."

"Lyss!" Mavva broke in. "Do you really want to do this? It's horribly dangerous. I don't think I realized it at first. It was all like a gerthddyn's tale or suchlike. But—"

Alyssa gathered her breath with a gulp. "I will not let Cradoc die in vain. If this book will help bring the gwerbret round, then I'll do my best to get it to Cerrmor and the advocates there. Our cause is just, and justice we shall have."

When she glanced at Cavan, she found him smiling at her in honest admiration. She felt, very briefly, brave.

CHAPTER 3

EVEN THOUGH CRADOC HAD taught rhetoric as a master in Lady Rhodda Hall, to give the women's collegium its proper name, the women rode at the end of the funeral procession, except for Lady Tay, who was allowed to ride next to Malyc Penvardd just behind the cart that carried Cradoc's body. None of the women were surprised that the rest of them were consigned to the position of least prestige behind the Bardic Guild, the noble-born men of King's, and the priestly neophytes of Wmm's Scribal. No one complained, either, since it suited their plans so well.

The procession formed up in the old market square. Alyssa and her silver dagger took the very last place of all. She was wearing a pair of Rhys's knee breeches under her skirt to allow her to sit astride her gentle dun palfrey. She carried the banker's draft and the loan note for the book sewn onto her underskirt. To protect the documents, Dovina had cut several hunks of silk off the bottom of one of her dresses and made a many-layered envelope.

Getting a procession of such a size ordered and moving took some while. While she waited her turn to ride out through the north alleyway into the streets of the town, Alyssa had plenty of time to wonder if she were doing the right thing. Had it not been for Cradoc's sake, she might have surrendered to her doubts, but he had fought several battles with the collegium authorities and his own guild before he'd been allowed to teach her rhetoric and bardic lore. All of the collegium women were trained in expressing themselves clearly, but Alyssa had received the further instruction normally reserved for men. He fought for me, she reminded herself. It's my duty to fight for what he championed.

And she would be riding with Cavan, a danger of another sort. She wondered why he attracted her so much. He was far from the handsomest man she'd ever seen. His face tended toward the square, his mouth was a bit wide and thin, and he apparently combed his hair once every week or so judging from the tangled way it fell over his ears. But his energy! He seemed to blaze at times like one of Lughcarn's famous forges. His gray eyes snapped with it, and when he smiled, she felt as if she'd stepped up to a hearth after being outside on a winter's day.

But a silver dagger, she reminded herself. It's no matter that you're hungry when the meat on the table's gone bad.

At last the men from Wmm's Scribal urged their horses forward. The women just ahead brought their mounts to the ready. Cavan rode up next to her and made her a half-bow from the saddle.

"I've been thinking," he said. "You'd best ride a bit ahead of me. I don't mind posing as your servant till we get free of this mob."

"Only till then, eh?" But she smiled at him. "Good idea."

She clucked to her horse and followed the other women riders out of the market square.

All along their route through Aberwyn, townsfolk lined the streets or sat in the upper windows of the buildings to watch. As the procession passed them, both men and women keened and called out their farewells to Cradoc, who had died in his attempt to bring them justice. Bolder folk ran outside and walked silently behind the riders. At moments Alyssa felt her eyes fill with tears, but always she brushed them away. Cradoc would have wanted strength, not mourning, from his best pupil.

When they passed the walls of the gwerbretal dun, however, nothing but silence greeted them.

At the northern city gate, Alyssa turned in the saddle and looked back. Several hundred walkers had joined the procession. Many of the men, she realized, carried stout sticks, some as thick as clubs. Cavan rode up close to her.

"I don't like the looks of this mob," he said.

"Mob? It's their right to attend a funeral. The Bardic Guild's putting on a feast for all the mourners, and it's bound to be a huge one. They don't stint when it comes to food."

"I still don't like it. Too many angry men among them."

The procession slowed at the narrow gate. The riders closed up their ranks and trickled through into the silence of the market gardens and pastures beyond the city walls. About half a mile ahead stood the grove of ancient oaks where Cradoc would join the bards who had gone on to the Otherlands before him. The road led up to the grove, then divided. One half circled round the trees and ran west; the other headed roughly north along the river Gwyn.

The priests of Bel, who presided over funerals, had set up a holding area for the horses of the attendees beside the north-running road in a stretch of pastureland. Riders were dismounting; horses were tossing their heads and stamping impatiently; grooms ran back and forth under a cloud of dust. In the confusion it was a simple matter for Alyssa and Cavan to keep on the road rather than turning in to join the mob. If any of the priests or servants noticed them riding steadily north, no one called out a question or gave an alarm.

Since Dovina had been keeping a watch on Alyssa and her silver dagger, she did see their escape. Once she could tell that they were safely on their way, she turned her attention to the crowd. Here and there she spotted men who served her father. As she and the other students passed by them, she recognized the underchamberlain, a couple of footmen, and some of the grooms. Even more ominous was the presence of a couple of the younger sons of the Hippogriff, the clan that held Abernaudd under her father's old enemy, Gwerbret Tewdyr. Neither of them wore their clan colors of brown, green, and a rich gold, but she'd seen them at enough social events and religious festivals to know who they were. Neither attended any sort of collegium. Warriors, both of them, and she doubted that they'd come to mourn Cradoc.

The rest of those walking in the procession were another matter, townspeople, mostly, but here and there she saw men and women whose bent backs and rough clothing proclaimed them farmfolk. Many of the common-born mourners carried walking sticks—stout walking sticks, as far as she could tell, with the glint of metal bands upon them, tools that had nothing to do with the chunks of roast pork and bread that the guild was going to distribute. No doubt they were carrying table daggers as well, or good knives.

Although Cradoc's actual grave lay among the sacred oaks, the ceremonies took place some hundred yards away on a level lawn beside an artificial stream. The priests of Bel maintained a large wooden platform with a row of chairs for important people. By the time Dovina and the women students reached the lawn, two priests of Bel, a priest of Wmm, and Lady Tay were already seated. Most of the women went to stand at one side of the crowd where the townswomen had gathered but, as the gwerbret's daughter, Dovina found herself pointed to a chair right on the platform, though at the rear.

At the front of the platform Malyc Penvardd was conferring in whispers with an elderly priest. With them stood two more priests, wearing their traditional garb for the ceremony—long tunics caught at the waist with a leather belt, sandals on their otherwise bare feet. From the belts hung the small silver sickles of their office. Their legs were pasty-white; like most priests of that time they wore knee breeches and boots with their tunics in their daily lives. As she passed them, one of them broke off their conversation and turned to her.

"Allow me to escort you to your seat, your ladyship."

Although she curtsied out of respect for his god, she would rather have been escorted by a snake. At least, given the strict celibacy of his order, he refrained from offering her his arm.

"We did want a word with you," he said in a quiet voice. "Just to tell you that your father can count on our support."

"The support of the god is always welcome." Dovina forced out a smile. "My thanks."

For a moment his face showed confusion, as if he couldn't decide if he'd been rebuffed or not. He gave her a smile as oily as her own and led her to her chair.

Once she was seated, Dovina turned in her chair to look at the towering oaks of the grove. Men in Bardic Guild livery were guarding the wagon where Cradoc's body lay. Behind them lay cooking pits with the cooks standing ready to pull off the covering of sod and bring up the roast hogs. Tables mounded with loaves of bread stood off to one side. With her weak eyes, Dovina couldn't be sure, but she thought she saw Alyssa's father in charge and her older brother there as well. It made sense that the Bakers Guild would send their highest officials in respect. Dovina sent up a brief prayer of thanks that Alyssa had gotten on the road before the bakers saw her do so. She turned back before they noticed her watching them.

She had an easier time picking out details of the crowd that waited for the ceremony to begin, because they stood in strong light, not the shade of the trees. She disliked the way that the Aberwyn and Aber naudd men had placed themselves—never together, but always within hailing distance of each other. Now and then she saw the underchamberlain raise a casual hand and the others answer him with a quick wave or a nod of the head. The two gwerbretion of Aberwyn and Abernaudd were technically allies but in most things bitter rivals. That some of their sworn men would cooperate was ominous, she realized. She wondered again why Ladoic had refused to end Cradoc's fast. Some grim reason, she thought, that involves more lords than Father.

Malyc walked to the edge of the platform. When he raised both arms for silence, the crowd gave it to him. He lowered his arms and boomed out the first line of the gwerchan, the "last song," in Cradoc's honor.

"Voice of valor, silenced now, void-tossed . . ."

The crowd sighed as the poem unrolled in great waves of sound, emphasized now and then with soft moments of regret. Malyc never faltered once during the long performance, never dropped a syllable, never gasped nor caught his breath. By the time the gwerchan finished, many people in the crowd wept, men as well as women.

Malyc stepped back to allow his second, Callyn, to come forward to speak. An apprentice handed Malyc a discreet goblet of something to soothe his throat as Callyn raised his arms in turn to quiet the crowd.

"My friends," he began, "today is a dark day for Aberwyn. One of our great men, anchor of the people, strong as an iron mace, has been laid low by arrogance and a vast disrespect for the sacred laws of our kind. What must the gods think of a man who lets a bard starve outside his—"

"Hold your tongue!"

"Treason!"

"You're slandering our gwerbret!"

The voices rang out in a well-rehearsed chorus, like chimes of a bell. The underchamberlain and the other Fox men had slithered their way forward to the front of the crowd. The two Abernaudd men stood close by them. Shocked beyond belief, Callyn did naught but stare—only for a tiny space of time, but too long a one.

"Filthy liar!" the underchamberlain roared. "Slander!"

A burly fellow with a leather apron over his clothes grabbed him by the shoulder, spun him around, and punched him so hard under the chin that the underchamberlain left his feet and fell hard. The other Fox men yelled and tried to push their way toward him. Screams broke out. Women tried to get free. Men jostled to get closer. Screaming, yelling, little eddies of fighting around the Fox men like water swirling around rocks in a stream—Malyc dropped the goblet and ran to the edge of the platform. His voice boomed out like thunder over the crowd.

"Stop! Fellow citizens! Stop, I beg you! This is no way to honor Cradoc!" Over and over he repeated it more loudly than Dovina had ever imagined a man could shout. "I beg you, stop, calm, stop."

"Listen to our bard!" Callyn joined in. "Listen to the Penvardd!"

And slowly, a few at a time, the men in the crowd did, stepping back, catching the arm of a companion who looked inclined to continue the fighting, muttering soft words while the women called to each other and gathered in little groups to surround and thus hobble the troublemakers. The Fox men grabbed the underchamberlain, hauled him to his feet, and dragged him, as floppy as a rag doll but upright, out of the crowd.

Dovina suddenly realized that she'd stood up. She breathed out with a sharp sigh and sat down again. Lady Tay leaned over the back of her chair to speak to her.

"That was entirely too close to another riot."

"It was, my lady," Dovina said. "I think me we'd all best leave before the feasting starts."

"I agree. I've spotted far too many ale barrels. I'm surprised at your father, stooping so low."

"Do you think he sent those men, my lady? He wouldn't. You forget. The men in his service will do almost anything to curry favor. I'd bet high that the underchamberlain organized this little expedition."

"Ah. I see what you mean. Much more likely, indeed."

But what about those Abernaudd men? Dovina asked herself. She saw two men leaving the crowd and hurrying in the direction of the waiting horses, but with her poor eyesight, she could no longer tell who they were.

It took Lady Tay some while to gather the scholars and get them organized to leave. As Dovina was climbing down from the platform, Malyc caught up with her. He helped her descend, then leaned her way to talk in a quiet voice—quiet by his standards at least. His voice finally showed the strain with just the beginnings of hoarseness here and there.

"My lady, I owe you a courtesy. Soon enough your father will know about this, but I wanted to give you a bit of a warning. The guild is thinking of filing a formal suit against the gwerbret for his treatment of Cradoc."

"Good," Dovina said. "It was despicable."

"I trust you won't see fit to tell your father?"

"I shall wait for the formal announcement. No doubt it will come soon enough."

"As soon as we decide how to proceed." Malyc hesitated, visibly thinking something through. "I know I can trust your discretion, my lady. I see no reason to file suit the way things stand. Why ask the gwerbret to take the matter into his court?"

"No reason on earth. We all know what his verdict would be."

"If my plan carries the day in the guildhall, we'll petition the Prince Regent to establish a justiciar here on the western border. If he does, then we'll take the actual suit there. If he doesn't—well, there's no use in continuing to fight that particular battle."

"I'm afraid I have to agree. All you can do is try to outflank him. This should be very interesting. I shall endeavor to be in the great hall when the messenger arrives."

It's going to be quite a display, Dovina thought, when Father hears about this. She felt a little stab of fear, a sense that more lay behind

the Bardic Guild's desire for fair courts than she'd been allowed
to see.

ince Alyssa and Cavan had traveled several miles down the
road before the crowd erupted, they of course had no idea
what had happened at the funeral. In the bright sunshine, free of
stone walls and gloom, Alyssa felt almost happy, but losing Cradoc
ached like a fever in her heart. When Cavan urged his horse up next
to hers, she turned in the saddle to glance his way.

"I hate to miss hearing Cradoc's gwerchan," Alyssa said. "But it
has to be."

"Just so. I'll wager you could compose him a splendid tribute of
your own."

"Mayhap. I'd like to think so."

"This road we're on. Does it run the whole way to Haen Marn?"

"It doesn't, but it'll take us to the actual road. There are inns
and suchlike on the way. Lots of people travel there, you see, for the
healing."

"It must be a hard journey for someone who's gravely ill."

"There are canal boats for them. Well, at least, the canals run
most of the way."

"Not all of it?"

"The noble-born who live around there—" She hesitated.

"Are stubborn old bastards?" He grinned at her. "I know their
kind. I've had to listen to too many of them, muttering over their
mead, saying all these canals and the mail coaches are only going to
unsettle the common folk. Let them know too much. Don't need all
this cursed learning to read, either."

"Just that!" She smiled in return. "Anyway, about the boats, we'll
reach the river harbor by tonight, and you'll see."

The road fell lower in gentle slopes until they'd left the coastal
hills behind. The fog had long since burned off, and the warm sun
was a welcome luxury. The road here ran beside the Gwyn on their
right hand and rich farmland on their left. In the fields the winter
wheat had sprung up and dusted the land with pale green. In the
meadows white cows with rusty-red ears grazed on the new grass.

Young calves followed their mothers on spindly legs or took a few venturesome steps away.

"A question for you." Cavan turned in his saddle to look at Alyssa. "Why exactly are we going to Haen Marn?"

"What? Didn't anyone tell you?"

"I suppose there wasn't time. I know we're supposed to be fetching some old book, but that can't be the real reason."

"But it is. It's not any old book, but an ancient volume about the customs of the Dawntime, when gwerbretion were elected by the people to be judges, not overlords."

"Elected? Judges? Ye gods! I've never heard of such a thing."

"Neither had Dovina's father until she told him about it. He refused to believe it, of course. It'll be a right fair shock when we prove it to him. Maybe he'll be less stubborn about keeping his grip on the law courts."

"He's not the only one who's going to refuse to believe it. Every gwerbret in the kingdom will squall. Do you truly think it's going to make a difference, what some old book says? This whole thing sounds daft to me."

"It's not the book itself. It's what the Advocates Guild in Cerrmor can make of it. It's only a gesture, in a way, but in this war a gesture's like a skirmish. It's not the real battle. Winning the war will take a long time."

"That's one way to think of it, I suppose. But I don't see how it'll do much good."

"It's a legal precedent that can lead to a compromise. Give us men who are proper judges, and we shan't say a word about your rank. We're not saying that the gwerbretion ought to be abolished. Just that they shouldn't be in charge of the everyday law courts."

"Legal precedent?" He paused to grin at her. "You sound like a priest of Bel."

"I'd take that as a compliment if you weren't smirking."

Cavan winced. For some little while he studied the road ahead in silence. "My apologies," he said at last. "You're not like any lass I've ever known, you see, and at times I don't know what to say to you."

He spoke so quietly, so sincerely, that she believed him. "Well," she said, "I've never met a noble-born man turned silver dagger before, either."

"The second, fair maid, trumps the first. Think of me as dishonored scum. The rest of the kingdom does." He tossed his head and grinned, but she could hear pain in his voice. Tempted though she was, she knew better than to ask a silver dagger what shame had earned him the long road. After a moment's strained silence he spoke again.

"You know, I never got to hear your speech, thanks to that foulmouthed dog in the market square. Could you recite a bit of it while we ride?"

"In truth, I was almost finished. My teacher always urged me to keep important speeches short. Listeners' minds tend to wander if you go on too much. Do you truly want to hear it?"

"I do." He was looking at her without a trace of his smile, and his eyes seemed utterly sincere, but she remembered Dovina's warning against the flattery of noble-born men. *They learn it at their father's knee, and I wouldn't trust it one bit.*

"You were interrupted," he continued, "right where you asked what we could all expect after the way Cradoc was treated. Nothing at all, was your answer."

He'd remembered. He must have been paying honest attention at the time. She took a calm breath, cleared her throat, and began speaking, while Cavan listened with every indication of interest. She finished up with a brief tribute to Cradoc.

"A man whose eyes saw a better future now sees only the dark of the Otherlands. A man whose mouth spoke for all of us has been silenced. Aberwyn, O Aberwyn, will you honor him, or will you forget him to your shame?"

She took a deep breath and made a slight bow from the saddle. Cavan grinned at her. "Splendid!" he said. "No wonder the gwerbret sent a spy! He must have known you could move men's hearts with words."

"I doubt if he's ever heard of me, much less heard me speak." Yet she had to admit that his praise pleased her, flattery or not.

All morning, as they rode beside the river, they often saw a pair of squat barges, piled with sacks and barrels, gliding downstream with the current. In their sterns stood the horses that would haul them back up again. Once they saw a more unusual craft on the river. A galley shot by upstream, rowed by a crew of twelve men in Fox clan colors. Messages from the gwerbret, Alyssa assumed, heading for the negotiations with the Bears. Cavan shaded his eyes with one broad hand and watched it pass.

"Interesting," he said. "I think I saw Travaberiel in that boat, riding as a passenger."

"The Westfolk herald from Wmm's Scribal?"

"The very one. Huh. He mentioned that the Westfolk are getting embroiled in whatever the controversy is. Things must be getting worse."

"Did Travaberiel tell you more? Heralds always do know more."

"Only that it's about some land." Cavan thought for a moment. "Two lords claim the same stretch of it, but it's right on the border."

"I knew that." She grinned at him. "The Westfolk have an ancient legal precedent for claim to a lot of land that Eldidd men covet. It's come to war before, back in 718, over the forests near Haen Marn. Which is why we've gotten hints of support from the Westfolk for our cause. They can't come right out and get accused of meddling, of course, but they have a lot to gain if we can get some impartial courts."

Cavan was studying her with a small tilt of his head and narrowed eyes.

"What's wrong?" Alyssa said.

"Naught, nothing at all! I've just never known a lass with your grasp of this sort of thing. That's all."

"There are a lot of us in the collegium."

He seemed to be about to speak, then gave her a watery sort of smile. Since she had no idea what he might mean by it, she let the matter drop.

The sun had traveled about halfway to the western horizon when they reached the road to Haen Marn, or to be precise, the two roads, one by land, one by water. The river forked around a small island. The Gwynaver's natural channel continued north, and a deep canal headed west next to the towpath, a broad road of beaten earth bordered by a grassy verge. Out on the island stood a tower, built straight with a peaked slate roof in the modern style. As they turned onto the west-running road, Alyssa pointed out a huge winch standing on the island.

"The toll keepers live in that tower. There's a chain across the canal, you see, well under the water when it's slack, but they can raise it if any barge looks like it's trying to sneak past without paying."

"That must make the gwerbret a fair bit of coin."

"Mayhap. My father told me that His Grace does spend a fair bit to keep the canal open and safe. The guilds help, too. Haen Marn brings a lot of trade through Aberwyn. The pilgrims need bread to eat like everyone else."

A few miles on, they heard a shout from behind them on the road. Alyssa motioned to Cavan to follow and turned her horse onto the grassy verge. Plodding along the towpath came a pair of big gray horses, followed by a bargeman on foot who held their reins. They were hauling a narrowboat, painted a pleasant green. She pointed out two cots lying in the bow and two more in the stern. On each lay a person bundled in blankets. A woman walked back and forth between the patients.

"They make them as comfortable as they can," she said. "But still, it's a hard journey if you're ill. Most of these patients for Haen Marn are desperate for a cure. They've tried everything close to where they dwell."

Toward sunset they came to a small village set back from the road. Unlike most villages in the western provinces, it included four inns and a couple of temples, one to Nwth, the god of merchants, and one to Sebanna, the goddess of healing. Alyssa led her silver dagger to a large inn that stood behind a whitewashed wall.

"We stayed here when I helped bring my father to Haen Marn," she said. "It's the second-most expensive one, but the cheaper pair are awful."

"I take it you've got the coin to pay for it?"

"I do indeed."

They dismounted at the open gates and led their horses into the nicely swept stableyard in front of the two-story inn. A stout young man with a leather apron over his shirt and breeches came hurrying out to greet them. He bowed to Alyssa, but took one look at Cavan and sneered.

"No silver daggers in our inn," he announced. "You're most welcome, good maid, but your guard here should try the Running Horse down by the canal."

Alyssa shot Cavan a nervous glance, but he seemed resigned to this sort of abuse.

"Oh, come now," she said. "Can't he sleep out in your stables? We passed the Running Horse on our way in, and I'll wager your stables are cleaner."

"Safer, anyway." The lad considered for a moment. "I'll ask my da."

The father, equally stout, came out when the lad called. The two innkeeps put their heads together briefly, then agreed to house Cavan with the horses. Alyssa did persuade them to let her silver dagger eat with her. While he tended their stock, she went inside to look over the tavern room, which held only a few patrons, this early in the spring. At one table sat a family, a mother, her husband or perhaps a brother by the look of him, and three children, one so skinny and pale, with such thin hair and deep-set eyes, that it was hard to tell if it was a lass or a lad. They, no doubt, were on their way to or from Haen Marn.

A more unusual group of travelers sat near a window, three women without a man to guard them. The innkeep pointed them out.

"We have a suite for women traveling alone," he said. "Will you share it with them?"

"By all means. It'll be safer than the common beds."

"Just that. She's a merchant wife with her daughter and their maid."

The wife, a slender woman with gray streaks in her dark hair, and the young woman, who had to be the daughter, judging from their resemblance, both wore blue linen dresses kirtled and shawled in green and white checks. The daughter, who was perhaps seventeen, wore the flowered headscarf of a married woman, but the mother, the black scarf of a widow. The elderly maid wore plain gray, but her dress and shawl looked new and of decent quality. When Alyssa introduced herself they all smiled pleasantly and introduced themselves in turn. They hailed from Abernaudd, the only other port city in Eldidd. The mother, Gratta, offered her a seat at their table.

"My thanks, goodwife," Alyssa said. "But will you mind if my bodyguard sits just behind us? He's a silver dagger, you see, hired by my Scholars' Guild."

Gratta and her daughter, Lanna, exchanged glances, and Gratta considered for some moments. "Oh, I don't truly see any harm in it," she said at last, "if you'll vouch for him."

"I will. He's got decent manners for one of his kind."

Alyssa sat down on the bench next to the maid and opposite the two women. A servant hurried over with a basket of warm bread and a bowl of butter. A second lass offered them pale beer.

"Mutton soon," she announced, then scurried away again.

"I hope it's not boiled into pulp," Gratta said. "But one doesn't expect much better when one is traveling."

"Too true, alas," Alyssa said. "Are you on the way to Haen Marn?"

"We've just come from there, actually."

Lanna blushed and toyed with a bit of bread. Finally she spoke in a small, soft voice. "I've been married for nearly two years, and no baby yet."

"Oh, how sad!" Alyssa said. "I do hope the healers could help you."

"They gave me lots of good advice. I'm to—" She stopped speaking and gazed across the room.

Alyssa, whose back was to the door, turned on the bench and followed her gaze. Cavan was standing just inside, and the two serving maids were trying to make him leave. With a sigh she got up.

"Excuse me," she said. "That's my guard."

"Oh!" Lanna said. "He's awfully handsome."

Gratta and the maid both scowled at her so fiercely that the lass blushed. Alyssa hurried off and reached the door just as the innkeep himself ordered the servants to stand aside. Cavan made him a half-bow and followed Alyssa back to her table. She pointed to the bench just behind hers.

"If you'll just sit there?" she said with a bright smile. "The ladies have agreed that you may eat nearby."

"Just like one of the dogs?" Cavan kept his voice low. "Still, that's more consideration than a silver dagger usually gets."

Alyssa nodded her agreement and took her place at table again. When the food arrived, the saddle of mutton had been decently roasted, not boiled, and pickled cabbage and soda bread studded with bits of apple accompanied it. For some while they all ate in silence.

"Quite nice." Gratta waved her table dagger at the food. "What a relief! One eats well at Haen Marn, of course, but some of the places on the route—" She shook her head and shuddered. "I'm afraid you don't have good fare ahead of you, Alyssa, at least when you're after crossing the Pyrdon border."

"Alas! I suppose the local lords are rounding up all the food they can. In case things come to war, y'know."

"We did hear rumors about that." Gratta dabbed at her lips with her handkerchief, then tucked it away in her kirtle. "I did my best to gather what information I could. The guild needs it with the summer's work about to start."

"Do you handle your husband's trading, now?"

"I do. Not that I ride on caravan myself, of course. My poor dear husband's apprentices do that." Gratta sighed in honest sadness. "I do miss him so! But about the feud. The whole thing seems rather odd to me, but then I am a townswoman."

Cavan turned around on his bench to listen.

"It's a rural matter, then?" Alyssa said.

"Not entirely. Horses are valuable, especially in this part of the kingdom, so I suppose the matter concerns far more folk than the farmers. As far as I could tell, it's a dispute over a large stretch of good pastureland. The farmfolk want to plow and plant. The West-folk horseherders have some ancient claim, which Gwerbret Standyc of the Bear is trying to get set aside."

"Set aside? By whom?"

"The priests of Bel. The gwerbret's own court has of course ruled in his favor, but the Westfolk called upon their own customs to deny the judgment. Not that I know what those customs are." Gratta shook her head in mild bafflement. "Eventually, I suppose, the matter will reach court—or the courts, I should say. Our High King and the King of the Westfolk will have to untangle it. Well, the councillors will do the untangling, of course, but the kings will have to agree."

Cavan leaned over and murmured a few words in Alyssa's ear. She asked his question for him.

"Do you think it will come to open war before the royal heralds step in?"

"I most certainly hope not! Ladoic of Aberwyn is concerned in some way, too, and fortunately he's being the very voice of reason."

The thought of Gwerbret Ladoic as the voice of reason struck

Alyssa as so strange that she nearly laughed aloud. She stopped herself and turned the noise into a polite cough.

"My apologies," Alyssa said. "Now, I did hear that Ladoic holds the allegiance of some of the folk involved. The farmers, I thought."

"Nah nah nah, it's the Westfolk that have appealed to him." Gratta had a sip of her ale. "I have no idea why."

Alyssa did know, but she was tired after a long day's riding, and the yellow beer was proving stronger than its color would indicate. It wasn't until after the other women had left to go up to the suite that her trained memory finally found the information she wanted. By then, Cavan had joined her at her table and was busily finishing up the shards of yeasted bread and soda bread the others had left behind. His own meal had been rather scant. Alyssa leaned on one elbow on the table and yawned as she watched him. He finished the last of the scraps and picked up his tankard of ale again.

"So the Westfolk are right in the middle of the trouble in Pyrdon," Cavan said.

"Indeed. You saw Trav going upriver on the galley, remember. Gwerbret Ladoic must have inherited the Maelwaedd ties with the Westfolk. They go back hundreds of years, and they made a strong alliance twixt Aberwyn and the Westlands. There was an exchange of vassals to seal the pact."

"That would explain it, then, why they appealed to him."

"Just that. As far as the Westfolk are concerned, Ladoic's clan are newcomers to Aberwyn." She paused for a smile. "They live so long, a hundred years to them counts for very little."

"So I've heard. Some of the great old clans close to the king think of the Western Fox in the same way—newcomers. Upstarts, even."

"The noble-born take that kind of thing seriously, don't you?"

"Not me, not anymore. I used to, but you know what they say, the gods don't like to watch a proud man strut. They throw things under his feet."

Alyssa winced at the bitterness in his voice. Cavan concentrated on his ale for a bit, then wiped his mouth on his sleeve and looked at her again.

"Tell me summat," Cavan said. "Why is Dovina so feisty, anyway? She's got everything a lass might want in life, land of her own and beauty."

"Hah! She also has to live with her father. And make a proper marriage whether she wants one or not. She'd truly rather live in the collegium her whole life than be some minor lord's lady."

"I thought all lasses wanted to marry."

"Most men would agree with you." Alyssa paused for a smile. "And they'd be wrong."

With that she took the candle lantern from the table and marched off to the chamber she'd share with Gratta and Lanna.

Dovina had managed to convince her father to allow her a last night at the collegium. Not only did the women have a ceremonial dinner planned to honor the dead bard, but she needed to retrieve her possessions from the private chamber her rank had given her. While Ladoic had no respect for the dinner, he was adamant that she leave none of her things behind.

"You'll not be going back there," he said. "Not after all that trouble at the burying."

"I'd be safer here than in the dun, if that's what's truly worrying you."

"You'd think so, most like, but I don't. Can't you see what your meddling's caused? People muttering in the streets! Cursed near another riot at the funeral! If that wretched Malyc hadn't calmed that mob—"

"If your ever-so-loyal retainer hadn't stuck a dirty spoon in the stew, it never would have soured."

"He had every right to speak."

"Oh, come now, Father! It's not that he spoke. It's what he said."

"Well, he paid for it handsomely. The fellow that swung on him was a blacksmith. Broke his jaw." Dovina winced. Such injuries never healed up properly.

"If you hadn't let Cradoc starve," she said, "there'd be no trouble. Why didn't you just offer to discuss the matter? You could have dragged it out for years."

Ladoic started to speak, then merely glowered. Dovina laid a hand on his arm.

"Father, what's so wrong? There's more to this, isn't there? Some complication, some thing I don't know?"

"There's always more than you know!" He hesitated again, then shrugged. "You need to be married, lass. Take up your position in life. I don't want you squirming out of going to Cerrmor. Then you'll truly be safe, under your husband's protection."

"Assuming I accept this suitor you've found. You can't force me to marry him, you know. It would be going against the venerable traditions of our clan, and I know how much you respect them."

Ladoic growled under his breath, but he refrained from arguing further. Dovina was profoundly relieved when he left her at the collegia gates and rode off without wanting admittance.

Malyc Penvardd presided over the dinner, a grim affair as scholar after scholar stood up from her place at table to speak her tribute to Cradoc. Thanks to her rank, Dovina sat next to Lady Tay at the head table. She spoke her thanks to Cradoc's memory first, which gave her the time she needed to prepare the necessary lie. The moment that the last speaker sat down, Lady Tay turned to her.

"Where's Alyssa?" she said. "Is she ill?"

"Overwhelmed by grief, my lady," Dovina said. "She wanted to go back to her family for the night, where she could talk with her mother and have a bit of privacy. I know we should have told you and our chaperones, but you were all so busy planning this dinner—"

"Well, so we were. Will she return to us on the morrow?"

"So I was led to expect. In the morning. Alas, just when I'll be leaving you, or I'd make sure of it."

"Ah, your father!" Lady Tay snorted in annoyance. "I do hope you'll be allowed to return to finish your studies. You're so close to gaining your scholar's badge and device!"

"Even if I accept this suitor, I'll fight for a long betrothal."

"Good. And may you win the battle!"

Seated as she was, Dovina could overhear much of the conversation between Lady Tay and the Penvardd, or, to be precise, she overheard Malyc's furious tirade and Lady Tay's occasional word of agreement.

"The guild won't forget this," Malyc said at one point. "Eventually His Grace did do the honorable thing and returned Cradoc to us for burial, but the delay! And of course, there's the death. He allowed Cradoc to starve when a word or two from him would have saved our guild brother. I'm sending messages to the Dun Deverry guild. They'll petition the High King himself."

"Or the regent, that is." Lady Tay managed to squeeze in a few words.

"Indeed, the Prince Regent, and about our petition for a justiciar here. Ladoic's court won't be able to dismiss a suit there even if the wretched priests of Bel connive with him." Malyc lifted his goblet for a sip of wine, glanced Dovina's way, and turned scarlet. "My lady, forgive me for speaking so boldly about your esteemed father! I fear me that Cradoc's death has addled my mind."

"Fear not, Your Honor!" Dovina smiled at him. "A bard may speak the truth at will, and I doubt if anyone in Aberwyn would argue against my father being arrogant."

"You're very kind to say so." Malyc had a long swallow of the wine. "My thanks."

Early in the morning, the gwerbret appeared at the gates with a carriage, a groom, and a maidservant to transport his daughter and her baggage back to the dun. The maidservant carried out Dovina's goods, though Dovina insisted on bringing her armload of books out herself, much to her father's annoyance. After a bit of confusion, the servants got everything stowed and themselves aboard as well. They set off and rattled through the cobbled streets up the long hill to the dun.

Although the Fox clan had spent a small fortune in taxes to make their dun as fashionable as possible, the high walls surrounded a massive clutter: new towers, old brochs, a fancy flower garden in the front, a welter of storage sheds and animal pens in the rear. All around the walls stood stables for horses at ground level and barracks for the warband one story up. Some of the barracks had a further rickety structure on top that provided sleeping quarters for the lower-ranked servants.

The carriage let its noble passengers dismount at the carved wooden door to the great hall, then clattered away to the carriage house round the back. Lower-ranked grooms ran after it. House servants and pages lined the steps as Dovina and Ladoic climbed them.

The chamberlain, Lord Veccan, opened the door with a flourish and bowed the noble-born inside. Servants followed and trotted off to attend to their various duties.

"Ah, the ancestral hall!" Dovina said. "It still stinks as badly as ever."

"I suppose you prefer the smell of your musty old books," Ladoic said.

"As a matter of fact, Father, I do."

Aberwyn's great hall lay in the oldest part of the gwerbretal complex, in the central broch built by the early Maelwaedd clan. Some hundred feet across and two stories high, the hall held enough plank tables and backless benches to feed her father's warband of a hundred and fifty men. A good half of them sat there at the moment, drinking ale and jesting with the maidservants who waited upon them. When the noble-born entered, the men rose to their feet with a clatter of scabbards and shouts of welcome. Ladoic acknowledged them with a grin and a wave, which released them to sit down again.

On the far side of the hall, directly opposite the door, stood a dais for the tables of honor with their proper chairs. Although mats of woven rushes covered the lower floor, the dais sported Bardek carpets. All of the tables were unoccupied except for the gwerbret's own. Two of her mother's ferrets lay curled up on the embroidered linen cloth. They lay so still that at first Dovina wondered if they were dead, but as she walked closer, she noticed their little brown sides trembling as they breathed. On the floor under the table, her brothers' big tan boarhounds snored and twitched.

The brothers themselves sat at one end of the table with full glass tankards of dark beer and brooded over a game of carnoic. As usual, on his side of the board Gwarl had a large heap of Adonyc's markers. Dovina wondered at times why Donno would even play, since he always lost.

Adonyc, Tieryn Dun Gwerbyn and the heir to Aberwyn, was some years older than both his siblings. Blond, both men, they had the narrow pale eyes and high cheekbones typical of Cerrmor men, a reminder that as clans went, the Fox was new to Eldidd and to the ranks of the nobility. While Gwarl's face was slender, and his eyes lively, there was something about Adonyc's face that always reminded people of cold bread pudding, rather thick, squarish, with slightly protuberant eyes like gooseberries.

When Dovina and Ladoic climbed the low steps to the dais, both brothers rose and bowed to their father, though the tilt of their shoulders made it clear they were excluding their sister. Dovina decided against a hypocritical curtsy.

"Well, well," Gwarl said to Dovina. "The nuisance is back, is she? We shan't have a moment's peace from now on."

"Hold your tongue," Ladoic said. "Don't set her off!" He glanced around the hall. "Where's your mother?"

"Feeling faint up in the women's hall," Adonyc said. "She left her stinking weasels behind, though, so she might come down again soon."

"Here!" Ladoic frowned at the sleeping ferrets. "You've not been giving them wine again, have you? You know that upsets your mother."

"So I told him," Adonyc said. "Twice."

Gwarl winced. Ladoic cuffed him on the side of the head. "Don't," the gwerbret said. "You know how she carries on if one of the cursed things dies. I will not have her troubled, you stupid young cub!"

Gwarl nodded and cringed. Ladoic hit him again, but not very hard.

"I shall go attend upon Mother," Dovina said. "I'll leave the drunken weasels with you lads, like matched with like."

Adonyc swore under his breath. The dogs lifted their heads for a look around in case interesting trouble was brewing. The ferrets woke and yawned with a waft of stink.

"Just go," Ladoic said to Dovina. "I'll send one of the servants up with the cursed ferrets."

"Better make that one of the men," Gwarl said. "Someone who owns a pair of leather gloves."

When Ladoic bellowed an order, a skinny servingman hurried up to the dais. He wore striped breeches and a red and brown vest over his shirt. His lower jaw was bruised blue and purple, and another bruise marked his forehead—from hitting the cobblestones, Dovina assumed.

"Ah, Ogwimyr!" Dovina said. "You must be the fellow who started the riot in the old marketplace."

"Naught of the sort, my lady!" The servingman made a small bow in her direction. "It was that cursed silver dagger's fault, attacking an innocent man. He was all fired up, I suppose, by that wench."

"Truly? I've heard a very different account of the trouble."

"We've already thrashed all that out!" Ladoic stepped forward. "None of your affair, Dovva!"

"Well, Father, but I'm rather interested—"

"I don't give the fart of a two-copper pig if you are or not! I've too much on my mind at the moment to—" He paused and took a deep breath to calm his voice. "My apology, but I don't care to discuss it now. Mayhap later. My men are searching for the wretched silver dagger, and once we haul him in, we'll hear his side of it."

"Well and good, then." Dovina curtsied. "I'll go attend upon Mother."

He smiled, pleased, and she headed for the stone stairs winding around the wall. Ogwimyr followed with an armload of struggling ferrets. About halfway up he yelped in pain as one of them bit him. Dovina made a mental note to get the weasels some extra meat from dinner.

The women's hall occupied half of the next floor up, across the landing from the gwerbretal apartments. When Dovina opened the door, her mother's maidservant, Magla, hurried over to take the ferrets.

"Don't bother to curtsy," Dovina said to her. "You've got trouble enough. Gwarl fed them wine again."

Magla, young and plump with raven-dark hair, sighed in annoyance and hauled the wriggling ferrets in.

"How is Mother?" Dovina dropped her voice to a whisper.

"Having bad days again. We've had the herbwoman in twice. She helps, but naught seems to cure."

"It's that inflammation of the womb. It lies very deep. I just wish she'd let us take her to Haen Marn."

"I'm just so afraid, my lady, that the journey would kill her."

"So is she, and truly, it's a long way away."

Magla sighed in agreement.

Bardek carpets lay thick on the floor of the semicircular room, and bright tapestries hung all along the curved wall. On little tables sat silver figurines and, here and there, showy enameled jars and dishes, filled with dried rose petals and spices in a vain attempt to hide the smell of ferret. In the midst of the color and sparkles, Lady Rhosyan was sitting in her favorite cushioned chair over by a window that looked out onto the rose garden far below. Like her sons she had pale eyes and high cheekbones, though her hair had gone mostly gray. Four children, one of them born dead, and two miscarriages in her first fifteen years of marriage had left her thin, ill, and, blessedly enough, incapable of conceiving again. Most days, like now, she could be found semi-reclining with her feet upon an embroidered footstool. Dovina smiled, sincerely this time, and leaned over to kiss her mother's cheek. Rhosyan patted her hand in welcome.

"So he dragged you home, did he?" Rhosyan said. "Poor darling! But I do think you'll like this new suitor."

"That would be a welcome change. Have you met him?"

"I've not, but I've got a portrait of him." Rhosyan raised a pale hand and waved vaguely in Magla's direction. "Put my little furry babies in their den and bring me that little picture."

By the time Magla found the picture among the clutter, other servants had brought up Dovina's luggage and gone again. Dovina retrieved her reading-glass from a saddlebag and studied the portrait, a small thing that barely covered her outstretched hand. It showed a dark-haired young man with a face certainly not handsome but pleasant enough, with wide eyes that, as far as she could tell, were gray. What intrigued her, however, was the stack of books on the small table beside him. The artist had unfortunately represented their titles with squiggles of paint, not words.

"I've had lots of reports of Merryc from women I know at court," Rhosyan said. "They tell me he's much interested in the history of the kingdom. And in breeding horses, of course, but then, one expects that in a young lord."

"Does he have land, then? Or is he mostly interested in marrying mine?"

"None of his own, but he's not the usual land-hungry younger son. His mother despaired of ever marrying him off because he absolutely demands an educated wife."

Dovina lowered her reading-glass and gaped.

"Well?" Rhosyan grinned and raised an eyebrow.

"Ye gods," Dovina said. "This trip to Cerrmor might be worthwhile, after all."

"Having those letter pouches going to and fro has certainly been a great help when it comes to arranging marriages! I have written to his mother—Lady Amara of the White Wolf, that is—you know her."

"Of course I do! Well, if this fellow's one of her sons, he might not be as bad as I feared."

"Just so." Rhosyan paused and looked toward the door. "What is it?"

A maidservant from the great hall staff took two steps into the chamber and curtsied. "My lady, you have a visitor. Lady Taclynniva of Lady Rhodda Hall. Are you receiving?"

"Most assuredly," Rhosyan said. "Do show her straight up, and then fetch Bardek wine and some little cakes."

The maidservant curtsied again and left.

Dovina sat down on a nearby chair and considered strategies. Dressed in a walking costume of blue, green, and pale tan, Lady Tay swept into the women's hall in a storm of tartan shawl and skirt.

"You little weasel!" Lady Tay said to Dovina. "Did you truly think you could get away with this?"

Rhosyan rolled her eyes and sighed. "And what has my beloved daughter done now?"

"Worked a most elaborate ruse, Mother." Dovina rose and curtsied to Lady Tay. "I knew we couldn't keep it hidden forever. May I ask how my lady found out?"

"Sirra—that's Alyssa's poor mother—came to me this morning, worried to distraction about her daughter. One of the gwerbret's men came to the bakery to ask about Alyssa."

"It's a cursed good thing we got her out of Aberwyn, then."

"Dearest," Rhosyan put in, "don't say cursed like that. It's so common."

"My apologies, Mother."

"If I may finish? When I found out Alyssa had disappeared, I managed to loosen Mavva's tongue with a few threats." Lady Tay scowled at Dovina. "None of which I intended to carry out, mind."

She divested herself of the shawl, which she tossed over the back of a nearby chair. "Not that she held out long. She's quite sincerely worried about Alyssa."

"I'm not. She's most resourceful, and we did supply her with an armed guard."

"A silver dagger! A wretched silver dagger, and now her honor is utterly ruined. Everyone will think the worst, whether it's happened or not."

Rhosyan cleared her throat. "Would you two please sit down and explain?"

"Of course, Mother." Dovina hesitated and gazed across the room. Although she could see things at a distance more clearly than things close by, still her weak eyes refused to focus on the edge of the door. "Is that door closed?"

Rhosyan glanced its way. "It's not. Magla!"

Her maid hurried in from the ferret chamber. When Rhosyan pointed at the door, she walked over and jerked it open. Skinny Ogwimyr staggered into the room. Rhosyan got up and gave him an iced smile.

"Has my lord sent you to me?" she said. "What does he wish?"

"Naught, my lady, naught." His face had gone quite pale. "I, er, well, we did wonder if your weasels be well and, er, all that."

"Quite well, my thanks. They'll sleep off my son's cruelty."

Ogwimyr bowed low, then turned and scampered away. Dovina hoped that he'd trip and fall down the stairs, but they heard no thump and yelping. *He'll bear watching,* Dovina thought. *I wonder if he's spying at Father's order? Mayhap just to see if he can learn summat he can trade for Father's favor.*

Magla shut the door with a small smile and curtsied.

"Well done," Rhosyan said and seated herself.

Lady Tay continued looking at the closed door with narrow eyes. "I wonder," she said. "That fellow fits the description Alyssa's mother gave me. The man wasn't a town marshal, she told me, but he was wearing the gwerbret's livery. A nasty little skinny sort."

"It easily could be Oggo, then," Rhosyan said. "Now, Dovva, what is all this?"

"Do you happen to remember my friend, Alyssa?"

"I do. I met her at your collegium's fair. Do sit down, Dovva! It makes me nervous, seeing you hovering like that."

As they settled themselves, the maidservant returned with the refreshments. She laid the tray on a small table and retreated to allow Rhosyan to pour.

"You may go, lass," Rhosyan said. "And do make sure that the door is well and truly shut, will you? My thanks."

The maidservant did so. Lady Tay accepted a goblet half full of white wine, then added water from the silver pitcher on the tray. Dovina took a cake to nibble while Lady Tay finished the tale of Alyssa's escape and Dovina's plan for the book. Much to Dovina's relief, her mother laughed.

"It would do no harm," Rhosyan remarked, "to gyve the falcon of gwerbretal pride."

"Gwalch and then valch," Dovina echoed the rhyme. "That's a nice rhyme and figure, Mother."

"My thanks, but your scheme is utterly daft! It's going to take a fair bit more than one old book to change your father's mind."

"Or the mind of any other powerful man," Lady Tay said.

"No doubt." Dovina paused to brush a few cake crumbs from her dress. "It's but the tip of the knife that's going to cut the meat. The Cerrmor Advocates Guild will be able to sharpen the blade when Alyssa gives them the precedent. And we had to have the ancient book, my lady. My father won't be the only man to accuse us of forgery without it."

"Perhaps so." Lady Tay took a small sip of wine. "But I still think it's daft."

"I fear me that I agree," Rhosyan said. "Your father's peers will have summat to say about all this."

"It's not the gwerbretion who matter, Mother. It's the Cerrmor guild and the Prince Regent."

"The guild will doubtless seize upon it with howls of glee," Lady Tay said. "The prince is another matter."

"Then I'll have to think of summat else. This is just the first thrust in the duel."

"Goddess help!" Rhosyan rolled her eyes. "Dovva, your schemes are always as tangled as a child's first knitting!"

"I tried the simple one first. But remember, Alyssa's been to Haen Marn before. They know her there."

"And does she realize what this little jaunt might cost her?" Lady Tay said. "Her honor, if naught else."

"She's a guildwoman, my lady. She has greater freedom in these matters than we do."

"True, I suppose."

Rhosyan leaned forward in her chair. "Her father's the head of the Bakers' Guild, isn't he? That's probably enough to ensure her a marriage to a man of her own class no matter what happens."

"I'd always hoped she'd do better than that," Lady Tay said.

"If she wants to marry at all," Dovina said. "Couldn't you find her a position at the collegium, if worst comes to worst?"

"Oh, certainly!" Tay's voice turned heavy with irony. "And put the child out in fosterage, you mean?"

All three women winced and fell silent. *The worst, indeed,* Dovina thought. But with the thought came an idea.

"A chair of rhetoric might be endowed for her," Dovina said, "if the right people could be persuaded."

"If you can find a weapon to extort the coin from your father, you mean?" Rhosyan lifted one eyebrow and smiled.

"Just that, Mother. I've always managed before. Let me think on it. We poor weak females have to use what weapons we can."

Lady Tay snorted in disgust. "Don't simper! Your father's not in the chamber at the moment." She glanced Rhosyan's way. "I trust my lady feels no need to pass this information along?"

"Of course not. He never listens to what I say, anyway, so why should I bother?"

"True spoken." Lady Tay considered the situation for some moments. "I hope she and her silver dagger stay safe, is all. I gather that the situation with that border feud is growing dangerous."

"Indeed. Ladoic's very concerned. I can tell because he's gotten quite nasty lately." Rhosyan glanced at Dovina. "You know what it means, when he bellows and snarls at us and the servants."

"I do, truly. I took that into account when we were laying our plan." Dovina hesitated, then spoke carefully. "A question for you, Mother. Did Father truly think Cradoc would die?"

"He didn't," Rhosyan said. "He was horrified when it happened. All along he kept saying that the bard was bound to give up soon, or that his guild would force him to eat."

"It should have been obvious that they wouldn't."

"Don't be quite so sharp-tongued, dearest. Please?"

"My apologies, Mother."

Lady Tay made a small coughing sound, as if to remind them of her presence where she couldn't help but overhear.

"About this silver dagger," Lady Tay said. "Do you know anything about the man?"

Dovina considered telling her that Cavan was one of Gwerbret Lughcarn's sons, but she feared that her mother might let the information slip. Father listens to her more than she realizes, Dovina reminded herself.

"I don't know for certain," she said instead, "but I suspect him of being noble-born."

"That's hardly a recommendation when it comes to behaving well around lasses."

"Just so," Rhosyan said. "Let's hope that Alyssa stays her usual sensible self, and that the silver dagger behaves honorably toward her."

Lady Tay snorted in profound skepticism and held out her goblet for more wine.

Circumstances were forcing Alyssa to be sensible where Cavan was concerned. As they traveled from inn to inn on their way north, every innkeeper relegated him to the stables like one of the horses while she shared a decorous chamber with other women. She knew that she should be pleased. A love affair, a bastard child—her life in the collegium would end in dishonor and shame. But at times as they rode together, and the sun caught his hair and turned it gold, and he smiled at her as warmly as the sun, the memory of that kiss in the marketplace rose to trouble her.

Whenever they passed a shady copse or sheltered wall, she would notice him looking at these possible trysting spots with longing. She was always tempted to suggest they stop and rest while they ate their midday meal, but always—at least so far—she'd resisted. Besides, they were never truly alone on the road. Pilgrims returning from Haen Marn passed them, some still ill, but most healed. Others heading for the holy island caught up with them, then left them behind in their hurry.

Canal boats glided up and down near the towpath, but now and then, out in the middle of the canal, a galley shot by with its rowers working hard at the oars. Whenever the rowers wore the colors of the Fox clan, Cavan always pointed them out, and Alyssa would wonder if some of those boats carried messages branding herself and Cavan fugitives. One Aberwyn boat they sighted, however, bore a different kind of burden. Prominent in the prow lay a long box-like shape draped in black. She could just make out a second drape, a narrow banner in the Bear clan's colors of blue and dark yellow.

"Young Lord Grif, I'll wager," Alyssa said. "Going home to his father in honorable return."

"So it looks. Huh. I'd guess that war's inevitable now."

"A very good guess, I'd say. And if the Westfolk choose to join in, who can say how bad it will be? I wish I could talk with Dovina. Maybe we can find another silver dagger to ride messages."

"I wouldn't be surprised if we'll run across several." Cavan paused for a sigh. "They'll have come hoping for a hire, and it looks like they'll find one."

As she usually could, Dovina had managed to wheedle her father into giving her a few pieces of information about the trouble with the Bear clan. That evening, when she lingered in the great hall with him after a particularly good meal, he unburdened himself further. The Westfolk were indeed involved, the matter was growing more dangerous daily, and no doubt it would explode like a dwarven fire arrow when Lord Grif's body arrived home.

"Curse the young cub, anyway!" Ladoic said. "What was he doing in my city? Spying, most like! Causing trouble!"

"Oh, come now, Father. He's the third son. He was hoping to be accepted into Wmm's priesthood one day."

"Third son, eh? Well, then, I can probably afford his wyrd price." Ladoic had a long swallow of ale, which he preferred to the new fashion in hops-flavored beer. "I'll admit it, lass, it troubles my heart thinking about the other two dead lads. I've given that young butcher's family twice his lwdd price, and the guild scholar's kin a fair bit, too."

"That was good of you." *And also,* Dovina thought to herself, *it'll help calm the outcry against you.* "Their poor mothers! What about the woman who lost an eye?"

"Paid that too, of course. Very sad, that! But I wish you'd see that you're helping those wretched bards stir up a pot of poisoned trouble, you and your scholars."

"What made the pot boil over was your warband charging into the crowd."

Ladoic growled under his breath, then calmed himself. "You have a point," he said. "Your brother's not got enough experience of such matters, is the trouble. He lost his head and command of his men both. But truly, these things are going to happen in these delicate situations."

"You have a point, too, Father. By the by, I saw Gwarl ride out this morning with ten of your men."

Ladoic looked over her head at the far wall. "Just exercising their horses, I wager."

"Father! You didn't send them after the silver dagger, did you?"

He said nothing, but his glower at the innocent stones told her what she needed to know.

"I don't understand why you'd put Gwarl in command after what happened before. He's too young to make decisions like—"

"How else is he going to get the experience he needs, eh?"

She decided that arguing further would only make things worse. She stood up and curtsied.

"If I may speak—"

"Since when have you ever held your tongue?" At last he looked her way.

"The people are truly concerned about the courts. It's not as if the Bardic Guild came up with this idea in the first place."

"Imph." He drank from his tankard. "We'll be traveling to Cerrmor by ship. So you can bring all the clothes and such as you women always seem to want."

She knew from long experience that she'd have to accept the change of subject. She was used to waiting for the right times to have these calm talks with her father.

In the morning, however, she realized that the right time would doubtless not come soon, if ever. The Bardic Guild's messengers arrived just as Dovina and her mother were leaving the breakfast table in the great hall. Although Rhosyan hurried up the stairs with her maid in attendance, Dovina lingered on the bottom step to watch as Ladoic broke the seal on the folded packet of pabrus, shook the pages out smooth, and glanced at the writing. His face slowly darkened to a dangerous shade of red.

"Nallyc!" Although he kept his voice steady, the name boomed through the hall. "Get your arse up here!"

With his black robes flapping around him, the councillor ran for the dais like a startled raven seeking a perch. Ladoic shoved the handful of pabrus into his hands, then slowly and carefully exhaled. He picked up his tankard and sipped from it while Nallyc read through the documents.

"I see why Your Grace is distressed," Nallyc said eventually. "But truly, it was honorable of them to notify you."

"Horseshit! They're trying to outflank us on the road to battle, aren't they?" He glanced Dovina's way, then back to the councillor. "Read it aloud, will you?"

For a moment Nallyc merely stared at the offending words while Dovina fretted. *Read it, old man!* she thought. Finally he sighed with a shake of his head. "We wish to inform you that we are appealing directly to the Prince Regent on the matter of appointing a justiciar on the western border to judge such affairs as the recent death of our guildsman Cradoc of Cannobaen." He coughed and shook his head again. "I see."

"The regent's as eager as a stud around mares to plant his men all over the kingdom. And if we get his cursed justiciar, then the pisspot bards will file suit against me. Am I right?"

"You are, Your Grace—well, in my opinion, anyway. We should get in a law-speaking priest to confirm it."

Father's not quite as furious as I thought he'd be, Dovina thought. She sat down on a step to continue watching.

Ladoic stood up and bellowed for his scribes. Like Nallyc the two of them arrived on the run with their satchels in hand. Once they were ready, Ladoic sat down again.

"I'll want seven of these messages sent," he said. "I'll give you the names when we're done."

The message was brief. He told the recipients about the petition, remarked that this was a threat that "none of us" could ignore, and ended with an invitation to meet and discuss the matter further. The list of names he rattled off made Dovina turn cold, all five western gwerbretion and two from central Deverry. He'd even included Standyc. *Rebellion?* she thought. *Surely not!*

With the scribes hard at work, Ladoic stood up and started toward the staircase. Dovina rose and curtsied to him.

"Father?" she said. "They're giving you grief, aren't they? The other gwerbretion?"

He started to snarl, checked himself, and smiled in a tight-lipped way. "I'm the man in the first line of the shield wall. That's how they see it. If I go down, the line's broken, and this cursed court argument spreads into their territories."

"I wish you'd told me this earlier. I heard the list of names. Some of them come from upstart clans, don't they? I wonder about their sense of honor."

"You see things clearly, don't you? Despite your watery eyes. Ah, bad cess to the god who made you female!"

With that he brushed past her and hurried up the stairs. Once he was well away, Dovina returned to the dais. The scribes had gathered up their things and left for some better place to work. Only two pages remained, clearing away Ladoic's interrupted meal. She knew one of them well, the son of a lord who held land in fealty to Aberwyn.

"Darro!" She summoned him with a flick of her hand. "I have an errand in town for you."

With a grin he trotted over and bowed. Going into town was much preferable to the usual afternoon job required of the pages, mucking out the stables and garderobes.

"See if you can find a silver dagger or some other messenger who's available for a long ride. Make sure he knows he'll be well paid. If you find one, bring him to the dun and have him wait outside the gates. Then fetch me."

"Of course, my lady."

Dovina fished in the pouch tucked into her kirtle and brought out a couple of small coins.

"If anyone asks," she said, "tell them I want to send a very private letter to a lord of my acquaintance. The mails won't do."

His eyes widened in hopeful curiosity.

"That's all you need to know." She handed over the coins.

He grinned again, slipped the coins into his own pouch, and hurried off. *A little false gossip to chase the truth away,* Dovina thought. *Let's hope it works.*

While he searched, Dovina wrote Alyssa a long letter and sealed it into an old-fashioned silver message tube. From her jewelry box she took a small silver square stamped with her father's seal, an official token that would allow her messenger to change horses at any loyal lord's dun. Should the lord get an inferior horse or none at all in return, the token ensured that the gwerbret would make good the loss. She'd taken the precaution, some years before, of stealing a handful of these pieces from the chief scribe's chamber.

Long before the noon meal Darro returned with the news that he'd found a silver dagger in a local tavern. Dovina had him accompany her. As she walked across the ward to the dun gates, she saw a youngish man, dark-haired and clean-shaven, standing just outside and holding the reins of a dun gelding. His clothes, though roadstained, were in reasonably good repair, and he carried a broadsword on his belt. When she drew close enough to see the fine points, he turned out to be remarkably good-looking. She found herself surprised by this, as if she'd expected that all silver daggers would be weaselly or brutish or at best like Alyssa's Cavan, decent-looking provided you liked a touch of wild animal in a man.

When she walked outside the gates to join him, the silver dagger started to kneel, but she waved him up.

"No need for that," she said. "Your name?"

"Benoic, my lady."

"And you're in Aberwyn because?"

"I heard there was a feud brewing. Work for my sword, I thought."

For several moments she considered him. He was, she supposed, as trustworthy as any silver dagger, which meant he'd be completely loyal as long as he was paid—a cut above the average mercenary.

"Tell me summat," she said. "Do you know a silver dagger named Cavan of Lughcarn?"

He smiled. "I do, my lady, and a good friend he is."

"Excellent! I have a hire for you." She glanced back at the dun gates, where two guards were lounging against the stone wall. "Here, come walk a ways with me. Darro, you stay here."

They went some hundred yards away from possible eavesdroppers before Dovina explained the errand to Benoic. It turned out that he came originally from Pyrdon and knew the territory around Haen Marn quite well. Along with the message tube and token, she handed him coins, a pair of Eldidd brazens, to provision him on the journey.

"At the end of my letter," she said, "there's a message to the recipient, saying to pay you well. If she never gets the letter—"

"Understood, my lady." He made her a bob of a bow. "I swear on my silver dagger that I'll put it into her hands and no one else's."

Dovina returned to the dun gates. She and Darro stood watching while Benoic mounted up and rode off.

"Not a word of this to anyone," she said to the page, "or I won't take you to Cerrmor with me."

"Cerrmor?" He grinned, all wide-eyed. "I could go to Cerrmor?"

"If you say naught a word—or wait, you can hint that I've sent a letter to a man I fancied, ending things, like, now that my father wants to betroth me to someone else."

He made her a deep and courtly bow. "Your heart must ache, my lady," he said, still grinning. "And his, too."

Alyssa and Cavan had reached a proper town, Lynarth. They paused their horses and considered the town walls, a tall, thick half-circle facing the road with the open side directly fronting the river. A flimsy wooden bridge, easily destroyed in case of siege, crossed the river to a huddle of shacks and tumble-down houses on the far bank. Men wearing hauberks stood at the iron gates. Some carried pikes, a few had clubs, and the rest, swords of various ages and sorts. None wore any sort of formal livery.

"Local militia," Cavan told Alyssa. "Looks like they've been recruited just recently, too."

"No doubt they have been. When the lords feud, the people crouch in fear."

"Nicely put."

"It's just an old proverb."

"Truly? I've never heard it before."

"Doubtless the noble-born don't repeat it."

Cavan blushed.

At the gates, they dismounted. Two of the militia men came forward and greeted them politely enough.

"Where are you headed, silver dagger?" the elder said.

"Haen Marn. I've been paid to escort the lady there."

"Be here long?"

"Only the one night. I assume we can find a decent place to stay?"

The militiaman nodded, then looked them both over slowly and carefully. He had narrow blue eyes in his weather-beaten face, and a full mouth pursed in thought under his gray mustache. At length he shrugged.

"Go in, then," he said. "But if you stay longer, you'll have to report to the mayor. The innkeep will tell you where."

He turned and walked away with a wave to the others, who stepped back and cleared the gates. As they led their horses down the winding main street, Alyssa noticed townsfolk hurrying about their business as if they hated being away from their homes.

They found an inn easily enough, but for the evening meal the dining room was so crowded that the innkeeper denied Cavan a place at table. The silver dagger had to sit on the floor at Alyssa's feet like a dog and hold his bowl of stew in his lap. She assumed that he found it humiliating, but his position brought him advantages. Alyssa could slip him extra food, and he could hear the gossip and news from the other diners.

A stout fellow wearing the checked waistcoat of a merchant had just returned from escorting his wife to Haen Marn and back. The wife, a pale and exhausted little thing with scant dark hair, leaned against him while she picked at her dinner and let him do all the talking—a habit, Alyssa supposed, that preceded her illness, whatever it might have been.

"Not sure what I think of Ladoic of Aberwyn," the merchant said. "Good of him to try to keep the peace, eh? But siding with the

Westfolk—don't know about that. We need to stick to our own kind. And stick up for 'em, too, when sword hits shield."

"Aberwyn has ties with the King of the Westlands that go back hundreds of years," Alyssa said. "And the folk bring in a fair bit of trade all along the western border of his rhan."

"Huh, happen the coin explains it, then. Now, Standyc of Pyrdon, he wants those border lands under his rule. Puffed up like a frog, he is, talking about taxes and bringing in the free farmers to pay 'em, Deverry men, that is, not those long-eared barbarians."

"So he's thinking of the coin, too."

The merchant paused to shovel in a mouthful of turnips in gravy. "Well, true spoken." He wiped his mouth on the back of his hand. "But you never know where you are with the Westfolk. I've heard they eat snakes."

Probably tastier than this stew, Alyssa thought, but she smiled rather than speaking the thought aloud. Not long after, the merchant helped his wife rise from table and led her off to their chamber. Alyssa snagged the woman's untouched portion of bread and handed it to Cavan before the merchant returned.

irect news from Aberwyn soon reached Cavan and his hire. In the morning they left Lynarth with an anxious eye for clouds that scurried in before a strong west wind. Eventually the sky turned so dark and damp-looking that they decided to stop early. They had reached Draegrhyn, a town that stood just south of the border with Pyrdon. Ahead lay the Bears' new gwerbretrhyn of Cernmetyn. Once they crossed that border, they'd legally be beyond Ladoic's reach.

"Who knows if he'll abide by the law, though," Cavan said.

"Truly. We'll not have much recourse if he doesn't, either."

"That's why we're making this journey, innit?"

Alyssa rewarded him with a smile.

They found accommodation in a shabby inn, too small to have a separate chamber for women. Nor was the innkeep too fussy to shelter a silver dagger. Just before the rain started, Cavan was tending their riding horses in high hopes for a bed shared with Alyssa and no other travelers when another silver dagger led his stumbling-tired horse, both of them sweat-stained and dusty from the roads, into the innyard.

"Benoic!" Cavan called out. "Hell's arse! You look like a badger's leavings!"

Benoic raised a hand in greeting and nodded, as exhausted as his horse. "Been riding urgent messages."

"Ah. To the local lord?"

"To the lass you're guarding. From the Lady Dovina of Aberwyn."

To a fighting man in Deverry, the needs of horses always came first. Simmering with curiosity though he was, Cavan tended Benoic's horse along with the other beasts while Benoic made himself fit to deliver the messages. He poured a bucket of cold well water over his head to wash off the worst of the dirt and wake himself up, then staggered into the inn. Once the horses were watered, fed, and in their stalls, Cavan hurried after him.

Alyssa was sitting on the end of a bench beside a greasy table and reading a curling sheet of pabrus in the light from a nearby window. His eyes half-shut, Benoic knelt at her feet and leaned against the table leg. When Cavan knelt beside his fellow silver dagger, Alyssa looked up.

"Can you read?" she said.

Benoic shook his head no, but Cavan held out a hand for the letter.

When Alyssa gave it to him, he scanned it fast, then summarized it for Benoic's sake. Someone had been eavesdropping on Dovina and her mother in the women's hall and found out that "the silver dagger in the marketplace quarrel" had left Aberwyn. Gwerbret Ladoic promptly sent his town marshals around to find out more.

"They now know that Cavan rode north," Dovina wrote. "I'm afraid that he thinks you rode with him. Certainly he knows you're missing. Father seems inclined to blame the King's Collegium men for everything, a delusion in which I shall encourage him. He's sending a squad from his warband north to catch Cavan, though, which means he'll catch you, too. You'll have to admit you were eloping out of love and no other reason if that happens."

Cavan looked up and stared wide-eyed at Alyssa.

"She means we should lie, of course." Alyssa sounded weary. "To protect me."

"Oh." Of course, curse it!

Cavan returned to the letter. At the end, Dovina stressed that using the new post service to answer her would be unsafe.

"Father is having the mails searched. My wretched dolt of a younger brother, by the way, is in charge of the squad following you. He'll probably botch the job somehow, but we can't be sure of that."

Cavan winced. His Grace was deadly serious, then, about stopping them.

"Luckily this other silver dagger turned up," Dovina continued. "I gave him a token as a speeded courier. Please pay him well when you reach your destination. Once you get across the border into Standyc's rhan, the pursuers will have to turn back."

"She's right about them turning back," Cavan said. "With things as they are, if some of Aberwyn's men took us on one of the Bear clan's roads it would be an act of war."

"Good. How far are we from the border?"

"About twelve miles." Benoic spoke up.

"Excellent!" Alyssa took the letter back. "I suppose it's too late to ride out now."

"My horse won't manage another mile without rest." He glanced at Cavan. "I don't suppose you've got a spare mount."

"No such luck. And you won't be able to ride that horse fast on the morrow, not without risking him."

Benoic winced. "As desperate as a silver dagger without a horse" was an Eldidd proverb and a true one.

"If you've got Lady Dovina's token," Alyssa said, "the local lord will give you a remount, but we don't dare go with you." She frowned in thought. "And it had best wait till the morning, too. The sun's setting. The dun gates will be closed."

"There's more bad news, my lady." Benoic elevated Alyssa's rank. "I heard it when I changed mounts. Cavvo, Gwerbret Ladoic's posted letters of bounty on you. The lord I spoke with offered me the chance at it." Benoic paused for a twisted grin. "A hundred Eldidd brazens if I bring you in."

"Is that all? The mingy bastards!"

"It's enough to put a lot of hounds on your trail."

"Here, you're not going to try to earn it, are you?"

"After the way you saved my neck up in Cerrgonney?" Benoic

looked Alyssa's way. "We were riding together in some lord's feud. I never did learn what started it or who was to blame. But it came to bloodshed, and I'd have been dead if it weren't for him." He glanced at Cavan. "Cursed if I'll turn you over for a handful of coin. But there are plenty of other men who won't be so high-minded."

"Wait a moment," Alyssa said. "You said some lord or other told you about it? The one who gave you the new horse?"

"Not him, actually." Benoic paused to rub his chin with one hand. "It was a bit odd, now that you mention it. I changed horses at Lord Orryc's dun. He's one of Ladoic's vassals and a generous man. Just at noon, this was. So once his groom picked out a horse, and I'd finished the meal they set me, I went out to the ward to saddle up. Another lord followed me, a friend of Orryc's, I guess he was, because he'd been eating with his lordship at the head table. And he made a point of telling me about the bounty."

"What was his name?" Alyssa said.

"He never told me. Just said, a tip for you, silver dagger, and went on about the letter of bounty."

"That's more than a bit odd," Cavan said. "Most lords don't bother helping out the likes of us."

"True spoken." Benoic fought back a yawn. "His tartan was brown and yellow with a thin stripe of a rusty black. Never saw his device."

"Huh. That's from over in Deverry proper. The Oaktree clan, and their gwerbret's dun is close to the Eldidd border, but I don't remember much else about them."

"News about this letter must have spread fast. Cursed bad luck, Cavvo."

Cavan turned to Alyssa. He was expecting her to come up with some sort of cleverness, and she didn't disappoint him.

"Such a pity," Alyssa said, "that Cavan's so ill from that old head wound. Not, of course, that his real name is Cavan. We might as well start calling him Valyn now, just to make sure we're used to doing so."

Benoic laughed, one quick whoop. Cavan set his hands on his hips and glared at her.

"I don't suppose," Cavan said, "that you might let me in on the joke."

Alyssa rolled her eyes skyward. "My dear silver dagger," she said with a grin. "If you stop shaving, and we bandage up your head, who's to recognize you? You can get dizzy spells and find it hard to remember things."

"Lie, you mean."

"You look so sour. What—"

"All this cursed lying! It's dishonorable."

Benoic groaned and rolled his eyes. "He's noble-born, you know. Cavvo, be reasonable! You're dishonored already. What counts now is keeping you alive."

"I suppose."

"Oh, hush!" Alyssa said. "Benoic's right."

"Oh, very well!" Cavan made her a mock bow. "I ride at your orders, my lady."

"Good. There's no time to argue if Gwarl's already on the road."

Cavan had never known a lass with her resourcefulness before, and he wasn't sure if he found it annoying or fascinating. A bit of both, he decided with a shrug. He got up from the floor and yelled at the innkeep to bring them dark beer.

The innkeep allowed Alyssa's silver daggers to eat at table with her, doubtless because the food deserved no better. The mutton had been boiled tasteless, the bread was stale, and Alyssa picked a dead cockroach out of her barley porridge and shoved the bowl away. Benoic and Cavan, however, ate theirs and shared her portion between them, too, though they did pick the roaches out first.

The quality of the food prompted a lot of sour comments from the other customers. Alyssa overheard a number of complaints about the coming war, the weather, the Westfolk, the taxes, and just about everything else that touched the complainers' lives. One even advanced a nasty opinion of Haen Marn, though that got shouted down fast enough.

"Well," the grumbler continued, "talk all you want, but I hear the place is crawling with spirits."

"Oh, ye gods!" another fellow said. "It's always the Wildfolk, innit? Or the mighty dwimmer or evil curses or now and then a woman who gave birth to six rabbits. Think, man! None of it's likely to happen."

The sour fellow scowled, but he did say, "I'll give you the rabbit story. I don't believe that one for one single moment. How would a buck even mount her? He'd fall short, like."

The men at that table all laughed, and Alyssa had to smile herself. Cavan rolled his eyes, and Benoic just went on eating.

"The west is full of strange things," Alyssa said to Cavan. "You'll be surprised, I think. But truly, no litters of half-human baby bunnies."

After dinner the innkeep helped them carry their gear up to one of the common rooms. Alyssa examined the smoke-stained wall behind the one square bed. Along with candle soot she saw the small black and rust colored stains where previous occupants had squashed bedbugs.

"We'll all sleep in your hayloft," she told the innkeep. "If that's acceptable to you, my goodman."

Since he had no objection, they all trooped back downstairs again and went out to the stables. The hayloft smelled only of mice, not known to bite travelers in their sleep. Alyssa announced that it would do and gave the innkeep the night's fee.

"We'll be leaving early on the morrow," she said. "As early as we can, truly."

"Good luck on the road, then. And mind you don't tip that there lantern and burn the place down."

"I can assure you that we have no desire to roast." Alyssa smiled to take any sting out of her words. "The candle's almost burned down, anyway."

In the little space of light remaining, the three of them bundled up hay and straw into improvised mattresses and spread out their bedrolls. Alyssa made her bed on the other side of a rotting wood partition from the men. She noticed Cavan watching her with a deeply sad expression, which she suspected him of exaggerating for effect. Benoic took off his sword belt, slung it down at the head of his blankets, then lay down, boots and all. He sighed once and fell asleep.

Before she went to her blankets, Alyssa looked through the clothes she'd been given and found an extra petticoat of plain muslin. She tore off some long strips to bandage Cavan's head on the morrow.

She took off her breeches and boots, then snuggled down into her nest of straw. Although she wanted to make plans for the road ahead, she fell asleep almost as quickly as Benoic.

Cavan lay awake for a long time and listened to Alyssa's soft breathing on the other side of the partition. In his mind he went over and over their route from Aberwyn and tried to figure how fast a mounted squad could travel it. Now and then his mind threatened to remind him that the gwerbret could and probably would hang him if he were captured, but he shoved that thought away. What counted, he told himself, was getting Alyssa safely away. If he died fighting in a scrap on the road, so much the better, as long as she could reach Haen Marn.

He could only hope she'd mourn him. On that less than happy thought, he finally fell asleep.

Dovina heard about the bounty on Cavan's head from Darro, who'd attached himself to her as her special page. Doubtless he wanted to ensure he got that trip to Cerrmor, but the arrangement suited her as well. He'd heard about the bounty from one of the men in the warband, he told her.

"A hundred brazens, my lady! Such a lot of coin! I wish I were a warrior." He pretended to hold a sword and mimed a few passes. "I could be rich."

"You've got a few years ahead of you before that happens." She smiled at him. "But here's a couple of coppers to get you started."

Darro smiled and bowed. Dovina went storming downstairs. On the dais in the great hall, she found her father drinking ale at the head of the honor table. He'd tipped his chair back so he could rest his feet on the seat of the chair to his left. When she marched up to him, he lowered his tankard and sighed.

"What is it now?" he said.

"The letter of bounty you put out for that silver dagger, the one who gave Ogwimyr what he deserved."

"He cursed near caused a riot."

"Ogwimyr did, you mean?"

"I do not, and you know it!"

"It hardly matters. The real instigator of the worst rioting is Gwarl."

"Enough!" Ladoic raised one hand flat for silence. When he spoke again, he sounded more curious than angry. "What's Ogwimyr to you, anyway?"

Dovina had heard enough about the incident to have a firm idea of what had happened. "Oggo called my dear friend Alyssa a two-penny whore. He said all the women at the collegium were, too. The silver dagger answered the slight."

Ladoic rolled his eyes and had a long swallow of ale. "Now this," he said, "is the way drink should taste. None of that new beer for me, nasty with hops."

"Father, I shan't be put off this easily. I happen to be a scholar at that collegium. I'm assuming that Oggo included me in the descrip-tion. What else would the people in the marketplace think?"

"I hadn't thought of that." Ladoic slammed his half-full tankard down on the table. Ale sloshed like an angry sea. "Oggo! Get up here!"

Ogwymir scurried over, his back bent as if he were trying to bow and run at the same time. Dovina set her hands on her hips and stepped back to watch as he knelt beside the gwerbret's chair.

"This business of the lass who was giving that cursed speech in the marketplace," Ladoic said. "I've been told you called the lasses at the collegium two-copper whores."

Ogwymir glanced at Dovina and bit his lower lip.

"Well?" Ladoic said.

"Only the one lass, Your Grace." His voice squeaked toward the end of his reply. "The one speaking."

"Hah! I doubt me if the townsfolk made such a nice distinction. Do you think I don't know about the nasty things they say about the lasses there?" Ladoic paused for effect. "My daughter's one of them, isn't she?"

"I never meant, I mean, Your Grace, just the things she was say-ing, not the Lady Dovina I mean of course not I—"

Ladoic held up a hand. Ogwymir fell silent. His face had gone quite pale.

"Don't," Ladoic said. "Don't ever say such things again. I do not wish to hear of you saying such things again. Do you understand me?"

"I do, Your Grace. A thousand apologies, I—"

"That's enough. Go!"

Ogwimyr crept off like a whipped hound.

"Oggo won't be slandering you again," Ladoic said, "but the bounty stands. I want that silver dagger back here for a fair trial before I hang him."

"Fair? You call that—"

"A jest, Dovva. You shouldn't be so cursed serious all the time. It's not becoming in a woman."

And he laughed. All Dovina could do was simper, curtsy, and leave.

CHAPTER 4

THROUGH THE SLITS AND holes in the stable roof, Cavan could see silver in the dawn sky. He rolled free of his blankets without waking Benoic, pulled on his boots, slung his sword belt over his shoulder, and got up. Benoic kept on snoring. Cavan climbed down the ladder from the loft, buckled on the sword belt, and went down the line of stalls to fetch their horses out. Benoic's chestnut walked without being urged, planted its feet without any sign of pain, and tossed its head with a snort at the cool outdoor air, but even so, Cavan decided, Benno was going to need a fresh mount if they were going to ride at a cavalry pace.

He'd just given each horse a nosebag of oats when Alyssa came out of the stable. She was yawning while she ran both hands through her dirty hair, her eyes looked puffed and gummy, but in the silvery light she struck him as more beautiful than any courtly lady. Once he would have seen her as prey, this common-born lass. Now she was far above and beyond him. Regret struck him like a blow, both for the way he would have seen her and for their positions now.

"What's so wrong?" Alyssa looked at him sharply.

"Naught, naught. Just tired. Is Benoic awake?"

"He is. Or at least, he muttered to himself when I walked by."

"A good sign, that. If he's not down by the time the horses are saddled, I'll fetch him."

Alyssa went to the well near the watering trough and hauled up a bucket of water. She set it on the well's edge, then dipped her hands in it and splashed water on her face. Twisted strands of hay clung to the back of her tunic. Smiling, he went over and picked them off.

"My thanks," she said.

"There's a bit left."

He brushed the fragments off with the side of his hand. At his touch she stiffened, but she said nothing, nor did she move away.

"My apologies," he said.

"No need." Her voice trembled, ever so slightly.

"Lyss, if I weren't a cursed silver dagger—"

"But you are." She turned to face him. "Please, no more."

Once he would have said more, wheedled, begged, pushed his suit. This time, with a sigh he nodded and turned away rather than cause her any distress.

They decided that they'd rather ride hungry than eat more of the inn's food. While he saddled the horses, Alyssa took her linen strips and went into the inn's kitchen hut. She came back with a few artistic blood stains on the cloth and bound his head so that they'd show. Cavan returned to the hayloft and told Benoic they were leaving. Benoic yawned hugely and sat up in his blankets.

"You'd best get on the road," he said. "I'll catch up with you on the other side of the border if I can. If you can reach it."

"With Ladoic's squad on their way."

"True." Benoic yawned again. "Worse yet if he sent messages to one of his vassals. They're closer."

True enough, Cavan thought. He was intending to push the horses and travel fast, but the night's rain had turned the road muddy and slow. As they plodded along, he kept turning in the saddle to look back, but the mud, of course, refused to send up the dust cloud that would have warned him of enemies coming. Toward noon he gave the horses a brief rest, but he and Alyssa stayed standing to eat a scrap of bread each. He cleaned the worst of the mud from the horses' hooves and got all of them back on the road.

By then the sun had been out for some hours, and the road had dried out except in the deep wagon ruts. Alyssa took the lead, Cavan the rear, when he decided they should ride single file. Eventually, when the sun had gone well past zenith, Alyssa saw a massive cairn about half a mile ahead with a squared-off pillar rising from it. She could just make out what appeared to be the statue of an animal at the very top.

"Look!" She pointed ahead. "A carved stone. I'll wager that's the border."

"Must be!" Cavan said. "Thank the gods!"

He turned in his saddle to take another look backward and swore. Alyssa looked, too, and saw what they'd been dreading—a cloud of dust, far too large and high to be raised by a single horse's hooves. The mud-streaked rutted road ahead was still too uncertain for a gallop.

"Hurry!" he said. "Trot!"

At the fastest pace they could manage they headed for the border of the Bears' territory. The dust cloud behind them followed, gaining but slowly. A silver horn rang out behind them. The dust cloud traveled faster and resolved itself into a band of armed men.

"Hold and stand!" A voice called out, no more than a faint thread of sound. "Stand, curse you! In the name of Aberwyn."

Alyssa kicked her horse to a faster trot. Cavan followed her. They reached the cairn and saw indeed a bear rampant crowning the pillar, but to either side of the road stretched nothing but fields, green with new hay.

"If they take us, who's to stop them?" Cavan called out. "You ride as fast as you can. I'll put up a bit of a fight."

"Don't! Someone's coming."

Down the road ahead of them another dust cloud came hurrying. Silver horns sounded ahead and behind. Men yelled out the names of their gwerbretion: "Ladoic!" "Standyc!" Cavan urged his horse up next to Alyssa.

"Get to the side of the road! If there's a scrap, head into the field!"

She followed him over.

The Bear warband, close to home, could risk a brief burst of gallop on the wretched road, while Aberwyn's men had to put their horses' safety first. In a whooping, cat-calling mob, the Bear warband surrounded Alyssa and Cavan, then pulled up to an orderly halt. They were a scruffy lot, armed with broadswords in the old manner and wearing odd scraps of mail and plate, doubtless all they thought they'd need for a ride around their lord's borders. A quick uncertain count told her that there were at least eighteen of them.

The Aberwyn men were better armed on better horses, but there were only ten of them. Gwarl snarled and swore, but he had no choice but to yell, "Back off and retreat." The Aberwyn squad stopped about twenty yards down the road and waited. Gwarl rode closer alone.

"Now, lass," the Bear captain said, "what's all this?"

"Oh, good sir, first of all, you have all the thanks and praise I can heap upon you." Alyssa put a convincing quiver and snivel into her voice. "You see, my father's an important guildsman back home, and he refused to let me marry Valyn here, the man I love above all else in the world." She shot Cavan a love-sick glance. "So when we ran away, he must have gone to the gwerbret."

"Ah, to fetch you back again, like. Well, if you were my daughter, I'd have done the same, but since you're not, it's none of my affair." He rose in the stirrups and called out to Gwarl. "Leave the lass alone! She's done naught against the laws of your rhan or mine, my lord, and I know and you know that Gwerbret Standyc will take grave exception to using force on his roads."

"They were on Aberwyn roads when we first spotted them!" Gwarl called back. "And what, pray tell, were you up to? Planning to raid into our territory?"

"We patrol the borders, my lord, regular-like." The captain made him a half-bow from the saddle. "Just in case there's trouble. Our gwerbret's a peaceable man."

Gwarl stiffened at the implication, "unlike yours." One of the older men in the Aberwyn warband urged his horse forward. He leaned in his saddle and whispered to Gwarl, who smiled.

"Captain, look here," Gwarl said. "The lass may be lying, she may not, but I can swear on my honor that this man has a bounty on his head. He's wanted by the courts in Aberwyn. I'd say her father has good reason to want her taken and brought back to him."

"Oh, indeed?" The captain turned to Alyssa and raised an eyebrow. "Well, if that's true, lass, you might be better off going with this lordship here. If he gives me a pledge as to your safety."

Alyssa noticed some of the men in the warband smirking. She was a dishonored woman in their eyes now. And Cavan would hang.

"Good captain, I beg you! Don't send me back! Lord Gwarl's an honorable man, I'm sure, but—"

"Hold!" the captain snarled. "Lord Gwarl, is it? The man who charged into the crowd in Aberwyn? Men died in that, lass."

The men behind him swore or muttered under their breath. Gwarl began backing his horse. Too late Alyssa realized what she'd done. One of those dead men was the younger son of Gwerbret Standyc. The Bear men all urged their horses a few steps forward, but the captain raised one hand, flat, palm outward. They held their position at that.

"Oh, indeed?" The captain's cold voice measured out each word as carefully as a baker measuring yeast. "Does the lass speak true, my lord?"

Gwarl swallowed heavily. He'd gone a bit pale. If he were captured, Standyc would hang him without a moment's worry for the inevitable war that would follow. The Bear's men laid hands on sword hilts. So did the men behind Gwarl. Cavan turned to Alyssa and mouthed the words, "get ready to run." She answered with a silent "you, too." The captain noticed and gave her a curt nod of the head.

"Get off the road," he snapped, "and take your cursed silver dagger with you." He turned back to Gwarl. "If his lordship will allow?"

Gwarl was already reaching for his saber. Alyssa jerked her horse's head around and kicked him to make him run. They darted into the meadow with Cavan right behind them. Out on the road yells exploded and the clatter of hooves as the two warbands met. Metal shrieked on metal and thumped on shields.

"Don't look back!" Cavan shouted to her. "Just ride! Over there through the grass!"

He pointed across the meadow to a thicket of trees.

Although Alyssa heard him, the horrifying noise behind her seemed to have cast a dwimmer spell. She sat transfixed on horseback and heard a man scream in agony. Swearing in a string of vile oaths, Cavan grabbed the reins from her with one hand and led her away as fast the horses could trot. Don't look, she told herself, don't look! But of course she did look back and saw a body lying in the road, a bleeding horse falling to its knees, another man, an Aberwyn man, retreating with his face blood-red. No one had had time to don their helms, she realized.

"Lyss!" Cavan shouted at her. "Look at me!"

She managed to do that, and the spell broke. As he led her into the safety of a copse of trees, she began to weep, a stubborn trickle of tears that persisted no matter how hard she fought them.

"Here, here!" Cavan said. "What's so wrong?"

"My fault, and they're dead."

"Fault? You saved us both. Don't you know what Gwarl's warband would have done to you on the way back to the town? You'd have been lucky to reach Aberwyn alive."

The tears stopped. She did know, had heard stories all her life about what men did to women they considered sluts and thus fair game.

"Besides," Cavan continued, "Gwarl's gotten what's coming to him. The Bear's men will take his body back to their lord tonight, and young what's-his-name will be avenged."

Her voice caught in her throat and choked her, but she stammered out a few words.

"This means war, doesn't it?"

"It does." Cavan sounded almost cheerful. "But here, don't blame yourself. It would have happened anyway. What matters now is staying safe and getting to Haen Marn."

On the other side of the meadow they rejoined the road. Alyssa felt herself trembling beyond her power to stop. Her hands, her face, felt icy cold in the spring sunshine.

"Cavan?" she said, and her voice shook. "Which of them won?"

"I can't tell from here, but I'd wager high it's the Bears. Numbers always tell, always, despite what the bards sing in those old sagas. There were twice as many of them as there were Foxes. And none of the Fox men were wearing armor."

Benoic caught up with them when the sun hung low in the sky. He was riding a black gelding instead of the chestnut, and he told them that the lord who'd given him the remount had been pleased to do so.

"The chestnut was his, it seems," Benoic said. "He'd given it to another messenger some while back."

"So he won't be worrying about getting the black returned?" Cavan said.

"I doubt it, but won't we be going back that way?"

"You might be, but Lyss and I won't."

"And I'd be glad of your sword," Alyssa said, "if you'd like to keep riding with us."

Inwardly Cavan sighed: would he never get a chance alone with her? He reminded himself that he was unworthy, but somehow, watching her lithe body and bright smiles, he was finding humility hard to come by. Still, he was a practical man in his way.

"We need you," Cavan said. "There's no doubt about that."

"Then I'm on!" Benoic made Alyssa a half-bow from the saddle. "I'll be glad of the hire, and truly, you'll need another sword. Here, Cavvo, what's going on? I rode past a place where there'd been a nasty scrap, from the look of the blood in the road and all. A couple of farmfolk were out, cutting up some dead horses for the meat, and they told me it was the Bear against some Western Fox men."

"It was that, all right."

"They said the Bear captain rode off with some lord's head on the point of his sword."

"He did what?"

"Took his head. The farmfolk swore to it." Benoic grimaced with a little shudder. "I couldn't half believe it at first! Ye gods, with all the laws and curses and the like against taking heads? I may be only a silver dagger, but it turned my guts, it did."

Alyssa went dead-white. Cavan leaned over in the saddle and grabbed her horse's reins.

"What's all this?" Benoic said. "My apologies for rattling on like that."

"It's ghastly, is all." Alyssa choked out the words. "In this day and age!"

"Most assuredly it's that," Cavan said. "Here, try to put it out of your mind. We'd best get to Haen Marn as fast as we possibly can. Standyc won't give us grief, but we've got to get beyond Ladoic's reach."

Benoic looked faintly puzzled.

"That head," Cavan continued, "most likely belonged to Lord Gwarl, Aberwyn's younger son."

"By the Lord of Hell's great scaly balls." Benoic was whispering. "War. It's certain now."

"True spoken." Alyssa's voice had steadied, though her face still was pale. "Haen Marn's a sacred rhan, you know. No one dares draw a sword there. We'll be safe once we reach it."

"If we do," Benoic said. "Cavvo, you've got a broadsword hidden in your blankets, from the look of that roll. Change it now. That fine-sword won't do us much good if things come to a scrap on the road."

"Or in a tavern, truly. Done, then."

Along this stretch of the canal, bordered by woodland, the tow-path narrowed. Cavan put Alyssa in the lead to spare her the dust, and he and Benoic rode side by side behind. They stayed close to her, however, and loosened their swords in their scabbards. Once they came free of the woods, they rode three abreast with Alyssa safely in the middle. The path and canal ran through fields at first, but the farther north they traveled, the more they saw pastureland, dotted with white cows with rusty-red ears. Occasionally they saw fenced pastures sheltering solid-looking carthorses with rich brown coats and white markings. To distract her from brooding, Cavan pointed them out to Alyssa.

"Probably bred for the canal boat trade," he remarked.

"Indeed." Her voice still sounded thin and dry with fear. "The traffic to Haen Marn's heavy in the spring and summer."

"I'm looking forward to seeing the place."

"Huh," Benoic said. "I wonder if that strange old woman's still there."

"Who?" Cavan said.

"A while past I got a hire guarding a healer of sorts who was going to Haen Marn to look for some kind of book. She had a cursed strange beast with her, a huge spotted cat, and I'm not having a jest on you, Cavvo, I swear it. The beast was as well trained as a lady's lapdog."

"What was her name?"

"Um, Rommardda, summat like that."

"What? You met the Rommardda? From Cerrgonney?"

"That's where she was from, true enough. But the Rommardda?"

"It's a title, not truly a name at all, though she uses it like one. We saw her in Lughcarn now and then, come to oversee a new smelter or bless a forge or suchlike."

"Bless? She's a priestess, like, you mean?"

Cavan cursed his own big mouth. He'd come close to revealing a secret of the iron craft. "In a way, truly, but she doesn't live shut up in a temple."

"Well, she was traveling around, sure enough, her and her cat beast. Cathvar, his name was. I swear she knew—ah well—strange lore, but doubtless just a daft fancy on my part."

Benoic seemed to have already figured out that the Rommardda was a dwimmerwoman, but Cavan decided against confirming it. As the second son of Lughcarn's gwerbret, he'd been sworn to the secret rites of metal-working as a lad. He might have dishonored his noble rank, but he refused to dishonor the Iron Brotherhood and his ritual position as the Sword of Fire. The Brotherhood, a Lughcarn tradition, stood halfway between a craft guild and a dwimmer lodge, though many thought their rituals were just for show, little fables and bits of lore and nothing more. Mostly the Brothers did charity work, helping the poor in Lughcarn, especially those injured in the dangerous craft of coaxing pure metal out of rock. Cavan had loved the work, the lore, and the rituals.

Now he'd lost it all.

As they rode north that day, Cavan found himself remembering the position he might have held in Lughcarn's rich trade and craft, if only he hadn't thrown everything away in a stupid brawl in a tavern. He might have been living in comfort as an overseer of dues and taxes, with plenty of coin to support an educated wife like Alyssa, or even running one of the law courts as other younger sons did—not that she would have let him handle matters in the traditional manner. He smiled at the thought of her facing down his blustering father with talk of justice and tradition.

No hope for that now, he realized. He also realized something else: soon he'd be facing Rommardda. He choked back a groan of pure shame, that she would see him like this.

"What's wrong?" Alyssa turned in her saddle to look at him.

"Ah, ah, naught."

"You've gone white as milk."

"Just, um, thinking."

"None of my affair if you don't wish to tell me." She returned to looking at the road ahead.

And why, he thought to himself, *have I met a woman like this now, when I can't possibly have her? Part of my punishment, mayhap, for being such a cursed stupid fool.*

From the south, the canal system ran all the way to Haen Marn, though it traveled no further north and only a short way to the east. That night, when Alyssa and her two silver daggers took shelter in an inn, Alyssa heard that Gwerbret Standyc did want to extend it, but he needed more coin to do so.

"Not a lot of folk up here, lass," a merchant told her. "So not a lot of dues and taxes. If he can open land to free farmers off to the west, well then, he'll have the means." He sighed and shook his head. "But the war with Aberwyn is going to throw a meat axe into that scheme."

"You think there's bound to be a war now?" Alyssa said.

"How can there not be? Lord Grif dead first, and now the Aberwyn lad?"

"Some might say it balanced out, like."

"True, if there was anyone out here with the authority to say it." He smiled with a twist of his mouth. "And if they listened to him. Damned arrogant, our local lords. The honor of the thing! Makes me sick, listening to them. Huh! Not worth a weasel's stinking arse, if you ask me."

"But there's the Westfolk behind all this." Another merchant leaned forward and shook his table dagger in the air for emphasis. "I don't trust 'em, I don't, those cat-eyed bastards, out for everything they can get."

"Oh, come now!" the first merchant said. "They're scrupulous fair traders, they are."

"Huh! Because they know we're watching every move their cursed skinny fingers make!"

The conversation died there.

Although Alyssa had been thinking about finishing the journey by canal, the more she considered it, the weaker the idea seemed. Once they were on a boat they'd have nowhere to run if Standyc decided to take them for a bargaining point with Aberwyn. Benoic and Cavan both agreed.

"The road's a better choice," Benoic said. "We can always cut away from it to hide if we have to. Besides, we'll be reaching Haen Marn soon enough."

After the meal, Cavan and Benoic left the inn to go sleep in the stables. Lantern in hand, Alyssa walked with them out into the stableyard for a private word. Over by the stable building three men were standing in a little group. Benoic swore under his breath. The three raised drawn swords and strolled over. She saw the gleam of dagger blades in their left hands.

"All right, Cavvo," one of them said. "You're coming with us to Aberwyn. Alive or dead. Your decision."

"Curse you and your balls both!" Cavan slid his sword free of the sheath. "It's the bounty, innit?"

"You'll have to get past me, too." Benoic drew his as well. "Renno, I'm surprised at you, running a coward's errand. And Wilyn, you mule's cunt!"

"Don't be a fool, Benno!" Renno said. "Our quarrel's not with you. Three against two, man! Think!"

"Lyss!" Cavan spoke without looking away from the approaching danger. "Run! Get inside!"

Good advice—she had no intention of following it. She knew that silver daggers settled their own quarrels, refused the aid of the laws, and all the rest of it. She cared not one whit. She held the lantern up and screamed.

"Help! Murder! Rape! Help! Thieves thieves thieves!"

Benoic and Cavan stepped in front of her as she screamed again with lungs grown strong from bardic training. The three bounty hunters hesitated just long enough. The inn doors behind her flew open with a spill of light. Men, a lot of men, rushed out yelling and waving weapons. Iron-bound cudgels, a meat cleaver, a couple of antique broadswords gleamed as her defenders ran through the spill of light from the open doors. Alyssa hurried out of the way and held the lantern high while she screamed again, wordlessly, this time, to add to the effect. The three bounty hunters shamelessly ran for the gates with the bolder members of the crowd in pursuit.

The merchant she'd been speaking to at dinner trotted over to her. He carried a quarterstaff.

"Are you safe, good maid?" he said.

"I am now, good sir! My thanks, my very most sincere thanks, oh I was so frightened to see them prowling around. Looking for your trade goods, I should imagine." She paused for a couple of sobs that she hoped sounded convincing. "If it hadn't been for my two guards, who knows what they would have done to me?"

"There, there, lass, don't let yourself dwell on it. You're safe now, and doubtless that lot are running for their lives."

It was late before the men who'd gone searching for the supposed thieves returned. They'd never found them, but they had found their horses, tied up not far from the inn. The leader of the search party brought them back inside the stableyard, and the innkeep locked and bolted the gates.

"We'll go through our goods in the morning light," the merchant told Alyssa. "If aught's missing, then these horses will make up for it, like."

"No doubt your local lord will want to hear about this."

"Him? Huh!" The merchant spat onto the ground. "Oh, he'd rule on the matter fast enough, him and one of the priests from the temple, but what good would that do? We'd still have to hunt these thieves down ourselves."

"You could hire a silver dagger, I suppose. They really are better than thieves."

"Huh. You've found the only honest pair in the kingdom, most like! Me and the lads will keep our eyes open and have a look around.

I wager they're still in town since we've got their mounts. I don't care if it takes us all day."

Alyssa smiled and dropped him a heartfelt curtsy. As she told her silver daggers, they could ride safely enough on the morrow.

"Assuming we ride fast, anyway," she said.

"Just so," Benoic said. "Truly, my lady, I admire your quick wits. You saved our lives, sure enough."

"You couldn't have won the scrap?"

"Not by half," Cavan said. "Here's how it goes. Two of them engage me and Benno. The third stabs one of us from the side. That leaves three men on one, and the one's dispatched like a chicken for the pot."

"And yet," she turned to Benoic, "you'd stand with him?"

"I told you. He saved my wretched life once. My thanks, my lady, and I call you that because you're noble to me. If we had yelled for aid, would anyone have listened? Not to a cursed silver dagger. A lass crying out—truly a different matter."

"So I'd hoped when I did it. It just aches my heart to think of men of your own guild—"

"When you ride the long road," Cavan interrupted, "you can't consider such fine points of honor."

"And a hundred brazens is a lot of coin," Benoic said, "even split three ways."

Alyssa supposed it was, enough to spend a winter in a silver dagger's inn somewhere, safe from the snow and alive for a few months more. *Silver daggers always say they have no honor,* she thought, *except about their hires. You don't want to believe them, but there we are.*

"I wonder if they've got enough coin to buy more horses," she said.

"I wouldn't be surprised. Someone put them onto me fast enough. That noble lord who made sure Benno knew about the bounty, maybe. But I'll wager they got a few coins along with the news."

"We'll have a day's start on them at least," Benoic continued, "and a cursed good thing, too. They'll be coming after us." He grinned in a surprisingly cheerful way. "They won't be taking it kindly, outsmarted by a lass."

"True enough," Cavan said, and he looked and sounded grim. "We'd best get to the sacred rhan as fast as possible."

The news of Lord Gwarl's death arrived in Aberwyn early on a bright sunny day. Two of the Fox men had survived the battle with minor wounds. They'd had the sense to flee the unequal and hopeless fight and managed to reach one of Ladoic's vassals further south. With their cuts bound, fresh horses, and a token to change their mounts for more, they'd ridden day and night to reach Aberwyn with the news.

Both Dovina and her mother were in the great hall, breakfasting with Ladoic, when the two filthy and stumbling-weary men staggered up to the dais. One of them pitched forward into the straw when he tried to kneel. He'd fainted. Ladoic got to his feet and hurried over, bellowing for servants to come help.

"Your Grace," the other stammered out, "the Bear caught us on their side of the border. Lost, Your Grace. Eight of our men and—" He paused to throw back his head and gulp for air. Tears ran through the clotted dust on his face. "Lord Gwarl is dead."

Dovina found herself standing without being aware she'd risen. Behind her Rhosyan screamed. Dovina spun around and caught her mother's arm.

"Come away, Mother! Up to the women's hall."

Rhosyan screamed again and shook her head no. Dovina hauled her bodily to her feet. The messenger was pouring out details, horrible details.

"They took his head, Your Grace. Right there in the road. I saw them when I looked back. The captain—the point of his sword—"

Rhosyan fell silent, her face stretched and dead pale, her eyes wide, her mouth working. Dovina half-shoved, half-carried her mother to the stairway. Darro came running to help, and together they managed at last to get her upstairs and into the women's hall. Her maid hurried over and led her to her chair while Dovina told the lass a version of the news that omitted the horrible details. In but a few moments Ladoic rushed in and hurried to Rhosyan's side.

"Why did you send him?" Rhosyan was gasping for breath between words. "Why? Don't you have sworn men for that?" She paused for a brief flurry of tears. "Well, don't you?"

Ladoic's face had drained to a corpse-like gray. He knelt beside his wife but said nothing. All he could do was open and shut his mouth like a landed fish. Dovina knelt at her mother's opposite side and clasped her hand in both of hers while Rhosyan sobbed aloud. Her maid hovered behind the chair.

At length Ladoic rose and collected himself with a deep sigh that seemed torn out of him.

"My love, forgive me," he said. "I beg you. Forgive me."

Rhosyan never looked his way, merely continued to sob. Ladoic turned on his heel and strode out of the chamber.

Dovina stayed with her mother until somewhere in the middle of the afternoon, when Rhosyan finally grew exhausted. With her maid's help, Dovina got her mother to drink some unwatered wine, then got her into her bed and perched next to her. She stayed, stroking her mother's hair, until Rhosyan slept. Dovina got up and motioned to the maid to take her place.

"I'm going down to see to the gwerbret," she whispered. "Stay with her."

"Of course, my lady."

Dovina found her father pacing back and forth on the dais in the great hall. Standing around him were the captain of his warband and his councillors, talking of provisions, horses, riders, spare weaponry. When he saw her, Ladoic raised a hand for silence.

"I'll return in a moment," he said. "Dovva, come walk a bit with me."

They went into a side chamber for their talk. Dovina braced herself, sure he was going to blame her meddling in politics for Gwarl's death, but his actual response shocked her.

"I should have listened to you," Ladoic said. "I never should have sent him."

It was Dovina's turn for the wordless stare while he twisted his mouth into something that might have been meant for an ironic smile. At last she found words.

"Father, it's done now and over."

"So it is, so it is, and there's no bringing him back from the Otherlands. Standyc will pay for this, him and his cursed Bears! Insulting the honor of my clan this way! They could have taken the lad and impoverished me with the ransom, couldn't they? For your mother's sake I would have paid it."

"But not for your own?"

"I'd have rather paid Standyc back in his own blood." His voice had dropped to a growl. For a moment he trembled. With a sharp sigh and a breath, he controlled himself. "I'll miss Gwarro. He had twice the wits of his brother."

"He did at that." Dovina felt her own voice clot with tears. She'd never loved her brother, but he was bloodkin, and she would miss him, nasty little remarks and all. "He was too young to die."

"Truly. Well, Standyc will regret this yet. I'm going to start by demanding he turn over the man who took the head. So I can hang him. Breaking every law! Barbaric!" He shook himself like a wet dog. "Standyc won't comply, of course, so there we'll be."

At war, she thought, no matter who else pays with their crops and young men and daughters. She might have spoken against it, but she knew she had no hope of averting so much as one needless death.

"As you think fit, Father," she said. "I take it we're not going to Cerrmor."

"We're not."

"Good. I can stay with Mother, then."

He nodded, then hurried back to his men and the planning for the war.

But just before sunset a pair of royal speeded couriers arrived with messages that changed everything. Dovina was up in the women's hall when she heard the great bronze bells at the harbor temples ring. She leaned out of a window and listened, counting. Three pulls on Manannan's bell, answered by three pulls on the Goddess's—a royal galley had just rowed into harbor. She hurried to the door of her mother's chamber and saw her safely asleep with Magla in the chair beside her.

"Did you hear the harbor bells?" Dovina said.

"I did, my lady. Could it be the king coming here?"

"I truly doubt that, but it'll be a message from him, sure enough. I'll be going downstairs in a bit. Should my mother wake, send a page to fetch me."

Dovina waited upstairs to give the message time to reach the dun. When she came down, she found two men in the royal livery of red and gold kneeling at her father's side as he sat at table. Councillor Nallyc sat at his other side and whispered to Ladoic, who nodded agreement now and then. When Dovina hesitated to join them, Ladoic waved her forward and pointed to her usual chair.

"Here's a second ugly blow to the day." Ladoic tossed a curled sheet of pabrus in her direction. "Read it." He glanced at a hovering page. "Take these two men to the kitchen hut. Get them fresh food to take back to the galley."

With much bowing and murmured thanks, the men rose and hurried away. Dovina picked up the parchment and smoothed it out. Nallyc looked both surprised and annoyed that she'd been given the message, while Ladoic leaned back in his chair, sipped his ale, and stared across the hall to a row of heraldic shields hung up under the rafters.

The letter began with many courteous greetings, recitation of Ladoic's titles and honors, and ritual hopes that he and his kinfok were well, a rather unfortunate courtesy considering the other news of the day. The meat of the message, however nicely phrased, read as an outright order from the Prince Regent.

"You will honor us by coming to Cerrmor before taking any action against Standyc, gwerbret of the Bear clan holdings, in the matter of this dispute over certain fields and pastures. We have sent the same request —" *Request?* Dovina thought. *Hah!* "— to Standyc, that he wait upon us immediately. We trust that you will make all possible speed in journeying thither, where we shall join you as promptly as the kingdom's affairs allow. Any violence that may break out between you and your men and those of Standyc will be assessed as damage against the laws and the kingship, whether such unpleasantness occur in your territories or in Cerrmor or on the road to Cerrmor."

Dovina rolled the letter back up and handed it to Nallyc, who returned it to the polished silver message tube, ornamented with etched wyverns, in which it had arrived. Ladoic looked at her with one eyebrow raised.

"I gather we're going to Cerrmor after all," Dovina said.

"Most assuredly." Ladoic set his tankard down on the table. "But not for a few days. I'll send messages back to the regent with his messengers to tell him of Gwarl's death."

"Good. I doubt if Mother will be strong enough to come with us, and I don't want to leave her straightaway."

"No more do I. Ye gods, this cursed day must have flown out of the gates of hell!"

"Truly. You know, you'd best send a copy of this decree to Donno. And of course the news, but we don't want him marching off on his own to avenge his brother."

"He wouldn't be so stupid. I lie—of course he would. Nallyc, get a scribe up here! We need to send Tieryn Adonyc a cursed strong message."

"Indeed, Your Grace." The councillor rose in a flapping swirl of black robes. "I quite agree. Shall I also send a separate note to his own adviser? From me, like, begging him to exert all possible influence."

"Excellent idea! Do that, and my thanks."

The delay in leaving for Cerrmor gave Dovina the chance to visit Lady Rhodda Hall and consult with her allies. On the morrow, once she'd made sure that Rhosyan felt stronger, she took Darro and returned to the scholar's compound. She left her page with the groom and pony cart outside the gates and went in alone. She was just crossing the lawn to the collegium when Mavva came running to meet her.

"Is there any news?" Mavva blurted out. "I've been so worried."

"None, but there won't be for some while, truly. Is Lady Tay here today?"

"She is. I gather she knows about it."

"Most definitely, and that's just as well. I think she's willing to help us if she can. We'll have to be careful how we phrase things, so she can't be blamed should my father find out she knew."

"Splendid!" Mavva paused to look around her in such a suspicious way that she might as well have shouted that they were discussing a secret. "When are you leaving for Cerrmor?"

"In a few days." Dovina debated telling her about Gwarl, but the news would spread quick enough without her whipping it along. "I'm hoping that Alyssa will arrive soon after we get there."

"I wish I could go with you."

As they walked back to the hive together, Dovina had a sudden idea. "Mayhap you could. We could pretend you were my maid—nah nah nah, that would be too demeaning."

"I wouldn't mind, if it meant I could go. After all, I'm only a commoner."

"You're not only anything, Mavva. You're a scholar. Never forget that."

Mavva smiled like the breaking dawn. Dovina went on thinking.

"I've got it. You can be my fellow guardian of the bookhoard. Well, if Lady Tay says you may leave the collegium, of course. Let's find her and ask."

Lady Tay was working in her private study on the second floor of the main broch. When they came in, she wiped her pen on a bit of rag and laid it down on her desk. Both younger women curtsied.

"I'm here to cause more trouble," Dovina said. "If you'll forgive me, my lady."

"Indeed?" Lady Tay raised an eyebrow. "What is it now?"

"Soon I'll be dragged off to Cerrmor by my father. I'd like Mavva to go with me as a fellow guardian of our bookhoard."

"Ah, I see. Your plot. Will Alyssa be in Cerrmor?"

"I can hope, my lady."

Lady Tay waved at the bench in front of her desk. Dovina and Mavva sat down and waited while the lady stared out of the window in apparent thought. Finally she sighed and looked their way again.

"Dovina, will your father provide for Mavva as part of your retinue?"

"I'll insist, my lady. I've got lots of dresses, Mavva, so you don't have to worry about looking well turned out."

"My thanks, my lady. I really was worrying about that."

"Very well, then," Lady Tay said. "Now, we do have a certain amount of coin that could go with you. It's part of the gift from Queen Carramaena of the Westlands. From what I've heard of her, she'll be well pleased to see it spent on books. There are some shops near the law courts in Cerrmor that might have some titles that we should have in our hoard."

"Near the law courts." Dovina glanced at Mavva. "No doubt we could find an escort to take us there. My alleged betrothed is a bookish man."

"Indeed? Well and good, then." Lady Tay considered for a moment more. "I'll give you a list of books we could use, but if you see some treasure, I'll trust your judgment."

"My thanks, my lady." Dovina felt herself blush at the compliment. "I'll do my best to choose well."

"I'm sure you will. Has there been any news of our wandering scholar and her silver dagger?"

"None, my lady."

When Dovina returned to the dun, she found her father drinking at the table of honor with Adonyc seated to his right. Both men had bound black ribands around their heads as a sign of mourning, and she reminded herself that she needed to do the same. She curtsied to Ladoic, ignored her brother, and started for the staircase, only to pause when she realized that they were talking about the bardic demand for a justiciar.

"The regent isn't going to trouble himself for their sake," Adonyc was saying. "Pack of vermin, really, gnawing away at our sacred traditions."

"I wouldn't be so certain of that," Ladoic said. "There's a precedent up in Cerrgonney."

"They don't have a gwerbret up there. That's the trouble. They need to apportion out the land into proper rhannau and find the right men to rule them."

"And deal with the aftermath?"

Adonyc opened his mouth to speak, then merely shrugged and drank his ale. *Feuds upon feuds*, Dovina thought. *A lot of men dead.*

"If he does appoint a justiciar here, it would be interesting." Dovina came back to stand at her father's left. "From a legal standpoint, that is."

"You'd think so," Adonyc said. "You're like one of Mother's stinking ferrets, always snapping and skulking around."

"If you're so worried about vermin, then you need ferrets. If you took more of an interest in the laws, you'd see this as a—"

"Oh, you think you know everything! They never should have sent you to that cursed collegium!"

"Donno, hold your tongue." Ladoic sounded weary rather than angry. "We've got enough trouble as it is."

"My apologies, Father. But ye gods, here's Gwarl dead and his body dishonored, and all we can do is wait for the cursed regent to give his opinion? It gripes my heart!"

"Indeed?" Ladoic reached for his tankard. "And what would you do instead?"

Dovina waited to see if Adonyc would dig himself his usual pit.

"Well, to begin with," Adonyc said, "I'd find a few of these rabble-rousers and hang them. That would silence the rest, eh?"

"It would be the worst thing you could do," Ladoic said. "Stir everything up all over again."

"Faugh, they're all cowards, not a fighting man in the lot! I'm surprised that Crayloc or Cronoc or whatever his name was didn't give up his suit long before he starved."

"So was I." Ladoic's voice was dangerously level. "Most surprised indeed."

"So you were hoping —" Dovina started to speak, but Adonyc raised his voice and drowned her out.

"Put the fear of death into them," Adonyc said. "You've already got rid of that one. Time to put the rest in their place. Somewhere else than here."

Dovina stepped forward, but her father got in first.

"Do you truly think I should somehow or other rid the rhan of bards?" Ladoic sounded incredulous.

"Of course not! Just the troublesome ones."

Dovina raised her voice in turn. "The bards are the voice of the people."

"Well, tell them to hold their tongues, too." Adonyc laughed as if he'd made a joke. "What do they need a voice for?"

"And what would you do without the guilds to lend you coin?" Dovina said. "As, for instance, in times of war?"

"I'm not talking about them."

"Oh, but you are! How would the clothsellers of Dun Gwerbyn take it if you told them they had no voice in your affairs? I can't think of anything that would tighten a guild's purse strings faster than that."

Adonyc turned to the gwerbret in mute appeal. Ladoic had a long swallow of ale before he spoke.

"She's right," was all he said.

Adonyc got up and stalked off and down the little steps from the dais. Without looking back he crossed the great hall to one of the tables where his honor guard of twenty men were seated. The captain rose from the chair at the head of it to bow. Adonyc sat down with his back firmly toward the dais. The captain took a seat elsewhere.

Ladoic muttered something that might have been a laugh and turned to Dovina. "How does your mother fare?"

"A little better, Father."

"Good. We truly do need to leave for Cerrmor soon. Tomorrow, I was thinking."

"Is Donno coming with us?"

"He's not."

"Good."

"He's only saying what I heard from a lot of the other lords. The Council of Electors, the other gwerbretion. Think on that, will you?"

"Was that why you let Cradoc starve?"

Ladoic looked at her for a long moment with an utterly neutral expression on his face, then returned to contemplating the row of heraldic shields. She realized that he'd answered her question in the only way he could.

chapter 5

bAEN MARN LAY IN no one's territory but its own, on
the shores of the southernmost of the Peddrolocion, the
Four Lakes that sit between Deverrian and Westfolk
territory, though in truth, its lake formed a fifth. The Westfolk
swore that there'd been only four lakes in the past, and that Haen
Marn had arrived out of nowhere one day. Just plopped itself down
and its lake with it, the Westfolk sages said. No one in Deverry believed them, as far as Cavan knew. Whether the sacred rhan lay just
west of Fox territory or just beyond that of the Bears had also been a
matter of some dispute for several hundred years, but only the heralds and the great lords cared. It existed, it was open to anyone needing healing, and that was all that mattered to most people. All around
the lake lay farms that paid taxes in kind, and grateful patients often
gave gifts of coin or merchant goods. Freed from a great lord's rule,
Haen Marn prospered.

The two silver daggers and their scholar hire rode west through a
pass between two hills. (The canal traveled in a tunnel dug by
dwarven engineers and forbidden to riders.) Cavan kept turning in
the saddle to look behind them, but the distance stayed free of the
dust cloud that would mean pursuit. At the crest of the pass they
paused to look down to the long narrow valley, where sacred lakes
gleamed in the afternoon sun. At the foot of the pass, the canal

emerged and joined a river that left the valley—somewhere to the west.

Cavan could make no sense of the silvery stripes of water, neither river nor canal. That is, the canal seemed obvious enough. It came out of the tunnel and joined a river, but one he'd not seen before. Try as he might, he could not see where this west-flowing river left the valley, and yet it had to leave it somewhere. Finally he gave it up as a bad job. He could clearly see that a town spread out beside this river, and beyond the town, a road led through meadows to the walled complex on the shore of the nearest lake. Out in the water lay the sacred island of Haen Marn, green and white from blooming apple trees. Beyond the lakes hills rose, dark with pine forests.

Late in the day, when mist was rising from the placid waters of the lake, they reached the place where the road widened, the canal ended, and the town began. Dun Sebanna existed solely to serve the patients and their escorts with its clusters of inns and temples to all the various gods that anyone had ever heard of, whether Deverrian or Westfolk. Even Alshandra, the central goddess of the far northern folk known as Gel da'Thae, had a sacred shrine there. While the laws would have dealt harshly with any madman who violated the sacred nature of the settlement, high stone walls surrounded it—just in case a madman came their way.

As the city gates closed for the night behind them, Benoic asked a town watchman if any other silver daggers had arrived that day.

"From the east, it would be."

"None," the fellow said. "Friends of yours on their way?"

"Not friends, but troublemakers. Some merchants in the last place we stayed were convinced these lads had been taking the wrong kind of look at their merchandise. Three men, and one of them has red hair and a mustache to match."

"My thanks for the tip, lad. I'm surprised you'd speak against members of your own band."

"Who knows if they're truly silver daggers?" Benoic shrugged and laid a hand on the hilt of his own. "These have been stolen from battlefields before."

Although this slur against their guild bothered Cavan, he held his tongue and nodded as if he agreed. Benoic had spoken the truth about one of their assailants, that third fellow who'd hung back from a possible fight. Neither Cavan nor Benoic had recognized him. In the poor light neither had been able to see if he carried the silver dagger, although they'd seen the glimmer of a sword blade clearly enough.

Since they had no need to seek the sanctuary of a temple for that one night, they found shelter in a decent inn catering to guildspeople. Much to Cavan's surprise, the innkeep made no objection to silver daggers.

"All be welcome at Haen Marn," he remarked. "We have a gentleman's common room with good beds, lads." He turned to Alyssa. "And privacy for the ladies as well."

"Splendid," she said. "I don't know how long we'll be staying."

"From the look of them bandages on that lad's head, it'll be a few days at least, eh?" He glanced at the sky and the lowering sun. "Dinner soon."

Late in the evening, once Alyssa had gone to the women's common chamber, Benoic bought the innkeep a tankard of his own ale. Over this friendly gesture, Cavan told the tale that he and Benoic had invented between them. It held enough truth to satisfy him.

"Now, the lass who's hired us?" Cavan said. "She's here to fetch a very valuable thing for her guild. We're sworn not to tell you what it may be, but you can doubtless guess that she's carrying a fair bit of coin."

"Makes sense, truly."

"There's already been one thief who paid high for trying to steal it." Cavan touched the fake bandages around his head. "We'd just as soon not have any trouble with another. I'm sure you feel the same."

"Indeed! Not in my inn!"

"So," Benoic took up the tale, "we'll be taking turns prowling around during the night. One of us should stay near the door to that women's chamber. But we don't want you to think we're up to no good."

"It's a good thing you warned me," the innkeep said, "or I would have been calling the town watch."

"There shouldn't be any trouble if we're on guard," Benoic said. "Thieves are not the most courageous lot in the kingdom."

With two silver daggers to ensure it did so, the night passed quietly. Some while after sunrise, Cavan was sitting on the floor across the corridor from the door of the women's chamber when Alyssa came out, carrying her sack of clothing.

"You're up early," she said with a laugh.

"I've been up for a while, truly." Cavan got up and stretched his back. "Let's get some breakfast. I'll fetch Benno. We'd best find a safer place to stay. Those lads might catch up to us by evening."

"Just so. I'm thinking that the temple of Wmm might help a wandering scholar and her guards. I've got the letters from Rhys to show them. The temple of the Goddess would shelter me, no doubt, but it's you those men are after."

"They wouldn't mind doing you a bad turn, too, I'll wager."

"True enough." Alyssa paused for a moment, then took a deep breath. "Let's see what we can find."

After they'd eaten, and Benoic had tended their horses, they fetched their gear and left the inn. In the narrow streets they led the horses past temple after temple, inn after inn. Everywhere they saw people who were visibly ill or injured, hobbling along or being carried in litters, surrounded by family or sitting begging alone. Street vendors cried their goods. Tavern keepers stood in their doorways and hectored the passersby. When they followed a lane down to the river, they found it brown and stinking with garbage, like all rivers that ran through towns. They retreated back to the main road.

"It's cursed different than I'd been thinking," Cavan remarked. "All this noise and confusion."

"The town's not much," Alyssa said. "Haen Marn itself is different. You'll see."

If we can reach it, Cavan thought. Since he was painfully aware that he was the cause of their danger, he was considering simply turning himself over for the bounty in return for the hunters' sworn vow to leave Alyssa alone. Benoic could then take Alyssa on to Cerrmor in safety. He'd not been able to force himself to make the suggestion aloud, though he knew he'd go through with it if he had to.

Finally Benoic asked a shopkeeper where they might find the temple of Wmm. They'd passed it, of course, and had to go back the way they'd come. Well away from the main road Wmm and his advocates occupied a compound behind curved walls, smooth and pale with Bardekian plaster and whitewash. At intervals along the tops of the walls stood statues of pelicans, Wmm's sacred bird. The young neophyte at the gates read the letter from Rhys, smiled and bowed, and told Alyssa she was welcome.

"I'm afraid your men-at-arms will have to wait out here," he said.

Cavan wasn't in the least surprised. While she went inside, he held the reins of the horses to allow Benoic, who'd taken the longest watch of the night, to sit on the ground against the wall and sleep. Cavan kept watch on the crowd strolling by, but he saw no sign of the three bounty hunters. They might still be in the town, he reminded himself, going from inn to inn with some story, asking after a pair of silver daggers with a lass.

Alyssa returned remarkably quickly, grinning in triumph and holding a thick packet of folded pabrus. The horses raised their heads with a jingle of bridles as she hurried over. Benoic woke, scrambled to his feet, and yawned.

"Luck?" Cavan said.

"Better than luck. Letters of introduction to the Lady of Haen Marn herself, and to Perra of Cannobaen."

"Is she the chief healer?" Cavan said.

"Perra? She used to take care of patients, but not anymore. She's the one who oversees everything else, the food, the servants, that sort of thing. I had the honor of meeting her once. But that isn't all." Alyssa waved the pabrus at him. "We might be allowed to stay in the guest house, even. It would be a great honor."

"Ye gods!" Benoic said. "Honored indeed!"

"Just so. And I've been told we don't need to worry about our safety. His Holiness was quite firm on that point. Trust in Haen Marn, he said. And he winked at me."

Benoic looked as if he were about to speak, then kept silent. *Dwimmer,* Cavan thought. *What else would it be? And I'll wager that Benoic's thinking the same cursed thing.*

"A question, if you don't mind," Benoic said. "Why would Wmm's men be so willing to help us?"

"They approve of our cause," Alyssa said. "They'd like to see the laws of the land written down in books, something permanent, like, that the priests of Bel couldn't change at whim if it suited them and the lord whose court they spoke in."

"I see." Benoic said nothing for a few moments. "Huh! A fight between priests, is it? Gladdens my heart that I'm not in the middle of it."

"Oh, but you are." Alyssa grinned at him. "The cat guarding the cheese had better protect his tail against mice while he's at it."

"Are you daft?" Cavan broke in. "Or outright mad? It's a war between two of the most powerful priesthoods in Deverry, and you can smile like that?"

"'Tis better than weeping, innit?" She laid a friendly hand on his arm. "Cavvo, forgive me. I didn't truly realize at first how complicated the situation is. Nor did Dovina. But it's a fair bit late to back out now."

Cavan groaned and shot Benoic a glance. Benoic merely sighed and shrugged. *Truly,* Cavan thought, *too late now!*

They led their horses to the town gates, then mounted and rode out. The river road led through long meadows, green with the spring grass and dotted with daisies and buttercups, bright in the warm sun. Birds sang in the willows on the riverbank. Here and there Cavan saw fat white cows with rusty-red ears. A couple of lads with black and white dogs watched over them. Everything seemed oddly still, despite the birds and the smooth murmur of the river, quiet and yet expectant, as if the very grass knew some great thing was about to happen. He'd felt this sort of stillness before, when the Iron Brotherhood met for a ritual, the lesser officers all in place, the ordinary members standing in their half-circle, waiting for that night's Wielder of the Mace to come from the robing tent and start the proceedings. The crackling of the ritual fire in their midst would seem to be sounding in some other world, just as the birds' chatter did here on the road to Haen Marn.

Benoic began singing an old air about spring and happier times, and Alyssa joined in on the descant. Cavan nearly yelped aloud in surprise. They hadn't felt the stillness, then, if they could break it so easily.

Benoic and Alyssa had just finished their song when they reached the gates of the healing complex at the shore of the lake. A decorative stone wall, not much higher than a mounted rider's head, surrounded it on three sides, while the lake itself formed the fourth wall. Wooden gates stood wide open to reveal a view of a grassy meadow and a scatter of low wooden buildings, newly whitewashed and thatched. Beyond those, off to Cavan's right and close to the lakeshore, stood a tall, long wooden building with glass in its lower windows—the guesthouse, he assumed.

Out on the long lawn, various people sat on benches or lay on wheeled pallets to take the sun. Some of the patients seemed deathly ill; others were chatting with friends or attendants. Right near the gates a group of boys dressed in white clothes with pale blue and gray tabards sat in a circle and played some sort of dice game. Benoic called out a halloo and dismounted. As Cavan and Alyssa followed his lead, one of the pages got up and came running.

"Are you here for healing?" the lad said. "Come in if you come in peace."

"Most assuredly in peace," Alyssa said. She reached inside her tunic and pulled out the folded sheets of pabrus. "Can you read, lad? I have a letter of introduction to Perra of Cannobaen."

"I can, good maid, and if you'll come with me, I'll take you straight to her. She receives visitors in the guesthouse." He bowed to Alyssa, then turned to call to the circle of pages. "Fallo, come here! These silver daggers need to stable their horses."

Another boy scrambled up and came trotting over with a nod in their direction. Silver daggers might have been welcome in Haen Marn, but no one was going to bow to them.

"Stables are this way." Fallo jerked a thumb in the vague direction of his left. "Follow me."

Fallo led the way through the cluster of cottages. Most had open windows—for the fresh air, Cavan assumed. As they passed by, he could smell herbal potions and perfumes that couldn't quite cover the scent of human waste and that indefinable stale sourness of the long-term sickroom. Once he heard a woman moaning and a man murmuring to her in a desperate attempt to help her rest. He saw attendants carrying food to several cottages and others taking away chamber pots.

The stables turned out to be clean and well-tended. Each horse had a decent stall, and Fallo brought out a sack of Haen Marn's oats for their nosebags. He showed them the tack room and pointed out a chest where they could stow their horse gear, then left the men to their own devices.

"What now?" Cavan said. "I've no idea how long Alyssa will be."

"Might as well go back to the meadow."

"You've visited the place, right? Why are there so many pages around?"

"They're being trained here as healers. Most are the sons of merchants and the like, but there's usually a younger son or two from a noble family, one with too many sons for their oldest brothers to trust." Benoic sighed and looked away. "I came here because I was part of the escort for my lord's lady. Back when I was still an honorable man."

"Was she very ill?"

"She died here. She should have come much sooner, they told my lord." Benoic shrugged with an uneasy twist of a shoulder. "She had stones growing inside her. I don't know where."

Cavan made a sympathetic noise and led the way outside.

After the dim light in the stables, the sun outside made him blink and almost stumble. A flock of ravens flew from the stable roof with a flash of black wings, glinting bluish in the bright sun. As they passed overhead, they called out in a chorus of squawks. Cavan shuddered.

"Ill omen!"

"Not here," Benoic said. "Ravens are sacred to the spirits of the island. I don't know why."

Let's hope it's a good omen for me, Cavan thought. *Maybe Rommardda's ridden on, and I won't have to face her.* But the first person Cavan saw as he and Benoic returned to the lawn by the gates was Cathvar, lounging on the sunny grass. The leopard glanced their way, then rose, stretching with a flick of his tail.

"There's my friend," Benoic said. "He did me a good turn last year, he did."

"Bit Lord Aeryn's arse?"

"Better than that. Scared the bastard's horse. His ever-so-noble lordship ended up arse over cock in a muddy ditch."

Cavan laughed aloud. Benoic had told him why he'd become a silver dagger, thrown out of another lord's warband when Aeryn had falsely accused him of theft. Some might have doubted the tale, but Benoic was the kind of man you could believe—he'd shown that more than once in the time Cavan had known him.

"Here," Benoic continued. "You told me you know Rommardda. Why does a beast like this one obey her?"

"Oh, she's got a kind way with animals."

Benoic rolled his eyes heavenward. "You can do better than that, Cavvo!"

"What makes you think I'd know?"

"True. Well and good, then."

As if he knew that they were discussing him, the leopard started to stroll over to join them. Some yards away the flock of ravens settled onto the grass. Cathvar saw them, stopped walking, and crouched, his behind high, his foreparts low to the ground. His muscles bunched. He leaped, pounced on the grass beside the flock, and dashed among the birds. With weary-sounding squawks they all flew safely away. As if he were proud of himself, the leopard came prancing over to Benoic.

"Well met," Benoic said to him. "It gladdens my heart to see you again. I'll wager your mistress is here, too."

Cathvar turned his head and looked toward the guesthouse. An elderly woman, wrapped in loose gray dresses held in with a plain blue kirtle, came out of the front door and hurried down the path. The Rommardda tended to look like a lively bundle of laundry, being as she was short, plump, and gave no thought whatsoever to womanly things such as what she wore. Her messy gray braids sat off-center on her head looking all the world like a handle on the laundry basket. Despite her obvious age and enveloping dresses, she came trotting over to them with plenty of energy to spare. Cavan bowed to her, and she smiled at him.

"Ah, Cavan of Lughcarn!" she said. "So you're here, are you? Good. We'll have a nice long talk while Goodmaid Alyssa gets the arrangements settled."

"If you say so, honored one." Cavan tried to sound pleased, but even to his own ears his voice sounded like mourning. "I'm sure you have much to say to me."

She smiled and turned to Benoic. "It gladdens my heart to see you again, lad."

"My thanks, good dame. I'm surprised you'd still be here."

"Oh, I've gone and come back more than once since last I saw you.

There is so much lore here! Well worth a trip to a healer like me. What happened to your friend? I fear me I've forgotten his name."

"Ddary? He's riding in the Otherlands. We saw some hard fighting up in Cerrgonney."

"How very sad! My heart aches for you and him both."

"That's what happens to silver daggers, sooner or later." Benoic dismissed the sympathy with a shrug.

Indeed, Cavan thought, *and one day my wyrd will take me, too. Just as well, truly. Just as well.*

A lyssa had met Rommardda but only briefly, as she and the page went into the guesthouse. The lad introduced them, then hurried her along a corridor to a small chamber, paneled in some pale wood. At the big windows, filled with good glass, a tall young woman, dressed in the pale blue and white of Haen Marn, sat at a narrow table that was scattered with pieces of parchment and scribes' tools. She looked up and smiled.

"Lady Perra will be here in a moment." She waved vaguely at the wall to her right. "There are chairs."

"My thanks," Alyssa said and sat down.

She would have asked the scribe's name, but the lass returned to her work with a little frown of concentration. She was Bardekian, from Orystinna to judge from the rich dark brown of her skin and her curly black hair, as glossy as a raven's wing. She looked familiar, though only vaguely so, with her deep-set dark eyes and generous mouth, but she gave no sign of recognizing Alyssa. Alyssa had seen many Bardekian merchants, some of them women, in Aberwyn, had in fact sold plenty of them bread and cakes when she still was a child working in her father's shop. Perhaps this young woman had once been a customer.

In but a moment, indeed, the door opened, and a woman of indeterminate age swept into the room accompanied by a pair of pages. She wore her pale hair, mostly blonde, partly gray, twisted up in a messy bun, and her blue dresses, unlike Rommardda's, were both clean and neatly arranged under her tartan kirtle. Alyssa rose and curtsied.

"So, young Alyssa," Perra said. "It gladdens my heart to see you again."

"And mine to see you, my lady. I have so much to thank you for. My life at the collegium has been wonderful."

"Good! What brings you to me?"

"I've come to fetch a book that the collegium lent to Haen Marn. Have you heard about the trouble in Aberwyn?"

"About the courts and the gwerbretion? I have. It's not just in Aberwyn. All of the western provinces are boiling over with it."

Alyssa caught her breath. "I hadn't realized, my lady."

"These are complicated times." Perra smiled with an ironic twist of her mouth. "Now, speaking of time, I have a good many things to do today, so we'll talk more on the morrow. I'll have you brought over to the manse—on the island, that is—as soon as I have a spare moment." She beckoned to the pages. "Honored Scholar Alyssa and her guards will sleep in the guesthouse. Show her to a chamber upstairs, and give the two lads cots in the servants' quarters. Alyssa will eat at the students' table, and her guards with the servants."

"Er, my lady?" Alyssa said. "I have the guards because we've been threatened. Could they sleep closer to my chamber? We've got bounty hunters chasing us."

Perra raised startled eyebrows.

"Gwerbret Ladoic set the bounty," Alyssa continued. "Just on one of the silver daggers at first, but I'm all mixed up in it, too. I was speaking out in the marketplace, you see, when—"

Perra raised a hand for silence. "We need to have a long talk on the morrow. But as for the bounty men, you've got nothing to fear. Haen Marn has some guards now. They're new since you were here last. I'd feel sorry for anyone who crossed them."

One of the pages chuckled, and the scribe looked up with a grin and a nod of agreement.

"Very well, then," Alyssa said. "My thanks."

Alyssa's chamber turned out to be small but nicely appointed, with a comfortable narrow bed, a carved chest for her belongings, and a cushioned chair. The window gave her a view of the lake and the island. For some while after the pages left, she leaned on the windowsill and looked out, studying the manse, a long wooden building set around with apple trees. Over the roof of the manse and between the trees she could just see the top of a stone tower. A pleasant place, it looked in the afternoon sun, and yet, the more she saw of it, the stranger it seemed. If she glanced away to look at something else, then back again, she could have sworn the manse had moved—just slightly, a bit to the left, or perhaps the tower seemed taller than she remembered. The apple trees, however, always appeared exactly as she'd seen them previously.

Finally she gave up looking rather than risk a headache. During her previous visit to Haen Marn, some years before, she'd been too worried about her father and too involved in his care to pay much attention to the manse. She began to wonder if some of the wild rumors about Haen Marn and the mysterious forces of the dwimmer could possibly be true.

Someone knocked on the chamber door, then walked briskly in. A young maidservant had brought her a china basin and a bucket of warm water.

"Oh, lovely!" Alyssa said. "I could use a wash before dinner."

"So I thought, good maid." The lass set the basin down on the wooden chest and the bucket on the floor beside it. "Our house matron told me to tell you that you're free to walk around where you'd like outside. Dinner will be in a bit. There's a gong they ring."

"Right. I remember that from when I was here before."

The lass curtsied and left. Alyssa washed, then put on her last clean tunic and her scholar's skirt to go out and about. Haen Marn had a wash house, she remembered. On the morrow she could bundle up her filthy clothes with those from her silver daggers and pay to get them done. She still had some of the money left that Dovina and the others at the collegium had advanced her, though she'd need to use the draft to pay her two guards.

Alyssa left her chamber and hurried down the wide staircase that led to the front door of the guesthouse. Benoic was waiting for her at the foot.

"Where's Cavan?" she said.

"Talking with a woman named Rommardda. She knew him from his Lughcarn days," Benoic said. "He wasn't too happy at being dragged off for a private chat. I guess she's got some authority there in the iron trade and all."

"He probably doesn't like being reminded that he's an exile."

"Could well be that. But he looked so hangdog that there must be more to it."

Alyssa hesitated, but her scholar's curiosity nagged and itched. "Benoic, I don't suppose you'd tell me why Cavan carries the dagger?"

"You're quite right, my lady. I won't." He smiled to take the sting out of the words. "We don't spread tales like that."

"I know, I know. I just wonder. Well, I'd really like to know because —" She stopped herself from saying more.

Benoic looked away with a thoughtful twist of his mouth, just as if he understood her unspoken thought, "because I'm rather sweet on him." Finally he nodded, as if agreeing with himself.

"I can tell you this much," he said. "It was none of the usual reasons. There were lies told about him. I truly doubt if he deserved the dagger at all."

"My thanks. I'll not ask you again, I promise."

"Then my thanks to you."

He'd told her enough. She'd been afraid that he was some horrible criminal, hiding his crime under his good manners. But if someone had lied, if he didn't truly deserve his exile, she could lay that fear aside.

As he followed Rommardda across the complex, Cavan stripped off the fake bandages Alyssa had wound round his head and shoved them inside his shirt for want of a pocket big enough to hold them. Cathvar trotted over to join them when they reached a long, low stone building out beyond the kitchen. Glazed windows lined the wall that, as far as Cavan could tell, faced north.

"The scriptorium," Rommardda told him. "I spend so much time here that I've been given a private chamber. There are so many books to copy! The guild's given me coin to hire a pair of scribes and to pay for the binding, but I like to keep my hand in myself on a short treatise or two."

Tall wooden desks stood in a row under the windows. Each had a narrow ledge for scribal tools, a rack to hold the material being copied, and a big writing board that could be propped at a steep angle for the actual writing of new pages. Behind each desk stood a pair of low shelves where leather-bound volumes stood upright, each attached to the bookcase but on a chain long enough for the book to reach the desk. As they walked the length of the room, Cathvar ran ahead, then stopped right in front of them. He sat down and scratched his neck with a hind foot.

"Fleas, I suppose," Rommardda said. "The days are growing warmer."

At the far end of the chamber, Rommardda opened a door and led Cavan and the leopard both into a wood-paneled room just large enough to hold two chairs, one on either side of a low table. A large rather dirty blue cushion lay under the table. Cathvar claimed that, and Rommardda took one chair and gestured at the other.

"Sit," she said. "I've not seen you since you were exiled. I'm wondering what's brought you here." She paused in an ominous manner. "Among other things."

Cavan sat.

"First," Rommardda said, "about that sentence of exile. I gather he drew first, or you would have been hanged. I should have thought you had the right to defend yourself."

"He did draw first, but there was a man at the hearing who claimed I did."

"Your charming younger brother, was it?"

"It was. You know how he's always hated me, the rat-faced little snot. And he's our father's favorite, so of course his lie carried weight."

"But they didn't hang you."

"The other witnesses all denied it. But they did claim I goaded him into it."

"Did you?"

Cavan winced. He knew from experience that lying to Rommardda was stupid. "I did," he said. "He was insulting me. So I called him a coward who wouldn't have the guts for a real fight. It was the honor of the thing."

"Ye gods, I am so sick of men prattling about their honor! Well, you've got none left now to worry about."

Cavan found no answer to that.

"But I wonder," she continued, "just what started the whole affair."

"It was that little tavern up on the hill in Lughcarn, a clean, decent place run by decent folk. The daughter was serving that night, and this ugly—" He paused to think of a substitute for "chunk of horseshit." "This ugly vermin wouldn't leave her alone. Finally he pawed her when she was trying to take a flagon to someone's table, and he called her names I won't repeat when she drew back and asked him to stop. So I got up and tried to teach him some manners." He paused again, remembering. "It got out of hand, thanks to my wretched temper."

"I see. You've always been a gallant man around women. It's other men that bring out the worst in you."

Her voice, the look in her eyes, her posture, even, had all softened.

"True spoken," Cavan said. "I'll not deny it."

"Good. You might think about it a bit. I'll admit, lad, that I don't know what to do about you. I've always thought you had great promise to do summat important with your life, but, as you say, your wretched temper." She shook her head. "I suppose you've been expelled from the Iron Brotherhood."

"I have. That's the worst shame of all."

Rommardda leaned back in her chair and considered him for a long moment. "You valued the Brotherhood highly, didn't you?"

"I did. Oh, I know we mostly gathered coin and gave alms."

"Valuable work, in itself. The injured iron men appreciate every coin. Those accidents at the smelters!" She shuddered as if to cast off the memories. "Why dismiss all that?"

"A lot of men, outsiders I mean, made fun of the rituals and the like. I fear me I've gotten into a few fights over their sneers, too. But truly, I always felt there was summat more there."

"More? Like dwimmer?"

"Just that."

"You're not a fool, I'll say that for you, but you're a hot-tempered man, Cavan, and the dwimmer may not be for you because of that."

Cavan had been afraid of just that for years, but her words still felt like a slap across the face.

"However," Rommardda continued, "there's always hope. Learn to control yourself. Consider the iron, when the blacksmith hauls the bloom from the smelter. Is it pure?"

"It's not. It's full of bits and grains of slag."

"And when he beats the bloom on the anvil, all those impurities break free and fly upward, little glowing sparks."

"They do, truly."

"Your nature is the bloom, hot from the fire. Purify it, and then perhaps we'll talk more of dwimmer. But that temper! You could turn it into steel, fit for working, but it might take a long time on the anvil."

"My thanks." He was stammering, floating on a tide of sudden hope. "Truly, I'll do my best. I regret what I've done, I truly do."

"No doubt, but what's past is past, and can't be undone. Now, tell me why you've come to Haen Marn."

He needed to swallow several times before he could speak. The grief he knew well, but this hope! It took an effort of will for him to gather his wits.

"I was hired by a bunch of scholars in Aberwyn to guard Alyssa vairc Sirra. She's here to pick up an old book. They think it can help in their suits to change the gwerbretal courts."

"Title of this book?"

"Dwvoryc's Annals of the Dawntime."

Rommardda laughed in a peal of good humor. "Brilliant of them!" she said. "If the right people take it seriously, it will help indeed."

With that she let him go.

Cavan saw very little of Alyssa during the rest of that day. At dinner she ate on one side of the cavernous, dimly lit great hall while he and Benoic ate at the other side. The servants seated with them mostly ignored them, silver daggers as they were. The food at least was good and plentiful.

"No cockroaches in this stew," Benoic remarked.

"Indeed. And the bread's fresh, not two days old."

They ate fast and left as soon as they were done. In the cool evening air they walked around the entire complex to see how easily a determined bounty hunter could sneak in during the night. The outer wall stood too low for Cavan's liking, and Benoic agreed.

"All that rough stonework in pretty patterns," Benoic said. "Might as well lean a ladder up against it and be done with it."

The guesthouse itself presented more problems. They'd be up on the top floor while Alyssa was sleeping downstairs. If someone crept in to do her harm, they'd never hear even if she managed to cry out for help. They stopped their circuit at the lakeshore near the back of the guesthouse and looked it over in the scarlet sunset light. Behind them the lake rippled and gleamed with the reflection like streaks of blood and gold on the calm water.

"All rough wood and unglazed windows." Benoic waved at the guesthouse. "But maybe we're overestimating the enemy. Those three young bucks would be glad to get hold of her if it was easy, but it's you they're really after. Money over revenge would be my wager."

"I tend to agree. I just don't want to be proved wrong. It would be a bitter wager to lose." Cavan glanced around and saw one of the pages heading for the guesthouse. "Lad! Come here a moment."

The lad did as he was bid and strolled over with a pleasant smile.

"A question or two for you," Cavan said. "When do they bar the gates in the outer wall? Midnight? Or an earlier watch?"

"At sunset, usually. Later in the dead of winter, when the sun goes down so early. They open them again at dawn, or earlier in winter. There's a bell outside that someone can ring if they need help. The night porter will open the gates for them if they're ill or suchlike."

"Will he let just anyone in?" Cavan said.

"If they need our aid, of course he will."

"What if they're here to cause trouble? Like, say, they have a grudge against someone inside. Do you have a night watch?"

"We don't need one. The island protects its own."

Cavan could think of a number of scathing replies, but from the lad's puzzled smile he could assume they'd be useless.

"Are you afraid of someone like that?" the page said.

"We are," Benoic said. "Three silver daggers who have a quarrel with Cavan here."

"You'd best speak to the night porter, then. He'll be having his breakfast about now in the kitchen hut."

The page turned and pointed to the far side of the guesthouse, then hurried on his way.

Kitchen lads and cooks filled the kitchen hut with confusion, and the huge hearth filled it with smoke, but they did find the night porter eating bread and bacon as he sat on a little bench in one corner of the long rectangular room. Encouragingly enough, he was a tall burly fellow with a large knife in his belt. A quarterstaff leaned against the wall next to him. Cavan knelt down next to him and told him their tale while he went on eating. Eventually he wiped his mouth on his sleeve and nodded.

"Not much I can do against three men," he said, "but I can sound an alarm, and then Haen Marn will do the rest."

"People keep telling us that the place is going to keep us safe," Cavan said. "I know it's a sanctuary, but these lads won't have any respect for that."

The man laughed, revealing a couple of missing teeth. "It's a bit more than that, laddie. A fair bit more than that. If these trouble-makers show up, you'll see what I mean." With that he picked up a chunk of bread and returned to sopping bacon grease.

The audience had obviously ended. Cavan and Benoic retreated before the cook threw them out.

"I'll have a word with Alyssa," Cavan said. "I'll tell her to stay in her chamber no matter what she hears outside."

Cavan eventually found Alyssa in the entrance way of the guesthouse, where she was chatting with another young woman in the lantern light. At Cavan's approach the other lass made some excuse and frankly fled. Alyssa smiled with a shake of her head.

"Everyone seems to think you're as dangerous as a dwarven fire arrow," she said.

"Not dangerous, just scum that might spread plague." Cavan tried to smile at his sour jest but failed. "Be that as it may, I'm thinking of keeping a watch tonight. They shut the gates to this place, but if our three friends decide to cause a little trouble, they can climb that wall easily enough."

"Do you think they will?"

"I don't know. They might. It's not just the coin they're after now. They'll want to get a bit of their own back after those merchants chased them all over town."

In the lantern light he could see her turn a little pale. *Good,* he thought, *she knows it's serious.*

"So please," Cavan continued, "stay in your chamber tonight. Until well after dawn, say, and no matter what you may hear outside."

"Well and good, then, I will. By the by, I was just finding out how to turn Dovina's draft into the coins to pay you and Benoic with. I'll do that on the morrow."

"My thanks, but there's no hurry. We've got a long way to go to reach Cerrmor."

Alyssa went straight to her chamber. She set her lit candle down on a little table at the foot of the bed, then returned to the window and gazed out at the lake and the island. In the dim blue gloaming she could barely tell water from land except for the little stripes of clarity where the windows of the distant manse glowed with the flickering yellow of candlelight and firelight. Even more than during the day the manse seemed to move, twitching like a dreaming cat. At other times it seemed to grow just a bit larger, then smaller again. The apple trees, however, stayed where they'd been planted.

"Maybe I'm going daft!" she said aloud.

She turned to look in another direction. She could see some of the small cottages. Their windows glowed with candlelight, but they stayed solid and motionless. Among them she saw someone walking. What were they? Two people, she thought at first, vaguely human in shape, more like shadows than persons. They traveled along the length of one cottage and through the spill of light from a window—except they disappeared in the light. They emerged on the other side of the patch, then slowly rose into the air. Birds? Much too large for birds, and they lacked wings. They merely drifted over the roofs of the cottages like dandelion seeds blown into summer air—huge, though, and as they came toward the manse, she could see that while they had heads and a torso, and two appendages that might have been arms, they lacked legs. Billows of darkness hung where legs might have been.

Alyssa took a sharp step back from the window. One of the creatures—if that's what they were—drifted closer. Words formed in her mind.

Be not afraid. We are here on watch. We are not evil.

"I meant no insult. You startled me, is all. You weren't here before."

True. The gardener called us forth.

With the words came a feeling of peace like the sound of a lullaby. The shapes drifted away and out of her sight. Alyssa closed the shutters over the window to keep out the damp night air. *Dwimmer!* she thought. Lady Tay's modern teachings, all their student talk about "old wives' tales" and nonsense, were tearing apart and fraying in her mind like a piece of old, moth-ridden cloth.

Later, as she was getting into bed, she remembered their remark about "the gardener." Another of Haen Marn's puzzles, she supposed, and let it lie.

"No sign of anything amiss," Benoic said. "They're more likely to come once it's light, anyway. I've been thinking, Cavvo. If they climb in here in the middle of the night, how are they going to find us?"

"That's true. They can't go barging into every cottage, and the guesthouse has a porter of its own."

"The pages have to be in bed, too. The lads told me that the woman in charge of them is strict about that. I doubt any of the patients or healers know who we are. So there won't be anyone about they can ask."

Cavan turned slowly in a circle to look over the complex around them. They'd made a circuit of the entire place from dungheaps to stables to guesthouse and now stood near the gates. The night porter had already closed and barred them, and he was sitting in a little wooden booth nearby. By the light of his lantern they could see him industriously picking his teeth.

"Doesn't look like he's expecting trouble," Benoic said.

"It doesn't at that. Tell you what. Let's go back and get some sleep. We can get up with the dawn."

With a wave to the night porter, they left the gates and headed toward the guesthouse. They were about halfway across the long lawn when Benoic happened to glance up at the sky.

"Mother of all the gods!" He sounded as if he were choking. "What's that?"

Two black creatures, partially human in shape, drifted above them. The hair on the back of Cavan's neck and on his arms stood up in sudden chill like winter frost. The creatures sank lower. The darkness hanging from them like draped cloaks swirled and shifted.

Be not afraid. We are here on watch, just as you are.

Benoic yelped and bolted for the guesthouse. Cavan managed to choke out a mangled version of "my thanks," then followed his lead. They rushed inside and saw the house porter laughing at them.

"I take it you've met the night watch," he said.

Benoic growled like the leopard and strode off for the back stairs.

"So we have," Cavan said. "Here, what would happen to someone if one of those—whatever they are—sat on him, like?"

"I've no idea, but I'll wager it wouldn't be pretty."

"I wouldn't bet against you." He collected his wits with a shudder and a shake of his head. "Well, good night to you, then."

Cavan and Benoic had a pair of cots at one end of a long row of them, in a chamber where the various menservants slept. When Cavan came in, Benoic had already taken off his boots and sword belt and was lying half-asleep on top of his blankets. The chamber was hot from all the rising heat of the house below. In winter, Cavan supposed, it would be murderously cold, just as most barracks were. He lay down and fell asleep before he was quite aware of doing it.

He woke to see gray light outside the tiny window. Dawn, he supposed. Snores and the occasional sigh told him that the other men still slept. He hauled himself out of bed and looked around for chamber pots. He found several, but all of them brimmed full. He'd have to find a privy. He picked up his boots and sword belt and carried them out of the chamber for silence's sake.

Just outside the door he stopped to strap on the belt. Should he go out alone? If the gates were open, and the day porter had taken over, would the night porter have warned him about the bounty hunters? Cavan went back into the sleeping chamber and woke Benoic. He murmured an explanation.

"Wise of you," Benoic whispered. "Let me just get belt and boots."

At the foot of the stairs they pulled on their boots, then headed out to the row of privies that stood behind the stables. In the east the light brightened and turned a few streaky clouds pink. Cavan kept looking up at the sky, but he saw no sign of the guard creatures.

"Not going to rain," Cavan said. "No doubt it won't while we're here and sheltered."

"It'll pour as soon as we get back on the road."

Once they'd run the errand they'd come for, they started back toward the guesthouse. To avoid the maze of cottages, they kept to the lakeshore. Not far from the stable area a long gray pier poked out into the still water. A matching pier jutted out from the island.

"Huh!" Benoic said. "Who's that? One of our lads, I think."

Cavan looked toward the guesthouse, where Benoic was pointing. A tall fellow with a thick thatch of red hair walked toward them with cautious steps. At his belt a silver point winked in the rising light. Only one man it could be—Renno paused, drew his sword, and whistled three sharp notes. A signal, Cavan assumed. He and Benoic both drew. Benoic stepped around to stand back to back with Cavan.

"Here comes another of them," Benoic said. "But it's only Wilyn. We've got a chance this time."

Renno stopped some ten feet away from them and smiled over his raised blade. "A share for you, Benno," he said, "if you'll just walk away. Silver dagger's honor. A full third. Our former friend decided he wasn't man enough to stick with the hire."

"Shove it up your arse," Benoic said. "One coin at a time."

"Well and good, then. I—" He stopped, cursed, and then yelped aloud.

From some distance behind, Cavan heard Wilyn scream full throat. He thought their alarm might be a ruse until Renno spun around and broke into a run, slipping and stumbling in the dew-wet grass. Cavan looked up and saw a creature of darkness moving after Renno in a streak of black cloud. Wilyn kept screaming. Grooms came racing out of the stables. Pages rushed out of the guesthouse. As he ran after Renno, Cavan yelled, "We were attacked!"

We know. We are not blind.

A second creature appeared, and a third. The grooms were bellowing, "Stop, stop!" The pages were calling out, "Just stop, and they won't hurt you!" Renno in blind panic reached the pier, ran onto it, and raced to the end. The creatures drifted after him but made no move to sink lower. Their skirts of darkness spread out, then held motionless. Renno took a step back and teetered on the edge.

The pages began yelling "Nah, nah, don't jump, don't!" Their high boys' voices rang with sincere terror. "Give up! Just give up!"

For a brief moment Renno wavered, then flung his useless sword straight at one of the creatures. The metal flashed in the sun, missed the billowing darkness, and clattered onto the pier below. A bluish light flashed. Instead of the creatures, three unusually large ravens began to circle, drifting lower as they did so. Renno stooped, grabbed the hilt of his sword, and swore at the touch. He let the weapon drop and threw himself into the water. He floundered, flopped, managed to get himself onto his stomach, and started swimming for the island. The pages screamed.

Near the opposite pier on the island stood a boathouse. The doors snapped open, and a long narrowboat with a fancy prow like a dragon's head pulled out. The six rowers bent to their oars. In the stern a young lad banged incessantly on a big bronze gong. A short, stocky man with a boathook stood in the prow, ready to pull Renno free of the water, Cavan assumed. He sheathed his sword and watched as the boat headed for Renno—too late.

Something was rising from the water, a great gray shape, the back of a beast, as smooth and solid as polished stone. The rowers began to yell and curse at the top of their lungs. A long neck snaked up, a small oval head appeared, a mouth opened. Teeth, ye gods, fangs! The neck whipped like a snake and sank the fangs into Renno. The bounty hunter had time for just one twisted scream of agony before head, neck, and Renno all disappeared under the water. A spreading red stain floated on the surface for a few moments before the ripples from the approaching boat broke it up and washed it away.

"Haen Marn protects its own, indeed," Benoic said. "Or the Lord of Hell does."

Cavan spun around and saw Benoic standing nearby. His face had gone dead-pale. Cavan figured that his own probably had, too. Some of the pages were frankly weeping.

"Where's Wilyn?" Cavan said.

"The grooms got him. He's the lucky one, eh? They'll haul him up before the Lord and Lady of the Isle, they told me. You're not allowed to disrupt the peace of Haen Marn." Benoic tried to laugh, but the sound came out as a giggle. "It's bad for the patients, they say."

"No doubt." Cavan distrusted his own voice so much that he said nothing more.

Cavan walked out on the pier to retrieve Renno's sword. If one of the pages took it, he figured, the lad would try to play warrior with it and hurt himself or one of his fellows. He squatted down and reached for the hilt, but cautiously. An unnatural warmth still radiated from the leather wrapping. It must have been extremely hot when Renno touched it. Cavan shuddered. He took off his waistcoat and wrapped it around the hilt before he picked it up. By the time he got back to Benoic, the dwimmer heat had cooled.

chapter 6

A LYSSA HAD WOKEN WHEN she heard the first screams. She flung the blanket back and got up, rushed to the window, and leaned out dangerously far to watch the entire confrontation, including Renno's death. She stepped away from the window and realized that she was shaking and cold from sheer revulsion. She reminded herself that Renno would have gladly killed Cavan for the bounty and probably raped her, too, if he'd had a chance at it.

"But the way he screamed. And those ravens!"

And the blood staining the water—she could see it so clearly in her mind that she wondered if she'd ever be free of the memory.

Once she'd dressed she went down to the great hall for breakfast. The students ate at communal tables of eight places set against the opposite wall from the servants' seating. She took a seat at one end of a table where four pages were sitting at the other, but no one sat in between. A servant brought her porridge with a generous dollop of butter and some dried apple slices, but she found it hard to eat. The young lads at the other end of the table were having no such trouble. As they gobbled down their porridge they talked of nothing but the silver dagger's horrible death—with details. One of the older boys noticed Alyssa and moved down a chair to speak with her.

"Good morrow, good maid," he said. "We were wondering sum-mat. The silver dagger that's your guard? Why did those fellows want to kill him?"

"Coin. I don't understand it, truly. I suppose it was gambling debts." She stood up and pushed her barely touched bowl in his di-rection. "Do you want to finish this?"

"I do. My thanks!" He grabbed the bowl before any of the others had a chance at it.

As she was leaving the great hall, she met Lady Perra's scribe, the young Bardekian woman. Seeing her for the second time primed Alyssa's memory. That's why she seemed so familiar!

"I thought I'd find you here," the scribe said. "Lady Perra would like you to come over to the island right now for your talk. She has to deal with the incident later."

Alyssa didn't need to ask her which incident she might mean.

"Of course," Alyssa said. "I have some papers I need to fetch up in my chamber, and then I'll go straight there. How do I summon the ferry? And may I ask your name? I don't mean to be rude."

"Not rude at all. It's Hwlia."

"Of House Elaeno?"

"Indeed I am! How did you guess?"

"Your brother Hwlio spoke at my collegium in Aberwyn a year or so ago."

"Well met, then!"

"You look much like him, you see."

"I do, I know. I'm a fair bit younger, but the resemblance is cer-tainly there. He's in Cerrmor these days, by the way." Her voice smiled with pride. "He was appointed ambassador to the city by our archon."

"Wonderful!" In more ways than one, Alyssa was thinking. This could be very useful! "I was so impressed with his knowledge of our laws. So important for his job there."

"It is, indeed. Now, as for the ferry, there's a silver horn attached to a boulder on the shore. Blow that, then go out on the pier, and the boatmen will come across."

"My thanks, Hwlia."

Yet Alyssa's stomach twisted at the thought of walking out onto the pier where Renno had dived to his death. She walked slowly along the lakeshore and paused often to watch the people hurrying between the cottages and the kitchen building to fetch food for those too ill to fetch it themselves. Now and then she saw someone walking very slowly with a cane or crutch while an attendant hovered, ready to help, as the patient made their way to breakfast.

She'd almost reached the pier when she saw Travaberiel attending upon an elderly man. Trav saw her, waved, and steered the elder in her direction. As they drew close she saw that the elder had to be very old indeed, as his white hair was sparse and his face, heavily lined.

"And a good morning to you, Alyssa," Trav said. "This is my master in my guild, Ebañy Salamonderiel."

"Good morning to you." Alyssa curtsied.

Ebañy grinned and plucked a silk rose out of Travaberiel's right ear, or so it seemed. He handed it to her with a shaky flourish.

"Thank you, good sir," she said. "You're awfully good at those tricks."

"I should be." His voice wavered on the words. "I've been doing them for many a year now."

They smiled all round, and Alyssa returned the rose. "I must go. I've been summoned to see Lady Perra."

"You'd best not keep her waiting, indeed," Trav said. "We'll be here on the morrow. At least that long."

"Perhaps," Ebañy said. "I hear the harps calling me."

Travaberiel winced. Alyssa curtsied again for want of anything to say. As she hurried off, she glanced back to see Travaberiel helping his master sit on one of the wooden benches. *He's so frail,* she thought. *I wonder if he's come to Haen Marn to die?* The sunny day, the sparkling lake, the lawns—they were so beautiful that she tried to push the morbid thought out of her mind. Yet she knew that death lay all around her, that even the brilliant healers of Haen Marn lost more patients than they could save.

The dragonboat came immediately in answer to her summons. When Alyssa scrambled aboard, the head boatman had her sit down in the middle, away from the sides of the boat.

"We don't need a second disaster," he said.

"I quite understand. Is the noise from the gong supposed to keep them off?"

"It did once. It still scares the little ones. But the old ones, they've gotten used to it. We'll have to do summat about that, and as soon as we can."

Much to Alyssa's relief, none of the beasts, big or little, showed themselves during the brief trip across. The boatman helped her disembark, then pointed to a flagstone path.

"Follow that to the manse," he said, "but don't step off it, or you might not get there. The island plays tricks, it does, until it gets to know you, like."

"I can well believe that, good sir!"

The flagstone path behaved itself and took her right to the front door of the manse, which also seemed to be on its best behavior. The walls stayed where they were, the door felt solid, and the page who ushered her into the great hall was a perfectly normal lad.

"I'm Alyssa vairc Sirra, the scholar from Aberwyn."

"Right. Lady Perra said to show you right up. This way."

The great hall looked to hold at least fifty guests at its tables. Braided rushes covered the floor, and strange carvings and marks covered the walls. Big swags of symbols and tiny pictures ran from corner to corner of each wall, though they parted around the huge stone hearth at one side. At the far end a staircase led up. Alyssa followed the page to a corridor with three doors spaced along it. The page opened the nearest.

"My lady? The scholar from Aberwyn is here."

"Come in!"

Alyssa did, and the page closed the door behind her. Near a glazed window Lady Perra sat behind a table littered with books and pieces of pabrus. In front of the table stood a half-round wooden chair with a cushioned seat. At the lady's gesture, Alyssa curtsied, then sat. Perra gave her a pleasant smile.

"Now then," she said. "What brings you to us?"

"We'd—the collegium—would like to request the return of a book." Alyssa handed her the pabrus loan note. "We need it for a legal matter we have underway."

Perra read the note. She quirked an eyebrow Alyssa's way. "I may have heard summat about that legal matter. The question of the law courts?"

"Just that. Removing them from gwerbretal control. Dwvoryc says—"

"I've read it. You're quite right that it's a crucial text, but I'm afraid you really can't have the Nevyn copy back. The book's far too old and crumbly to survive a trip to Aberwyn."

"Farther than that, my lady. We need to take it to Cerrmor so we can lay our complaint before the Prince Regent."

"Cerrmor?" Perra winced. "That's much worse, indeed. You poor lass! You look so disappointed."

"It's just that I've come such a long way to fail."

"You're not going to fail. We'll give you summat just as good. We have some truly old copies that aren't particularly valuable as things in themselves. Here, if I validate a copy, will anyone dare to argue with it?"

"They won't, indeed." Alyssa smiled in relief. "My humble thanks!"

"But I'll show you why," Perra said. "Or better yet, let me summon the man who oversees our bookhoard."

The protocol at Haen Marn struck Alyssa as less than formal. Perra went to the window, leaned out, and called, "Glaeryn! Come up a moment, will you?"

A dark voice answered from directly below, "I will. Let me just wash my hands."

Perra smiled and turned from the window. "He's been working in the herb garden, I see. It's not truly his work, but now and then he likes to help out a bit. We call him the gardener."

Soon enough a fellow strode into the room, tall and lean, his dark hair an unruly thatch, his plain shirt and breeches smeared with dirt here and there. He was neither handsome nor ugly, ordinary in every way, except he carried himself like a prince. He nodded pleasantly Alyssa's way, but his eyes! Dark Eldidd blue, and they seemed to pierce her very soul. *The gardener*, she thought. *This must be who the spirits meant.*

"Ah, the scholar from Aberwyn," he said.

"She'd like to see the bookhoard," Perra said. "She—"

"The window's open. I could hear you both quite clearly. The Prince Regent can come look at the book if he insists." Glaeryn made a snorting sound. "He can travel. It can't."

Perra laughed and nodded her agreement. Alyssa got up and curtsied for want of anything to say. She'd never heard anyone speak so freely of the man who was king in everything but name.

"How old are you, lass?" Glaeryn said. "Do you know?"

"I'll be twenty come Lugh's Feast, good sir."

"Then this book is nearly forty times as old as you are. Come along. I'll show you."

Alyssa followed Glaeryn down the corridor to a big half-round of a room. All around the edge stood shelves with books safely chained to them. In the center a big pottery stove, vented with a pipe through the roof, exhaled a pleasant warmth to keep the precious volumes dry. Not far from the stove a long narrow table held six glass boxes. Glaeryn pointed them out.

"Those protect books so old they might crumble away if we let people handle them," he said. "The Nevyn Book's one of them. In truth, it's the second of Nevyn's books. We have one more that he owned, a book of dweomer lore, but that's not on public display."

"Uh, excuse me, good sire, but a book of what kind of lore?"

Glaeryn laughed. "Dway-oh-mer is the way the word was pronounced a long time ago. You know it as dwimmer."

"My thanks. I must remember to tell my friend Mavva that. She's fascinated by how words change. Nevyn was someone's name? Not the man the histories call King Maryn's sorcerer, was he?"

"He was, at that, but the histories aren't entirely accurate. He did do the Red Wyvern a good turn or two, but there was a bit more to him."

Another gardener, he was—Alyssa waited, hoping for more of the tale, but Glaeryn merely gestured to her to follow him and headed for the table. He was smiling as if he'd made some sort of jest, and his dark blue eyes had changed, a normal gaze, though tinged with a jest.

Even though the Nevyn copy had been in the collegium's book-hoard when Alyssa had arrived as a student, she'd never seen it, because it had been kept wrapped in a locked drawer, safe from careless hands. Glaeryn opened the hinged lid of the glass box and brought out more of a bundle than a book. Once it had had leather covers, but the spine had shredded along most of its length, leaving the covers attached by a few inches here and there. The gilt on the cover had mostly rubbed off. The stamped letters had become so shallow that Alyssa could just barely pick out Dwvoryc's name.

Glaeryn laid the book down gently and opened it a few pages in.

He smoothed the old-fashioned parchments with fingers so affectionate that he might have been stroking a pet cat or greeting an old friend. While the writing stood out clearly, the edges of the thick pages had begun to split with age.

"I do see, good sir," Alyssa said. "Of course it should stay here in this room. Forever, doubtless. Well, as long as it lasts."

"But now you can say you've seen it," Glaeryn said. "Swear to it, even, should you have to."

"Indeed." She paused to read half a page. "The language is so old. Mavva would love this. Stiff, like, and all those little words at the beginning of every sentence! Did the folk really speak like that?"

"They did. Or tried to at least. I've no doubt that the fine points fell away quickly as time went on."

Glaeryn put the book back in its box. He escorted Alyssa back to Perra's office, then returned to his work in the garden. Alyssa wasn't sure if she were sorry or relieved to see him go. Perra waved her into the chair by her worktable.

"You're not in this plot alone, are you?" Perra said.

"I'm not. Most of my collegium is, and in particular, Lady Dovina of Aberwyn."

"The gwerbret's own daughter?" Perra's eyebrows shot up. "Ye gods! This is a serious matter then."

"It is. Without her we'd not get very far. She's going to be in Cerrmor, and I'm to meet her there with the book. Her father's arranging her a betrothal, which is why she's going."

"I see. About those silver daggers, your guards. I'm very glad you have someone to protect you, but you do realize, don't you, that you're now in a bad position?"

"I do. My woman's honor is as dead as a kitten in a wash bucket."

"Just so, but beyond that. Have you thought about what might happen to you if the Prince Regent should agree with you? If the gwerbret's angry, and from what I know about Ladoic, he will be, you might never be able to return to Aberwyn, not even with Lady Dovina's protection."

For a long moment Alyssa could neither think nor speak. She felt as if an icy hand had grabbed her neck and squeezed.

"You understand, I see," Perra said, but gently. "Do you have family in Aberwyn?"

"I do. My whole family. You don't think the gwerbret will harm them, do you?"

"I don't. Ladoic's a better man than all his blustering makes people believe. When it comes to you, though, if you've thwarted him, there's no telling. Well, your friends will do what they can. I've met Lady Tay several times, and with her scholars she's as fierce as a wolf with her cubs. But I'm wondering if you'll ever see your family again. If Lady Dovina can't guarantee you a safe harbor after all this is over, come back to me. We'll find a position for you here."

"My thanks." Alyssa clasped her hands in her lap to keep them from shaking. "Truly, my thanks, but I've no talent for healing."

"More goes on at Haen Marn than healing. We're the overlords for this entire area, you know. Here, come with me. I need to attend upon the Lord and Lady of Haen Marn, and I think you'll find this interesting."

They returned to the great hall, where a small crowd had assembled at the end of the room nearest the front door. A man of the Mountain Folk sat in the center seat of a long table. A priest of Bel sat at his right, and at his left, a priestess of Sebanna, regal in her long white robes and red headscarf. At each end a scribe was taking notes on long rolls of pabrus. Cavan and Benoic sat on a bench in front and off to the side, while two guards stood on either side of a kneeling man—the surviving bounty hunter, Alyssa assumed.

"That's Kov son of Kovolla in the middle," Perra whispered. "The Lord of Haen Marn."

Alyssa nodded to show she'd heard. Lord Kov leaned forward to look directly at the kneeling man.

"Very well, Wilyn of Cengarn," Kov said. "We've heard the evidence of the two silver daggers. Do you dispute this in any way? You have the right to dispute any detail of it should you want to."

"Only one, your lordship," Wilyn said. "I didn't join Renno willingly. I owed him a cursed lot of money, your lordship, from the gambling, and he swore he'd get me handed over to the galleys down at the coast if I didn't pay him right up. I never wanted to hunt down a fellow silver dagger, but my share would have paid Renno off. I knew it was a stupid idea, your lordship, and a dishonorable one, but I—"

"Enough!" Kov raised a hand for silence. "Renno's no longer

available to back your story up or deny it. Do you swear it's true on your silver dagger?"

"I do, your lordship." Wilyn spoke promptly and openly, but Alyssa wondered if the little weasel was simply a practiced liar.

Kov turned to the two silver daggers. "Do you lads believe him?"

"I do, my lord," Benoic said. "It would break a vow for me to tell you why he has the dagger, so just let me say that I have reason to believe him."

Kov grinned at the dodge, a gesture that made his square dwarven face almost attractive.

"I believe him, too," Cavan said. "But if he comes after me again, I'll—"

Benoic elbowed him so hard that Cavan broke off. He said nothing more, merely glowered and rubbed his side where the elbow had hit.

"Do either of you have any questions?" Kov said. "Any civil questions, that is?"

Benoic shot Cavan a nasty look that kept him quiet before he spoke. "Wilyn, who was that third man, the one who bowed out of the fight?"

"He gave his name as Lannac. That's all I know about him. He wasn't any silver dagger, I'd swear to that, for all he claimed to be. He had a dagger with the three little knobs, but they were different, like, just a little too small. We never saw the actual blade out of its sheath."

"Interesting." Kov looked at Wilyn again. "Did he offer you lads money for your help?"

"He didn't, my lord. Just a share of the bounty. Thirty-three brazens each for me and Renno. That bounty, it seemed cursed high to me, for what Cavan's been accused of."

"It may be. I have no jurisdiction over another lord's letters of bounty," Kov said. "As for you —" this to Wilyn "— the charge against you is disturbing the peace of Haen Marn and offering violence in a holy sanctuary." He turned to the priestess. "Your Holiness?"

"Assessing a fine on a man with not a coin to his name is a waste of time." She spoke in a pleasantly high but firm voice. "Since no violence took place, I suggest he be transported to the Desolation."

Wilyn's face drained to a ghastly sort of white. He swayed a little as he knelt. Alyssa felt a brief pang of sympathy. The Desolation, those newly settled lands just north of Cerrgonney, was a wild, harsh place, known for horrendous winters.

"Or," the priestess continued, "labor on one of Haen Marn's own farms for some few years would also erase that debt."

"Please, my lady!" Wilyn's voice wavered and swooped. "I'll gladly work for Haen Marn. Please!"

The priestess smiled and nodded her agreement.

"Done then," Kov said. "Wilyn, you will labor for a farmer who needs the work for two years and a day. Until then, your horse and gear, your sword and dagger will remain here in trust. You will receive a signed receipt for these things. I would advise you not to try wandering away from the farm. One of the raven spirits will be keeping an eye on you."

Wilyn swallowed several times before he spoke, but his voice had regained its strength. "Very well, your lordship."

"You'll eat better than you would on the long road, anyway," Kov said with a grin. "Think of it as a blessing."

Wilyn tried to smile but failed.

At a gesture from Perra, Alyssa turned away. The lady led her to a small side door, and they went out together.

"I've been thinking," Perra said, "that we need someone here to speak for the people who are being accused. Very few crimes happen at Haen Marn, but we're responsible for the town, too."

"I see. That's a truly novel idea, my lady, but it strikes me as a good one. Well, for what my opinion's worth."

"You seem to have thought a good deal more than I have about such things." Perra smiled at her. "So, as I said, should you need a place in life, come back to us here."

"My thanks." Alyssa curtsied as deeply as she could. "My humble thanks."

Perra returned to her work, and Alyssa met up with her two silver daggers. Benoic was jesting about the future ahead of Wilyn, and Cavan was grinning as he listened to a long ramble about mucking out cowsheds. *At least we don't have to worry about that pair any longer,* Alyssa thought. *But there might be other men after the bounty.*

The bounty. A new thought struck her hard. *Ye gods, how are we going to get Cavan into Cerrmor?* Her clumsy ruse of the wounded Valyn would fail miserably around men who knew him from his noble-born days. Cerrmor, as the second most important city in the kingdom, usually did have some of the noble-born visiting there for various reasons. Leaving him on the road somewhere would be even more dangerous, for her, as well as for him.

Simple thievery accounted for one of those dangers. When Alyssa turned over Dovina's draft at the treasury on the island, the amount of coin shocked her, far too much for the small pouch she'd brought with her. The bursar was no stranger to the situation, apparently, because he handed Alyssa a plain cloth pouch from a box of them on his worktable.

"You're not leaving Haen Marn alone, are you?" he said.

"I'm not. I have two silver daggers waiting right outside the door."

He smiled and bowed.

Alyssa collected her guards, and together they went down to the pier, where the dragonboat waited. She noticed a thick cloud of flies swarming around something lying on the beach, maybe fifteen yards from the pier, so many flies that they looked like a pillar of smoke. The stench of whatever it was drifted toward them.

"Lord of Hell's arse!" Benoic said to the boatman. "What is that? Dead fish?"

"Naught so clean." He paused to swallow heavily, as if he choked back the urge to vomit. "I've sent for a couple of pages to take it away and bury it, but the lads are in no hurry to follow the order."

"Can't blame them. But what—"

"It's the remains of that red-haired halfwit. The cursed beast what ate him appeared a little while ago and vomited up that pile. Bits of clothes, it looks like. I saw summat that gleamed like silver. Maybe that dagger of yours."

Cavan and Benoic exchanged a weary glance.

"Like a cat with hair in its guts," the boatman said to Alyssa. "You've doubtless seen that." He was looking at her with concern, as if he expected her to faint.

"Many a time," she said, "but mice don't carry silver daggers. It can't have been good for the poor thing's digestion."

The boatman started to reply, then merely looked sicker than ever.

"Which one of us?" Benoic said to Cavan. "Do you have your dice with you? Mine are in my saddlebags."

"Mine, too, but I owe you for making me hold my wretched tongue during the hearing." Cavan turned to the boatman. "Can you wait a bit?"

"If you'd like. But don't linger. I want to get away from that, I do."

"Alyssa?" Cavan said. "Do you have a kerchief I could borrow?"

"Here." She fished it out of her kirtle and handed it to him.

"My thanks."

Cavan tied the kerchief around his head to cover his nose and mouth. He walked down to the stinking heap on the sandy shore. Some, at least, of the flies fled at his approach. He waved at the rest with his left hand and with his right drew his sword. He used the point to poke around in the shredded cloth until he'd gotten the silver dagger free of the mess. When he flipped a human bone out of the way, Alyssa lost her nerve and almost her stomach. She turned away and kept her gaze firmly on the guesthouse across the water. She heard splashing and a few curses before Cavan returned to the ferry with wet boots but a reasonably clean silver dagger.

"You're the senior." Cavan handed it to Benoic.

"I'll take it to the nearest smith when I can." Benoic frowned at the dagger. "Look! The leather wrap on the hilt's eaten nearly through, but ye gods, this is witch's metal!"

Alyssa forced herself to look at the blade as he held it up—shiny and unmarked, not a trace of the etching that the acids of the beast's stomach would have made on ordinary steel.

"Not witches!" the boatman said. "Dwarven work, and don't you lads forget it."

"We won't." Benoic grinned at him. "We can go across now, good sir."

The boat deposited them safely on the landside pier without any interference from the beasts of the lake. As they walked off to dry land, Alyssa glanced back at the island. A pair of pages with shovels were marching toward the mess on the shore. The flies had returned.

"You've got the strongest guts of any lass I've ever met," Cavan said.

"I suppose I should thank you. I never thought I'd need them, and I wish I didn't."

Both silver daggers laughed, but in a kind sort of way. Alyssa glanced around and pointed to one of the polished wooden benches.

"Let's sit down. I've got the coin for your hire," she said. "At least so far. I still need to get to Cerrmor."

"I shan't be leaving you," Cavan said.

"If you have need of me, I'll stay on, too." Benoic made her a bob of a bow. "When will we be leaving Haen Marn?"

"I'm not sure. The man who's in charge of their bookhoard is preparing a letter for me and a copy of the book, and then Lady Perra has to sign and seal it. You know, once we have it, I'm not even sure which road to take."

"I'll think about it," Benoic said. "I know this stretch of country fairly well."

"Good," Cavan said. "I don't."

Both men looked at her, but all she could do was shrug to show her ignorance. *Goddess help!* she thought. *I'm as much of an outcast now as they are!*

At dinner that night, Alyssa found her next move in the elaborate game of carnoic she was playing with her wyrd. She found a place at one of the students' tables, while Cavan and Benoic ate with the other men at a table across the great hall. She had just been served when, much to her surprise, Rommardda and her leopard friend strolled over.

"May I join you?" Rommardda laid her hand on the back of the empty chair next to Alyssa's.

"Of course!" Alyssa started to stand in order to curtsy, but Rommardda stopped her with a little wave of her other hand.

The elder woman sat down, arranging her skirts under her, and Cathvar lay down beside her chair. A servant hurried over with a bowl of steaming vegetables and set it down with a little bow.

"Are there any bones from the kitchen tonight?" Rommardda said. "No fowl, only meat bones."

"I'll see, my lady, and bring some for his esteemed spottiness if there are."

Rommardda grinned, and Cathvar thumped his tail once on the floor. The servant hurried off again.

"I swear, my lady," Alyssa said, "that Cathvar understands our talk."

"He does, at least for simple sayings, and especially if it concerns food." She reached down and stroked the leopard's head. "He's quite intelligent."

The servant returned with a bowl containing scraps of meat and two large bones from legs of mutton, which Cathvar accepted with a gracious nod of his head. For a little while they ate in silence, or at least, the two women did. Cathvar slurped and munched and now and then cracked a bit of bone.

"This afternoon," Rommardda said abruptly, "I was poking around in some ancient parchments from the Herald Guild. They've taken to storing important records here for safekeeping. I came across summat that should interest you."

"Indeed, my lady? I'm grateful you'd take the time."

Rommardda picked up her goblet of watered wine and considered it for a moment before she spoke. "In your studies you must have come across the various controversies about the Maelwaedd line of gwerbretion. Their connections to the Westfolk, that is."

"I have."

"When the line finally died out, back a hundred years or so ago, the High King and the Council of Electors awarded the rhan to the Western Fox. Or I should say, when they thought that it had died out. Childbed had certainly failed the Maelwaedds, not a new heir in sight. What they didn't know, however, was that there was another possible claimant. Since he never came forward, one can hardly blame them."

Alyssa laid down her table knife and turned in her chair. She had the feeling that she was gaping in shock and made an effort to look dignified.

"Quite a surprising bit of news, innit?" Rommardda said. "Here's another. That claimant's still alive, and he has a son."

"He must be a man of the Westfolk, then."

"He is, one of their heralds. His name is Maelaber. He's not from a pure Westfolk line, mind. His mother was Gwerbret Rhodry Maelwaedd's daughter—you've heard of him?"

"I have indeed. I attend Lady Rhodda Hall."

"Of course! Well, Maelaber's Rhodry Maelwaedd's daughter's son. She herself had Westfolk blood, because her father was a half-breed. Not that anyone knew it at the time."

"But the son was illegitimate, wasn't he?"

"Not by the laws of the Westfolk. Still, your point is an important one. I doubt very much indeed that he could ever win a suit in the High King's courts. But the news of his very existence might be of great use to you and your cause."

Alyssa nodded. Her mind was racing, putting together ideas, scraps of wording, and proper rhetorical figures she might use in a speech. If Ladoic refused to give in about the courts, they could perhaps bring suit over his right to rule—but what would that do to Dovina? The cold doubt made her come back to the moment. Rommardda was waiting for an answer.

"Forgive me, my lady! Of great use, indeed! A nice tough bit of gristle for His Grace to chew upon. It would be in his best interests to settle our suit as quickly as possible."

"Just so."

"I'm ever so grateful to you for this information. A thousand thanks!"

"You're most welcome. In return, will you listen to a bit of advice from a nosy old woman? A thing that's not truly any of my affair, but I worry."

"I should be glad of your wisdom. I'll wager it's about Cavan."

"You are bright, aren't you?" Rommardda smiled, then turned serious again. "Indeed. I know him well. He's a good lad at heart, but he's too quick with his temper and his sword. I doubt me if he'd ever stoop so low as to beat a woman, mind. But he's bound to get himself into trouble over and over again, and any woman who loves him will be sharing in that trouble."

For a moment Alyssa felt close to tears. The very depth of her disappointment showed her just how dangerously fond of him she'd become.

"You'll be much better off with a man of your own kind," Rommardda continued. "A guildsman who knows the value of an educated wife. Or even, for that matter, a bard, a man who understands your love of learning."

Alyssa found her voice at last. "I've always thought I'd never marry at all, my lady. I truly do understand your concern. I share it. If I didn't, I probably would have been stupid already, foolish enough to—well, no doubt you can guess."

"Indeed I can. Hold to your resolve, dear. Cavan cannot help being the man he is."

Alyssa was about to speak when Cathvar raised his head and growled. A man was making his way through the crowd toward Rommardda. In the uncertain lantern light it took her a moment to recognize Travaberiel. Ap Maelaber! That's the heir's son! Apparently Cathvar had recognized him as well, because the leopard returned to his mutton bones.

"Ah, Trav!" Rommardda said. "I was thinking of summoning you this evening."

"Like a demon, eh?" Travaberiel pulled out the empty chair on the other side of Rommardda and sat down.

"Not quite, or so I hope. Alyssa and Cavan are making ready to leave Haen Marn. I doubt me if it will be safe for them to ride straight back into Eldidd."

"I share your doubts, what with war brewing and all. Riding all the way to Cerrmor will take weeks, too." Trav leaned forward to look at Alyssa. "And you don't dare take a coach."

"Truly we don't," Alyssa said. "We'd be pulled off by some lord's men or another's quick enough."

"Just so. I'll recommend you travel south through Westfolk country. And take a ship to Cerrmor from Mandra. That's the town right on the coast, not far from Cannobaen."

"They'll need a guide if they do that." Rommardda cleared her throat and gave him a pointed glance. "There could be trouble of a different kind if they don't. And someone's got to negotiate for the ship."

He laughed. "Oh, very well," he said in a moment. "I should have seen that arrow flying my way. I'll travel with you, Alyssa, if that pleases you."

"It does indeed. You have my thanks, my very deepest thanks."

"Mine, too," Rommardda said. "I have a letter for you to deliver, a very important letter, to your father. He should be at the horse fair."

"He will be. He never misses one."

Alyssa leaned forward to speak to him. "Do you think the Westfolk king and queen will be there? I've been told that they sometimes visit the fair. I'd love to meet Queen Carramaena. She's done so much for my collegium."

"She'll appear if Daralanteriel does, but I've no idea if he will or not," Trav said. "She's a marvel, truly. She looks like a human woman, but she matches our king in years."

"Truly? Does anyone know why?"

"Oh, there are odd little legends and rumors." Rommardda leaned forward. "I doubt if anyone knows the truth of that." Her voice carried an odd sense of a warning, one which Trav seemed to understand.

"That's true," he said. "The folk will say the strangest things."

Alyssa hesitated, aching with curiosity, but she refused to be rude to people who were going out of their way to help her.

"How interesting." She paused for a pleasant smile. "You know, if we're heading for the coast, I'd best send Benoic to Dovina with messages."

Rommardda and Travaberiel exchanged a look that once again puzzled her. It seemed Trav was asking a question, and she'd answered, but they'd not said a word.

"I doubt me if that's necessary," Trav said eventually. "There's been news. The gwerbret and his entourage will be leaving for Cerrmor in the next few days. The Prince Regent summoned them."

"I see. But I'll still need to send Benoic to Aberwyn. Lady Tay will want to know how we fare. And my family! Ye gods, I should have thought of them long before this. My poor mother!"

Rommardda said nothing, but the little twist of her mouth and raised eyebrow spoke her agreement. Alyssa winced.

"Well, if it'll be safe for Benoic to ride into Eldidd," Alyssa continued. "No one will be hunting him for bounty or suchlike, but there's the war brewing."

"No longer," Rommardda said. "One of the patients who arrived yesterday told us that the Prince Regent has forbidden any warfare until he's adjudicated the complaints."

"Really? How wonderful! This sounds like a good omen to me, my lady."

"To me, too. I think the circle around our king is finally realizing that all this feuding and bloodshed's not in the best interest of the kingdom. What they can do about it is another matter entirely, of course."

"Of course. But mayhap our cause might be of more interest to them than I'd feared it would be." Rommardda's mention of patients arriving had jogged Alyssa's memory. She turned to Travaberiel. "Your master?" she said. "How does he fare tonight?"

"Not well, alas. I suspect he'll be leaving us for the Otherlands soon. Not this night. Perhaps the next, the healers tell me."

"That saddens my heart to hear! You have my sympathies."

"His time's come, truly. It's best to go when staying's become meaningless." He turned to Rommardda. "But I can't leave here until—"

"Of course. I understand that. I'll come vigil with you tonight."

"My thanks." His voice trembled on the edge of tears. "He'll be glad of that, too."

Someone else arrived not long after to join the vigil for Ebañy Salamonderiel. When Alyssa left the great hall, Trav came with her. In the pleasant sunset light they stood chatting about the journey to Mandra. Alyssa was asking about buying provisions when she heard a strange sound, coming from some distance.

"What's that?" she said. "It sounds like a drum."

"So it does. Odd." Trav cocked his head to listen. "Unless it's a— must be! Drums aren't that loud."

Indeed, the sound had turned to beats like thunder or an enormous hand slapping the air.

"Must be what?" Alyssa said.

"A dragon. Look!" He pointed off to the west. "There he is."

Flying out of the sunset came a gleaming white beast that could only be a dragon, enormous, his scales glittering, his huge wings drumming the air. All over Haen Marn shouts broke out—greetings, shrieks, cries of "what by the gods is that?" The dragon glided in a vast circle over the complex. Trav tipped back his head and cupped his hands around his mouth.

"Devar!" he shouted. "Devar! Outside the gates!"

The dragon dipped his huge head to acknowledge the request, then flapped his wings twice and turned and headed for the gates. Trav turned and started jogging after him, then paused and glanced back.

"Ebañy's nephew!" he called back. "My apologies, but I'd best go tell him how his uncle fares."

He turned and ran off again. Alyssa stood watching through the open gates as the dragon landed with a few dainty steps forward until he could come to a full stop. He furled his wings next to his body and waited for Travaberiel to reach him. Now that he was closer, she could see that his scales were more silver than white and touched with pale blue here and there.

"Lyss!" It was Cavan, running full tilt toward her. "Lyss, are you all right?"

"Of course I am. The dragon won't hurt anyone. He's here to see his uncle, or so I've been told."

He caught her by the arm and tried to turn her toward the guesthouse. She pulled away.

"That's a feeble jest," he said.

"It's not a jest at all."

He scowled at her.

"Haven't you seen dragons before?" she said.

"And I suppose you have?"

"I have indeed. They visit Aberwyn now and then." She paused to search her memory. "They have some ancient connection to the gwerbretrhyn through the Maelwaedds. The chronicles are truly vague about how and why, though."

Cavan started to speak, then merely shrugged. They stood together and watched through the open gates as Travaberiel and the dragon conversed. She could hear the massive rumble of Devar's voice, though her Elvish was too poor for her to understand more than the occasional word.

"Very well," Cavan said at last. "The dragon's a civilized fellow, and I worried for naught."

Travaberiel left the dragon and came hurrying back through the gates. At his shout, three pages ran out of the guesthouse to join him. From what Alyssa could overhear, Trav was giving them orders of some sort. The lads trooped off to the guest cottages. Trav called out to Cavan.

"Cavvo! Could you lend me a hand? I need your muscle."

Cavan trotted off to help with the mysterious errand. Alyssa found a bench and sat down to watch. Not long after the pages and the two men reappeared, carrying a litter. Wrapped in blankets upon it lay Ebañy. They carried him out of the gates and laid the litter down in front of the dragon, who bent his head to speak to his uncle in a soft rumble. Something glistened on the dragon's face. Alyssa got up without thinking and walked to the gates to see. Indeed, those were tears, and the dragon's eyes, she realized, were dark blue and oddly human in shape.

Devar stretched out his neck and laid his head flat on the ground. Cavan and Travaberiel between them lifted Ebañy from the litter and helped him sit between two of the massive flat spikes on the dragon's shoulders. Trav took a coil of rope from under the blankets on the litter and tied the elder securely in place, then wrapped him in the blankets and tied those down, too.

"He begged to die at home," Travaberiel said. "Up on the northern border, that is."

"Can the dragon get him free of all those ropes?" Alyssa said.

"Gordyn's there at the tower, Ebañy's apprentice." Travaberiel's voice caught. "Or truly, my apprentice now."

By then the sunset had faded to the somber blue gloaming. The pages picked up the empty litter and carried it back inside the gates. Devar took a few steps, spread his wings, and ran forward with a leap. The huge drumbeats echoed over Haen Marn as he flew away, heading to the northern sky, where a few stars already glimmered in the darkening night.

Travaberiel covered his face with both hands and sobbed. Cavan patted him on the back in a useless gesture. Alyssa linked her arm through Travaberiel's and led him, still sobbing, back to the guesthouse. Its windows gleamed with lantern light, and Rommardda stood waiting, a dark figure against the golden glow through the doorway.

It took a long time that night for Travaberiel to collect himself. Cavan had to admit that he found it easier to accept the presence of a vast dragon than the sight of another man weeping. Grief was understandable, of course, as was weeping over the loss, provided you did it somewhere privately. He remembered being a child, too young to be sent off as a page for his training, when he lost his mother. He also remembered how his father had beaten him for sobbing so loudly at her burying.

Eventually he left Trav to the ministrations of the two women and fled the guesthouse. He found Benoic, and they went to the stables to tend their horses.

"Alyssa mentioned summat to me about riding messages but later rather than sooner," Benoic said. "But I'll be heading out with you."

"Gladdens my heart. She knows her own business best."

"She does at that. Frightening, in a way, to see that in a lass." Benoic grinned at him. "Better you than me."

"Huh!" Cavan returned the grin. "I've no idea when we'll be leaving. There's some delay about that cursed book."

They both learned more about Alyssa's plans that same evening. They'd left the stables and gone for a stroll at the water's edge, though not too near, when they saw her carrying a lantern toward them. They met at one of the ever-present wooden benches.

"I've been told that the book and the letter should be ready the day after tomorrow," Alyssa said. "A wait, but a good thing, because we'll be traveling through Westfolk country, and there aren't any inns there. I'll need you lads to go into Dun Sebanna and buy supplies."

"Westfolk country?" Cavan said. "Why?"

"It'll be safer. Trav's going with us. Rommardda set everything up at dinner, you see, and this is the first chance I've had to tell you. She's been ever so helpful and kind."

"Splendid." But Cavan had to admit to himself that the thought of Rommardda and Alyssa laying plans together made him profoundly nervous.

"Benoic," Alyssa continued, "when it comes time to ride those messages, they won't be for Lady Dovina. She's on her way to Cerrmor. They'll be for other women, like my poor mother. She must be frantic by now. You can ride with us to the coast. It'll be out of the way, but safer."

"Much safer." Benoic nodded her way in lieu of a bow. "Of course I'll take them on."

"Hold a moment," Cavan said. "How do you know Dovina's not going to be there?"

"Rommardda told me. I've no idea how she knows, but I wasn't going to argue with her."

"Dwimmer. She has it, you know, and I'll wager that Trav does as well."

"Oh, come now!" Alyssa said. "Now who's jesting? Although—those ravens."

"For one thing, truly. Come now! I'm not jesting, and you know it."

Alyssa started to make some comment, but Benoic interrupted.

"I'll back Cavvo on this. I've seen her use it to get horses to accept that leopard of hers. Alyssa, here! Do you really think she tamed that beast with bits of meat and kind words?"

"It's no ordinary beast, either," Cavan said. "I'd bet high on that."

"Oh, very well! You're right, both of you," Alyssa said. "But dwimmer? It's so hard to believe."

"This whole place stinks of it," Benoic said. "Haven't you noticed?"

"True spoken. I have, truly."

"Well then?"

Cavan had the enjoyable experience of seeing her flustered. For some moments she stayed silent, merely sat scowling in the lantern light. All at once she laughed with a rueful shake of her head.

"Dwimmer it is," Alyssa said. "I think me I just didn't want to admit it could be true. Odd. At the collegium we study Mael the Seer's works so carefully, and they're full of hints that such a thing exists. But we're taught to ignore that. Old superstition, Lady Tay always calls it. This is the modern era, and no one but farm wives believes in that old stuff."

"Then the farm wives know a thing or two your school mistresses don't," Cavan said. "And that's that."

For all the rest of that evening Alyssa said barely two words to anyone, thinking, he supposed, about dwimmer and his revelations concerning it. Realizing that he knew more about at least one subject than she did pleased him. In the morning, however, when she counted out coins so they could buy supplies, he was back to being the silver dagger, and her, the important person who'd hired him.

The dwimmer lore in the person of Travaberiel joined Cavan and Benoic while they ate breakfast. He sat himself down at the servant's side of the hall without the least bit of fuss and grabbed a hunk of bread from a passing basket.

"I've just spoken with Alyssa," he said. "I've arranged a Westfolk escort for us. You'll have to trust me on this, but there's danger once we leave the sacred rhan."

"Doesn't take dwimmer to know that," Cavan said. "But I'll be glad of the escort."

Travaberiel grinned and saluted him with a cup of water. "I take it you've seen me for what I am."

"You're not much good at hiding it," Benoic said.

"True enough! Very well, then. We'll ride through the pass on the morrow and meet them on the other side."

"Done, then," Cavan said. "We'll be off to town in a bit to get what we'll need."

So many travelers passed through Dun Sebanna that Benoic and Cavan found plenty of goods for sale in permanent shops, unlike the situation in most Deverry towns. The prices for food and leather sacks and the like struck him as ridiculously high, but Benoic could haggle like a farmwife, and the coin had ultimately come from Lady Dovina, so Cavan devoted himself to keeping watch outside each shop rather than arguing. They weren't free yet of that letter of bounty and the trouble it brought.

What had happened to the mysterious Lannac? Had he really given up the bounty hunt? During the abortive attack in the inn, Cavan had seen the third man only by lantern light. Cavan remembered the fellow mostly as a shape, of average height, thin rather than stout, with a finesword in one hand and a dagger in the other. That dagger—it never caught the light and gleamed the way a true silver dagger would. Wilyn had certainly told the truth about that. When Alyssa started screaming, the fellow had been the first to turn and run. That Cavan did remember—the third lad ran, then Wilyn followed, and finally Renno, cursing them both, bolted for the gate.

Something else floated to the surface of Cavan's memory, a feeling only, a twinge in his mind. He made himself remember walking out into the innyard, seeing the three men—he couldn't quite place it— wait! A twinge indeed, a sharp stab of danger warning, and oddly enough, another warning that came to him like a stench from a privy or maybe rotten meat. Neither out of place in an innyard, of course, but he knew that the innyard was blameless. He'd had warnings of danger come to him in the past, always vague images that formed around his various senses—a shout only he could hear, a flash of light, and now this stench.

Evil, he thought. *Evil on the hoof.*

Benoic emerged from a shop carrying a roll of heavy canvas. "We're doubtless in for rain this time of year," he said. "So I bought a lean-to. This town is a marvel! No waiting for a market fair, just ask around for what you need."

Cavan smiled and nodded. Benoic dumped the roll at his feet and darted across the street to yet another shop. Should I tell him? Cavan asked himself. Nah nah nah, it sounds like summat from a bard's tale. But I'll remember.

Eventually Benoic had acquired so many supplies that they realized they needed a pack animal. The horse market stood over by the north gate. Under a few trees and some rickety sheds, six sturdy-looking horses and a couple of mules stood tethered for sale. While Benoic examined the stock in the company of a pale-haired man who looked like he had Westfolk blood, Cavan leaned back against the wooden rail fence with their previous purchases piled beside him. He rested his elbows on the top rail and yawned, drowsy in the hot sun.

The haggling had just reached the second mule when a tall, stout fellow came walking up. He looked young and dressed like a merchant, with checked blue and white trousers and a fine linen shirt, both of which looked newly sewn, as did his plain gray waistcoat. He carried a wooden staff, but so clumsily that Cavan doubted it was a weapon he knew how to use. The oddest thing about him, however, was his hair, a mere covering of black stubble over his skull. Lice, Cavan assumed, and he'd had to shave his head to get them gone. He smiled at Cavan and glanced at his sword belt.

"A silver dagger, are you?" he said. "Looking for a hire?"

"I'm not, my thanks," Cavan said.

"Ah, too bad. I could use a proper guard." He hesitated, looking Benoic's way. "I take it he's with you?"

"He is. Also hired at the moment."

"Ah." Again the hesitation. "Oh, wait, you must be with that lass, the one from Aberwyn, I think it is?"

"I may be, I may be not. Who wants to know?"

"Just some idle talk around," he said. "I've heard that she's in trouble with the law down in Eldidd. She's a guildwoman, right?"

Cavan straightened up and took a step away from the fence. The merchant took a step back. He gave Cavan a tremulous smile and slid one hand into his breeches pocket. He brought out a couple of coins to rub together when he spoke. Silver glinted between his soft, pink fingers.

"I was wondering," the merchant said, "if that was true. This sort of thing can, um, er, affect trade, y'know. So I was just curious, what guild does she represent?"

"It's none of your affair." Cavan kept his voice level. "And silver daggers take only one hire at a time."

"I see. Er, well, um, my thanks."

The merchant walked away fast, hurrying toward the crowded streets deeper in the town. Cavan crossed his arms over his chest and watched him go. Merchant? My arse!

"What was all that?" Benoic came up to the fence.

"I don't know, but it bodes ill. Someone asking too many questions about our hire. Pretending to be summat he's not, too."

"Huh. We'd best get out of here. I bought the gray jenny mule, by the by. He threw in a decent pack saddle to sweeten the deal."

"Good. Let's load her up and get back to Haen Marn. Alyssa should have that book by now."

And yet, Cavan thought, *this fellow had brought no stench of evil along with him. No doubt because he's a clumsy oaf! It's the other one that'll bear watching out for.*

Preparing the gwerbret's retinue for the Cerrmor trip was not as simple as getting two silver daggers and a rebel lass on the road. As a high-ranking nobleman invited by the regent, Ladoic was entitled to bring an escort of twenty-five men from his warband as well as whatever servants and retainers he wished. Dovina, as his daughter, was entitled to a page, a maid, her choice of chaperone, the chaperone's maid and page, and, if she wished, a groom, two horses, and a ladies' open carriage. To the chamberlain's great relief, Dovina was more than willing to forgo the carriage and horses.

"I shan't need a maid, either," she told him. "My page and then my friend Mavva as chaperone will be all I require. Mavva and I are used to caring for ourselves in the collegium, but I'll need Darro for messages."

"Between you and your new betrothed, no doubt," Lord Veccan said with a wink. "It must be such an exciting time for you!"

"Indeed." Dovina arranged a smile for this useful fiction. "Very exciting."

"But my lady, if I may offer a bit of advice, truly, you do need to bring a maid."

"Why? You know, when I first went to the collegium, I was shocked, and, I'll admit it, vexed that I couldn't bring servants. The only token of my rank was that I got a bed to myself in the common sleeping room. But you know, after a few months I understood why. If I'd surrounded myself with all the trappings I was entitled to, I would have set myself apart. I would have missed one of the best things about attending the collegium, the feeling of being part of a community of scholars. I loved that. I still do."

Veccan considered all this with a thoughtful twist of his mouth, not his usual smug little smile.

"I see your point, my lady," he said at last. "But in Cerrmor you'll be surrounded with people who take such trappings with deadly seriousness. If you appear without the right number of servants, they'll wonder why. Are you in disgrace? Is your father short up for coin? Nasty natterings like that."

Dovina considered, then sighed aloud. "You're right," she said. "I should have thought of that. My thanks for your advice, my lord. My mother's maid can doubtless recommend a suitable lass. Or two of them, one for me, one for Mavva."

"Well and good, then. But you can certainly forgo the carriage. I'll insist that the Cerrmor town council provide the horses for His Grace's escort. That will simplify things even more."

"Will they even need mounts? I doubt if we'll leave the city."

"Of course they won't need them, not in any true sense, but can you imagine the men agreeing to walk anywhere?"

"No, I can't. You're right a second time."

"So. We should leave on the outbound tide tomorrow night. If you and your friend could have your clothing and such packed by morning?"

"Easily done. I'll send a message to Mavva and then get started. I shan't be taking too much."

He bowed and hurried away. Dovina took a deep breath. It's begun, she told herself. The first move in our very long game! You'll need wiles and guile a lot more than fancy clothes. And oh, by the Goddess's mercy, I do hope Alyssa's well and on her way!

chapter 7

Early in the morning a page brought Alyssa her copy of the Annals, several sealed letters of authentication from Lady Perra, and a long letter explaining how to use the book's testimony should things come to court. Since the book itself arrived wrapped in cloth and further packed in a waxed leather bag, Alyssa had to restrain her longing to have a look at it. When they rode out, she carried it in her saddlebags on her own horse rather than letting Cavan pack it onto the mule.

Travaberiel and the two silver daggers kept them moving briskly along. The pass through the hills made them nervous, they told her. Too good a place to lay an ambuscade—and yet they rode through without any trouble. By the time they reached the open land along the river valley, the sun hung past zenith, and the horses and mule needed rest. Travaberiel rode up next to Alyssa.

"My friends should be here soon," he said. "Let's go down to the riverbank and let it guard our backs until they arrive."

The men unsaddled the animals and let them roll, then brought them to the water to drink. Alyssa sat on the soft grass in the pleasant sun and wondered if this was the way fine ladies felt, with someone to do everything that needed doing while they took their leisure. The fine ladies, of course, wouldn't be wondering if their lives were in danger the way she was. Once the horses were tended, Cavan sat down next to her. He said nothing, but his solid presence eased her fear.

And Travaberiel would warn them, she reminded herself, if danger lay ahead. At times her mind returned to the inescapable truth: dwimmer was real. All that modern thought on the subject was wrong. Intellectually she could accept the truth. Emotionally it annoyed her like a buzzing wasp. She could wave it away, but always it came back: the things they taught you were wrong. Call it dwimmer or dweomer, strange things happened in the world, and some few people could control them. *It's not fair!* she thought. *All that careful study upended like a clumsy cart in a market! Old superstition, indeed!*

At least the dwimmer folk she'd encountered had all been kind, helpful, devoted to helping the sick and easing the lot of the common folk caught up in legal matters. She could remember other tales of another kind of dwimmer, an evil thing worked for selfish ends. *That can't be true,* she thought. *Bards make up that sort of thing for their tales. Don't they? Or is that why people try so hard to pretend that dwimmer doesn't exist?*

She shuddered as if a cold wind had touched her. Cavan turned to her in some concern. Her suspicions seemed too puerile to share.

"It's naught," she said. "Just worrying about the road ahead."

Dwimmerman or no, Travaberiel had apparently appointed himself their chamberlain. He rooted through the mule packs and brought out food. They were all eating bread and meat from the market when they saw riders approaching through the tall grass. Some eight Westfolk drove a small herd of horses, maybe twenty head on a quick count, and led pack animals as well. Big dogs, half-wolf from the look of them, trotted along with them. When the riders came close, Alyssa was startled to see that four of them were women. All of them, men and women both, carried hunting bows and wore quivers of arrows and long knives on their belts. When Travaberiel hurried out to meet them, one of the men dismounted. They walked a short distance away from everyone and talked. The rest of the Westfolk began unsaddling their riding and packhorses.

"We won't be covering any more ground today," Benoic said with a sigh. "The Westfolk never hurry."

Two of the Westfolk began leading horses, a few at a time, to the river to drink while others stayed out with the herd. Travaberiel returned with a fellow he introduced as Jenandar.

"We've been traveling fast to catch up with you," Jenandar said. "We need to tend our stock."

"Very well," Alyssa said. "I'll wager we're safe now anyway, now that you're all here."

He grinned and patted the hilt of his sheathed knife.

As Benoic had predicted, the Westfolk proceeded to set up camp. They tethered out the horses, set the dogs to watching them, and brought out a skin of mead to pass around with the introductions. Alyssa had seen Westfolk many a time in Aberwyn, and she knew something of their complicated language, too. Although Cavan had considerable trouble, she easily learned their names and pointed out to him that they all were related to one another in equally complicated ways.

"All those little pieces of the names have meaning," she told him. "They can tell you quite a lot about a group like this—an alar. Alar's the word for group."

"If you say so," Cavan said. "I take it that woman named Graelamala is the one who owns the horses."

"They own them in common. She does look like she's in command, though."

"We let her handle the haggling at the horse fair," Jenandar put in. "She's the best at it."

Out among the horses Graelamala was testing each tether stake by stepping on it with her full weight. Since she looked to be over six feet tall, her weight was doubtless sufficient.

Two of the other women, Elajario and Jonnadario, Jenandar's sisters, sat with Alyssa when the Westfolk men took over cooking the evening meal. Both of the women appeared to be young, though with the Westfolk one never knew their age. Despite their strangely curled and pointed ears, they were beautiful, with hair as pale as moonbeams and deep-set violet eyes, slit vertically like a cat's. They were also as heavily armed as the rest of their group.

"Travaberiel tells me there's four men following you," Elajario said. "With your two silver daggers, that gives us good odds if it comes to a fight, ten against four."

"Huh!" Jonnadario understood more of Deverrian than she could speak. "Won't be any fight. Unless they can't count to ten."

"I take it," Alyssa said, "that you're both archers."

"Just that," Ela said. "The knives are a last resort, if things come to some kind of battle."

"Have you ever fought in one?"

"I have. When we took back the western cities." She looked away, and her eyes darkened. "A long time ago now, and I don't like remembering it."

"I shan't bring it up again. My apologies."

"And you, Alyssa?" Joh said. "You fight with what?"

"Words. That's all I have."

Joh laughed like bells chiming. Ela scowled at her.

"Words have their power," Ela said. "The right words can be a sword of fire."

Joh looked chastened.

"I hope my words will burn in the right ears," Alyssa said. "The only knives I know how to use are for slicing loaves of bread. My father's a baker."

With that the conversation turned to and stayed upon the subject of families.

In the morning, when it was time to break camp, Ela and Joh rode with Alyssa, just behind the two silver daggers in the line of march. Alyssa noticed Joh studying the two silver daggers as shrewdly as if they were going on sale themselves. She assumed that Joh distrusted them.

"They're decent men for silver daggers," Alyssa said.

"Good to know," Joh said. "The one with the sandy-brown hair, Cavan, he is yours?"

"Not exactly mine. What—"

"I watched him last night. He is sweet on you, I think, and you on him?"

"She's at it again," Ela interrupted. "She's desperate to have children. She's looking for one of your men to put out to stud. They're so amazingly fertile."

Joh leaned over in the saddle and cuffed her hard on the arm. Ela merely laughed.

"Well, in that case, I'd rather you didn't press Cavan into your service," Alyssa said, as demurely as she could. "But the other silver dagger might be interested in a hire. His name's Benoic."

All three of them laughed, and Cavan turned in the saddle to look back with suspicious eyes. Alyssa simpered at him in her best Dovina imitation. He turned back again.

"Does it shock you, Alyssa?" Ela said. "So many Deverry women practically faint at the way we arrange these things."

"It does. I won't deny it."

"Oh, huh!" Joh said. "We shock other Westfolk. Not about the getting of babies, but about everything else."

"True spoken." Ela sounded abruptly wistful. "We're wild women, Alyssa, the moon-struck ones. That's what the Westfolk women who live in towns or serve the king's court call us. We're throwbacks to the old days, when my people lived free with their horses out on the plains."

"Townsfolk!" Joh wrinkled her nose in a sneer. "Well, from the far south, anyway."

"Mandra, you mean?" Alyssa said.

"Not so much there, but the folk from the far south, the islands. Anmurdio and beyond."

"They come from a very different way of living," Ela broke in. "They call us savages."

"Wild women, is it?" Alyssa said. "I'm not, only a rebel of sorts."

"Traveling with the silver dagger?" Joh grinned at her. "Good choice."

"Oh, spare us!" Ela said. "Babies, babies, babies! Well, I hope you get one this time. So you can talk about summat else."

They laughed on the edge of giggling, as only sisters can. Alyssa watched in amazement. Married women whom she knew talked about pregnancy, of course, either longing for or dreading another one. But the two sisters were joking and teasing each other, neither of them married, apparently, as lightly as if they were arguing over a favorite sweetmeat.

"May I ask you summat?" Alyssa said.

"Of course," Ela said.

"Do the Westfolk marry? In some legally binding way, like we do in Deverry?"

Ela explained the question to Joh in Elvish. The three women talked back and forth until Alyssa understood that no, the Westfolk made very few legal commitments about anything other than the support of those very welcome children.

"There are reasons." Ela's voice had turned cautious, her words careful. "It's hard for us to know how long we can keep a promise like that."

They were ducking a difficult subject—their long lives. No one in western Deverry was quite sure how long the Westfolk lived, and even less did they know how many years a mixed blood child might have. Alyssa had spoken with a good many people in Aberwyn who resented the Westfolk bitterly, them with their hundreds of years while Deverry folk only rarely lived past sixty.

"I understand," Alyssa said. "I have friends who want children that badly, too."

Ela and Joh smiled, and the difficult moment ended.

They traveled a decent distance south, that day, before the lowering sun warned them to make camp. They found a spot where the river curved, and its scour had created a small sandy beach. That night everyone except Alyssa and Graelamala, the Westfolk leader, took turns standing a watch. At intervals Alyssa woke to see the sentinels coming back to their blankets. She always saw Travaberiel, wide awake and walking here and there, on guard in his own way.

In the morning the Westfolk insisted on taking the time to bathe in the river while the horses grazed and rested. Nothing Travaberiel said could convince Graelamala to move fast. Their horses had to be in good condition to sell.

"There's a storm on the way," Trav said to her. "A big one."

"None of us will shrink if we get wet. Huh, you're as delicate as a townsman."

"Oh, very well!" Trav threw his hands in the air and stomped off, muttering to himself in Elvish.

Alyssa bathed with the Westfolk women down at the far end of the beach. Both Ela and Joh took their weapons with them and laid them near at hand. Alyssa took the chance to wash out her loinwrap and spread it in the sun to dry. The time was near for her monthly bleeding to start, and she had no ready supply of rags to protect her clothing. Ela gave her the answer.

"Pull the long grass," she said. "That's what we do. Stuff it into your loincloth."

"Of course! And then I can just dump it somewhere and get fresh. I wish I was a wild woman like you!"

"We teach you," Joh said. "Keep riding with us."

They gathered their weapons and Alyssa her laundry. As they walked back to camp, they saw the men, also freshly bathed, lying on the sunny sand, decorously wrapped in the crucial places. Cavan lay on his back, half-asleep. Alyssa tried to act as indifferent as the Westfolk women, but she found herself studying Cavan's mostly naked body, the hard muscles, the soft pale hair on his chest, every detail and curve that spoke of strength and vigor and a hard life of riding and fighting. With a yawn he opened his eyes and smiled at her. She felt desire like a spear of fire thrust through her whole body. In something like panic she turned away and hurried after her friends.

"That Benoic!" Joh said. "My my. Indeed. I must smile at him more." She paused, thinking. "He has a scar on his side. I must be sympathetic and ask how. Fighting men like that."

"Always on the hunt," Ela said with a mock-sigh. "What would our mother think if she only knew!"

"Huh! She was just like me, or you wouldn't be here."

Alyssa knew what her mother would think if she were the one hunting. Horrified would be the word. Sirra had picked out a rising young guildsman as a prospect for her daughter's betrothal, but fortunately—or so Alyssa thought of it—she'd gotten her place at the collegium. Bren had married her younger sister Arrana instead. He was a nice boy, not bad-looking, hard-working, too. Alyssa had not been able to make herself the slightest bit interested in marrying him.

After a leisurely noontime meal, Graelamala finally decided that their horses had rested enough.

"Time to ride," she said. "Travaberiel looks frantic to get on the road."

"Just so," Joh said. "Benoic, ride with me, will you? I have summat to ask you. About those Deverry swords, the old broad ones. You still use them?"

"When we know we're in for a battle, we do."

"Ah, I see."

They walked off together. During the rest of their journey, Benoic usually dropped back to ride next to Joh, who always welcomed him with a soft smile. He looked stunned at moments, Alyssa realized, like a man who couldn't believe his luck.

Originally the spring horse fair had taken place at the Lake of the Leaping Trout, but once Haen Marn had established its rhan there, the fairs had been forced to move. They kept moving thanks to their success. The more Westfolk herders brought in horses to sell, the faster the available grass vanished, eaten down almost to the ground. The sheep they brought along to serve as the main dish at feasts would have left the ground bare had they been allowed to graze for any length of time. Thus custom, usage, and a fair amount of arguing among the horse traders had established a new pattern. The Westfolk moved their herds along the west side of the Aver Delonderiel, and the Deverrian merchants brought their caravans of trade goods to the east side. Together they built three bridges at roughly equal distances from one another. At each bridge the fair lingered for eight days, then moved south to the next. Finally, at the Westfolk town of Mandra, the fair ended for the season.

Although she'd never seen one, Alyssa knew a great deal about the Westfolk horse fairs. Men came from all over the western provinces to buy and sell at them. Every spring some of the Aberwyn merchants put together an expedition to acquire the specially bred geldings that made such splendid hunting and battle horses. The Westfolk wanted trade goods, mostly, rather than coin, so the merchants bought heavily from local craftsmen. Everyone shared in the prosperity, even the bakers. Alyssa's father and brother sold pound upon pound of hardtack and flatbreads to provision these caravans.

As well as the trading, the fair featured horse races. The Westfolk had started them just to show off the stock, but now frenzied betting took place as well. Cavan had heard of them, and he sounded so enthusiastic about the races that Alyssa had to remind him that the point of going to the fair wasn't to bet away every penny of his wages.

"We'll need every coin we have to reach Cerrmor," she told him. "Trav's friends are going to want to be paid, you know, for taking us there."

"True enough." He gave her a grin. "I'll try to remember that."

On a morning when the sky threatened rain, Alyssa's caravan of a Westfolk dwimmerman, two silver daggers, and a troupe of Westfolk with their herd caught up with the horse fair at the second bridge, about halfway to the Westfolk town of Mandra. They passed the sheep first, about a mile north of the bridge. The flock, guarded by dogs as well as shepherds, was pastured away from the valuable horses to avoid giving them ovine parasites. Before they reached the actual fair, they smelled it. The leavings of so many animals, including the traders on both sides, left an unmissable mark on the warm spring air. The cloudy sky seemed to hang close, and the air lay heavy around them, making the stench worse.

"You get used to it." Travaberiel paused for a small choking noise. "Eventually."

Benoic had bought Alyssa a pomander in Dun Sebanna for just this occasion. She held her reins in one hand, took the silver ball out of her kirtle, and held it to her nose.

"It'll rain soon," Cavan said. "That'll clear things out a bit."

When the road topped a low rise, they saw the fair at last.

"There it is!" Trav said. "It's a cursed good thing we got here early in the day. We need to find proper shelter."

"Good gods!" Alyssa said. "It's enormous."

The fair spread out along both sides of the river. On the west bank, horses grazed. Downstream stood elven tents, at least thirty of them, Alyssa estimated. On the east, mules and merchants camped downstream from a cluster of knocked-together wooden booths. Men and Westfolk both gathered around or strolled back and forth between them.

"They sell all sorts of things," Trav said. "Ale and mead—a lot of that."

In the midst of all this stood the bridge itself, made of wood but standing on proper stone pillars on each bank. Now and then a merchant and his servants led their latest purchases across. As soon as their hooves hit the hollow-sounding boards, the horses tossed their heads and pulled uneasily on the lead ropes, but the men calmed them and guided them across. These Western Hunters, as the breed was known, were too valuable to "encourage" with whips or sticks.

Since they were already on the west side of the river, Graelamala could take her herd and her people directly out to the grass beyond the fair. Benoic lingered a moment. He rode up to Alyssa and leaned in the saddle to speak to her.

"Do you have need of me?"

"None." She smiled at him. "Go help Joh tether her horses, if you'd like."

He grinned, made her a half-bow, and rode off after the Westfolk.

Trav led Alyssa and Cavan past the horse herds to the cluster of Westfolk camps. In the silvery light from the approaching storm, their brightly painted tents gleamed in a long scatter across the beaten-down grass. As they dismounted, a young Westfolk man, slender and not very tall, hurried to meet them.

"There's Linderyn," Travaberiel said.

Alyssa's first impression was that Linderyn had to be part owl. He had large dark eyes, a sharp beakish nose, and his pale hair, cropped short, stood up from his forehead in two soft peaks. After a round of introductions he stood watching, hands on his hips, as Cavan and Travaberiel unloaded the pack mule. Her tiny lean-to caught his attention.

"That little bit of canvas won't keep you dry, Alyssa," Linderyn said. "I'll let you use my tent. Trav, Cavvo, and I will impose on Trav's father."

"My very great thanks." Alyssa wondered how she could possibly find the courage—no, the affrontery—to speak, but the other men had wandered away out of earshot. I'm a wild woman now, she reminded herself. "But I'd rather Cavan stayed with me."

"Very well, then." Linderyn glanced at the sky. "He'd best get your gear stowed away. This rain's not going to hold off for long. The other silver dagger?"

"He's over there." Alyssa pointed to the edge of the cluster of tents. "He's found a place to stay."

"Good. Let me get things arranged, then."

And that was all there was to it, her momentous decision. Alyssa smiled and curtsied as Linderyn hurried off to tell the others. She watched as Joh and Benoic began to set up her small peaked tent, just large enough for two people. She hoped that her new friend would soon have the child she wanted, and that she herself escaped a similar gift. A scrap of linen, she reminded herself, you soak it in mead or vinegar, wrap it around a smooth pebble, and—the idea spoiled the romantic glow of her scheme, but then, a baby would spoil a great deal more.

Linderyn's round tent, painted with images of birds and trees, though she could see no owls among them, stood ready for them. The dwimmerman had cleared out his own bedding. She carried some of her own gear inside, but Cavan insisted on hauling most of it as well as his own. They dumped their possessions on the floor cloth in untidy heaps and hurried back outside. Both of them wanted to see something of the fair before the rain hit.

"There's a big horse fair like this near Lughcarn," Cavan said. "My father and his equerry went yearly, of course. I always wanted to see it, but he'd never take me, only my youngest brother."

"He didn't take the eldest? The heir?"

"Not even him. But the youngest, Careg, was his little favorite. He knew how to flatter and wheedle and twist our father round. He learned how from my sisters."

"Did you ever get to the fair? After they sent you away, like."

"They exiled me in Slaughter-Month. No fairs then, not for a long time."

He forced out a smile, but Alyssa caught her breath. "They sent you away in the dead of winter with only a silver coin and a horse."

"The usual terms of exile, truly. Oh, they let me keep a warm cloak and an extra pair of boots, too."

His face revealed nothing, his eyes open as usual, his mouth absolutely neutral—not a twitch, not the hint of a frown. If his father had appeared at that moment, Alyssa would have thrown together a flyting song on the spot, gwerbret or no.

"Old tales," Cavan said in a moment. "Let's go have a look, shall we? I'm wondering if some of our enemies have followed us here. I want to get a good look at the crowd."

"That third bounty hunter?"

"For one. And the man with the shaved head. I'll recognize him if I see him."

With a glance at the darkening sky, she followed him across the bridge to the east bank. A good many merchants who had naught to do with the trade in horses came to the fair. Off to one side, on the other side of the tent camps from the horse herds, stood a confusion of booths and pedlars. Some of the booths were cleverly constructed of wood so they could be taken apart, loaded onto a wagon and moved to the next camp. Others were mere stacks of firewood. Pedlars moved through the crowd with small goods piled in baskets. Here and there a farmer knelt behind a blanket spread with cheeses or fruit or vegetables. Brewers sold their ale and beer out of the barrel. Over it all hung the scent of roasting lamb and pork and the sound of Westfolk harps and song.

As they wandered from booth to booth, Cavan made a great show of pointing to various things for sale, but he kept on guard. As they walked, he kept glancing at the people around them. He paused often to look over a display of hunting knives here or leather pouches there, but even as he studied the merchandise, he'd pause for a quick look around. Eventually they came to a booth with fine jewelry laid out on a dark woad-blue cloth. Brooches and bracelets, mostly silver with touches of gold and gems, were sewn to the cloth, nailed to the wood beneath it. This time Alyssa was the one to pause for a better look.

The smith, a Westfolk man with emerald eyes, made her a little bob of a bow and smiled. His oddly long fingers moved among the merchandise like pale spiders as he pointed out finger rings and brooches, bangles and bracelets of silver and bronze. At one side of the display lay a line of betrothal brooches, made of two silver wires cleverly wound and spiraled to look like a single strand at first glance. She did her best to ignore them, though her rebellious eyes insisted on turning toward a particularly fine one, set with two red stones in the embrace of the silver. You're not likely to ever get a betrothal brooch now, she reminded herself. Rebels and wild women don't.

"Does summat interest you, fair maid?" the jeweler said.

"I'm just admiring your skill, good sir. You do lovely work."

He smiled and bowed again. She nodded in response and led the way from the booth.

They paused again at a cutler's to let Cavan haggle over a hoof pick with a stag-horn handle. Alyssa walked a few steps away and studied the crowd—mostly men, the merchants, their muleteers and horsehandlers. All the other women she saw were Westfolk, striding through the fair with their long knives at their sides. Off to the north of her she heard a sudden noise—the crowd murmuring and moving. The men nearest her began to drift in that direction to see what the excitement might be, but in a moment it appeared on its own. A smug-looking merchant was leading one of the most beautiful horses she'd ever seen, a Western Hunter gelding whose golden coat shone like polished metal. It walked proudly, head up, eyes pricked, feet lifted high as its new owner led it through on a halter rope.

"Oh, splendid!" Cavan came up beside her. "I wonder what he traded away for that. Half his fortune, I should think."

"He'll get it back and more from some high-ranking lord," Alyssa said. "Probably paid for with bribes from the law courts."

One of the bystanders near her turned to give her a smile. "Well said, lass!"

She returned the smile, but Cavan laid a firm hand on her arm.

"Seen enough for now?" Cavan said. "I was thinking of a tankard of beer and maybe a stick of that roast lamb."

"Splendid idea!" She looked at the slate-gray sky. "We'd best hurry. Rain's on its way."

Hurry they did, because he kept her moving fast. Once they were well away from the fellow who'd spoken to her, "Lyss," he said, "you've got to hold your tongue about the courts! We don't know who might be listening."

She winced in a little shudder of fear. "True spoken. Apologies."

"Well and good, then. Now let's go get summat to eat."

They'd barely finished their meal when, with a roll of thunder, the rain began in big spatters. Alyssa and Cavan ran back to their borrowed tent and reached it before the downpour began. Alyssa rummaged through a mule pack and brought out a punched tin candle lantern and a candle.

"How are you going to light that?" Cavan said, grinning. "I'll wager that no one in this camp thought to have a fire ready."

"You'll see."

Alyssa brought out a tin box of sulfur matches and a scratch stone. When she struck one, Cavan caught his breath in surprise. She lit the candle and shook the match out.

"An alchemist back home invented these," she said. "A couple of our merchants are vying for the right to sell them elsewhere."

"Splendid! I could have used them many a time on the road."

Cavan stared at the glowing candle for a long moment, then knelt down by the untidy heap of goods that they'd dumped in the tent earlier. Alyssa looked around the tent and found a safe place for the lantern. He unrolled his bedroll and spread his blankets out on one side of the fire pit. Alyssa knelt by hers and undid the straps holding the roll in place. She was surprised that her hands weren't shaking, just from the gravity of her decision.

"We shouldn't be sharing a tent," Cavan said. "Your womanly honor—"

"My womanly honor?" Alyssa paused for a bark of a laugh. "Do you truly think that matters any more? Cavvo, I'm as much an outcast as you are."

"What? Lyss, that makes no sense—"

"Doesn't it? Do you think Gwerbret Ladoic won't notice that I brought the book to Cerrmor to use as evidence against him? Do you think Travaberiel turning up with a claim on his rhan will gladden his heart? And who's bringing Trav with her?"

Slack-jawed, Cavan stared at her.

"Do you think I'll be able to just go back to Aberwyn and take up my studies, all peaceful, like? Marry some guildsman just like naught's happened?"

He made a strangled sound that might have been "Ye gods."

"I may never even see my family again," Alyssa continued. "I'll miss my mam so badly, but if I try to visit them, it could well mean as much trouble for them as it would for me."

"True spoken. Ye gods, Lyss! You're right. I've not seen that. My apologies."

He stayed kneeling, staring at the floor cloth of the tent as if he were thinking something through. She stood up and shook her blankets out, then laid them next to his.

"What—" Cavan began, then let his voice trail away.

"I've got naught to lose, have I?"

She knelt down on the blankets, a mere arm's reach away from him. He studied her face as intently as if he were trying to see her soul through her eyes.

"I don't suppose you do," he said at last. "But I'm still not worthy of you."

"That's for me to judge, not you."

Outside the tent, the wind picked up with a sound like a distant voice. She shivered with a little toss of her head.

"Frightened?" he said.

"I'm not. This cursed rain! I feel so cold."

"Oh, well, then." He held out his hand. "Let me keep you warm."

She smiled and laid her hand in his. He drew her close and kissed her with a passion that sparked her own.

When Cavan woke, the candle had long since burned down. The sky showed gray through the smoke hole of the tent, but the rain had stopped. He could hear that the camp outside had started its day. Distantly a dog barked, a mule brayed, men's voices murmured. Cavan rolled out of the blankets as quietly as he could. Alyssa turned over, smiling in her sleep, and nestled down in the warmth. He felt torn between wanting to kiss her awake and letting her rest, caught between thinking "she's mine at last" and "ye gods, what I have done to her!"

He dressed, then stood and watched her sleep until he started fearing he'd wake her. He slipped out of the tent and made sure that he guided the tent flap silently back into place. He'd crept away from the beds of other women without waking them to avoid any kind of conversation or commitment. This time was different.

The various merchants had long been up and working. He saw none of the pedlars or the farmers with their blanket stalls, but the merchants with booths were grumbling together as they wiped the wood dry. Some had already spread out their goods, but they seemed more concerned with inspecting than selling them. Cavan went straight to the Westfolk silversmith. He smiled and nodded in greeting.

"Those silver betrothal brooches," Cavan said. "Got any left?"

"The priciest ones, of course."

"Good. The one set with red stones?"

"Right here. I noticed your lass fancied it."

My lass, Cavan thought. *She is now, for all the good it'll ever do her.* It took most of the coin from his hire to pay the smith, but he considered it the biggest bargain he'd ever made.

Cavan entered the tent as quietly as he could, but she sat up, still naked, when he knelt down beside her.

"I've got summat to give you." He offered her a hand clasped around the brooch. "For what it's worth."

When she held out her open hand, he dropped the silver brooch into it. She gasped in delight.

"It's truly lovely! Thank you!" She looked up with a grin. Out of habit, she'd used the polite form, "chi," for "you." She repeated her thanks with the familiar form, "ti." "We probably know each other well enough now."

He laughed and caught her by the shoulders for a kiss.

"This brooch is so lovely," she said. "It's the second-best thing anyone ever gave me."

"Only second?" He tried to keep his voice light, but he knew that disappointment stained it.

"You gave me the best thing last night."

For a moment he missed her meaning, but the way she grinned at him jogged his mind. He kissed her again, caressed her, and they lay back down together in the blankets.

The sun hid behind thinning clouds by the time Alyssa and Cavan left the tent in search of much-needed food. Fortunately the fair had returned to its usual busy self. They ate bread slathered with butter, roast pork, and a handful each of dried apples. Cavan washed down his share with a tankard of dark beer, but she found someone selling boiled water. She used her own tin cup to drink a ladleful.

As they headed back to the tents, a pair of men walked between them, hurried off with an apology—but Alyssa was left some six feet away from her silver dagger. As she turned to go back to him, someone laid a heavy hand on her shoulder. She twisted around and broke free to see a grinning fellow dressed in rough wool clothes.

"Here's a real lass!" he said. "None of those cursed ears, eh? How much for a tumble, wench?"

"Not for sale," Alyssa said. "Keep your paws off!"

"Ah, just give me a kiss, then."

Cavan charged up beside her, grabbed the fellow by the arm with one hand, and hit him so hard in the guts with the other that the fellow staggered and went down. He struggled but managed to get to his knees. Alyssa jumped back just in time as he spewed the contents of his stomach at her feet. Cavan grabbed him by the hair. She saw his silver dagger flash.

"Stop! Don't cut him!"

Cavan held his hand with the dagger just at the man's throat. All around them men were shouting, pushing forward to reach out for Cavan, but then holding back, stepping away fast when he swirled around to face them.

"Don't!" Alyssa threw every bit of force she had into the words. "Stop it! No bloodshed!"

Cavan shook his head like a man who's been stunned. He took a deep breath and looked at her. She could see from his eyes that the berserker fit had left him.

"It's over, good sirs," Alyssa said. "Cavvo, put the knife away. Please?"

"By all means." Cavan sheathed the dagger. "My thanks for stopping me. Ye gods!"

Some of the men standing round swore softly under their breaths. The fellow who'd touched her got to his feet. He was pasty-white and stank of vomit, but he stood steadily enough.

"It's a good thing, lad," one of the men said to Cavan, "that you listened to your lass there."

"Indeed," Cavan said. "He was too drunk to know what he was doing."

The fellow took a few steps backward, then kept going, shrank into the crowd.

"You!" Alyssa snapped. "Wait! I want to—"

Too late! He'd gotten clear of the circle. Before anyone could stop him, he turned and ran, dodging through the passersby. In the crowd, he disappeared so fast that Alyssa realized she'd have to let him go. The men around them drifted away, a few at a time, on their own business. Alyssa waited until the last of them had gone, and she kept her voice down.

"He wasn't drunk," she said to Cavan. "I've smelled enough men who stank of a night's binge to know the difference. They'd come rolling into the baker's shop when we first opened of a morning, seeking summat to sop up the drink before they went home to furious wives. He did that to provoke you, Cavan. Get you hauled before the Master of the Fair."

"Where he could claim the bounty?" Cavan also spoke just above a whisper.

"Just that."

"And leave you without a guard. Let's get back to the Westfolk side of the camp."

"And find Travaberiel. He needs to know about this." She laughed, but from nerves not humor. "Well, at least that fellow got a good bit more trouble than he bargained for."

When he heard the tale, Trav sent Jenandar over to the east side of the fair to see what he could learn.

"Things are getting much more complicated than I like," Trav said. "A few spies following us are one thing. Attempts at causing trouble is another. You two had best stay in the tent and leave the scouting to me."

"Gladly," Cavan said. "No more drink for me, either. It only makes my temper worse."

"Good that you can see it. Let me talk with Linderyn, look around, that sort of thing."

"We'll go back to Linderyn's tent," Alyssa said. "It'll be safer that way."

It was some while later that Travaberiel joined them in their borrowed refuge. He seated himself next to her before he spoke. "The man who attacked you? He may have been found. Cavvo, you got a good look at him, didn't you? We need you to view the corpse."

"Corpse?" Cavan snapped.

"Just that. He was found washed up in an eddy of the river. Drowned, they thought at first. Plausible, if he was drunk. Then someone noticed the fresh bruise on the side of his face." Travaberiel pointed at his own temple. "He must have been struck down and then dumped into the water."

"I don't want to leave Alyssa here alone," Cavan said.

"Quite right." He stood up. "Ela and Joh are right outside."

When Travaberiel lifted the tent flap, the two elven sisters came in. Joh carried a leather sack. Travaberiel said a few words to them in Elvish, then ushered Cavan outside. Talking in low voices they hurried off.

"We just heard!" Joh sang out. "The attack! How do you fare?"

"Not hurt at all, just shaken," Alyssa said. "Where's Benoic?"

"Getting clothes on," Joh said. "I have something to give you, the spare knife."

Joh rummaged through the sack she carried and eventually brought out a knife in a black sheath. She drew it with a flourish to reveal a long, narrow blade, sharp on both sides. Black leather strips wrapped the hilt. Both the hilt and the sheath gleamed with a faint bluish overtone from whatever dye the maker had used. Alyssa thought instantly of ravens.

"It's so beautiful," she said. "I've never seen a blade like this."

"From a fight long time gone now," Joh said. "I kept it, but they— Travaberiel's kind told me, not for me. For some other I meet one day."

"I remember that," Ela said. "Truly, I think it's yours, Alyssa. We've met because you're riding a dangerous errand, after all. One that they sanction."

"They? You mean dwimmer folk."

"Just that. Joh found that knife in the ruins of Rinbaladelan. It was—"

"Stop!" Joh continued speaking in a long stream of Elvish.

Alyssa could pick out only a few words, one of which meant a vow sworn to a god. She decided against prying further.

"Here." Joh held the knife out. "All that doesn't matter. It's for you."

Stammering thanks, Alyssa took the knife. They showed her how to attach the sheath to her skirt's belt and how to draw it fast should she have need of it.

"I might well need it," Alyssa told them. "There's a fair bit more danger to fetching a book than I thought there would be. Even with guards."

"So it seems," Ela said. "Now, if a man should grab at you or threaten, remember to strike low and strike up. Hit them in their manhood with all your strength. Let me show you the grip."

The two Westfolk women were still teaching her when Cavan and Travaberiel returned with Benoic in tow. They both exclaimed over the knife. Cavan reached for it, but Joh stepped away from his reach.

"Ask Alyssa," she said.

Cavan looked at her and smiled. "You may," she said. "Carefully."

He took it in both hands and turned it this way and that while Benoic moved close to see.

"Mountain folk made it," Joh explained. "Special steel only they make."

"I've heard of that," Benoic said. "Not the same alloy as the silver daggers, though. It has something to do with the charcoal in the smelting. I think. I don't know."

Everyone looked at Cavan, their sole representative of the Lughcarn ironworks.

"I can't tell you," he said. "The dwarven smiths keep their secrets."

He handed the knife to Alyssa. She sheathed it at her belt and let her tunic drop over it to hide it.

"What about that corpse?" Alyssa said.

"It was him, all right," Cavan said. "Someone ensured he couldn't spill a secret."

Not even making love to Alyssa could soothe Cavan's spirit that night. He lay awake with her asleep in his arms while he brooded over the day's events. His cursed ill temper! He'd let it rage without a single thought, not even a feeble attempt to control himself. He'd had a chance but failed to rise to Rommardda's challenge. *I could have killed him,* he thought. *I wanted to. Thank the Holy Goddess, Lyss stopped me!*

But then some foul bastard went and did the job.

Dangerous enemies. He spent a long while, that night, going over everything that had happened since they'd left Aberwyn. The conclusion was obvious. Noble lords and perhaps a priest or two were determined to keep the law courts firmly in their hands. Anyone, even a young woman, a commoner no less, who posed any sort of threat would be dealt with by whatever means necessary. Once they returned to Deverry territory, what would she have to protect her? A couple of silver daggers! Maybe only one, if Benoic decided to stay with his elven mistress. With the bounty on his head, Cavan realized, he couldn't even trust the members of his band enough to hire more silver daggers.

And that stench of evil—someone more dangerous than a noble lord had hired Renno and Wilyn.

Finally he did sleep, only to have troubled dreams that meant nothing but left him exhausted.

"We need to get back on the road," Travaberiel said. "I've spoken to Graelamala. She and the horses will stay here, but Jenandar, Joh, and Benoic will come with us to Mandra. The horse fair will reach there eventually, and they can rejoin her alar then."

"Sounds good," Cavan said. "I take it that Joh's almost as good with weapons as a man."

"Almost?" Travaberiel laughed, one sharp bark. "Better than most. I wouldn't cross her. Benoic's a braver man than me, I tell you."

Alyssa had to smile at Cavan's shocked expression. They were standing outside their borrowed tent while they talked. All around them the fair went on, as noisy and busy as always, just as if a dead man hadn't been fetched out of the river only the day before.

"I'd like to make a start today," Trav continued. "But first we've got to go talk with my father. I've got that letter from Rommardda to deliver. Cavvo, come with us, will you?"

"Of course. Just in case."

Travaberiel led the way through the elven encampment. In front of his tent, Maelaber, who looked look so much like Trav that no one would ever doubt the relationship, was sitting on a leather cushion. He was talking with a pair of friends who squatted in front of him. They stood up to leave after exchanging a few polite greetings with Trav. Maelaber also got to his feet, saw Alyssa, and nodded her way.

"Speak in Deverrian, will you?" he said to Trav. "Let's not be rude."

"You're right." Trav made her a half-bow from the waist. "My apologies!"

"I'm studying Elvish," Alyssa said, "but I've not got much beyond introducing oneself and chatting about the weather."

"Useful enough, but limited, truly," Trav said with a grin. "I was just telling my father here that I've got a very important letter for him."

"We'll leave you to the reading of it," said one of the friends. "We'll see you at the feast, Maelaber."

Once they'd left, Maelaber took Alyssa and Trav inside his tent for privacy, but Cavan insisted on staying outside on guard.

"Someone might want to eavesdrop," Cavan said. "I want to get a good look at him, in that case."

"True enough, and my thanks." Maelaber opened the tent flap. "If you two will just come inside?"

They sat on leather cushions under the smoke hole for the light while the elder herald began to read Rommardda's letter. He looked up with a frown and what sounded like a curse in the Westfolk language.

"The last thing I'd ever want in life," he said, "would be to rule Aberwyn. Ye gods! Has she taken leave of her senses?"

"Read it all first," Trav said, "then we'll talk."

Maelaber scowled at him, but he did finish reading. "Very well, she's not taken leave of her senses, but I shan't go along with this anyway. My claim? Hah! It's much too tenuous to stand up in any court, no matter how impartial, and thank the Divine Ones for that, too."

"All we're asking," Travaberiel said, "is for you to pretend you're interested in reopening the matter."

"And what good will that do? None. More harm than good, I'd say. I've no intention of infuriating Gwerbret Ladoic. He's been a good friend to the Westfolk too many times." He tossed the letter into Travaberiel's lap. "Tell Rommardda I'll have no part in this."

Alyssa felt like an archer who's seen his arrows broken right in front of him.

"Well, good sir," Alyssa said, "I'm in no position to argue with you, but truly, we need every weapon we can find."

"This one's no weapon at all. My apologies, lass. Your cause is a good one, just and right and all that, but I can't help you." Maelaber crossed his arms over his chest and glared at his son. "I don't want to argue any more, either. I'm not going to Cerrmor and make a fool of myself in front of the Prince Regent."

Travaberiel winced. With a sigh he took the letter and began rolling it up again.

Alyssa tried again. "But the gwerbret—"

"You don't understand. Ladoic can be a stupid stubborn man when the fit takes him, but the fits don't rule his entire life. Our treaties with him are the only security the Westfolk have on the coastal border. The horse fairs matter to your people, truly, but not enough to protect us."

"Protect you, good sir? May I ask you from what?"

"From your people, of course. Come now, lass. You must have studied the history of the west in that collegium of yours."

Alyssa sighed and looked away. "I have. I can't blame you, good sir. I'm taken by surprise, I suppose, by your high opinion of our gwerbret."

"The view is different from our side of the river. But beyond all that, the Westfolk aren't as welcome in the rest of the kingdom as they are in Aberwyn." He glanced at Travaberiel. "The Wise One's spent too much time in Lughcarn and the like. You may tell her I said so, too, when next you see her."

"Done, then," Travaberiel said. "I'll come with you to Cerrmor, Alyssa, to make sure you get there safely."

"You'd best not stay in Cerrmor." Maelaber spoke before Alyssa could get a word in. "Rommardda mentioned that feud between the Bears and the Maelwaedds. Standyc won't appreciate Westfolk poking their nose in."

Alyssa started to thank Travaberiel for his offer, but he held up one hand for silence. She heard Cavan's voice, sharp and threatening, just outside the tent. Trav got to his feet fast and had the tent flap open before she or Maelaber could rise.

"What's all this?" Travaberiel stepped outside.

Alyssa followed him in time to see Ela and Joh running up to help Cavan, who was struggling with a portly man, dressed like a merchant, who had oddly short dark hair. As soon as Joh laid a hand on him, the fellow squalled.

"Do not touch me, woman!"

"Hah!" Cavan said. "You're one of Bel's priests, aren't you? I thought so."

The man stopped fighting. Joh laughed and ran an impious hand over the stubble on the priest's head.

"Now you must get purified," she said, grinning. "Not my god!"

His face turned bright red. When Cavan let him go, he made a great show of pulling down his shirt and smoothing himself generally.

"Here," Trav repeated, "what's all this?"

Trapped, the priest scowled back and forth between the herald and the silver dagger, as if trying to decide which was worse. Finally he sighed with a loud exhale.

"We have a right to discover if someone plots against us," he said. "The laws have been in our hands and hearts forever."

"As far as I know," Trav said, "no one wants to change that. It's the gwerbretal courts that have become corrupt, not their sacred advisers."

The priest crossed his arms over his chest and stayed silent. For a change Alyssa was glad that their kind refused to listen to a woman's words. She knew perfectly well that a great many people wanted the laws wrested from priestly control, but why bother telling the truth? Instead she did her best to look humble. Cavan was looking the man over, narrow-eyed.

"A priest you were, at least," he said. "Where's your sickle? I can't believe a true priest would dress up but not have that in a pocket or suchlike. That waistcoat you're wearing's so cursed tight I could see the thing if it was there."

The priest's face blanched.

"The temples throw out garbage like the rest of us," Cavan continued. "I'd wager—"

The man made a growling noise deep in his throat and jerked up a hand, only to stop himself when Cavan laid a hand on the hilt of his finesword.

"I suggest," Travaberiel said to the priest, "that you stop following us. No good's going to come of it."

The priest merely glared the harder.

"Oh, by the hells," Trav continued, "just go, will you? Be gone and stay gone!"

"Now wait!" Cavan snapped. "I want to ask him—"

"He won't answer." Trav laid a hand on Cavan's arm. "Go on!" This last to the priest. "Leave before Cavvo slits your throat for you. I suggest you leave the horse fair, too."

Muttering under his breath, the disgraced priest strode off. Cavan watched him go with murderous eyes. Travaberiel kept his hand on his arm until the priest had disappeared into the thick of the crowd.

"I can follow his every move," Travaberiel said to Cavan. "Now that I've seen him in the flesh, I can scry him out with no trouble at all."

"Of course." Cavan forced out a smile. "Right you are."

More dwimmer. Alyssa felt as if she were sailing on an unknown and stormy sea. Every time the thought came to her, *dwimmer is real*, she felt as if she went to walk across the deck of a ship only to feel the footing fall away from her as the ship pitched in the waves.

Although they did manage to leave the fair and get on the road that afternoon, they only traveled for a few miles before the lowering sun bade them stop. After that first day, however, things went more smoothly without a herd of horses and a large Westfolk escort. The weather stayed fair, and the road, so important to the economy of the fairs, was a good one. Travaberiel reported several times a day that as far as he could see, no one followed them.

"I doubt if trouble waits for us in Mandra," he said. "Bel's priesthood isn't welcome there, but Wmm's is."

"Wait a moment," Alyssa said. "You actually do know that Wmm's priesthood wants the laws written down, don't you?"

"Of course. I just lied to that fat priest." Trav grinned at her. "I'd never lie about the dwimmer, but this has naught to do with that."

That night, Alyssa and Cavan laid out their blankets near a small fire. In the glow of the embers she lay awake, thinking about Maelaber's refusal. Cavan propped himself up on one elbow to look at her.

"What's so wrong?"

"You heard, didn't you, that Maelaber wouldn't help us?"

"Why should he?"

"Well, our cause—"

"Is perfectly just, but he has causes of his own. You've been lucky so far, Lyss, meeting people who've helped you. You can't expect that from everyone you ask."

She hesitated to answer, but only briefly. "You're right, aren't you? Things have been too easy so far."

"Easy? Truly, only getting caught in a riot when the bard died, the threat of hanging, and bounty hunters, and you nearly being turned over to Aberwyn's men, and dragons and—" He broke off in a mutter of laughter. "Easy, she says. Ye gods, you're as innocent as a little child, Lyss!"

She opened her mouth to argue, but the truth of his words stopped her. "I suppose I am. But I'm learning."

"Good. Here's another lesson for you. From now on, hold your tongue when we meet strangers on the road. Don't tell them what we've got or where we're going."

"I won't. You're right again."

In the last of the dying firelight she saw him smile. He lay down, and she could sleep at last.

As they rode south, a different sort of holy person joined their small caravan, one of the Gel da'Thae women who worshipped the goddess Alshandra. She was tall, with a mop of long black hair and skin pale as milk, though she wore so many tattoos that she appeared to be blue and green from a distance. As her kind always did, she was traveling alone and walking barefoot. Her only possessions were the sack on her back and the staff in her left hand, but she was the merriest person Alyssa had ever met. Her name was Rakina, which in her language meant "lucky," and she seemed to think it fitting.

"As long as I have my goddess, I have everything," she told them all, "but if you'll allow me to travel south with you, I'll feel a fair bit safer. The country out here, it's so flat and open." She allowed herself a shudder. "I was raised in hill country. You know where you are there."

"Be welcome," Alyssa said. "And join my fire for a meal."

"I have bread and need naught else." She smiled. "But the Goddess will bless you if you've got a bit of dried fruit to go with it."

"We do, indeed. You don't drink mead, do you?"

"Never. Pure water from her streams and river is enough."

That night, as they sat around a fire and chatted, Alyssa noticed Cavan watching Rakina with a question in his eyes. Eventually he spoke up.

"Tell me summat," Cavan said to Rakina. "Is it true that Alshandra's Travelers have the power to bless a marriage?"

"We do, good sir." Rakina glanced Alyssa's way. "Do you have need of such a thing?"

Alyssa and Cavan both spoke at once. He, "We most certainly do," and she, "Not in the least." She set her hands on her hips and gave him an angry stare—so that's what he thought about her desire to be a wild woman!

Rakina laughed with a toss of her head. "Well, if you do make up your minds, come to me in the morning, and I'll bless you in Her holy name before we travel on."

That night, as they lay side by side in their blankets at the edge of the camp, Alyssa and Cavan argued in whispers.

"You took the betrothal brooch, didn't you?" he said.

"I did. I don't want any man but you, and the brooch marks that."

"Marrying me would mark it more."

"Marrying you admits I did summat wrong that needs mending."

"What? I don't see that."

"Oh, come now, haven't you ever listened to the gossip? And there she is, summat he's picked up off the road, and now he's bringing it home? Or, marry her after he's bedded her, the slut? It's like he pissed in his tankard and now he's drinking the ale. That's what the old people all say, innit?"

"None that I've ever heard."

"Maybe it's different among the noble folk, then."

He was silent for some while. She turned over on her side with her back toward him. The long day's ride had left her sleepy, but her thoughts kept whirling around and around. He's only doing what he thinks is right. He's a pompous ass, and I don't care. You do care. You know you do. He laid a tentative hand on her shoulder.

"Lyss, please?" he said. "Won't you even speak to me?"

"About what? I've told you nay already, haven't I?"

"I don't understand why."

"I don't understand why you keep talking about it."

"Curse it! I love you, and I want us to marry. I know I'm not much of a prize—"

"That's got naught to do with it!"

"But how will I ever be able to face your mother, should I ever get to meet her? What will she think of me?"

"You dog!" Alyssa felt like slapping him, just because he'd pressed on the worst bruise of all. "That's not fair!"

"I'm not talking of fair or unfair. I'm thinking of what I've done to you and what that will mean to your kin and clan."

"The clan won't give a fart or a whistle about it."

"But your kin?"

In her mind Alyssa could see her mother's face, staring at her so reproachfully, so sadly, with tears glistening in her weary eyes.

"Oh, hold your tongue!"

"Hah! That means I'm right, doesn't it?"

She stared out at the dark plain beyond the camp and refused to answer him.

"Lyss, please, listen to me. I know full well you made your own choice in the matter. I know full well you did what you did because you wanted to, not out of pity for me or any other such stupid reason."

He'd finally said the right thing. She turned over to look at him. In the dim light from their dying fire she could just make out that he wasn't smiling, not in the least. He raised himself up on one elbow, and she could see the seriousness in his eyes.

"But I still feel like I've dishonored you," he said.

"You didn't dishonor me. For one thing, I don't feel dishonored."

"I do! I feel dishonorable because—"

She laid a hand over his mouth. "Well and good, then. We'll let her bless us for your sake."

He kissed the palm of her hand and lay back down. "Not yours? Agreed. For my sake, and you have my thanks."

"Truly?"

"Truly. You do."

Hearing that, she could go to sleep in a better frame of mind.

In the morning, when she told the priestess of her decision, everyone in camp congratulated her so much that she almost changed her mind. Only Joh understood. She gave Alyssa a wink and whispered, "Whatever keeps them happy, eh?"

Rakina led them away from camp and road both to the flowerdotted meadow at the edge of the wild grasslands. A white shawl covered her hair and draped over her shoulders. She carried a silver chalice in both hands. When Cavan and Alyssa knelt in front of her, she said a brief prayer, first in the Gel da'Thae language, then in Deverrian.

"May Alshandra grant you eternal joy in each other." She held up the chalice. "Wine mixes with water to the improvement of both. So does male mix with female."

She dipped her fingers into the mixture and sprinkled a few drops on both of them.

"Go forward in life together. And may peace be always between you."

"We shall," Cavan said.

"We shall," Alyssa repeated. "And we'll do our best about the peacefulness."

Rakina favored them with her sunrise-bright smile. "She will bless you forever and always!"

With the ceremony over, Cavan insisted on giving the last of his hire to Rakina as a contribution to her goddess. Alyssa reminded herself that the money was his to spend and no longer Dovina's. Thinking of Dovva made her smile.

Cavan took her hand. "What's the jest, Goodwife Alyssa?"

"I was just remembering that Lady Dovina's on her way to Cerrmor to meet her betrothed. How very odd that I've gotten myself married first."

"So you have." He grinned at her. "It gladdens my heart, and I hope yours, too."

"Of course, or I'd not have done it."

They shared a kiss, but Alyssa was thinking, I've done it indeed. I wonder what Mam's going to say? Naught good, if she even ever finds out. Dovina, knowing her, will doubtless find it droll.

PART 2

CERRMOR

When your kettle of soup is boiling over, be careful how you swing it off the fire.

Old Eldidd proverb

chapter 8

The GWERBRETAL sbIP baD left Aberwyn in splendid weather for sailing, or so Gwerbret Ladoic announced. As always, Dovina felt sick for much of the voyage and kept to the tiny cabin she shared with Mavva. Mavva had no such trouble. She came from a merchant family and had spent her childhood on boats. Whenever she urged Dovina to come out on deck for fresh air, Dovina would turn her face to the wall and groan into her pillow.

"Oh, come now," Mavva would say. "It's been such a pleasant trip! Lovely weather!"

Dovina would groan again, and eventually, Mavva would leave. Her new maid, an Eldidd lass with the typical blue eyes and dark hair, persisted in trying to feed her until Dovina threw a plate of cheese and sea biscuit at her. Dovina did apologize immediately, which disconcerted Polla almost as much as the thrown plate had. Dovina overheard her speaking to Mavva outside the door.

"I'm not used to a lady saying she's sorry," Polla said. "Usually they just act like naught's happened after they scream at you and suchlike."

Dovina felt worse than before and apologized again next time the maid came in, just to make sure she'd done so.

Dovina dressed and came out of the cabin for the first time on the afternoon they reached Cerrmor. The Fox clan's ship, a large merchanter modified here and there to make it more comfortable on its short voyages, glided into harbor but anchored offshore while two crew members rowed a herald to one of the many piers for the formalities. With one exception, no gwerbret or representative of the High King could enter the free city without permission. Since a large crowd of people waited on the pier to greet the Fox party, apparently the permission was going to be granted.

Dovina braced herself at the rail against the gentle rocking of the ship on the placid water. Mavva joined her, and together they studied the view. Cerrmor spread out and up on a gentle slope from the harbor district, cluttered with wooden warehouses and shipyards. Beyond the clutter, houses and shops lined curving streets that proceeded up to what appeared to be bigger buildings. Here and there sunlight glinted on what was probably glass.

"I hate my eyes," Dovina said. "I can't see a cursed thing clearly, not even in the distance."

"Well, it doesn't help," Mavva said, "that they've whitewashed everything. It all sort of blends together in the sunlight. Why is it so chilly here when it's so sunny?"

"Cerrmor's always cold and damp. It's all the fog. It probably just lifted before we got here."

"Um." Mavva pointed at the crowd on the pier. "Can you see that really tall fellow, the Bardekian? Over to our left standing next to whoever that is who's wearing the ugly red hat and the gold chains around his neck."

"The hat and chains mark the Lord Mayor of Cerrmor. I do see the Bardekian. He must be from Orystinna, he's so tall."

"He looks familiar somehow."

Silver horns sounded among the waiting crowd, the signal that permission had been granted to dock. As the ship glided toward the waiting pier, Dovina's eyes began to find their focus. The Bardekian took a step to the side, so that she saw him clearly at last.

"It's Hwlio from House Elaeno!" Dovina said. "He spoke at the collegia a year or so ago."

"That's right! He was brilliant, I thought."

"He was. This could be very useful. Do you remember what he spoke about?"

"The importance of written laws. And allowing all the people who live in the realm to read them whenever they wanted. Useful indeed!"

They exchanged wicked smiles. The ship glided the last few yards to the pier, where longshoremen stood waiting to secure her to the bollards. The waiting crowd cheered. The Aberwyn sailors did mysterious things with sails and ropes and eventually lowered the gangplank. Dovina felt deeply relieved when, at last, she and Mavva were allowed to leave the ship and gain the wooden wharf.

The solid ground she longed for had to wait, however. The mayor bowed to Ladoic, then began a long, rambling speech of welcome while the gwerbretal party stood shivering in the sea breeze. With a muttered insult to her own weak eyes, Dovina scanned the crowd behind the mayor for a glimpse of her betrothed-to-be. She saw several young men who looked much like the portrait she carried in her reticule, but only one of them wore a waistcoat in the red, white, and black plaid of Clan Daiver. That fellow was staring at the group around her, she realized, craning his neck, glancing this way and that as if he looked for a particular person. When she risked a smile and a nod in his direction, he raised one hand in a polite wave.

"Most likely Merryc," Mavva whispered. "He's not bad-looking at all."

"My thanks. I couldn't tell."

Ladoic shot them a nasty look, and they fell silent. Eventually, so did the mayor.

The mayor himself escorted them to waiting carriages. Their luggage and most of the servants would follow in an open wagon. Once everyone was safely stowed, the mayor took the seat opposite Ladoic and the two young women. Dovina's page climbed up beside the coachman, and they set off, rattling through the cobbled streets of Cerrmor.

"Now, the Prince Regent will arrive later," the mayor said. "The royals have a villa just a few miles from the city."

"So, he's not arrived yet?" Ladoic said. "Why?"

"He's been delayed in Dun Deverry, Your Grace. The King has good days and bad days, you see, and the prince needs must stay when his father's mind wanders."

"I see. What about Standyc of the Bear?"

"He's also yet to arrive, and we've not decided where to

accommodate him. We're rarely so honored as to have two gwerbretion visiting us. We are most unusually honored, because a third
man of your rank is also here. Tewdyr of Abernaudd."

Ladoic went very slightly stiff, and his eyes just barely narrowed.

"An honor indeed." Ladoic's voice was smooth—too smooth.

"And his wife?" Dovina put in. "Has she accompanied him?"

"Indeed she has, my lady. In fact, she's planned an elaborate fête
for this afternoon. You've arrived just in time."

Ladoic glanced skyward and appeared to be about to make a remark. Dovina placed a ladylike elbow into his ribs. He stayed silent.
Fortunately, the mayor noticed nothing. He was, Dovina figured,
buried in his own misery at having to entertain three gwerbretion
at once.

Their carriage came to a stuccoed wall and turned in through
wrought-iron gates. The municipal guesthouse, a four-story-high
stone mansion in the newest Bardekian style, vast and rectangular in
pale tan limestone, sparkled with glazed windows. The second and
third stories sported window boxes of greenery and spring flowers at
every window. When the carriage stopped in front of the entrance,
footmen in red waistcoats over white shirts and tan breeches rushed
to open the doors and help the ladies down.

A flight of low steps led up to double doors of dark wood, framed
by slender pillars. As Dovina and Mavva walked inside, a matronly
woman, wearing blue silk dresses clasped by a kirtle in red, white,
and black, came to meet them. She held out both hands and smiled.
Jeweled bangles glittered at each wrist.

"Dovina dear!" Lady Amara said. "So lovely to see you again!
And to meet your friend." She turned to Mavva. "You must be dying
of curiosity. I'm Amara, Lord Merryc's mother."

"This is Honored Scholar Mavva of Aberwyn," Dovina said.
"Fellow guardian dragon of our precious bookhoard."

Mavva smiled and dropped a curtsy. Dovina took Amara's hands
in hers. "It's lovely to see you, indeed. So! You're my mother's fellow
conspirator in this betrothal."

"Of course. Let me come with you up to your suite. I need to officially speak with you so you can meet Merryc in the proper manner."

"By all means. I do hope Mavva and I will share this suite?"

"You will. So proper of you to bring a chaperone. One who I'm sure is most reliable." She gave Mavva a wink.

Mavva blushed. "I hope to be so," she said. "My betrothed is studying to be a priest of Wmm, my lady, so I'll have to behave properly."

On a tide of polite laughter they hurried up the marble staircase together. *Mavva's doing so well*, Dovina thought, *and here I'm feeling rather overwhelmed myself!* Ladoic may have been a gwerbret, but his court looked like a Dawntime hovel compared to the wealth and polish around them.

Their suite matched the rest of the guesthouse. They'd been given three rooms, two with large, luxurious beds surrounded by embroidered hangings, and in the third, cushioned chairs and a settee done in red and white fabrics woven in a maze of braids and spirals. Servants rushed in behind the women, some with Mavva and Dovina's chests of clothing, others with trays of sweetmeats and a glass pitcher of wine with matching cups, which they set on a round table inlaid with mother-of-pearl. The two Aberwyn maids, Polla and Minna, hurried into the bedchambers and began to unpack. Darro trotted in and bowed to the ladies. He handed Dovina a silver message tube with the seal of a hippogriff rampant upon it, the device of the gwerbret of Abernaudd.

"Have you need of me, my lady?" he said to Dovina.

"Not at the moment. Go claim yourself a bed in the servants' quarters."

He bowed again and trotted out. The Cerrmor servants hurried after him, all together as if they were bits of driftwood carried on a strong tide. With a sigh of relief Lady Amara sat down on the settee by the table of refreshments.

"Shall I pour?"

"Please do," Dovina said. "I could use a little wine after that awful ship."

Mavva hovered, but at a gesture from Dovina she took a chair.

"Do you have your reading-glass?"

"I don't. It's in the clothing chest. Here, you'd best read this."

Mavva cracked the seal on the message and shook it out.

"It's an invitation to the fête this afternoon from Rhonalla of

Abernaudd." Mavva tossed the curled pabrus onto the table, then laid the tube more decorously beside it. Amara handed her a cup of wine.

"Things are going to be fraught," Dovina said. "With both Tewdyr and my father here."

Amara sighed. "True spoken. I'm assuming that he and your father still hate each other."

"I doubt if they'll ever stop, not after all these years. They talk about the honor of the thing, but it all comes down to revenue, doesn't it? Tewdyr will never forgive my father for building the second harbor." She glanced at Mavva. "There was quite a lot of boring intrigue around him getting that royal charter."

"Everyone in town assumed that, truly," Mavva said. "The gossip ran wild."

"Father got it, Tewdyr didn't, and the coin has flowed into Aberwyn ever since. But it's the honor of the thing. Of course."

The three of them laughed.

"And so Rhonalla's slinking around like the cat she is." Amara glanced at Mavva to include her. "The lady of Abernaudd, Tewdyr's second wife. She's related to the Prince Regent, you see, through her birth clan, the Sun, the gwerbretion of Cengarn, y'know. Royalty's a distant connection, but I'm sure she'll work it for all she's worth."

"Indeed," Dovina said. "This matter of the law courts is bound to interest her and her wretched husband."

"Ah. That." Amara hesitated. "You really must talk with my son about that, Dovva. Once you've gotten to know him a bit better. Which reminds me. We've not got much time to sit and gossip. Rhonalla's fête looms."

"I gather we really must go."

"Truly, you should. Now, it's a perfectly normal thing to do, to give the free city some coin and have them give your reception or feast for you. A nice sign of gwerbretal generosity and all that. But I suspect she's doing it for reasons." Amara emphasized the word "reasons" with a twitch of a well-plucked eyebrow.

Dovina turned to Mavva, who was looking confused. "She doesn't have much of a position, you see. Tewdyr has his sons from his first wife. All Rhonalla has is that one daughter and what influence she can scrape together. Her dowry wasn't all that much, either."

"Ah," Mavva said.

"No doubt she's a bit put out that you arrived in time for the fête," Amara continued, "but she could hardly fail to invite you. Oh well, we can make some use of it. You can meet Merryc then, all properly in public."

"We'd best wash and dress," Dovina said to Mavva. "I've brought some silk dresses for you. One's a sort of red wine color."

"That will be lovely with your dark hair, Mavva," Amara put in. "I see your maids are busy shaking out your clothes and the like. I'll leave you now, but rest assured, I'll be looking for you at the fête, and I'll come join you immediately."

By the time Dovina and Mavva were ready, the fête had begun. As they hurried down the long hallway to the grand marble staircase, they could hear laughter and chatter. Now and then the sound of harps reached them as well. They went down one floor, then stood hesitating and looking down from a safe distance.

Guests in their finery thronged the great hall. The women wore silk dresses, bright as a flower garden as they sat on cushioned chairs and gossiped. The men looked equally as grand in tartan waistcoats over linen shirts and fine deerskin breeches. Silver and gold glittered in the afternoon light streaming through the glass windows. Buttons, brooches, sword hilts, the women's hair ornaments, the clasps of belts and reticules all sparkled as their owners moved across the black and white tiled floor. At the far end of the enormous room a pair of harpers played near a well-laid buffet.

"At least there'll be food," Dovina said. "I'm starving."

"I'm not surprised. What did you eat on the trip? A handful of salted biscuits, that's all."

At the top of the staircase Dovina and Mavva waited to be announced. Dovina's page darted forward to speak to the chamberlain. Mavva's nerves had finally failed her. She trembled as she stared at the grand reception below.

"You look so lovely in that color," Dovina said. "You'd best remember that you're betrothed."

Mavva smiled, touched the brooch pinned at her clavicle, and grew a bit calmer.

The chamberlain cleared his throat and bellowed. "Lady Dovina of the Western Fox. Honored Scholar Mavva of Aberwyn."

Mavva took a deep breath. Dovina linked her arm in hers and together they descended to the first landing. Down below, Lady Amara made her way toward the stairs through the crowd. Accompanying her was a short, slender woman with black hair. She was wearing a silk dress of rich green, kirtled with the plaid of Abernaudd. Something sparkled just above her left breast. As they descended, it came into focus, and Dovina could see a circle of gold set with rubies and emeralds.

"That brooch!" Mavva whispered. "It's splendid."

"She wears it everywhere," Dovina said. "That's Lady Rhonalla."

"She looks so young."

"Tewdyr's second wife, remember."

They all met at the bottom of the stairs. Lady Amara made the introductions. Mavva and Dovina curtsied, and Rhonalla smiled. She was a pretty woman with raven-dark Eldidd hair but deep brown eyes, shrewd eyes that she was using to study every bit of their clothing and general air. *Veccan was right,* Dovina thought. *We need to put on a display here.*

"My dear Dovina! Your arrival was so fortunate!" Rhonalla spoke with little shrieks at the end of each utterance, but to be fair, Dovina thought, the great hall did ring with noise. "So kind of you to grace my little fête!"

"Oh, but it's a splendid affair." Dovina raised her own voice to be heard, though she omitted the shrieks. "You have my thanks for inviting us."

They stood smiling without another thing to say. Fortunately a servant came rushing up to Rhonalla with some problem about the refreshments. In a wave of regrets Rhonalla allowed herself to be swept away. Mavva let out a sigh of relief.

"Indeed," Amara said. "Find a quiet corner if you can. I see Merryc over there, and I'll just fetch him."

While she fetched, Dovina and Mavva searched and finally found an embayment near a Bardekian statue in black marble. A nearly naked warrior brandished a bronze spear as if he were keeping the worst of the noise away. In a little while Lady Amara hurried to join them. Behind her came a young man and woman, both with dark hair and facial features that were pleasant without being beautiful.

"That's Lady Belina, Amara's daughter," Dovina said. "I've met her. She's a collegium woman like us, but from Queen's up in Dun Deverry."

"Wonderful!" Mavva smiled in obvious relief. "Someone we can talk with."

"Indeed, and Goddess help, that must be Merryc."

Merryc it was. Amara made the formal introductions. Merryc bowed, Dovina curtsied, everyone smiled. Conversation lay dead while Merryc and Dovina stared at each other until Amara stepped in.

"Belina, my love," Amara said, "both Mavva and Dovina are scholars at the collegium in Aberwyn."

"We are indeed." Mavva took up the burden. "It's a very interesting course, centering around the works of Prince Mael. Do you know them, Lady Belina?"

"At my collegium we did read some of his books," Belina said. "But I fear me that the language was so old-fashioned that some of the meaning escaped me."

"You're in luck, then." Dovina recovered her manners at last. "Mavva's special study has been Mael's language. She's preparing an annotated word list, in fact, to help students It's really well done."

Belina smiled in sincere pleasure, and Mavva blushed.

"I should so like to see that when you've finished," Belina said to her. "Perhaps my collegium could acquire a copy?"

"Of course! But I'm not quite finished. As soon as I am, I can make one for you."

"You don't have a collegium scribe?"

"Us?" Dovina rolled her eyes. "Luxuries like that are only for the men's collegia."

"Oh, Goddess help! That's so old-fashioned!" Belina turned to her brother. "I wonder if summat might be done, a subsidy of some sort?"

"It might." Merryc smiled at her and made a half-bow in Dovina's direction. "Allow me to see what's possible."

"Gladly!" Dovina curtsied to him. "And my thanks."

Merryc smiled at her, Dovina smiled at him—both of them vacantly, two people who had just met, two people at the mercy of their family's arrangements. Dovina wondered if he, like her, was deciding if they could bear to sleep together. *At least he has nice muscles,* she thought, *where he should.* She knew perfectly well that her father had political reasons for insisting on this match, and no doubt Lady Amara had them as well. Clan Daiver could not afford sentimental motives.

"You must let us introduce you to some of the people here," Belina said. "Look, my ladies! There's Master Daen!" She pointed to a portly bald fellow wearing the checked waistcoat of a merchant house. "He has a splendid bookhoard down at the Advocates Guild."

"You'll have much in common, I should think," Merryc said.

"I should love to meet him." Dovina picked up the hint. So. This pair had a horse in their race, did they? Or was she reading too much into this exchange?

"I would, too," Mavva said. "I do so love books."

The rest of that afternoon passed in a whirl of important introductions, more or less sincere congratulations on the betrothal, and a great deal of idle chatter. Clan Daiver was land-poor by gwerbretal standards, but coin they had and, even more importantly, influence. Merryc's elder brother served in the High King's court along with the gwerbret's own son, one the Master of Protocol, the other the equerry. Their various sisters had all made good marriages, most to important nobility, one to a favored cousin of the High King himself. Dovina found herself courted so strenuously that she felt like screaming, "Go away all of you!" Instead of course she smiled and made small talk while Mavva did her best to answer questions and fend off the most insistent.

The afternoon finished at last with a formal banquet and speeches that rambled on while pork grease and fruit juices congealed on the official Free City of Cerrmor plates and cutlery. Dovina and Mavva fled to their suite as soon as they possibly could. They flopped down on the cushioned chairs.

"So quiet in here," Mavva said. "Lovely!"

"Indeed. I hope and pray that we've heard the last of the speeches."

"Still, meeting everyone like we did, that's bound to be important."

"Very! We're established. Now to ferret around and learn all the gossip we can."

Gossip came to them, however, in just a few moments, and not in a pleasant way. Polla came out of the bedroom and curtsied to Dovina and Mavva, whom she and Minna insisted on treating like a lady. Her bright Eldidd smile had vanished.

"What is it, Polla?" Dovina said.

"Summat happened, my lady, while you were at that there fetty. Do you know who Lady Rhonalla is?"

"Alas, I do."

"Well, me and Minna, we were helping the cooks set out food. And Lady Rhonalla's maid come up to me and drew me aside, like, out in the corridor, where it be quieter. She said that her lady wanted to speak with me. I was that startled! So I asked her why. Seems like her lady wanted to ask about you and your dealings and such. So I said I wouldn't do such a thing. And so she said there'd be coin in it for me if I would, like."

"Good gods!" Mavva broke in. "What did you say to her then?"

"Naught, because one of the cooks did come out, then, and I went back to my work. But I'll wager this maid, she'll hunt me down later."

"You'd win that wager most handily," Dovina said. "Hmm, what do you think of this, Mavva? Polla, you take her offer and then come tell me all about it. You can keep the coin."

Polla grinned and curtsied.

"If she makes you promise not to tell," Mavva said, "it won't count. Because you're really spying for us, not for her. So any mighty oaths or such won't matter to the gods."

"Well and good, then, my lady. That did trouble me a fair bit, but you're the ones who know all about the laws."

"And the same will apply to Minna, should they approach her, too. Where was she during the fête?"

"Serving behind the long table, my lady. So no one could've talked to her there."

The very next morning Rhonalla's maid approached Polla and Minna while they were carrying out the chamber pots to dump into the latrines behind the guesthouse. They came rushing back with the news and the freshly washed pots, which Minna put away before joining Polla for the report.

"We got a Cerrmor penny each, my lady," Polla said. "And the promise of more. Now, the lady has decided she'd best not risk speaking with us herself, but her maid's been with her for years, like, and so she'll ask us the questions when we get a proper chance to talk, like."

"Very well," Dovina said. "How much does a Cerrmor penny buy, do you know?"

"A hair riband or some sweets at the big market fair."

"Not a bad bribe, then," Mavva said.

"Indeed," Dovina said. "Now, let me think. I know! I'm very tired after the long journey, and I wish to sleep the afternoon away. So I won't need your services for some while."

"Excellent!" Mavva said. "And I need to study a book I brought with me, so Minna will be free, too."

Polla grinned and curtsied to both of them.

The afternoon's spying went well. Out behind the guesthouse were gardens, which included a small grassy area for the servants' use. While Minna and Polla were innocently taking the air and sun there, Rhonalla's maid, Corra, had joined them with a basket of mending.

"We talked about this and that," Polla reported, "and then the questions started."

"A fair flood of 'em," Minna put in.

"It was, indeed. What were you doing here? Who was this Lady Mavva? Was it really all about your betrothal? Had you said aught about whether or not you'd take Lord Merryc? What did we think of the gwerbret himself?"

"Which was quite wrong of 'em, I must say!" Minna said. "As if the likes of us would know aught about the gwerbret. So we made up a tale or two, just to fool her, like."

"Good for you!" Dovina grinned at her. "What did you say?"

"Everyone in Aberwyn knows about His Grace's awful temper, my lady. So we told her about that, and some things about his fine-blooded horses, not that she was much interested in the stables. So we said that he kept getting mysterious messages from the north, and no one knew who they were from, because he took them away from the great hall to read them in private, like."

"Excellent! That'll keep her going," Dovina said.

"Better yet," Mavva put in, "if we hear that tale somewhere, we'll know it comes from Rhonalla, because no one else will know it."

"So we thought. And so Corra gave us five pennies apiece."

"Good." Dovina had prepared for this moment. "And here's two more pennies each to go with them. There'll be a market fair three days from now, and of course you'll both have leave to go."

"My thanks, my lady! We'll have a splendid time, but we'd best be careful." Polla glanced at Minna. "We'll need a good tale to tell as to how we came by so much coin."

"Taking messages back and forth between our lady and her betrothed, if she'd not mind?" Minna looked at Dovina.

"Not at all," Dovina said. "Lots of secret messages! Fit for a bard's tale. My thanks. You can go now. We won't dress for dinner till later."

Once they were alone, Dovina turned to Mavva. "Well, we've made a good start on our ferreting. Let's see what else we can do while we wait for Alyssa." Dovina paused for a grin. "And of course, for the Prince Regent."

During their long ride down to the coast, Alyssa had been wondering if she would ever reach it, much less find a ship to take them to Cerrmor. Eventually, on a sunny day that made the ocean sparkle, her small caravan reached the low rise that overlooked Mandra. Back in the Dawntime, when the People of Bel first arrived in their new world, the Westfolk had lived in splendid cities up in the far western mountains, but a horde of Horsekin invaders had laid waste to them. Some survivors had fled across the ocean to islands south of Bardek; others had taken refuge on the grasslands to the east of the mountains. The islanders did their best to reproduce the rigid society they'd lost. The grasslanders became nomads, raising their horses and traveling where they willed. Over time, the two groups found each other again. These days, many folk came back and forth between the Southern Isles and the Westlands. Westfolk towns flourished once more.

For some moments Alyssa studied the view. "It really is different from Deverry towns, innit?" she said.

"Indeed," Travaberiel said. "Both places follow their own ways, too."

Below them the town of some two thousand Westfolk spread out around a shallow cove that lay just west of the river's swampy estuary. Inside the cove a long breakwater of dwarven concrete protected the actual harbor. The town itself had struck Alyssa as foreign because all the perfectly straight streets met in a tidy grid instead of rambling along in curves.

"I have friends here," Travaberiel told her. "They run an inn. Another friend lives close by, and she's someone I very much want you to meet."

"It would gladden my heart to do so," Alyssa said. "I take it she follows your craft."

"She does, or to be precise, she's a master of it, while I'm but a journeyman. Her name's Valandario."

They rode down into the town and the inn, a pleasant place catering to merchants. Benoic and Joh stayed behind with the gear and horses while Travaberiel took Alyssa and Cavan to see Valandario. Alyssa was expecting that a great master of dwimmer would live in a magical place like Haen Marn or perhaps a luxurious villa in the Bardekian style. Instead, Valandario had a small suite of rooms above a pottery.

Inside, however, the rooms were luxurious enough, decorated like an elven tent with embroidered cushions, Bardek carpets, wall hangings, and the like. On one wall hung an unstrung bow and a sword in a sheath, which Alyssa took as meaning she had a husband or male partner of some sort. Valandario herself dressed simply in a linen tunic over a pair of loose wool trousers, both dyed blue. Pale, very thin, with hair that might have been gray or ash-blonde, she was sitting on a pile of cushions with a patchwork cloth, further decorated with embroidery, spread out in front of her.

"Ah, there you are," she said to Travaberiel. She sounded oddly casual, as if he'd merely stepped out for a moment and come right back in. "Alyssa, greetings! I've heard much about you."

Alyssa curtsied. "I hope it was good, my lady."

"Very. Come sit down, both of you."

As they did so, Valandario folded up the cloth and put it into a small leather sack that lay on the floor beside her.

"Brae's not here?" Trav said.

"Out fishing. Crabbing, actually. It's the right time of year. Now, Alyssa, Travaberiel asked me to make some arrangements for you. I've found a ship, a small coaster, that will take you both to Cerrmor, but they only have room for three passengers. Even that will be a stretch."

"We'll have to leave one of our silver daggers behind, then," Trav said. "Curse it all! We need guards. What about one of the bigger trading ships?"

"Their captains won't interfere, and that's how they see it, interfering." She glanced at Alyssa. "Gwerbret Ladoic is very highly thought of around here, you see. I know he can be blunt and downright nasty at times. Most human men can and do. But he has a decent streak if you can reach it, and he's always been scrupulously fair in dealing with us."

"I see, my lady. I'll admit to being surprised. But then, I'm only a commoner, and he frightens me."

"No doubt." Valandario grinned at her. "Let me tell you a thing about the gwerbret. He very much admires boldness in a person and plain speaking. If you earn his admiration, he'll drop the tableslapping bluster and do what he can to help you."

"My thanks! This could be very useful indeed."

"Let us hope you get a chance to meet him, actually meet him, I mean, not merely see him go past in a procession. Trav, we have friends in Cerrmor, don't we? Can you get Alyssa in safely?"

"Most assuredly. It's her husband we need to worry about." Travaberiel thought for a long moment. "I may be able to arrange sanctuary at the Bardekian embassy. If we can reach it safely."

"If," Alyssa said. "Do you think we can?"

"If I didn't, I wouldn't try. We have some important people on our side, including the Bardekian ambassador and his wife." Trav glanced at Valandario. "You know her, I believe?"

"We've met."

A simple word, met, but Alyssa found herself wondering if some other meaning lay behind it, simply because Trav and Valandario both seemed to be trying very hard to sound casual. Was the ambassador's wife one of those mysterious "friends" Valandario had referred to? *That's the trouble with all this dwimmer,* she thought. *You start suspecting it everywhere!* The dwimmermaster smiled in a suspiciously vague manner and looked at Cavan. She started to speak, then paused to look him over with an unsettling attention. Cavan fidgeted and blushed.

"I know I'm only a silver dagger," he said, "but I intend to make Lyss the best husband I can be."

"I meant no insult, lad. My apologies."

"Accepted, of course." Cavan was staring at the carpet as he spoke.

The uncomfortable silence stretched out until Travaberiel broke it with a cough.

"Anyway," he said, "besides the Bardekians, there are others in Cerrmor who'll be on our side. For instance, Clan Daiver."

"Hah!" Alyssa said. "Dovina's betrothed belongs to that clan."

"So he does." Travaberiel grinned at her. "He most certainly does."

chapter 9

ONLY ONE GWERBRET IN all of Deverry had the freedom of the city of Cerrmor. Verrc, Gwerbret Daiver and head of the Two Rivers clan, had his apartments on the second floor of the clan's town house, a tall stone building with four floors and more chambers than most bothered to count. His late wife—for he was a widower—had done up his private study in masculine tans and white, just touched here and there with gold on the sconces and the brocades of the drapes. Brown leather covered the solid, comfortable chairs. Verrc himself generally sat at his dark oak desk. When his nephew, Lord Merryc, arrived, the old man gestured at a chair.

"You wanted to see me, Uncle?" Merryc sat down and stretched his long legs out in front of him.

"I did, to offer you my congratulations. On your betrothed. Pretty lass, isn't she? And with land of her own. I trust you'll accept her?"

"If she'll have me, I will. Men like me marry to please our clan, I know, but frankly, I'm quite pleased myself."

"Your mother has done you proud. Dovina has a nice little shape to her, too."

"She has, indeed." Merryc allowed himself a brief smile. "More to the point, I'm impressed with her quick wits. She'll need them."

"Because she's marrying into our clan, you mean? She will at that."

A manservant entered with a foaming glass pitcher of dark beer and two tankards. Verrc considered wine fit only for women. Merryc took one tankard and had an obligatory sip. Verrc had a good long swallow and wiped his gray mustache on his embroidered sleeve. The servant placed the pitcher, still on its tray, on the corner of the desk and retreated.

"And of course," Verrc continued, "she brings us a connection with Ladoic of Aberwyn. Very important, that. If naught else, you can draw her out about the real problem. Find out what he's thinking, where he stands, about these cursed law courts."

"If she can be drawn."

"See what you can do." He paused for another swallow of the beer. "A pretty face, but a nice parcel of land, too. Pays a good rent. Your mother looked into that first thing."

"Good. I've got a bit of coin of my own, but for a decent marriage we'll need more than that."

"Just so. Well, if she'll let you know where her father stands, come tell me. Don't write it down or send a page. Not with Tewdyr in the city and Standyc on his way here."

"Understood. If Ladoic finds out we've been gathering information, things could get difficult."

"Hah! Difficult enough already. Did you hear about Gwarl of Aberwyn?"

"I did. Ye gods, have things gotten that bad in the west, to have men taking heads again?"

"First one in a long time, and by every god, let's hope it's the last."

When he left his uncle, Merryc went to his mother's pink and white suite. She was sitting in a bay window with Lady Ledda, her serving woman, and working on a massive embroidery in a wooden frame. Merryc bowed to them both, then flopped down on a nearby cushioned settee.

"Did you speak with your uncle?" Amara said.

"I did. He approves of the betrothal."

"Do you?"

"Very much so. My thanks, Mam."

She smiled and ran her needle into the cloth. She turned a little to face him while Ledda stitched earnestly on.

"But I've heard summat that's a bit troubling, about Dovina and her father." Merryc hesitated, searching for just the right words. "They seem to understand each other oddly well, or so I've heard. As if they were perhaps too close for a father and daughter."

"Who told you that?" Amara leaned forward in her chair.

"No one outright told me. I heard servant lasses gossiping in the great hall. As soon as they saw me, they stopped. Of course, if it's only servants—"

"Merro, dearest, don't be a dolt. Maids gossip to their mistresses. Mistresses pass the gossip on to other women, and usually when their servants are present, too."

"I wonder." Ledda ran her needle into the cloth. "Could it be Rhonalla behind this?"

"An excellent guess." Amara paused for a ladylike snarl. "Merro, pay no attention. It's because of Dovina's poor mother. She's an invalid, you know, and almost never leaves the dun. Mostly she stays in the women's hall with her ferrets. It's rather common, in such cases. The daughter takes over some of the wife's duties, listens to the father, accompanies him to public events and places." She laughed with a sudden snort that wasn't in the least ladylike. "They fight like cats in the stableyard, Ladoic and his Dovva. They're too much alike, is the trouble. Not that either of them will ever admit it, not until the hells melt, anyway."

"Truly? Ye gods, what am I marrying, then?"

"Someone quite unlike you, my darling. Which will make all the difference."

"I'll hope you're right."

Ledda got up and curtsied to Amara. "If you'll excuse me, my lady, let me go ask Pharra if she's heard this rumor."

"Please do!" Amara glanced at Merryc. "Ledda's maid."

Ledda hurried from the chamber. When it came to matters of fine feelings and the subtleties among families, Merryc always deferred to his mother on the rational basis that she understood what he didn't. Ledda returned in just a few moments.

"Well, well, well!" the serving woman said. "Pharra tells me she heard it from Lady Rhonalla's maid, who heard it from Rhonalla herself."

"The nasty little vixen! Rhonalla, I mean, not her poor maid. My thanks, Ledda. You were quite right. Let us all keep our ears open for more of this gossip, shall we?"

"Of course, my lady," Ledda said.

"Just so," Merryc said. "One last thing, Mother. My page told me you're giving a fête here, not in the guesthouse."

"I am indeed. Rhonalla thinks she's ever so well-connected, but her husband doesn't have the freedom of the city, does he? This will show her that spending a lot of coin on a fête can't compete with having one's own town house to give it in."

Merryc smiled at her with a little shake of his head. She often denied caring about such things as rank and status, only to show that she cared very much. He stood up and bowed to the ladies. "I'd best be on my way. Belina and I promised to show Dovina and her companion the city gardens."

Cerrmor's famous gardens lay outside the east gate of the city. Although they were open to all during the day, a high stone wall surrounded the full three acres, and iron gates closed them off at night. Near the gates stood a long wooden roof, supported on poles rather than walls, where the carriages of the wealthy could wait safe from sudden rains. When they drove up, Merryc hopped out first and helped Dovina descend while the groom and the page helped the other two ladies. Dovina had been hoping that this candidate for betrothal would have decent manners, and so far, he'd passed that test.

The gardens stretched out green and pleasant before them. In the distance, Dovina could make out a small hill topped by a small round temple—to the spirit of water, Merryc told them.

"It shelters an artesian spring," he said. "There are other sources of water for the fountains, too, but I'm not sure of where or how they operate. You'll see why it's important."

As soon as they walked through the gates, Dovina did indeed see. Even with her weak eyes, she could pick out the play of fountains that rose like thrown diamonds from beautifully carved basins. Not far in they came to a pair, one on either side of the slate-inlaid path, that depicted the horses of the sea, a mare in one, a stallion in the other, rising from shallow ponds edged in white marble that matched that of the statues. In the basin water circulated in smooth ripples.

One of the gardeners knelt beside the stallion's station and pulled the little weeds that were growing round the base of the pillar. At the sight of the noble-born he started to rise, but Merryc smiled and waved at him to continue his work unbothered. He was an odd-looking fellow, not very tall, with brown hair as short as fur that grew down in a peak almost to his plumed eyebrows. As they walked on, they saw two more workers whose hair grew in exactly the same way, though one of these wore expensive blue linen breeches and a fine white shirt of Bardek silk. These gardeners stood beside a fountain where naked undines made of pale green marble consorted in jets of water, and water lilies grew all around. He was explaining something to his assistant in a language Dovina had never heard before.

"That's one of the engineers," Belina said. "They come from way up north near the Desolation. They're in charge of the city's water supply, too, and it's amazing how well they understand water and the pipes and all of that."

"Indeed," Merryc said. "When one of the pipes breaks, or there's summat of a problem with the sewers under the city, they find it so fast you'd think they could swim."

"No one would swim in the sewers!" Belina said.

"Well, true spoken, but when there's flooding, and —" this to Dovina "— we do get flooding in the winters now and then."

As they walked further in, among flower beds and shade trees, Belina and Mavva talked earnestly about the problems of annotating and copying ancient texts such as Prince Mael's writings. Eventually the two scholars insisted on sitting on a bench to "rest" but, in reality, to allow Merryc and Dovina to walk on together for a little privacy.

"Your collegium's emphasis on the works of Prince Mael interests me greatly," Merryc said. "They're certainly the best exposition of the honor code that I've ever read."

"They are that," Dovina said. "Some might find that code archaic, but certainly we needs must understand it."

"Very archaic, the books and the code both." He paused to study her face as if he were judging her reaction. "At times a concern with honor can be splendid. At others it presents a great danger."

"And not just to the honor-bound man himself." Dovina also paused, then dropped a word into the conversation. "Unfortunately."

He nodded his agreement.

"Sometimes," Dovina continued, "those around an honor-bound man suffer with him through no fault of their own."

"No fault and to no profit to them, either."

"Very well put, my lord."

They strolled on a little further and stopped by the next fountain, a small one for contrast. A tiny marble dragon clung to the rim of a gray stone basin. Its wings were spread, and it leaned over as if it were about to drink the rippling water.

"I'm hoping that you know the situation in Aberwyn." Merryc paused for a long moment. "I heard that there's been some trouble in the streets."

"There has, my lord." Dovina chose careful words. "Over the situation in the law courts, as I understand it."

"So I understood as well."

They contemplated each other in cautious silence. Merryc spoke first.

"I gather that the common people feel they have legitimate complaints about the gwerbretal courts."

"Indeed? Some of us find their complaints justified."

Merryc suddenly grinned, and his nondescript face became for that moment attractive. "So I'd hoped," he said. "Can we dispense with the fencing?"

"It would be a great relief. I take it you know more about the matter than you were going to admit at first."

"I wanted to know what you thought of it. I'd not drive you away with wrong opinions. Now that we've met, I'm quite pleased with your father's offer of a betrothal."

"I see. I'll admit I find it more congenial than I thought at first, too."

They both smiled, but Dovina decided that it was too soon to approve of him in any binding way.

"But about the courts," Dovina said. "I've learned since we got here that the trouble's not confined to Aberwyn."

"Very true. Your father is much more fair-minded, in fact, than many a gwerbret."

Dovina was shocked enough to find herself at a loss for words. Merryc seemed to misunderstand.

"I'm not saying that for idle flattery."

"It gladdens my heart that you find him so. Some of the others must be utterly awful then."

He laughed, and she joined him. "Lughcarn, for example," he said, "but I'd best not be indiscreet."

"Please do! A dear friend of mine has found herself entangled with a younger son of that clan, the one who's become a silver dagger."

"Cavan?"

"The same."

"It gladdens my heart that he's well enough to get himself entangled. He was a page in my father's court when we were both lads. His exile was—shall we say—troubling."

"Did you feel it deserved?"

"I did not, and I said so at the time."

"Then perhaps there's some hope for my friend. Is there any chance he'd ever be recalled?"

"I doubt it. His father's as stubborn as a mule, and his eldest brother won't want him back in their rhan. He's the jealous sort, Carlyn. And now I am being indiscreet. I really should hold my tongue, my lady. There are three sons in that family, you see, and four sisters. Carlyn's the heir, and Cavan's the second-born. Lughcarn's youngest son is here in Cerrmor at the moment."

"And you don't want him to overhear?"

"Just that. Careg's his name." Merryc looked briefly sour. "I suggest you avoid him. I do whenever I can. But the grim news is, the father, Gwerbret Caddalan himself, just happens to be visiting kinfolk who have a villa some miles east of here. Right on the coast, not far at all."

"The vultures are gathering?"

"Hawks, more like." He smiled with a grim twist of his mouth. "Hawks who think themselves eagles."

How much to tell him of their plot? Dovina was tempted to drop a few guarded hints, but still, she hardly knew the man who was going to be her husband. *Amara would have warned me if he were dangerous,* she thought. Still, she kept her language formal and guarded.

"Is summat wrong, my lady?" Merryc said. "You seem so distant."

"I have much on my mind, my lord. My apologies. Do you know when the Prince Regent will arrive?"

"Soon. He sent messengers ahead. My mother tells me that you have some interest in the legal matters before him."

"I do indeed, such as the request for a justiciar on the western border. Our chief bard did me the favor of warning me the lawsuit would come."

Merryc looked away, thinking. They walked a few yards further on, then paused again. "I have reason to believe," he said, "that the prince will hear the bards' request in formal court. I have no idea if he'll honor it or refuse it, of course."

"Of course. It should be interesting, either way."

A cool wind picked up and made her shiver in her light summer dress. Dovina turned and looked southward toward the ocean. Sure enough, a distant gray blur announced fog.

"The weather appears to be betraying us," Merryc said.

"Shall we rejoin the others?"

"By all means." He smiled at her with real warmth. "As my lady wishes. I'll see you again at our clan's fête. May I escort you when it's time?"

"I should be honored. My thanks."

Good! Dovina thought. *He likes this betrothal. I can use that as a weapon should I need one.*

That same morning, Dovina had received a note from Lady Amara about the afternoon fête. Mavva read it aloud once they were back in their suite.

"For the clan members, you know, and family, and a few family friends. Naught too formal. Only some thirty or forty people, and food, of course, and bards."

"Only." Dovina rolled her eyes and sighed. "Well, of course they have to show me off to the bloodkin. The food will probably be good, anyway, so we shan't be too horribly bored."

"Splendid," Mavva said. "I'm getting quite spoiled by these spreads. Going back to the collegium food is going to be difficult."

The fête, however, proved to be less tedious than Dovina had feared. They did meet a small army of Merryc's relatives, which necessitated a great deal of curtsying and bobbing in the hot and crowded great hall. At one point Merryc left Dovina's side to help an elderly great-aunt, who announced that she was feeling faint and needed to leave. Dovina and Mavva retreated to a settee some distance from the enormous buffet while she struggled to remember at least some of her new relatives' names. Mavva pointed out someone they knew.

"There's Hwlio," Mavva said. "The lady with him must be his wife."

"Markella, her name is. Ye gods, she's nearly as tall as he is!"

Hwlio had seen them as well. He waved, and the Bardekian couple made their way through the crowd and joined them. Markella was as beautiful as she was tall, with wide black eyes and thick masses of curly black hair, which she wore swept back with silver combs. While Hwlio's skin was the deep rich brown of Orystinna, Markella's was somewhat lighter, more of a deep tan, which meant her family came from the north coast of one of the main islands of the archipelago. Markella was also pregnant. The beaded kirtle on her red silk gown sat quite high. Mavva got up and with a curtsy offered Markella her seat on the settee.

"My sincere thanks." Markella sank into the cushions. "It really is time for my confinement, I suppose, but I'm not quite ready to be shut away from the world again."

"And do you have other children, then?" Dovina said.

"Only the one. She's with her nursemaid at the moment. Oh, well, at least I have my tiles to amuse me when I'm confined."

"Do you read the fortune tiles, my lady?" Mavva said.

"I do, but just for myself and my friends."

"I certainly didn't think you'd read in the marketplace," Mavva said, blushing. "My apologies!"

"Naught to apologize for."

Hwlio was looking at his wife with his thick eyebrows arched in such a hopeful manner that Dovina saw a possible ploy at work. Here where so many other people might overhear, an open invitation might have caused some wondering.

"I've always wanted to see how the tiles worked," Dovina said brightly. "It sounds so amusing."

Hwlio relaxed. *Message received*, Dovina thought.

"Oh, you must come and let me read yours, then," Markella said. "I'm certainly going to be at home most afternoons from now on."

"As long as I wouldn't be imposing—"

"Not in the least. I'd love to have your company. Mavva, of course this includes you."

"My thanks, my lady," Mavva said. "I'd love to come."

They chatted for a bit more, only to be interrupted by a Deverry man whom Markella introduced as Edry, her physician, a stout gray-haired fellow wearing a blue and white striped waistcoat with his breeches and linen shirt. Dovina recalled that the stripes indicated that he'd begun his medical training at Haen Marn.

"Now, now, my lady." Edry waggled a finger at her. "I don't want you staying too long here and tiring yourself."

"I was just thinking the same," Hwlio put in.

My word, Dovina thought, *they do have this well-planned!*

Markella laughed at both of them. "Then you'll have to haul me out of this settee," she said. "I'm afraid I'm not going to be able to get out by myself."

Grinning, Hwlio helped his wife up while Edry sent a servant to have Markella's sedan chair brought round to the front door. After the usual round of goodbyes and promises of an afternoon visit, Dovina and Mavva found themselves chatting with the physician.

"I must say," Dovina said, "the Bardekians strike me as far more rational than our own people. They respect things like books and learning a lot more, too."

"I quite agree," Edry said. "I studied physick in Bardek for several years, you see, and so I learned a great deal about their ways. I believe this sensible quality of mind owes much to their dark skin, a sign of their abundance of black bile. Their temperament thus tends toward the melancholy, which allows for serious thought and reflection upon weighty matters. The dark skin also mitigates the rays of the sun, which nurture the choleric humor. Thus our pale lords are quick to rage, while a Bardekian archon will take proper counsel before acting."

"Doesn't the sun's light increase the sanguine humor as well?" Mavva put in. "I remember reading that in one of Neb the Healer's writings."

"Quite so." He gave her a little nod. "And I'm afraid our Deverry lords have no shortage of the sanguine in their humors. It gives them the blithe confidence that they may always do as they please, no matter who objects. It's no wonder that the sun turns their pale skin red."

Out of simple coincidence and nothing more, at that moment the chamberlain announced a red-cheeked Gwerbret Tewdyr and Lady Rhonalla of Abernaudd. Dovina stifled a giggle with great difficulty.

Tewdyr, Gwerbret Abernaudd and head of the Hippogriff clan, was a tall, spindly man, quite gray in hair and mustache, and a good many years older than Rhonalla. He had shrewd little blue eyes, narrow at the moment, as he studied the crowd in the great hall. Dovina and Mavva exchanged a look, made a polite excuse to the physician, and drifted over to a quiet corner farther away.

"Where's your father?" Mavva said.

"I'm not sure." Dovina was doing her best to scan the room. "Wait! Is that him there, just coming away from the table where they're serving mead?"

"It is, indeed."

"I hope he's not had too much to drink."

Ladoic, however, seemed both sober and on the alert. He turned back, set the goblet of mead down onto the table, and walked away by a circuitous route through the crowd that kept him a good twenty yards away from Tewdyr. Dovina noticed that Rhonalla was guiding her husband in the opposite direction and liked her a little better. Eventually Ladoic fetched up in Dovina and Mavva's corner. They both curtsied, and he bowed, grinning.

"My thanks, Father," Dovina said. "You're splendid at dancing around Abernaudd and his wife."

"I'm not going to risk spoiling your fête," Ladoic said. "Look at Tewdyr there! Gone straight for the mead, hasn't he? He won't be right in his mind in a bit. If the pair of us get into some sort of a shouting match?" He shook his head. "I think I'll leave and avoid him. I've paid my regards to all of your new kinfolk."

"I haven't accepted Merryc yet!"

"We'll see about that." He grinned at her. "But I think me he's pleased enough with you."

"The question, my dear father, is am I pleased with him?"

"And are you?"

"I'm still deciding. Ancient traditions give me that right."

"Well, then, hurry up about it! Hah! I'll be going back to the guesthouse. Send your page there with a message if you need me."

He made a little bob of a half-bow to each of them, and then strode off. Dovina watched until he'd made it safely out of the door. She let out her breath with a little puff.

"There. That's one trouble avoided!"

But when Dovina and Mavva returned to their suite, trouble was waiting for them. As Darro opened the door for the two women, a piece of pabrus fluttered onto the carpet. He darted forward and picked it up. They went inside, and Mavva shut the door behind them.

"It's some kind of letter, my lady." Darro handed it to Dovina with a bow.

"Where did I leave my reading-glass?" Dovina in turn gave the pabrus to Mavva. "Do read it aloud, will you? Probably another wretched feast or such."

Mavva glanced at it and shook her head.

"If you value your life and health, have naught more to do with your impious rebellion. Evil falls upon the head of those who seek to undermine the ancient laws. You have been warned." She looked up, her face pale.

Dovina stared at her for a long moment until at last she found her voice. "Who could have written that? It sounds too polished to be one of the gwerbretion, and they would have had to write it themselves. You couldn't trust a councillor with a threat like that."

"The script's too finely penned, too," Mavva said. "Priests. That's what the language tells me, priests of Bel."

Darro made a squealing noise, quickly stifled. He looked more excited than frightened.

"Quite so," Dovina said. "Well, when I make enemies, I do a grand job of it, don't I?"

"So it seems." Mavva held the paper up to the fading light from the window. "No watermark. They must have cut this sheet to avoid one."

"What are you going to do, my lady?" Darro said.

"Nothing, of course." Dovina glanced at Mavva. "This makes me more determined than ever. What about you?"

"The same. How dare they threaten us! But honestly, I have to admit, I wish Rhys were here."

"Me, too. It'd be very useful if we could ask the Wmm priests for help. They know everything that's worth knowing. But he's not, and we can't, so let me think. I'm going to hide this bit of evidence. We'll need it."

Not an hour later they heard more of the danger around them when Darro returned to the suite. He bowed to both women, but his flushed face and wide eyes indicated he had something important on his mind.

"What is it?" Dovina said. "Never mind the courtesies."

"My thanks, my lady. The chamberlain told me to go out to the gardens to gather some of the early roses for your chambers. I'd just fetched a basket and knife when this young lord followed me out. He didn't say his name, but I'd recognize him again. It was growing dark but not that dark. So anyway we chatted for a bit, and then he asked me if I wanted to earn a silver piece. And I said how. I thought mayhap he wanted his horses exercised or such. He wanted me to talk about you, why you were in Cerrmor, and was it really all because of your betrothal. So I said I knew nothing above my station, and then I ran back inside. My apologies, I never got the roses."

"We can live without flowers," Dovina said. "Don't vex yourself about that!" She glanced at Mavva. "I think we may have to do summat about all this after all. I forgot that ferrets can get caught in traps."

"Indeed!" Mavva said. "Lady Amara?"

"My thought exactly. Darro, I'll need you to describe this young wretch to the lady. Here, let me write a note, and then you find out where Amara is and take it to her."

"I wonder," Mavva said, "if the chamberlain is part of this, or if he just doesn't want to refuse a request from a priest."

"I wonder, too. Odd that he should send Darro out at sunset, truly."

"Very odd indeed. Darro, I wonder if the other pages have seen or heard anything? Do you know any of them?"

"Only one, my lady. Berwyn. His father's rhan lies right next to ours, but on Gwerbret Tewdyr's side of the border. So he's been fostered to Abernaudd."

"How very interesting."

When Dovina winked at him, he grinned.

"I told him we could play carnoic if you gave me leave. This evening, that is, unless you need me for summat."

"I doubt very much if I will. Some of the other lads might like to play, too. A tournament, like. I'll stand you a Cerrmor penny for a prize."

"They'll be glad to join us now! My thanks, my lady."

"Good luck with the game. For now, go see if Lady Amara's free to speak with us."

Darro bowed and hurried out on his errand. The two women sat down to wait. When he returned, he brought Lady Amara with him. He bowed all round, then sat on the floor to wait for his turn to speak.

"Your page told me you'd received an upsetting letter?" Amara said. "From whom?"

"We don't know." Dovina handed her the pabrus. "They didn't sign it."

Amara sat down in a chair near the candelabra and read the letter. Her face turned as dark and grim as a warrior's. When Darro repeated what had happened in the rose garden, she was silent for a long time.

"I'll just wager that lord was Careg." She got up and moved to a chair farther from the heat and smoke of the candles. "My thanks, lad. You've done your lady good service today."

Darro murmured his thanks and looked modestly away. When Dovina gave him leave to go, he bowed all round and hurried out.

"Well!" Amara said. "This is a nasty little stew you've been served! I'll wager the priests of Bel wrote this. If they lose control of the courts, they lose a great deal of illicit revenue. Those temples are expensive to maintain."

"My lady?" Mavva sounded honestly shocked. "Are you saying the priests do take bribes?"

"It's common knowledge, my dear, here in Cerrmor and up in Dun Deverry, too." Amara scowled at the pabrus in her hand. "Not that anyone would dare try to prove it. Being ritually cursed is as good a threat as hanging."

"I remember a time when I was a child," Dovina said, "and I brushed my hand against what I thought was a bit of dirt on my bed hangings. It turned out to be a huge spider, and I screamed. I feel rather like that now."

"Both sick and frightened?" Mavva said. "Me, too. But, my lady Amara, there's a thing I don't understand. You and your clan seem to be on our side of this combat. May I ask why? Your clan's gwerbretal."

"In name, my dear, in name but not in actuality. Or, to be precise, not in the same actuality as others of gwerbretal rank. Our vast demesne covers some eight hundred acres, a very good-sized farm, it is, and we have milk cows and pigs and some lovely vegetable gardens and a small orchard." Amara paused for an ironic smile. "If one of our herdsmen or gardeners has a legal complaint, we may judge it. Otherwise, everything we have depends upon the royal clan. We serve it. In return, they are generous to us, more than generous at times. Our interests are their interests."

"And their interests lie with justice for the common people?" Mavva sounded puzzled. "I shouldn't have thought—"

"Not precisely that." Amara glanced Dovina's way, a quick glance, almost furtive.

"Go ahead and say it," Dovina said. "It's in the interests of the king to keep the gwerbretion under some restraints. Oh, come on, Mavva! Haven't we been complaining that my father and his peers can do whatever they like, whether it's fair or not? The Prince Regent isn't stupid. He can see where that leads."

"To a lot of petty little kingdoms," Mavva said. "Kingdoms in all but name, anyway."

"Just that." Amara looked relieved to have the matter out in the open. "And then there's the feuds, the stupid bloodshed and trampled crops and unpaid taxes and all the rest of it. How many of those start in a gwerbretal law court? Or in the lack of one, if it's between two of the gwerbretion? As in this matter of Ladoic and Standyc. Most, I'd say."

"Just so," Dovina said. "And the priests of Bel are that spider. I should have realized that they'd consider our reforms an attack on their privileges."

"It is an attack," Mavva said. "Wmm's priesthood are supplying the swords and arrows. The Bel priests must hate that even more."

"We have some proof of that right here." Amara waved the pabrus vaguely in Dovina's direction. "May I give this to my brother? Verrc will be most interested."

"By all means," Dovina said. "If we get any more, I'll give them over to you, too."

"Good, and my thanks. At least we're not up in Dun Deverry where all the gwerbretion have free access. We only have a few to deal with. Your father's one of them, come to think of it. You should tell him about this threat."

"I wasn't going to trouble him. He has much on his mind as it is."

"And this is part of it. I'll tell him if you'd rather not."

Dovina hesitated, then finally decided that Amara was right. "If you could, my lady, I'll be grateful."

At that, Polla appeared in the doorway that led into Dovina's bedchamber. No doubt she and Minna had been listening—not that Dovina blamed them. *I would have done the same,* she thought. "What is it?" she said aloud.

"Er, my ladies, Minna and I were helping out in the kitchens. And we heard the cooks grumbling, because there were two gwerbretion here already, and they'd got news that His Grace Caddalan of Lughcarn and a couple of other high-ranking lords were close by."

"One of Cengarn's sons, too," Minna put in. "The young one who's a tieryn."

"That's Lord Bryn," Amara said. "He stands to inherit the gwerbretrhyn when the old man dies."

"And His Grace Standyc is coming, of course," Polla said. "But they'd been warned about him a long while past."

"Ye gods!" Amara said. "Did they say all these men would be staying in the guesthouse?"

"They said they weren't, my lady, and they thanked the Goddess for it, too, but they figured they'd be in and out, like, ordering dinners and fetties."

"You have my thanks for this news, lass." Amara glanced at Dovina. "Worse and worse. I fear me that they have summat in mind."

"And we're not going to like it at all," Dovina said. "I doubt me if anyone will argue with that."

Gwerbret Verrc was indeed interested in the letter that most likely came from a priest of Bel. He studied it carefully while Merryc sat in his usual chair and watched. Eventually Verrc laid the letter down with a little snort of disgust.

"We need do summat about this," Verrc said.

"Just what I was thinking. I'm surprised the temple would stoop so low."

"Not the whole temple, lad. There are factions within factions. Never forget that. I've seen plenty of it, over the years. Infighting in the temple. Squabbling between them and other temples. The one we have here, a good man in charge. Not like some of 'em. He had a fair right mess to clean up, too, when he took over the head priest's job. He threw the worst of them out of the priesthood. Sent a few others off to this temple they have for priests who need a quiet place to think about things."

"Is that in Cerrgonney?"

"Worse yet. In the Desolation. Not much out there but farmers and the men who guard them. And a few criminals digging those ditches for the water."

"Sounds lovely."

"Very peaceful." Verrc flashed a grin. "And a good weapon for the head priests to wield."

"I wonder what His Holiness would think of this note, then."

"I wonder, too. I'd best have a little chat with Argyn."

His Holiness Argyn, the legally required priest of Bel for their rhan, lived on the Daiver demesne, such as it was, and tended a small shrine to the gods.

"Shall I fetch him?" Merryc said.

"Not necessary. I'll send him a message. He's always glad to get away from the farm and visit the city. He may be able to find out more about this."

"Let's hope he can."

"Indeed. By the by, a messenger from the Prince Regent rode in this morning. He's on his way. In fact, he'll be here on the morrow. Doubtless you'll see him before I do. Tell him that you need to discuss the matter."

"I will indeed, Uncle. Things could turn dangerous."

"Me and the other pages, we played our games of carnoic last night," Darro said. "I heard all sorts of nasty gossip. Tieryn Bryn's got a Westfolk mistress, and everyone says she's an evil sorceress. That was one of the best bits."

"I doubt if she's a sorceress at all," Dovina said. "What I want to know is what people are saying about us. What concerns us, reforming the courts, that sort of thing."

"Well, there was some of that."

"So I thought," Dovina said. "What does concern us? Tell me the worst first."

"Well, it's about Lord Merryc." Darro paused, started to speak, bit his lower lip, thought, and finally came out with it. "They say he's one of those men. The kind who like other men. They say he and the Prince Regent—" He blushed scarlet.

"I understand, no need to say more. What else?"

"That he only wants to marry you for your land."

"That's hardly gossip. Most lords do want land when they marry."

"But my lady, er, that other thing—is that true?"

"Not that I've noticed." She laid a hand on her bustline. "He certainly seems interested in more than my land."

Darro grinned, but a paler version of the blush returned.

"What it says to me," Dovina continued, "is that some people are so jealous they could spit. Every lord wishes he had the Prince Regent's favor, but Merryc's one of the few men who does. Did you hear that rumor from Lady Rhonalla's page?"

"I didn't, my lady. He wasn't allowed to come. I saw him in the great hall this morning, and he told me his lady had forbidden it."

"Oh, had she now?" Dovina allowed herself an evil grin. "Then she knows we're playing a different sort of game. Very good! Fetch my writing things and my reading-glass. I'll write Merryc a note.

You can give it to him before we go to the ceremony. Stress that it's very important. I do think Merryc needs to know what's being said."

Thanks to their special ties to the throne, representatives of Clan Daiver were expected to attend the Prince Regent's entry into Cerrmor. Dovina and Mavva traveled in Lady Amara's town carriage, an open affair that seated four in two facing seats. Darro clung to the back along with one of Amara's footmen, and another footman rode next to the coachman. Dovina noticed that both footmen wore fine swords in clear view of anyone who might consider making trouble. Amara chatted as if nothing at all were amiss.

"The prince will stay in his coastal residence just west of the city," Amara said. "It's a lovely large villa—that's what the Bardekians call those big houses in the country, villas—that used to belong to an offshoot of the Maelwaedd clan. There's still a fair bit of Maelwaedd blood, good Eldidd blood, in the royal line, even though it's been what—how many years?"

"Just over a hundred," Dovina said, "since the heralds decreed the line gone. Though you know, there's summat nagging at my memory. Mavva, isn't there an illegitimate heir somewhere for that clan?"

"I think so, my lady, but I don't truly remember. The heralds should know."

"It hardly matters, I'm sure," Amara said. "Now, once the mayor grants the Prince Regent entry, he'll be able to go back and forth without all this fuss. I'll be giving a reception for him, of course, as soon as I can consult with his chamberlain about days and times and suchlike."

Another cursed reception! Dovina thought, but she smiled brightly when Mavva said, "How lovely!" in a convincing tone of voice.

Although the prince's villa lay to the west, he would enter the city through the north gate thanks to the traditional ceremonies. The crowd waiting to see him gathered inside the city on a plaza. The defensive plan of the city made it impossible for them to wait on the road outside. High walls lined the road leading up to the north gate for some five hundred yards. Any would-be attacker would find his troops funneled through long lines of archers up above. A similar arrangement protected the west gate. To the east lay the gardens, and to the south, of course, was the ocean.

Just before Amara's carriage reached the plaza, Merryc rode up on a golden Western Hunter gelding. He made a half-bow from the saddle to the ladies.

"Did you read my note?" Dovina said.

"I certainly did," Merryc said. "My thanks. I'll attend to it."

Amara raised a curious eyebrow, but the coachman clucked to the horses, and they moved on. Merryc rode beside the carriage, but he stayed just a bit too far away for his mother to question him.

The north and west gates each opened onto roughly circular plazas, some hundred yards across, bisected by the main roads and bounded by the high stone city walls. The heavy wooden gates, twice as high as a tall man and bound in steel, were shut. Armed guards, a herald, and the mayor in full ceremonial garb stood above them on the catwalks, and workers stood ready at the huge winch.

A good-sized crowd of citizens filled the northern plaza, and a number of the noble-born in residence in the city had come down as well on horseback or in carriages. A few enterprising vendors were hawking bits of sweetbread and chunks of roast pork on sticks to the crowd, while a small troop of city guards tried to keep everyone in order. At the sight of the Clan Daiver tartan, the guard captain gave the carriage a place right beside the road.

"My lord Merryc," he said, "if you could sit on your mount just beside the ladies?"

"Gladly, Vrando," Merryc said. "You've got quite a crowd."

"Too many, but who can blame them? We don't get a look at the prince all that often. Should be soon, milord. Him and his escort, they're inside the outer walls already. Just waiting for us to open the city gates."

With a bow he hurried off. Dovina noticed Lady Rhonalla of Abernaudd's carriage just across the road from them. Rhonalla and her companion, Lady Gratta of the Stag clan, sat primly in the back, guarded by a pair of armed footmen. When Dovina waved, Rhonalla waved back.

"Oooh," Mavva said. "What a simpery little smile she has!"

"I want to keep her off-balance," Dovina said. "Let her think we suspect naught."

"Just so," Amara said. "Until we've gathered more evidence."

Silver horns sounded just outside the gates. The murmuring crowd fell silent. The herald called out in a booming voice, barely audible to the crowd except to those directly below. Dovina could just make out "Who demands entrance here?" and some phrase about "garbed in royal markings" or perhaps "garments." No one could hear the answer except the herald and the guards on the wall.

"Does the mayor of Cerrmor grant entrance?" the herald called out.

The mayor said something inaudible.

"Done, then!" the herald said. "Open the gates to Prince Gwardon of the Gold Wyvern, regent for our most honored High King, Maryn the Sixth!"

The workers set to at the winch handle. Silver horns called out again as the gates creaked and groaned and finally, with a great spray of dust, opened. The crowd cheered as the first contingent of the prince's escort, some twenty-five riders, came in at a stately walk. In the first rank rode two flag-bearers, one with the device of the gold wyvern of the royal line, the other with the prince's personal device of a silvery-blue dragon. Behind them rode the prince himself on a golden gelding to match Merryc's. He was younger than Dovina had expected, perhaps in his late twenties at the most, with raven-dark Eldidd hair and, as far as she could see with her weak eyes, a charming grin. He waved to the crowd, bowed from the saddle to Lady Rhonalla, then paused his horse briefly at Amara's carriage for a bow to her and the other women. That close Dovina could see that his eyes were Eldidd dark blue.

"Merro!" he called out. "Come ride with me!"

"Done, my liege!" Merryc bowed to him, then urged his horse forward to fall in beside the prince's mount.

The prince rode on, followed by the remaining twenty-five riders of his allotted escort, with Merryc at his side. Mavva ducked her head this way and that to look between the passing horses.

"Rhonalla looks like she could spit gall and vinegar," Mavva said eventually. "I wish you could see her face, Dovina. Sour as sour and twice as vicious. Hah! Now she's smiling again. Lady Gratta must have said summat to her about putting on a good face for the crowd."

Amara chuckled under her breath. "No doubt. She only got a bow from the prince, while Clan Daiver received a great deal more. Ah, good, look! Here come some of his servitors. The fellow riding the chestnut mare is his chamberlain. I shall ask him about the reception as soon as we all get back."

"Will you invite Rhonalla?" Dovina said.

"Of course. We need to keep an eye on her."

"Is the prince going to stay in your town house, my lady?" Mavva said.

"He has a town residence of his own, but he can only stay in it a single night at a time. Cerrmor guards its privileges very carefully. He has servants there year round, of course." Amara winked. "Unkind souls might call them spies, but I'd prefer to say that the prince likes to stay abreast of local news."

Mavva shook her head with a little shudder. "I'm glad I'm marrying a priest and not a noble lord, but really, Dovina, this marriage looks absolutely perfect for you."

All three of them laughed. The coachman clucked to his team, and the carriage turned into the road to head back to the guesthouse.

The Marked Prince's Cerrmor town house had once belonged to the gwerbretion of Cerrmor. It sat discreetly near the north gate, a squat tower complex in the old style in the midst of a cobbled ward. The outer walls held barracks and stables for his warband on those occasions when he was spending his one allowed night in the city. When they rode into the ward, the men dismounted and, at an order from the captain, took Merryc and the prince's horses off to stable them along with their own.

"I'm assuming you'll dine with me?" Gwardon said.

"I should be honored, my liege," Merryc said.

Although Merryc and Prince Gwardon had been friends since boyhood, they were still bound by rank. Gwardon expected full courtesies, though at times he himself dropped them, only to pick them up again when circumstances changed.

They went inside to the great hall, the entire ground floor of the broch with room enough at its tables for over a hundred men. The table of honor sat on the usual dais across from the door. Gwardon sat down at the head and yelled at a servant to bring bread and ale. Merryc waited to sit until Gwardon gave him leave to take the chair at his right hand.

"I need to thank you for those letters you sent," Gwardon said.

"We're dealing with a nasty little mess from the sound of it. A tangle of gwerbretal vipers."

"Very nasty, my liege. Let's see, we have Aberwyn and Abernaudd here in the city and then Lughcarn some four miles away. He just happens to be visiting his cousin."

"Of course, a mere coincidence." The prince grinned, then let it fade. "Abernaudd I can understand. What happens in Eldidd concerns him. I summoned Standyc and Ladoic, so that fault is mine. Lughcarn makes four. And the Stag clan—let's not forget them—their rhan's not far from Cerrmor."

"True spoken, my liege. So the trouble isn't just confined to the western border, is it?"

"Though it did start there. Who's left on the border? Pyrdon, for one, though I've not heard a word about him or from him when it comes to this matter."

"His law courts are said to be the most justly run in the entire kingdom."

"Which is significant, truly. What about Cengarn? How long before he just happens to be visiting someone in the vicinity?"

"His son's on the way, and his youngest sister's here already, Lady Rhonalla." Merryc reminded himself that she was Gwardon's cousin and spoke carefully. "My mother tells me, my liege, that she's been sending off daily letters to her brother."

"If that's all she's doing, we should be grateful. No nasty gossip?"

"That, too."

"When we were young, we used to play a game summat like carnoic, but made easy for children. There were lots of pieces, all different colors, on the board. If you were playing with Rhonnie, you had to memorize exactly where yours were at all times. Should you be distracted or have to leave the game for a moment, she'd move a couple of your pieces into a less advantageous position. What's the old saying? If the foal limps, the horse will go lame?"

Merryc allowed himself a polite snort of laughter. A servant appeared with tankards of ale and a basket of bread on a tray. She set everything down in front of the two men, curtsied deeply, and hurried away. Gwardon took a chunk of bread and a tankard and waved at Merryc to help himself.

"What kind of gossip?" Gwardon said.

"So far, mostly about me and the woman I may be betrothed to."

"May be?"

"She's not said me yea or nay yet, but then, she's the canny sort." Merryc smiled at the thought. "I'm hoping she'll accept me. Dovina of Aberwyn."

"My congratulations! I hope she does, too. This could be very useful, you having a link to the western border."

"More than a link, my liege. She has land of her own in Eldidd. Near some village or suchlike named Cannobaen."

"Better and better! I've heard of Cannobaen. It has ties to Wmmglaedd and to that Westfolk town further west, Mandra I think its name is. But about that gossip, if it gets too poisonous, I'll have a word with Rhonnie. She loves to curry favor with royalty, which generally means with me. It's one of her better vices."

"Then perhaps, my liege, you might read this." Merryc took Dovina's note out of his waistcoat pocket. "It concerns you, too."

The Bardekian merchants and diplomats mostly lived and worked in the southwest corner of Cerrmor, convenient to the ships but far enough from the clutter around the harbor to be a reasonably quiet district. High walls, stuccoed white, surrounded the compound of the official embassy to the free city. Inside, Hwlio and Markella had a modest residence, a square of rooms around an open court called an atrium. Dovina admired the tiled pool in the middle of the atrium, there to catch rainwater for the household, mostly, but it also sported a lovely statue of a nymph sitting at one corner and leaning over as if to see her reflection.

"The whole thing is Dwrgi work," Markella told her.

"What sort of work? I've not heard the term before."

"The Dwrgi are the people who've built the public gardens and the sewer system and the like. They come from up north somewhere."

"It's an odd name," Mavva put in. "Water dogs? Not very complimentary."

"Truly, but they don't seem to mind. Although, really, some people!" Markella shook her head. "I've heard that the Dwrgi can turn themselves into giant otters. Of all the silly things to believe!"

Markella escorted them into her sitting room, a pleasant space with windows that opened onto the atrium. The servants had arranged cushioned chairs around a square table, ready for the fortune-telling tiles, which Markella kept in a brightly painted wooden box in a nearby cabinet. She set the box on the table.

"Before we start," Markella said, "I have news. Hwlio is doing his best to provide Cavan, the silver dagger, sanctuary here at the embassy. We'd heard about the bounty on his head. It was proclaimed here in the usual way."

"He'll certainly need that!" Dovina said "Will the sanctuary apply to my friend Alyssa? She's journeying here with an important document."

"Or at least, we hope she's on the way," Mavva put in.

"The ruling of sanctuary will apply to both, then. Assuming Hwlio can persuade the council, but frankly, I'm fairly sure he can. Whether or not your friend's on the way, well, maybe the tiles will tell us." Markella reached for the box and smiled in a peculiar way, as if she were trying not to laugh.

She already knows, Dovina thought. *I don't see how she can, but she already knows.*

The tiles were indeed quite clear on that point. Alyssa and Cavan were heading for Cerrmor. They also remarked, almost in a "by the way," that an enemy of Dovina's had badly overreached herself.

erryc was sitting in the great hall of his clan's town house when a servant ushered in a young page. The boy wore the colors of the Western Fox.

"My lord?" the page said. "I've got a message for you."

The lad proffered a silver tube. Merryc fished in his waistcoat pocket, found a couple of pennies, and handed them over in exchange. The tube, he noticed, bore an engraving of the dragon of Aberwyn. He opened it, scanned it, and handed the empty tube back to the lad.

"Tell Gwerbret Ladoic I'll wait upon him directly."

"My thanks, my lord."

The meeting would have somewhat to do with the betrothal, he assumed, although by custom, such details should have been worked out between Amara and the gwerbret without involving Merryc himself. Ladoic, however, had a reputation of being impatient with courtly details. Well-deserved, it turned out, when Merryc arrived at His Grace's suite in the guesthouse. Ladoic himself opened the door and ushered him inside.

"I'm inviting you to a dinner," Ladoic announced, "but I'm not the one giving it. Let me show you summat."

They sat down in chairs in front of an empty hearth. A manservant brought a flask of mead and glasses. Merryc accepted a small drink for politeness' sake. Once the manservant had retired, Ladoic handed over a piece of pabrus.

"Tell me what you think of this," he said.

Merryc allowed himself a low whistle of surprise at the sender, Gwerbret Caddalan of Lughcarn.

"What's he doing here?" Merryc said. "Lughcarn's in the east, far away from the elven border."

"I wondered that myself. Read the rest of it."

Caddalan was staying at a cousin's villa just a few miles from Cerrmor. He was inviting Ladoic, Tewdyr of Aberwyn, Doryn, Gwerbret Buccbrael, and Tieryn Bryn of Cengarn to a dinner in order, as he put it, "to discuss the current threats of rebellion and treachery."

"Does he mean the controversy over the law courts?" Merryc said.

"Just that. I don't see where treachery comes into it. The rebels haven't been sneaking around. They've made their every move cursed obvious."

Ladoic sounded strangely unmoved by either the letter or the events. He appeared perfectly calm, as well as, perhaps—and even more strangely—amused. Probably at me, Merryc thought. I can't think of a cursed thing to say!

"I was wondering," Ladoic continued, "if you'd attend this meal with me. You're practically my son-in-law. And you're someone who has some influence with the prince."

"Some influence, Your Grace, but very little on weighty matters like these."

"But he listens to the news you bring him, eh?"

"He does that. Do you really want me to know what's said at this affair? I might feel moved to repeat it."

"Why else would I be asking you to go with me?"

Once again Merryc found himself speechless.

"Enough of this cursed fencing," Ladoic said. "Things are happening that I don't like, lad. I want your opinion of them, and I want you to know about them. There. That's the truth."

"My thanks. It will gladden my heart to go with you, then. It will be good to see Bryn, too. We spent two years at collegium together."

"Well and good, then. Do you know that they threatened your betrothed?"

"I did, but I thought it was the priests—"

"The wrong kind of priest can be bought. Used like a weapon, eh? They threatened my daughter. The cursed bastards actually threatened my daughter. And she's your betrothed, for that matter."

"True spoken. If I find out who sent that note—" Merryc laid his hand on his sword hilt.

"Good lad! So I asked myself, do I really want to be allies with swine like this? Not on your life!"

"I see, Your Grace. And I agree."

"Good. Be ready close to sundown. We'll be riding. None of these pinch-arse carriages for me, my thanks. And I'll be bringing some of my men with us." His voice turned oddly bland. "You never know what might happen on a dark road."

"Just so. I've no warband of my own, alas."

"Imph. We'll have to do summat about that eventually. Very well. We'll ride by your clan's house and send someone in to fetch you."

"Done then, and my thanks."

Caddalan's cousin, Tieryn Macyn, had a large dun with a rambling residence that could only be called a villa out of courtesy. In the center stood an old-fashioned broch with suites of rooms stuck onto it rather randomly, some of three stories, others of only one. The broch itself housed the great hall, very much in the old style, with two enormous hearths facing each other across the huge room. At one hearth some hundred men sat at long tables drinking, the combined warbands and escorts of the nobles who sat around a round table by the other hearth. As Macyn's chamberlain escorted them to the nobles' table, Merryc noticed that the lords were passing around a sheet of pabrus, reading bits aloud, and laughing.

"Ladoic, Gwerbret Aberwyn, and Lord Merryc of Daiver," the

chamberlain called out—yelled it, really, and long before they actually reached the table.

The laughter and chatter stopped cold. Caddalan slipped the pabrus inside his shirt.

"Evening, gentlemen," Ladoic said. "I see that the Bardic Guild's latest song has reached you."

Silence lasted a moment; then came the babble of everyone talking at once. Finally young Bryn stood up and bowed in Ladoic's direction.

"My apologies, Your Grace," he said. "We were laughing at the clever twists of words, not at you."

Beautifully done, Merryc thought, and the other lords all nodded and smiled. Except of course for Tewdyr—he snorted into his goblet of mead and muttered, "every word fits him, too." Without a thought Merryc stepped in front of Ladoic and went tense, waiting for the sound of a finesword being drawn. Bryn took a few steps in Tewdyr's direction.

"So it does," Ladoic said. "Malyc Penvardd's a clever man."

"And not above turning it against his betters." Caddalan glared at Tewdyr, who shrugged and had a long swallow of mead. "My lords, we have more important things to discuss, don't we?"

Again the nods and murmurs of agreement. The chamberlain stepped forward and showed Ladoic and Merryc to chairs directly opposite Tewdyr's, as far away, in other words, as he could, considering the shape of the table. Maidservants hurried forward with platters of little pastries filled with spiced meats and set them on the table where everyone could reach them. Bread followed, and more mead. Merryc had a polite sip, then let the goblet sit beside his plate. He noticed Bryn doing the same.

"Ladoic," Caddalan continued, "you've suffered more from this than any of us."

"Than anyone else has yet," Ladoic said. "Don't fool yourselves, my lords. This won't stop at Aberwyn."

"It'll roll east like a tide," Doryn said with his mouth full. He swallowed and spoke again. "Better stop it while we still can."

"Just so," Caddalan said. "We don't want another meddling royal justiciar like that stiff-necked bastard up in Cerrgonney."

Maidservants appeared with platters of roasted chickens and still more mead. The conversation continued, a farrago of fears, outrage, and an odd sort of puzzlement. The court system had worked for centuries, they agreed. Why should anyone want to change it? Merryc ached to say, "because it only works for you, no one else?" but he knew better. He ate his dinner and nodded as if agreeing when anyone looked his way. Eventually someone pointed out that their best weapon was Bel's priesthood.

"They agree with us, of course," Tewdyr said. "They stand to lose more than prestige if these cursed commoners have their way."

Everyone nodded solemnly. Doryn underscored the point with a belch. Along with dried apples soaked in white wine with honey, the noble-born chewed over ideas about enlisting the priesthood to their side. Merryc could stand the silence no longer.

"My lords," he said, "they're on your side already. The question is, how widely do you want this known?"

"Quite so." Bryn joined in—the first words he'd spoken for some while. "I've heard hints that they're keeping an eye on things already, out on the western border."

"Good," Caddalan said. "Those piss-poor bards! Unraveling years of tradition, hundreds of years!"

On a round of toasts to the old days and the old ways, the dinner party ended. As the lords stood up to leave, Merryc noticed Ladoic, still quite sober, walking over to Caddalan. He followed at a discreet distance just in case things turned ugly, but the two gwerbretion seemed to be determined to be polite.

"My apologies for the flyting song," Caddalan was saying. "Tewdyr brought it."

"I assumed that," Ladoic said. "But I wanted to ask if you want news of your second son, the exile."

Caddalan stiffened. Ladoic waited, then shrugged.

"I see," Ladoic said. "Just wondered. He got himself into some real trouble back in Aberwyn, and I've had to deal with it."

"Huh! I'm not surprised."

"Summat I don't understand," Ladoic continued. "He always struck me as a decent lad, a credit to his clan and all. I've often wished my own son had his wits. Hah! I see you trying to hide a smile. We all know that Adonyc's a dolt."

"Well, um, wouldn't call him that, exactly. I suppose you wonder why I exiled Cavan. He drew his sword first in a tavern fight and killed an important guildsman."

"Not good, that."

Merryc wanted to shout, "He did naught of the sort!" He made himself stay silent. Later, he would have a private word with Ladoic.

"It's his cursed temper." Caddalan went nattering on. "Ye gods, he drove me and the servants daft from the time he was a little lad, always arguing, refusing to do this or that, giving in to howls and fits when he couldn't have his way." Caddalan shook his head with a little shudder of rage.

Oho! Merryc thought to himself. *He was too much like you, Your Grace.*

"And then that cursed Iron Brotherhood! I wish I could just abolish the thing and be done with it."

"Wouldn't that cause a fair bit of trouble in your city?"

"Too much to risk. I told Cavan he was there to keep an eye on what went on at their meetings. That's why a gwerbret's son is a member, innit? Tell me what the wretched guildsmen are up to, I said. Hah! I won't be a spy, says he. A spy! Nasty word for it, eh? I swore a vow, says he, to keep things secret. He stood there and looked me in the eye and refused to tell me one cursed word."

Ladoic made a sympathetic noise.

"Now Careg has taken his place, and I hear what goes on. Well— what they'll say in front of him, but—" Caddalan paused. "Well, never mind that, eh? I'm better off rid of Cavan, and that's that."

With a nod to Merryc to follow, Ladoic turned to leave. When they walked over to the riders' side of the hall to gather the Aberwyn escort, Bryn hurried toward them. Merryc met him partway. No one else seemed to be paying them any attention.

"I was surprised to see you here," Bryn said.

"I'm about to become Ladoic's son-in-law," Merryc said.

"Ah. Congratulations! Dovina's a lovely lass."

"She is at that." Merryc allowed himself a smile. "Tell me summat. Has there been trouble in Cengarn over the courts of justice?"

"A fair bit, and for all the usual reasons." Bryn paused and glanced around for eavesdroppers. There were none. "We've got to allow some changes. It's become a disgrace."

"I thought you might see reason."

With the noise of all the escorts rising from table, hearing each other had become difficult. Merryc raised his voice.

"Come visit while you're here."

"I'll do that. Soon. I've got to return back west shortly."

They shook hands and parted, Bryn to gather his escort, Merryc to follow Ladoic out to the torchlit ward. While the Aberwyn escort readied the horses, he had his chance at that private word.

"Your Grace, I know Cavan well. He never would have murdered a man in a tavern brawl. He does have a temper, and if someone drew on him, he'd answer it fast enough. But kill a guildsman, someone who's not even armed? He'd never do such a thing. I swear it."

"Huh. Very well, I'll take that under advisement, then. Wasn't there a witness?"

"His younger brother, Lord Careg. Who of course profited by getting Cavan out of the way. As the third son, what prospects did he have?"

"I'll consider that, too. Here comes the captain with our horses. Let's ride."

Merryc had trouble sleeping that night. How far would the top ranks of nobility take their opposition to changes in the legal system? While the central lands around Dun Deverry lay under direct royal rule, fourteen gwerbretion all in all held large rhannau scattered around the kingdom. Some of the land in each was portioned out to tierynau, only a few of whom could act independently, and lords, who did what their tierynau told them to do. None of the gwerbretion would be happy to surrender the fees and income from their law courts. The priesthoods ruled similar hierarchies. Would all the head priests of Bel support whatever course of action the gwerbretion chose? Eventually the questions allowed Merryc to sleep, but he dreamed of battles.

In the morning Merryc decided he'd best consult with Dovina and went to the guesthouse. As he entered the great hall, he saw her page and hailed the lad.

"Where's your lady?"

"In her suite, my lord, with her chaperone and your sister. Shall I take her a message?"

"Not necessary. I'll attend upon them directly."

Dovina, Mavva, and Belina had holed up in the suite like foxes in their den. Before she'd come up, Belina had wheedled a plate of sweet breads out of the guesthouse cooks. Dovina parceled some out to Polla and Minna, who sat down on the floor in a corner to eat them. The three noblewomen were sharing the rest and talking idly of town gossip when someone knocked on the door: three quick raps, two spaced ones.

"It's Merro," Belina said. "We have this code."

At Dovina's gesture, Polla got up, wiped honey from her hands onto her skirt, then hurried to the door and opened it. Lord Merryc came in with bows all round.

"Good morrow to you," Dovina said. "What brings you to me?"

"News of a sort," Merryc said. "I attended an interesting dinner last night with your father. I thought I'd tell you what happened there and get your opinion. You know the situation in Aberwyn far better than I do."

Dovina smiled at him with true warmth. *This betrothal,* she thought, *looks better and better.*

"Do sit down, my lord, and join us." She glanced at Mavva. "You know, I think it's time we told him about the book."

Before they left Mandra, Alyssa sent Benoic to Aberwyn with messages for her mother and Lady Tay. Joh decided to go with him and then take him back with her to the Westfolk lands if he wanted to go.

"Never seen Aberwyn," she said. "Interesting, eh?"

"Hah!" Alyssa said. "It's Benno you want to keep an eye on."

Joh laughed and agreed.

The ship that Valandario had found for Alyssa and Cavan turned out to be a sleek if small caravel, already loaded with cargo for Cerrmor. The captain gallantly let Alyssa have his tiny cabin and told her he'd sleep out on the deck with Travaberiel and Cavan. Although he assured them that the ship was capable of deep-water sailing, for this trip they stayed close to the coast.

"Now if we get a storm," he warned them, "we'll have to put in to the nearest harbor. The Wise One said you need a fast trip, but I'm not risking my boat."

"Understood," Alyssa said. "A wrecked ship won't do us any good, either."

The weather, oddly enough, continued absolutely perfect for the entire voyage, day after day of a brisk but manageable wind that shifted its direction slightly with every twist of the coast so that it always came from dead behind them. The captain and the sailors all took to making the sign against witchcraft every time they came face to face with one of their passengers. Alyssa was tempted to do the same whenever she saw Travaberiel.

Late one night they arrived at Cerrmor, or rather, at a position at sea just outside the harbor. The sailors dropped anchor into the shallow water for the wait—sailing into harbor in pitch darkness meant risking a bad accident at a pier. By lantern light their passengers gathered their luggage near the gangplank and waited. Alyssa sat on deck with Cavan and Travaberiel and looked into the darkness covering the town. By starlight she could just make out the dark mass of buildings and the swirl of river water at the estuary. Once or twice a point of light gleamed in the town only to disappear.

After a long chilly wait, the eastern sky began to lighten, just a show of silver at the horizon at first.

"Light enough for our eyes," the captain said. "We'll take her in now."

"Good," Travaberiel said. "I've got to get these two to the Bardekian embassy before the town's awake."

The captain trotted off, yelling orders in Elvish. As the sky began to brighten, the ship glided into harbor and docked at one of the piers nearest the Bardekian quarter. When Alyssa noticed a group of some ten men waiting, her heart leaped in fear.

"Trav!" she said. "Those men! Are they city guards?"

Travaberiel leaned forward and clutched the rail while he looked.

"They're not," he said at last, "but men from the embassy. An escort."

Alyssa sighed in sharp relief.

"I'll stay on board here, then," Travaberiel continued. "We'll be pulling out when the tide changes."

"It will sadden my heart to see you go. Thank you for all your help. I don't know how to repay you!"

"No payment needed. Stay safe and win your case!"

As the group on the pier hurried forward, she recognized Hwlio of House Elaeno at their head. His men grabbed the baggage, helped Alyssa off the boat, then surrounded her and Cavan for their quick walk through the silent streets. Now and then a dog barked as they passed. Once or twice an early riser stopped walking to look at them, or a woman leaned out of an upper window to empty a chamber pot into the street, but no one challenged them.

They reached the embassy before the sun had truly risen. High walls, painted white, sheltered an imposing compound. Directly inside the ornamental brass gates stood the official embassy building itself, two broad stories of pale stone. To either side flagstone paths ran through low-growing greenery to outbuildings. Hwlio led them around the right-hand side of the embassy to a small square guesthouse set some distance from the walls. He opened the door and gestured at the men carrying the baggage to take it in.

"There's food laid out for you inside," Hwlio said. "I suggest you eat and sleep first, and we can all talk later."

"Excellent idea," Cavan said. "And you have my humble thanks."

CHAPTER 10

AVVA AND DOVINA WERE having breakfast in their suite when Darro hurried in with a message. He handed the silver tube to Dovina with a bow.

"A Bardek man gave me this for you, my lady," Darro said. "He's waiting for an answer."

"How very interesting!" Dovina laid her slice of bread and honey down on her plate and handed the tube to Mavva. "My reading-glass is in the other chamber."

Mavva slid the papyrus out, glanced at it, and whooped in delight.

"We'd love to have you come to dinner at the embassy this very evening," she read. "Someone has arrived that we know you'd enjoy meeting."

Dovina whooped in turn and clapped her hands with a loud smack.

"We'll send a carriage for you," Mavva continued. "If you could write your answer on the back of this note and return it, that might be wise."

"Wise, indeed," Dovina said.

Mavva stood up. "I have my writing case in my bedchamber. I'll just fetch it."

fter the long days on the ship, Alyssa was most grateful for the Bardek-style bathhouse attached to the embassy, but the soft bed in the guesthouse ran a close second, as Cavan agreed. They slept through the day, waking only when a servant came to tell them that dinner would be served in a short while.

"You have friends here to greet you, too," she said. "Lady Dovina and her chaperone. Shall I help you dress, my lady?"

"Thank you," Alyssa said. "Cavvo, get up! We can sleep later."

Once they'd dressed, the servant returned to lead them back to the main embassy building. In an elegant reception room Dovina and Mavva were sitting on a pale blue velvet settee and drinking small glasses of wine. Hwlio was sitting on a matching chair nearby, but Alyssa noticed that he was not drinking at all. As they walked in, Dovina set her glass down and got up to greet them. She caught Alyssa's hands in hers.

"So good to see you!" she said. "Did you get it?"

"I did indeed, or summat just as good, with a letter from the head of Haen Marn herself. I've got so much to tell you."

"And I have plenty to tell you, too."

Mavva got up to join them. "What's that brooch on your dress? Are you betrothed?"

"Married, actually." Alyssa turned to Cavan with a grin. "I never do anything easily, do I?"

"I just hope you've not made the mistake of your life," Cavan said. "I'm honored to be your husband."

"For a silver dagger," Dovina said, "you're well-spoken, at least. But congratulations to the pair of you!"

Cavan made a stiff bow in her direction.

"Come sit down, Lyss," Dovina continued. "We've got some scheming to do. We can celebrate your wedding after we make sure your husband doesn't hang."

"A splendid idea, that." Alyssa took a chair next to Hwlio. "Dovva, I absolutely have to ask! Is your betrothed acceptable?"

"Very, though I'm not ready to tell him that just yet. Lord Merryc of Daiver."

"I know Merro." Cavan sat down next to Alyssa. "He's a good man, my lady. It would be good to see him again if he could stand the company of an exile."

"He's looking forward to seeing you," Mavva said. "He's said so several times."

For a moment Alyssa thought that Cavan would weep, but he collected himself.

"My thanks," Cavan said. "That's good to hear."

A servant hurried in with a tray holding glasses and more wine, which she offered round. As she left, she spoke to Hwlio in Bardekian, and he answered in the same.

"Dinner soon, she tells me," Hwlio said. "Pork stewed with apricots and various vegetables."

"Sounds wonderful." Dovina paused to set her half-full glass down on a little table. "First we need to hear each other's news. Then, what shall we do about the bounty on Cavan's head? He can't live here at the embassy forever."

"Quite so," Alyssa said, "but wherever it is, I'd like him to live a fair bit longer."

"I can see the virtue in that, myself," Cavan said.

Over dinner, between bites of an excellent meal, Alyssa gave the others a report of their journey. Dovina added pieces of information that confirmed one of her fears. Some of the priests of Bel were involved, though apparently the local temple was deeply divided over the issue. With the little sweet cakes toward the end of dinner, the conversation turned to the current situation.

"Things have become dangerous," Dovina said. "I think you'd best leave the book here for now."

"In our bookhoard," Hwlio said. "The cottage is too easy to get into."

Servants have been bribed before, Alyssa thought, but she kept the thought to herself rather than insult the embassy staff. Cavan stood up with a half-bow in Hwlio's direction.

"If you'll excuse me, I'll fetch it right now."

"My thanks. Good idea." Hwlio turned in his chair and motioned to a stocky manservant waiting near the door. "You'll need a lantern."

"Of course, sir." He nodded at Cavan. "If the Deverry lord would come with me?"

Cavan rose, bowed to the ladies, and followed him out.

"I can't tell you how grateful I am for your help," Alyssa said. "It's beyond generous."

"You're welcome," Hwlio said, "but it's very much to our advantage. Consider. Our merchants do a lot of very profitable business in Cerrmor, don't they? It's a free city with its own laws, is why. They practically drool at the thought of expanding the trade to other Deverry ports. They even talk about setting up inland trading stations. What's stopped them, do you think?"

"Aha!" Dovina said. "They can't trust our courts to protect their interests."

"Or their property," Mavva put in. "If some lord decides he can fine them for some infraction or other, what can they do about it?"

"Don't forget the feuds," Alyssa said. "I come from a guild family. No one wants to see their hard work destroyed in a siege or suchlike."

"And there you are." Hwlio nodded at each of them in turn. "Without a proper law code, ye gods, without judges to rule on it, who's going to risk the family fortune to come trade in Deverry?"

"Only the bravest, or perhaps that's the most foolish," Mavva said. "And because of the risk, the prices on their goods are enormously high. You know, it would be to Deverry's advantage to make things more secure, like."

"Coins have voices," Hwlio said. "Let us hope the Prince Regent can hear them."

"There's one voice I know he listens to," Dovina said. "Lord Merryc's."

"Dovva, you've really got to accept him and be done with it," Mavva said.

"Oh, I know. I just keep thinking that there's got to be summat wrong with him that I've not seen yet, that's all."

"No one's going to be perfect!"

"True spoken. Maybe I'm too suspicious. But be that as it may, here's to the regent. He's in Cerrmor, or I should say, at his villa nearby."

They all raised their wine glasses in a toast to the prince. The servants took that as a signal and hurried in to clear the table. Hwlio led his guests back to the reception room.

Cavan returned shortly after with Alyssa's saddlebags. She took out the book, unwrapped it, and laid it triumphantly in Dovina's lap. In its pale leather binding, embossed with a design of interlaced birds and spirals, the massive volume looked oddly innocent for an object that could throw the kingdom into an uproar. Mavva picked up the letter that had come with it and began to read it silently.

"The actual Nevyn copy can't travel," Alyssa said. "I saw it, however, and can swear to its existence."

"No one will argue with this letter." Mavva looked up from the pabrus. "Signed by Lady Marnmara and Lord Kov as well as Adjudicator Perra herself. They swear this is a venerable and accurate copy of the Nevyn book, the oldest in their bookhoard, dating from before the Time of Troubles."

"Excellent!" Dovina stroked the book with gentle fingers. "Let us hope the prince is impressed. I'll ask Merro about how to approach him."

"Hah!" Mavva said. "You used Lord Merryc's nickname."

"So I did." Dovina mugged rue. "I suppose I'm weakening."

"It's a terrible thing, female weakness," Alyssa said with a grin.

"Look what it's got you into, indeed," Dovina said. "Now, here, we've got to figure out what we're going to do about the bounty."

Cavan sighed and slouched down in his chair, a gesture that failed at making him less visible.

"Tell me summat," Hwlio said. "I remember a bit about these laws, but not enough. Can the bounty on Cavan be paid anywhere, or does it have to be in Aberwyn?"

"It can be claimed anywhere that the gwerbret happens to be," Alyssa said, "but it can only be paid in Aberwyn by the servitor he appoints for the job. Otherwise he'd have to travel with all that coin."

"And once it's been assigned, do you have to turn the prisoner over immediately?"

"As soon as you get to Aberwyn. Within five days, assuming that the gwerbret's in residence. If not, you've got to assume responsibility for the prisoner until His Grace returns. Stand surety for him, is the phrase."

"But if the claimant never goes to Aberwyn—"

Alyssa stared at him, then grinned, and finally laughed, a long chuckle under her breath.

"The thing is," Hwlio said, "once the bounty's claimed, no one else can touch him. Am I right about that? Isn't his person sacrosanct under the laws?"

"You are and it is. So is the person that claimed the bounty. That's to prevent bounty hunters from fighting over the prisoner and probably killing him while they're at it."

"So I thought. But Alyssa, it strikes me that this is cursed dangerous. What if Ladoic has one of his famous fits of ill temper and just has his men take Cavan on the spot?"

"If we don't do summat," Cavan joined in, "they'll do that anyway. Here, what are the choices I have?" He held up a hand and ticked them off on his fingers. "Live my entire life as a fugitive, always running, always lying, until I finally die in battle over some petty lord's feud. Surrender and be hanged and done with it, which sounds better to me than that. Or try a bold move like the one you've come up with."

"I'm all for the bold move," Alyssa said. "Assuming His Grace will listen to me, I'll have a speech ready that should melt his heart."

"And," Dovina put in, "there's no reason that Cavan has to come along when you make your claim. Let's not risk that."

"Very true spoken," Hwlio said. "You both are welcome to be guests of the embassy as long as is necessary. By charter, no city guards or lord's men can enter here without my permission."

Alyssa spent the rest of the evening sketching out what she might say to Gwerbret Ladoic. First she'd have to gain his attention. Weeping and crawling and begging as a poor weak woman? A revolting idea, and one she discarded as soon as she thought of it. As she considered what Valandario had told her about the gwerbret, she also realized that such a stance was likely to fail. And how had the dwimmermaster described his usual manners? Table-slapping bluster. Maybe the gwerbret was a good bit less frightening than she'd always thought. She had practical problems to consider, too. Where would she find Ladoic? And who would be with him to witness her speech? There would have to be witnesses of the right sort. She would need to be very careful to avoid even the slightest trace of embarrassing or shaming him. Doing so in front of others would mean instant failure whether or not the laws were on her side.

"This is why we're fighting this battle," she told Cavan. "This is what Cradoc always told me. It has to be the laws, not the man, that define what justice is."

"I've come to understand that this last few weeks. Do you really think this daft scheme has a chance?"

"I do, because Dovina's on our side. I'll be going up to the guest-house tomorrow to talk with her."

"It gripes me that you've been placed in this position. Maybe I should just go back to the long road and—"

"Oh, hush! Trying to wriggle out of our marriage?"

"What? Of course not! I'm trying to spare you the shame."

"I don't want to be spared. I want to get that hypothetical noose off your neck."

He hesitated, his mouth a little slack, his eyes more than a little distressed. Finally he shrugged.

"Well and good, then. I'm grateful, you know. Never think other-wise. Grateful you'd marry me, grateful you won't let me hang." He laid a dramatic hand over his eyes. "Not that I deserve any of it."

"Idiot!"

He looked up with a laugh, and she joined in.

In the morning, Alyssa woke early and spent some while dressing. The embassy servants had washed her road-filthy clothing, not that she had much of a choice of clothes. Finally she decided that her best skirt and scholar's tunic would have to do. Finery would have been out of place, anyway, for a suppliant. She kissed Cavan farewell, said a few brave words that she didn't believe, and left for the guesthouse with an embassy guard, an enormously tall and heavily muscled fel-low named Gurra, for an escort. He must have had some Deverry blood in his clan, because his skin was a light brown rather than the very dark, almost bluish, black of Bardekian aristocrats like Hwlio. Gurra carried a finesword at one hip and a long Bardekian knife at the other. His narrow eyes below bushy eyebrows made him look frightening, but he turned out to be a soft-spoken man with a pleas-ant smile.

Dovina was waiting in her suite, though Mavva still slept. As Alyssa had suspected, Dovina already had a scheme in mind.

"Father's invited Tieryn Bryn to come here and eat breakfast with him and Merryc. They should be arriving shortly. Nallyc's joining them, and Bryn's councillor whats-his-name, and Merryc's uncle, too. The guesthouse has private rooms for this sort of thing. We can march in before they start eating."

"I can't tell you how glad I am to hear you say we."

"Scholars together forever!" Dovina grinned at her. "And besides, if I'm there, Father won't be able to bite you."

It took Alyssa a moment to realize that Dovina had made a joke. She managed to laugh.

For all her jesting, Dovina was as nervous as Alyssa, though for Cavan's sake. She knew her father well enough to know that at the worst, he'd treat Alyssa with cold courtesy—have us both tossed out, she thought, though politely. She had no idea what he'd do in answer to the petition. At the same time, she could see no other way to get her father to lift the bounty. Arguing would only turn him stubborn, or even more stubborn, as she phrased it to herself. While she couldn't see why her friend had wanted to marry an exile and a silver dagger, Dovina would do her best to make sure Alyssa's choice stayed alive.

When they went down to the great hall, a servant directed them to the private room. They followed other servants, laden with plates of sliced ham and fresh bread, into a sunny chamber, hung with fine tapestries of hunting scenes. Windows looked out onto the long lawn behind the guesthouse. The men sat at a round table near the windows. At first only Merryc noticed Dovina and Alyssa; the others seemed to have assumed they too were servants. He turned in his chair and started to greet them, but Dovina laid a finger on her lips. He smiled and said nothing.

Alyssa took a deep breath—Dovina could hear it quite clearly— and stepped forward.

"Your Grace!" Alyssa said. "I am a subject of yours from Aberwyn. It aches my heart to disturb you, but I have little choice. I call upon my right to petition the gwerbret."

Ladoic slewed around in his chair. The servants and councillors

froze, the other lords sat stone-still as well. Alyssa curtsied to them
and to the gwerbret. Ladoic looked her over, then noticed Dovina
standing off to one side. He quirked an eyebrow. She mouthed a
"Please listen."

"Very well." Ladoic turned to Alyssa. "You are?"

"Alyssa vairc Guildmaster Avar."

"I've heard your name. One of our rabble-rousers."

"One of the worst, Your Grace, but I'm here on a private matter."

Ladoic laughed, just a mutter under his breath, but a good sign
nonetheless.

"You've placed a bounty on the head of Cavan the silver dagger,
an exiled son of Caddalan of Lughcarn. I've come to claim it."

"Now that's a surprise! How did you capture a man like that?"

"He's my husband, Your Grace."

Tieryn Bryn had taken a sip of ale. He snorted and nearly spat it
out but managed to swallow in time. Dovina noticed Gwerbret Verrc
kick him under the table. Councillor Nallyc froze with a slice of
bread halfway to his mouth. Bryn's councillor pursed his full lips
into an O. Ladoic himself showed only a mild surprise.

"But you'd turn him over to me?" Ladoic said. "He must be a
cursed bad husband."

"He's a splendid husband, Your Grace," Alyssa said. "Our laws
say that I can't turn him over to you unless we're all in Aberwyn. But
I can lay claim to the bounty wherever you may be. And once I do,
it's mine and belongs to no other."

"True spoken."

"So, Your Grace, I have to take him to Aberwyn to hand him over
and receive the coin."

Ladoic abruptly understood. His eyes narrowed in anger. Dovina's whole body tensed in a fear so strong that she couldn't speak.
Alyssa waited, as calm as if she were merely studying the tapestries
behind him on the chamber wall. For some moments Ladoic kept
staring at Alyssa as if he couldn't believe her effrontery. She returned
his scrutiny with the same modest calm. Suddenly he laughed, a
pleasant bellow of sheer delight.

"Well done, lass. Very well done!" He turned to the other lords.
"You see what kind of folk I have in Aberwyn? It's no wonder I'm
proud of the place, eh?"

The others nodded and murmured a word or two. Merryc looked close to laughing out loud. Ladoic turned back to the petitioner.

"No doubt it'll be a long time before you and he see Aberwyn again, eh? Am I right?"

"You are indeed, Your Grace. But since I'm a guildsman's daughter, I'll point out that during that long time, you get to keep the coin."

Ladoic chuckled and smiled. "Very well, Alyssa vairc Avar," he said. "I accept your claim."

Dovina felt her jaw slacken of its own accord and her mouth fall open. She shut it again.

"My thanks, Your Grace." Alyssa curtsied to him. "My very humble thanks! I shall tell everyone I meet how generous and noble you are."

"No need for flattery! Cavan the silver dagger is now under my protection until you and he return to Aberwyn." Ladoic turned to the men at the table. "Let's see, the formula runs how? I think it's because the bounty has been assigned. Let no one give him or his wife a jot of trouble." He nodded at Councillor Nallyc. "Do we make a public proclamation or suchlike?"

Nallyc looked so stunned by what had just occurred that it took him a long moment to answer. "We ask His Grace, Gwerbret Daiver, if we may consult with the mayor, I should think."

"Of course you may," Verrc said. "Matters of law always come first in Cerrmor. The city will lend you a herald. Mayor's a fair bit sharper than he acts sometimes, and he'll go along with it, I'm sure."

"Excellent," Ladoic said. "We should attend to that today."

"Your Grace?" Merryc put in. "I'll be glad to act as your messenger. Cavan's an old friend of mine."

"Mine, too," Bryn said. "Anything I can do to help?"

"Take the official messages back to your father," Ladoic said. "And tell everyone you meet along the way. Very well, Goodwife Alyssa. You may leave our presence in safety. Your husband had better stay in his den at that embassy until Lord Merryc's spoken with the mayor. We want word to get about."

"Your Grace is ever so generous." Alyssa curtsied first to him, then to Verrc, then again to Bryn and finally Merryc. "I thank you all from the bottom of my heart."

Dovina started to follow Alyssa out, but Ladoic rose from his chair and signaled to her to linger a moment. As soon as the door shut behind Alyssa, the whispers and the talk broke out among the men who'd witnessed the scene. The servants looked as if they would burst from having to hold their tongues. Ladoic caught Dovina's hand and led her a little apart.

"Hah! Speechless, I see. Probably the first time in your life." He chuckled to himself. "Your friend has almost as much spirit as you do."

"So she does, Father." Dovina found her voice at last. "I'm so glad you find it acceptable."

"How could I not admire her, eh? The sheer unmitigated gall of the lass, but ye gods, it served her well. Reminds me of you. No wonder you're friends, whether she's a commoner or not."

"Just so. And she had the laws as her shield."

"You would say that!" But he continued smiling. "You'd best go join your friend. Merryc will probably tell you later what we're going to discuss here. Good lad, that one."

"I rather think so, too, but of course, I'm not quite ready to agree to the betrothal. A lass must know her own heart before she commits herself."

Ladoic snorted. "Get along with you! We'll talk later."

Once the two women and the servants had all left, the men got down to discussing the matter before this impromptu council: what to do if indeed the other gwerbretion started an armed rebellion. Merryc looked at Bryn and raised a questioning eyebrow.

"I was indeed approached," Bryn said. "I weaseled in the hopes of learning more. But as far as I can tell, no one truly wants an armed rebellion. They're hoping that if they hint and threaten, Gwardon will back down."

"The Prince Regent," Verrc put in, "isn't going to back down on anything."

"I know, Your Grace, which is why I weaseled. Maybe I'll hear more that way."

For a few moments they all ate in silence. Finally Ladoic wiped his mustache on his sleeve and put down his table dagger.

"The only one of us who could afford to arm a true rebellion would be Caddalan. Maybe it's a good thing he's a miser, eh?"

Everyone laughed but dutifully.

"There are other kinds of rebellion, my lords," Nallyc pointed out. "A refusal to pay taxes, for instance, or allow the king's men access to their cities."

"A cursed sight better than open warfare," Bryn said.

"It would turn to fighting soon enough, my lord."

The others nodded in agreement.

"Is there aught we can do about it?" Ladoic said. "Now, I mean."

The consensus, after a long and heated discussion, was that they couldn't. Watch and listen, try to sound out other lords who might be of the same mind as themselves—small things, but at the moment, nothing better presented itself.

When the meeting broke up, Bryn and Merryc left together. They walked outside and lingered on the steps of the guesthouse.

"I was thinking," Bryn said, "that we should stand Cavan a tankard or two. Once it's safe for him to leave the embassy grounds, anyway."

"Splendid idea," Merryc said. "Why don't you send your page with a message? I'm on my way to the mayor's. I'm just cursed glad there's summat we can do for our old friend."

"Me, too. Trust Cavan to marry a lass like that! She may be a baker's daughter, but ye gods, she's got the heart of a Bardek lion!"

"She'll need it, married to him."

The mayor had a public office above a tavern, which turned out to be closed when Merryc arrived. The barman, however, hinted that his lordship might well find Mayor Eddel at home.

The mayor and his family lived in apartments supplied by the city at the top of the civic broch down near the harbor. A tall tower rose four stories high in the midst of smaller, squatter towers of varying heights. Since he often ran unofficial errands for his uncle, Merryc knew the complex. He was expecting to wait for some long while in the public reception area down below, but as soon as he gave his name, a clerk escorted him up the four stories of a narrow winding staircase.

"Ye gods!" Merryc gasped. "These stairs!"

"You get used to them after a bit, my lord. Cursed good thing, too."

Eddel opened the door himself, a typical Cerrmor man with high cheekbones and narrow-set blue eyes. Although he'd lost most of the usual Cerrmor blond hair, he was on the young side of forty. With a bow he ushered Merryc inside to a small, sparsely furnished greeting room—a couple of plain chairs, a small table, and, on the wall, a sea-green cloth banner decorated with the device of the mayor's office, a pair of grappling badgers. The room, and Merryc could assume the entire set of chambers, smelled of frying onions.

"I was hoping you'd honor me with a visit, my lord," Eddel said. "Come sit down."

"My thanks." Merryc removed a small toy horse from one of the wooden chairs, then sat.

"Ah, the children!" Eddel said. "Don't pick up after themselves no matter what the wife says to them." He brushed some indeterminate crumbs off the seat of the other chair before he sat down. "I've been a bit worried, my lord, I don't mind telling you, about all these noble lords and gwerbretion turning up in my city."

"I know the folk here don't much care for the noble-born."

"Excepting your clan, of course. You're all family, like, and none of you swagger and sneer. But be that as it may, I hear things, you know, from those what wait upon the other kind."

"No doubt. Angry words? Threats?"

"Just that. Talk of war, my lord. And it's my job, like, to keep this city safe."

"Let me be blunt. There's talk of a rebellion against the Prince Regent, but so far it's only talk. It should have naught to do with Cerrmor. A matter of honor, mostly, a dangerous matter, but a thing among the noble lords only."

"So far, eh? These things tend to get out of hand."

"You're right enough. My uncle and I will be working to contain it. So will another gwerbret, one I can't name at the moment."

"Well and good, then. Free city or no, Cerrmor's bound to supply archers to the Marked Prince should he call upon us. I need to know when to summon a muster. It'll take us a day, like, to get everyone ready to go."

"I understand that. It's fifty archers, innit?"

"A hundred in times of open war, my lord. Fifty if the prince chooses to accept fewer."

And their provisions, Merryc knew, meant another thing to assemble, as well as weaponry from the armory. "Wouldn't hurt to put them on alert. As soon as I hear anything, I'll send you a message if I can't come myself."

"My thanks, my lord. Very fair of you." Eddel paused, thinking, then shrugged. "Now. What brings you to me?"

"A request. Gwerbret Ladoic of Aberwyn has just assigned the bounty on a fugitive, a silver dagger named Cavan of Lughcarn. The man's in town but in pledged custody. He might be seen on the streets. The gwerbret sent me to ask you for a public herald to proclaim that the bounty's been assigned and the fugitive's person is sacrosanct."

"Easily done, my lord. Let me get my keys, and we'll go down and fetch the bells."

The Justice Hall occupied the second floor of the tower. An antechamber led into a high-ceilinged chamber crammed with chairs and benches enough for at least a hundred people. At one end stood a dais with a table and a free-standing cabinet. Eddel unlocked the cabinet with a big iron key. On the inside of the door hung the city's golden Sword of Justice in its leather sheath. Eddel rummaged among the boxes and bags cluttering the shelves and at length brought out two big brass hand bells on wooden handles. He gave them to Merryc to hold while he locked up the cabinet again.

"Now we go out on the street, my lord, and I'll ring one of these ladies. The heralds live right round here, and if they're sleeping, it'll wake 'em up."

The bell rang loudly enough to wake the dead, Merryc decided, once he heard it clanging in the open air. Dwarven work, Eddel remarked, and as solid as always. Two heralds came running to the summons. One of them had pulled his red and white striped tabard over his head but had yet to fasten the ties at the sides, so that it flapped around him as he hurried up. The other carried his tabard bunched up in one hand and a chunk of bread in the other, part of his morning meal, Merryc assumed.

"Very good, lads," Eddel said. "We need a bit of news proclaimed around town."

The heralds may have lacked the polish of the royal staff up in Dun Deverry, but Eddel only needed to repeat the message twice for them both to have it perfectly memorized. Each took a bell and hurried off to spread the news that Cavan the silver dagger had been turned over to the proper authorities on his wife's pledge. None were to harass, harm, or murder him or her on pain of hanging.

"That should do it," Merryc said. "My thanks to you, Eddel. If I hear summat definite about the rebellion, I'll make sure you know."

Cavan had spent a miserable morning waiting for Alyssa's return. The embassy compound sported a walled garden—a long rectangle of grass around a rectangular pool, both bordered by red and yellow roses. Cavan walked around and around on a little flagstone path until he was sick of the sight of the flowers. Now and then he met a member of the embassy staff, or the gardener or another servant, all of whom greeted him politely and smiled. He always answered the same way, but he felt shamed to realize how uneasy it made him that everyone he saw had dark skin. Some of the embassy people were so dark that they seemed to gleam in the sunlight; others were more of a reddish brown, but all of them struck him as alien. He'd grown up in the north of the kingdom, and while he'd certainly been taught about Bardek and its people, he'd seen very few of them.

These people are saving your wretched life, he reminded himself. He returned to the guest cottage and flopped into a chair to brood until he was equally sick of calling himself a fool and a dolt. He sighed, got up, went to the window, looked out, sat down again. After some while of this it occurred to him that he was making the wait worse.

"I should find some way of . . . summat to do with myself . . ."

The walls had no suggestions to make. His mind returned to brooding and inevitably found his most painful loss, the rituals and lore of the Iron Brotherhood. It was in some ways an odd organization, peculiar to Lughcarn with its dangerous smelters and forges, a charity, really, dedicated to helping the workmen injured or sickened by the process of turning Cerrgonney ore into hammered steel. But thanks to visiting sages like Rommardda, the lodge had an overlay of dwimmer practices, such as regular meetings to work rituals of sorts. Ostensibly these rituals existed to bond the members of the lodge and remind them that charity was a service to the gods, just as holy as sacrifices in the temples.

Cavan had always wondered if they meant more, if they pointed the way to something splendid and mysterious. The lodge meetings had been the light of his life, back when he was the middle son of an important noble, a lad who existed only in case his older brother died. Now he'd lost them thanks to his own stupidity and the lies of his younger brother, that stinking flea on the Lord of Hell's balls . . . he stopped himself from thinking about Careg.

The rituals, now, there was a good thing to remember. In his mind he could see their meeting place so clearly, first the wild meadow in the torchlight, then the long procession to the hunting lodge they'd taken over for their rituals. At the door the sentinel would challenge and each member respond with the password and the name of their rank. Inside, by firelight, he saw again the big chamber and the banners, the officers in their positions with their swords, and he himself would take his place as Sword of Fire.

Gone, now. He could not bring himself to say the ritual words, not even to himself. He got up and paced over to the window again. Alyssa was hurrying down the little path, and he could see that she was smiling. The past is gone, he told himself. Let's see if you've got a future.

He crossed to the door and flung it open.

"We've won!" she called out. "He assigned me the bounty. You're safe!"

She ran to his arms. He kissed her, laughed, kissed her again and again until with a laugh of her own she wiggled free. He shut the door and stood grinning at her.

"Do you remember what the Westfolk dwimmerwoman told us?" Alyssa said. "Under the bluster, she said, Ladoic's a different man. Well, she was right. At first he was furious, and then he laughed and agreed with me. They're going to put the news about, Cavvo, that your person is sacrosanct, and then you can leave the embassy grounds."

"Safe! I can hardly believe it, Lyss!"

"No more can I, but it's true. Well, safe as long as we never go back to Aberwyn."

He stopped smiling. "Your family."

"Ah well, many a woman has to leave her clan behind when she marries." But her voice trembled on the words.

"Ye gods, forgive me! I'm not worthy—"

"Will you stop that? It's vexing, seeing a strong man grovel."

He sighed and sat down. In a moment she took the other chair.

"The future will do what it will do," Alyssa said. "I was offered a place at Haen Marn. And Dovina offered me a place here in Cerrmor for when she marries Lord Merryc. They'll have apartments in the clan's town house."

"You with your fine wits, little better than a serving woman?" A worse thought struck him. "The collegium."

"There's one here. No doubt I can win a place in it." But her voice nearly broke.

"Better you go back to Aberwyn, and I stay on the long road. That's the one cursed thing I'm good at, fighting in some other man's battle."

"Stop it! Do you think I want to lose you?"

"I don't know what to think. That's the sad truth of it."

She looked away with a little sigh. "I don't, either. But there's got to be a way out of this. Just give me time. Summat will occur to me."

"But—" He stopped at his sudden realization. "You know what, Lyss? I don't doubt that it will."

After he left the mayor, Merryc had gone straight back to the public guesthouse to give Dovina his report. Out in the courtyard he saw Gwerbret Tewdyr's captain and ten men of his escort standing by their horses. A fine ladies' carriage waited at the head of their line, and a laden cart at the end. Merryc dodged around the crowd and walked into the great hall. Bryn was leaning against the wall near the door.

"What's all this?" Merryc jerked his thumb in the direction of the crowd just outside.

"My dear cousin Rhonalla!" Bryn rolled his eyes heavenward. "She's leaving Cerrmor in a nasty snarling huff. I'm waiting to bow and bid her farewell whenever she and her companion get their lady-like selves down here."

"I see. Do you know why?"

"She had some sort of conference with the Prince Regent. She did not like what he said, whatever it might have been. I don't suppose you—"

"You know cursed well I know." Merryc grinned at him. "She was spreading some rather vile gossip around, some of it about my betrothed. Anything to damage Aberwyn, y'know. But she overreached herself. Some of the mud stuck to the prince himself. I'd guess he's just brushed it off."

"I see. Ah, there they are now!"

With her head held high, and her jeweled brooch glittering on her traveling cloak, Lady Rhonalla, dressed in black for the occasion, was descending the stairs, slowly, tragically, even, with the air of someone falsely accused going to her hanging. Burdened with jewelry cases and a bouquet of roses, Lady Gratta followed, chattering all the way.

"I'll leave you to your farewells," Merryc said. "She won't want to see me."

"Or you her, I should imagine. Well and good, then. I've sent Cavan that message about a tankard."

"Good."

Merryc turned to go, but he'd waited too long. Rhonalla left her companion behind and swept up to him in a rustle of fine silk skirts. When he bowed, she made no answering curtsy.

"I gather you were the one who told the prince those lies about me," she said. "Making trouble between my cousin and me!"

"Lies? None, my lady. Only the truth as I saw it."

She flushed scarlet.

"At least my husband understands what an insult I've suffered," she said. "He knows that it reflects on his honor as well as mine. He's taking the insult to heart. Your precious Dovina had a hand in this, I'll wager. She might regret it soon enough."

With that she turned away and swept off again. Bryn caught Merryc's glance, rolled his eyes, and hurried after her. *Trouble,* Merryc thought. *It's not just some woman's matter, not any more. Gwerbret Tewdyr's not the man to let any stain on his honor go unscrubbed.*

"Poor dear Rhonalla," Amara said.

"My heart bleeds for her," Dovina said. "Poor thing!" They shared a particularly nasty laugh.

"On the other hand," Mavva said, "Gwerbret Tewdyr is furious."

"True spoken," Dovina said. "True and very dangerous. I shouldn't let my glee get the better of me."

"No more should I," Amara said. "Mavva, have your maids heard anything more?"

"Quite a lot. Tewdyr's manservant has taken a liking to our Polla. He told her that His Grace is, and I quote, rampaging around about the insult to his wife."

Dovina winced.

"A pretty second wife and an elderly lord," Amara said. "Usually a recipe for trouble. He'll blame the prince for this, I should think."

"Indeed he does." Merryc appeared in the doorway. "May I join you?"

"By all means," Dovina said, "We'll need another chair."

Merryc smiled and came over to sit on the floor at her feet. "This will do well enough."

"As long as my lord is comfortable." Dovina returned the smile.

"Very, my thanks."

Amara folded her hands in her lap and radiated satisfaction. *She's done awfully well with this betrothal,* Dovina thought. *I'm surprised she's not purring like a cat.*

"As if His Highness doesn't have enough on his mind," Dovina said. "There's the matter of my father's wretched feud to deal with. I gather Standyc's here in Cerrmor."

"He is," Merryc said. "Are you going to the hearing, my lady?"

"When is it?"

"Tomorrow morning."

"I'd best be there. My father might need calming down."

"True enough. I have this afternoon free, my lady. Is there anywhere you and Mavva would like to go? I can escort you."

"There is indeed. We're waiting for Alyssa. She has letters to deliver to the Advocates Guild. One of them's from the temple of Wmm."

"From your betrothed, Mavva?" Amara said.

"Someone a bit more important than Rhys, my lady," Mavva said. "It's all rather complicated."

"And Merro, once she gets here," Dovina said, "we'll have her tell you about some things that happened after they left Haen Marn. The priesthood of Bel's definitely been taking a hand in this."

Although Merryc had no warband, he did have two men for bodyguards. Alyssa appreciated his bringing them both to join Gurra when he escorted her, Mavva, and Dovina to the Advocates Guild. Although the Cerrmor heralds were hard at work announcing her and Cavan's legal status, the news had yet to spread far enough for her to feel safe.

The guild owned a modest building in Old Town, the maze of narrow streets and timeworn buildings upriver from the new center of the city. Respectable if poor people lived there among the little shops and outdoor stands selling cheap food such as scraps of pork in bread or fried fish wrapped in a cabbage leaf. Many of the lodgings were so old and rickety that allowing cookfires inside would have presented far too great a danger to those renting them. One of these streets dead-ended in a section of wall, joined to a squat broch tower.

"This was once part of Dun Cerrmor," Merryc told them, "back in the Time of Troubles. There's a little garden in the back with an incredibly ancient tree and a spring, so the guild does have clean water if not much else."

Alyssa smiled politely at the joke.

"The wall must have housed stables then," Dovina said.

"Just that. Those wooden doors lead to lodgings of a sort—the old barracks. Mostly sailors who need a place between voyages."

Inside, however, the broch displayed a fair bit more wealth and comfort than its surroundings. The great hall held some twenty polished tables, but not for warbands. Scribes worked at some. Others held heaps of books, both bound in the Deverry style and scrolled in the Bardekian. Mavva made a little "oh" sound of longing under her breath.

"I don't suppose they'll let me touch them," she said.

"Some look almost as crumbly as ours," Dovina said. "So you'd better not."

A young man, dressed in fashionable doeskin knee breeches and a spotless white shirt, hurried up to their party. He bowed to Lord Merryc, who acknowledged him with a nod and a smile, then to the women in turn.

"What brings you to us, my lord and ladies?"

Alyssa stepped forward. "I have a letter to personally deliver to the guildmaster. It's from His Holiness Olnadd, high priest of Wmm on the Holy Island."

Merryc caught his breath with a little gulp.

"Someone more important than Rhys, indeed," Dovina muttered.

The lad waiting upon them bowed at the name. "If you'll just come with me? We have a reception room for visitors."

A well-appointed comfortable room, it turned out, with a scatter of cushioned chairs and huge tapestries on the walls. Their guide saw them settled, then hurried out to tell Lord Daen, the guildmaster, that they waited. He returned quite quickly with the lord himself, a third son of a poor clan who'd taken to the guild as much for love of learning as for lack of land. Daen was stout, middle-aged, and nearly bald, with narrow blue eyes that surveyed them all kindly enough.

Alyssa rose from her chair and curtsied. She took the message tube out of her kirtle and handed it over.

"I was told to deliver this to you, my lord, and only to you."

"Good." Daen hefted the tube. "My thanks. So, you're Alyssa vairc Sirra, are you? I've heard about your exploits."

"Good things, I hope, my lord."

"Good depending on the rank of the person telling me." He gave her a quick grin. "Good enough, in short. I've had a note from Malyc Penvardd, asking if you may speak at a hearing, if indeed there is one."

"He honors me, my lord. I hope not unduly."

"I hope not, too. Tell me about your education. Aberwyn's a long way away, and I don't know much about the collegium there."

"In our first two years, we did the three paths. Logic, grammar, and rhetoric. Most of the women go on to do geometry and astronomy, but I was allowed to study the bardic lore with the men at King's Collegium."

Daen's eyebrows rose. "Did you do well?"

"I won the Scholars' Cup that year, my lord, so some thought I did. There's always more to learn, though."

"How did the men you studied with take your victory?"

"Badly. Oh, they were furious." Alyssa couldn't stop herself from laughing, just briefly. "I loved every moment of it, after the grief they'd given me."

"I see. Well, it sounds to me that you're fit to speak at a hearing. It takes courage as much as learning, you know, to stand in front of the regent. Very well. If this putative hearing actually takes place, you have my permission."

"My thanks, my lord, my humble thanks." Alyssa curtsied again. "I'll do my best to keep from disgracing you."

"I've no doubt of that. There's someone here who wants to meet you, Alyssa." He turned to the others. "Would you like to see our bookhoard? It's the one thing we have to show off, you see. Most of our work here is rather tedious, or at least, it looks tedious to visitors."

Mavva nearly leaped from her chair to curtsy and agree.

Everyone rose and filed out after Lord Daen, leaving Alyssa alone to study the ancient tapestries and wait. Faded, torn in places, the weavings had all been sewn to new cloth to allow them to be displayed. One showed King Bran and the omen of the white sow that had told him where to found his holy city; another, Great Bel dispensing justice in the cloud-dun of the gods. The third, however, newer than the rest, displayed a story she'd not seen before. On a riverbank a group of strangely dressed men holding spears confronted a band of Deverry warriors. Alyssa was studying it when she heard the door open behind her.

"The founding of Cerrmor," a soft female voice said, "or at least, the negotiations with the people who originally owned this land."

Alyssa spun around to see a tall, slender woman with white hair, cropped off like a lad's, but a young-seeming face, handsome rather than pretty. She closed the door behind her and came over to look at the tapestry. She was wearing men's clothes, but on her they seemed oddly womanly, the breeches of very fine blue cloth, the shirt embroidered with flowers in the Westfolk style under a pale gray waistcoat.

"My name's Hild," she said.

Alyssa curtsied. "I'm Alyssa vairc Sirra, but I suppose they told you that."

Hild smiled and looked her full in the face. Alyssa felt that her gaze had impaled her, pinned her to the wall behind her, or turned her to stone, perhaps, because she could not look away. Hild's gaze seemed to judge her innermost soul, not just the superficialities of her face. With a little nod of approval, at last the elder woman looked away and released her.

"I'll give your ancestors some honor." Hild waved a hand at the tapestry. "They didn't slaughter and enslave those people. They paid them for the land with cattle. The tribe didn't understand what coin was, you see, but they herded cows and appreciated new stock."

"It gladdens my heart to hear that. Do you know what happened to them?"

"Their descendants are with us still, much mingled by marriage and all that. Such as my own clan." She paused briefly. "Look at the biggest person in the tapestry. Someone embroidered details to make their hair yellow and their eyes narrow. You see that today, don't you? Our spirit is very much alive in Cerrmor, at any rate."

"Your names, too. You don't hear names like Hild and Aeddyl out in the west."

Hild smiled. "It became a fashion, like, to give children the old names, back when Cerrmor became a free city. You see, our elders believed in various odd ideas. While they had leaders, they had no noble lords or kings. Everyone was of equal worth in their primitive tribes."

"I've read about such things. In the old days our people believed things like that, too."

"What do you think about them? The ideas, I mean."

Alyssa hesitated only briefly. Fear had no place in this chamber. "I wish we still believed them. I wish they could come again."

"Good. They might. Rivers change their beds now and then, and the wind blows where it wants to. Every sailor will tell you that it's grand, having the wind at your back."

"Uh, so I've been told. I don't quite understand—"

Hild spoke as if she'd not heard her. "Do you have a weapon? Or at least know how to use one?"

"I have this." Alyssa pulled up her tunic's hem and revealed the elven knife in its sheath. "A Westfolk woman showed me how to use it."

"Excellent! Huh, I always wondered whom that blade would claim."

"Well, I didn't claim it, exactly. I—"

"Nah nah nah, I meant it claimed you."

Dwimmer again! Alyssa thought.

"Carry it with you at all times," Hild said. "You may need it."

With a little nod her way, Hild turned and left. Alyssa was still staring at the closed door when she heard Lord Daen talking just outside. He opened the door with a flourish. The rest of her party waited in the corridor.

"Lord Merryc tells me you'd all best be getting back," Daen said. "My thanks for visiting, Goodwife Alyssa."

"My thanks to you, good sir. I'll treasure this meeting in my mind."

He smiled, then bowed her out of the chamber.

As they walked back through the narrow streets, Alyssa was thinking mostly about Hild. Who was she? That she had dwimmer seemed obvious. The wind's at our back—the times were ready to change? Is that what she meant? A shout from Gurra yanked her out of her reverie. Lord Merryc tapped her arm and guided her forward to rejoin the others. She'd fallen a bit behind.

"We're being followed," he said. "Come walk with Dovina and Mavva. My men will guard the rear, and I'll join Gurra at the front."

As he did so, she noticed that he'd laid his hand on the hilt of his finesword. A glance back showed her that the bodyguards were following his example. Hild's warning about her knife took on sudden meaning.

Possibly because of the precautions, they reached the guesthouse without incident. Once they were safely inside, Merryc remarked that he'd seen the spy before.

"He's an attendant at the Temple of Bel," Merryc said. "I'm not sure if he's a novice or only a servant, but he opened the door when I went there recently, running an errand for my uncle."

"Huh!" Dovina said. "These priests aren't very good at snooping, are they?"

"They're too used to having everything their way," Mavva said. "Well, or so my betrothed tells me."

"No doubt he's right," Merryc said. "Alyssa, when you want to return to the embassy, my bodyguards will go with you."

erryc left the company of the ladies and hurried off to join his uncle. That the Advocates Guild would welcome Alyssa and Dovina so warmly was something Verrc would want to hear. He found another guest there ahead of him, His Holiness Argyn, servant of Bel, priest of the Most Holy Shrine to the Great God that stood upon the estate of Clan Daiver. Since he was attached to a shrine, not a temple, Argyn wore ordinary clothes, a shirt under a waistcoat, gray breeches stained green in spots from his garden, boots instead of sandals. He did, however, wear the tiny silver sickle of his office hanging from his belt. A tall man with a pronounced belly, he settled himself in a chair with a comfortable sigh and accepted a tankard of dark beer.

"What the high priest doesn't know," Argyn said, "won't keep him awake at night."

"Just so," Verrc said with a grin. "How are things at the farm?"

The members of Clan Daiver tended to refer to their estate as the farm, being as it was one.

"Very well, Your Grace. The first roses are blooming in front of the shrine, and I've been planting some cabbages and other greens in my kitchen patch."

"Good. While you're here, will you be joining your brethren at the temple?"

"I already have this morning early, when we place the garlands on the statues. Important ceremony, though you should hear the neophytes sneezing in the morning chill. They're not used to bare legs yet."

"And then you joined them for the morning meal?"

"I did, the usual oatcakes and an egg or three." Argyn considered the gwerbret over the rim of his tankard. "What's all this, Your Grace? You don't usually care where I get my feed."

"I'm hoping you had a chance to pick up some gossip about—oh, various things."

"Ah." Argyn grinned and had a long swallow of ale. "I'm guessing it has summat to do with this matter of the law courts."

"You're good at guessing, Your Holiness."

Verrc nodded at Merryc to give him permission to speak.

"I've had some news about the goings-on out west," Merryc said. "Priests dressing up as merchants. A man knocked on the head and dumped into a river."

"Indeed. The news reached us, too. I heard some talk about that this morning. Wmm's priests have been sending letters around. They're right enough when they say it's a disgrace to every priesthood, not just ours."

How much of a disgrace? Merryc wondered. Argyn owed Clan Daiver a great deal, including freedom from the closed temple life that he hated, but there were limits to any man's loyalty when the gods had a prior claim on him.

"Murder tends to be disgraceful," Verrc said. "Especially when the killer's sworn to uphold the laws."

"Oh, the killer would have been found outside of the temple and paid for," Argyn said. "I'll wager that the fellow who did the hiring was turned out of our Cerrmor temple last year, when His Holiness took over. Still a dishonor to the priesthood. I mentioned I'd come to town at your behest, Your Grace. The head priest would like me to come back to temple for dinner with him after our visit. For a chat, he said. What do you say to that idea?"

"I'd say it's a good one," Verrc said. "He must have heard the talk that's going around. The holy blade harvests more coin than it does truth—that kind of remark."

"Indeed." Argyn paused, thinking. "The Lawspeakers are a priesthood within the priesthood. Some forget who's the trunk and who the branch." He held up one hand flat. "Not all, mind, some."

"Understood," Merryc said. "When there's an important hearing, who chooses the Lawspeaker?"

"Omens, of course." Argyn paused for a grin. "Omens need interpreting, however, and His Holiness Tauryn does that. He's a good man, but he has to be careful. He can't insult important men by keeping them shut up in the temple all the time. The Prince Regent's hearing, now? I'm less than fond of the brother they're sending for that. It will be interesting to hear how well he does."

While Alyssa was visiting the Advocates Guild, Cavan occupied himself by remembering the rituals of the Iron Brotherhood. Some marked the initiation and progress of the membership; others marked the installation of new officers; a third type marked the seasons of the year and the phases of the moon. Together they occupied several evenings a month, and after each the brothers met to discuss the business of the lodge—raising funds for injured ironworkers and their families, finding apprenticeships for children who had no interest in working metals, and the like. Most brothers hurried through the rituals as just so much showy ceremony, but Cavan had loved them. He could feel the power that flowed through the lodge when the ritual was in progress, power that mostly went to waste, but power nonetheless.

Rather than merely thinking about them, he found, he could recreate snippets of them in his mind—not the entire long procedures, but certain pieces of the ritual that had particularly impressed him. He sat bolt upright in a chair at the cottage and imagined himself sitting in the ritual chair assigned to the Sword of Fire while he spoke pieces of the ritual aloud or merely pictured someone else taking part.

At first his mind wavered from the imaginary ritual to the noises outside as servants walked past the cottage or birds chirped and the like. But as time passed, the inner world began to seem more real than all the distractions around him. He could smell the smoke of the ritual fire, hear words spoken by the misty figures around him, and yet he never slept. Part of him remained aware of his body, the light in the little chamber, and the feel of the chair under him. The rest of him, however, had drifted far away to the ritual tent in the fields outside Lughcarn and the fire that burned during each working.

The smoke! He could smell it so clearly that he was on his feet and standing before he even knew what had alarmed him. Pale gray smoke swirled in the little room. He rushed to a window and flung it open, then turned and ran into the bedroom. No fire. He saw not the slightest glint of flame and light. Nothing in the main room, either, and with the window open, the smoke had mostly fled.

From outside he heard excited voices calling out in Bardekian. Someone pounded on the door. Expecting a servant, he opened it to find himself face to face with Markella, the ambassador's wife, accompanied by one of her women. Behind her stood two menservants carrying buckets of water.

"There's no fire," Cavan said.

"So I see," she said. "May I speak with you for a moment?"

"Of course, my lady." He bowed to her.

Markella dismissed the menservants, who dumped the water onto a flower bed and trotted off. With her chaperone following, she led Cavan to the little garden. Vastly pregnant as she was, Markella sat on a small bench with the serving woman standing behind her. Cavan knelt on one knee on the grass nearby.

"I can't think of any clever way to lead up to this," Markella said. "So, were you working dwimmer just now?"

"What? I wasn't! I know naught about it, well, except for the things we did in Lughcarn. I mean, I belonged to this group, you see, that did charity things among the ironworkers, and we also met for, well, I suppose you'd call them rituals."

"I suppose I would, indeed. And?"

"Well, just now I was merely remembering some of them. I'm an exile, you see, and lost my standing at the lodge. But it all still means a great deal to me."

"That smoke. We all smelled it."

"Well, fire was part of our ritual. The smelting, you know, and working with iron. My title was Sword of Fire. I can tell you that much, but—"

"No need to reveal secrets. But did you call that smoke up?"

"I couldn't have. I don't know how. I was just remembering it."

Markella considered him for a long moment. She looked thoughtful, not angry or unkind. He felt a sudden flare of hope.

"Uh, my lady? What makes you ask?"

"I have a bit of talent that way. And there are—well, let's just say that these things send messages to someone who can hear them. I'd picked up summat, and then Olanna here came running to say the cottage was on fire."

"My apologies. I didn't mean to alarm everyone."

"It's quite all right. Are you studying with someone?"

"I'm not. I was told I shouldn't, that I'm unfit."

"By whom?"

"Rommardda of the North."

Her eyebrows quirked. "A woman worth listening to, certainly. But I wonder. I suspect you've got too much talent in these things to ignore." She rose from the bench. "You need to be trained. I can't promise you anything, but who knows? Let me send her a letter, shall we say? I'll ask."

"I'd be very grateful."

"Don't be. An untrained talent is a danger in more ways than one, so at the worst she just might want a working done that would close everything down for you. Are you willing to risk that?"

"I am. I'd risk anything to learn more. I've never wanted anything more in my entire life than learning about —" he could not quite force himself to use the word dwimmer "— these things."

She smiled. "Good answer. I'll also warn you that her decision will outrank mine. But let's just see."

Markella and her serving woman hurried away. Cavan rose and stood watching as they left the garden. For the second time in a few short days, he felt hope mingled with raw fear.

chapter 11

AFTER SOME DISCUSSION BETWEEN the regent's royal councillor and the mayor of Cerrmor, the hearing concerning the feud on the western border took place in the Justice Hall of the Cerrmor civic broch, a larger room than the justice chamber in the prince's little-used town house. Since the regent presided thanks to the mayor's courtesy, the usual title given to such things, malover, was laid aside, but the prince's decisions would have the force of royal law behind them. Before the proceedings began, a crowd of the curious assembled, but between the escorts of the nobility and the prince's bodyguards there were precious few seats left.

As part of Lady Amara's retinue, Dovina had arrived early. Their combined rank gave them good seats off to one side, close enough to the front for Dovina to be able to see. When she looked over the crowd, she saw Alyssa also off to one side, standing with Master Daen of the Guild. She must have visited the marketplace, because she'd bound her hair back with the flowered scarf of a married woman. With her rumpled skirt and plain tunic, she looked like a market woman herself, very much the commoner. *Thank the Goddess I went to the collegium,* Dovina thought. *I'd never have paid her the least attention if I hadn't.*

Before any of the men, lords and commoners alike, were allowed to enter the Hall of Justice they were required to disarm. With a clatter and a fair amount of grumbling, those who carried arms put their swords and daggers on long tables guarded by the regent's sworn men. Once everyone was seated, the mayor, golden sword in hand, climbed the steps up to the dais. Accompanied by his councillor, two guards, a priest of Bel, and Merryc, the Prince Regent came through a small door at the back of the dais, nodded to the mayor, and acknowledged the crowd with a wave of his hand. A few cheers rang out, hastily suppressed when Prince Gwardon scowled.

"This hearing is now open," Mayor Eddel said. "Under the jurisdiction of the High King in the person of his regent, Prince Gwardon Maryn." With a flourish Eddel handed the prince the Cerrmor Sword of Justice.

"My thanks," Gwardon said.

Eddel bowed and retreated to a corner. Merryc left the dais and found a place to stand near the door. The bodyguards stepped back. The bare-legged priest, dressed in his traditional tunic with a silver sickle at his belt, came forward and blessed the sword. The prince knocked the pommel thrice upon the table, then laid the sword down crosswise in front of him. The prince and the priest took chairs behind the table. The watching crowd fell silent except for one last cough and sniffle from the back.

"Your Holiness, Lawspeaker," Gwardon said to the priest, "is it just that even the highest lords in the land are subject to the laws of the gods?"

"It is both just and right, Your Highness." The priest had a deep voice that rolled through the entire room.

"Well and good, then. I have a matter to lay before you. The town heralds have proclaimed that Gwerbret Ladoic has granted the bounty on a certain silver dagger. Are we, the gwerbret and I, correct in thinking that the person of this man and of the one who claimed the bounty are now inviolate?"

"Until such time as the bounty has been paid over, that is quite correct. It's an ancient tradition with the force of law."

"But not law itself?"

Curse him! Dovina thought. *What's he trying to do? Undermine everything?*

"Not law, perhaps, my prince, but the ancient traditions run very deep and strong. In such cases, they must be obeyed."

"I see. You have my thanks."

Don't curse him after all, Dovina thought. *This will be blessedly useful!* The royal councillor leaned forward and murmured something. Gwardon and the priest both nodded their agreement.

"Done, then," the prince said. "Now. Two matters have been laid before me. The first is the question of disputed lands between Gwerbret Standyc of Pyrdon and certain magistrates of the people known as the Westfolk. By treaty Gwerbret Ladoic of Aberwyn is entitled to represent them and will do so when we reconvene on this matter."

On the word "reconvene" whispers spread in the crowd. The prince half-rose from his chair. The whispers stopped.

"We have received messages that two Westfolk magistrates wish to attend any discussion of that case to advise the gwerbret. Hence the delay." Gwardon spoke to the priest but loudly enough for the crowd to hear. "Today we will adjudicate on a graver matter. We call Gwerbret Standyc and Gwerbret Ladoic to come stand before the Sword of Justice."

Anyone of a lesser rank would have been required to kneel, but strict procedure tended to loosen in the presence of gwerbretion. The laws had long since recognized that insulting men of that rank was a good way to turn a legal proceeding into an outright brawl. Standyc and Ladoic walked up to the dais, bowed deeply to the prince and the priest, and then stood at either end of the long table.

"My thanks," Gwardon said. "We are here to investigate one grave and unclean crime: the taking of the head of Gwarl, son to Gwerbret Aberwyn, after a battle upon Pyrdon roads."

Noise broke out—gasps, whispers, outright oaths in the crowd. The prince allowed it to continue for a few moments before he silenced it.

"The charge has been laid," Gwardon continued, "that the captain of Gwerbret Standyc's warband committed this crime against our laws and those of the gods."

Standyc stepped forward fast.

"He did it at my orders, Your Highness," Standyc said.

"Your orders? Were you on the road that day?"

"I was not. I had spoken earlier in my great hall, saying that if ever I or any man in my service had the chance to bring me the head of one of Ladoic's sons, I would want it done and want to see the proof of it."

Dovina glanced around. The people in the crowd sat in dead silence, but their faces—disgust, horror. Lady Amara had laid her hand over her mouth. Mavva leaned forward a little in her chair, all attention.

"That was an evil day," Prince Gwardon said.

"So it was," Standyc said. "But—so if there's fault found, let it come to me, not him."

"If there's fault? Ye gods, how can you say that? Don't you know the sacred laws against such a—"

"Let me explain." Standyc raised a hand flat for silence as if the prince were but a commoner. "Your Highness, I beg you. Let me give you my reasons, and then judge."

"Very well." The prince sat back in his chair and listened with his arms crossed over his chest.

"They sent my son Griffydd home to me wrapped in linen in a wooden coffin, just slung into a wooden box. He was only a third son, born after some daughters, but in some ways he was my favorite. His wits were sharp, sharper than most men's twice his age, and he was a great lad for a jest, always merry, unless someone's plight touched him. He was always ready to offer his aid to any who needed it. He truly wanted to study for the priesthood. I never had to bully him into it. He loved learning, Your Highness." Standyc's voice quivered, but he cleared his throat and went on. "So, he came home in the coffin. My lady and I both wished to see him one last time, so we had the servants unwrap his body."

Dovina caught her breath. She knew how Grif had died, thrown to the ground and trampled by charging warhorses shod with good iron.

"It was foolish of us. Pieces, Your Highness. Bruised, bloody, his head half torn off, mangled—"

"Enough!" the prince said, but gently. "And so, when you thought of revenge, you turned to the old ways, the ancient ways of tradition."

Ladoic winced. *Knives cut both ways,* Dovina thought.

"Just so," Standyc said. "Grief can be a kind of madness, Your Highness. It seemed a fit vengeance to me at the time. Haven't we just heard about the power of ancient traditions?"

The priest scowled but stayed silent.

"My heart aches for your grief," Gwardon said. "But truly, it seems to me that your son's death was an accident, and the defilement of Ladoic's son, quite deliberate. Still, your griefs seem to me to be equal, and your losses in balance. I as a mere man am inclined to consider mercy."

Some of the listeners nodded. A few whispered to their companions. The priest cleared his throat and turned toward Gwardon.

"But of course," Gwardon spoke fast, "let us hear what our ancient laws say on the matter." He raised an eyebrow and waited for His Holiness to speak.

The Lawspeaker rose from his chair and looked over the crowded chamber for a long moment. He turned to the prince, and even with her weak eyes Dovina could see how furious he was. The prince had trampled their ancient privileges by speaking first for mercy. The chamber fell utterly silent and waited.

"The fault must be redressed," the priest said. "For more than a thousand years, Great Bel has let it be known that the taking of heads displeases him. It is a barbarity, a foul thing, suitable for savages, not men of standing." He paused for a dramatic moment. "Will you interfere with the will of the gods?" Another pause. "Your Highness?"

"Never would I," Gwardon said, "in matters that pertain to the gods. Is this such a one?"

The priest had the choice of backing down or establishing a legal precedent. He made a snorting sound, then finally said, "It is a matter pertaining to the will of the gods."

All graciousness, Gwardon bobbed his head in a gesture of submission to the priest's direction.

"Then speak, Your Holiness, and judge this man."

"The law requires that the taker of a head be hanged until dead," the priest said.

Curses broke out in the back of the chamber, quickly stifled as Standyc's men remembered where they were. Those seated turned to look, then turned back in a rustle of clothing and whispers.

"Would that be the man who did the deed, Your Holiness," Gwardon said, "or the man who gave the order?"

The priest was near trembling with raw anger. He had been forced into the position of giving the noble-born a reason to resent his priesthood's hold on the laws, and they, of course, would spread the tale. Standyc's captain's face had gone as white as milk.

The priest cleared his throat several times before speaking. "I would say the man who gave the order, Your Highness. He has asked that it fall upon him."

Several among Standyc's men swore under their breaths. One man grabbed at the place his sword hilt should have been. The gwerbret spun around and shook his head in a no, held up his hand for silence as well, before he turned back to the prince.

"Is there no ground for mercy?" Gwardon said to the priest. "None?"

The priest had had a moment to think. "I too am minded for mercy in this sad, sad affair. Bel is great, Bel is good, and he is the very epitome of mercy when the hearts of men show frailty, not evil attempt."

"Then shall we have mercy?" Gwardon said.

"Mercy we shall have. A pound of the purest gold and a pair of white bullocks, I think, for the temple sacrifices, would address Standyc's fault."

Poverty was a better fate than hanging, Dovina supposed. Unused as they were to thinking in terms of coin, Standyc's men cheered. When Gwardon half-rose from his chair and glared at them, they fell silent. Dovina moved to the edge of her chair, ready to dart forward and keep her father from disgracing himself. Ladoic was standing with his arms tightly crossed over his chest, hands tucked into his armpits, his head thrown slightly back as he considered the priest and the prince. The Prince Regent sat back down in his chair and considered him in turn.

"Will you accept this settlement?" Gwardon said. "Over the matter of your son's desecration only."

Ladoic's posture relaxed. He hooked his thumbs over his belt and continued his level stare for a long few moments, but Dovina knew he was struggling to keep from smiling. Finally he said, "I accept it, Your Highness."

"Done, then." The prince turned his head to look at Standyc. "I rule that his fault was accidental, yours deliberate. Will you accept the penance set by the Lawspeaker?"

Standyc swallowed several times before he answered. He stared straight ahead of him, and his face had sagged, especially around his mouth. "I will, Your Highness."

"Very good." The regent rose from his chair to look around the chamber. The last of the whispers stopped. "We will discuss the rest of the matters that require settlement at a later date in another hearing." He sat back down and picked up the Sword of Justice. "Adjourned." He knocked the pommel thrice on the table.

The crowd rose and swirled in little eddies, some people heading for the door, others joining friends for whispered conversations. Ladoic hurried out with Tieryn Bryn beside him, talking urgently. The prince and the law-speaking priest stayed behind, waiting, no doubt, for the room to clear. As she left the chamber, Dovina saw one of Standyc's pages leaning against the wall. She made her way over to him.

"Tell me summat, if you please," Dovina said. "How fares Gwerbret Standyc's lady? I heard that she viewed her son's body."

"It was an awful thing, my lady. She fainted when she saw it. So her women took her upstairs to their hall, and they were ever so worried. I heard from her maid that she refused to eat or get out of bed all the next day. She hadn't come down again by the time we had to leave to come here, so I don't know any more."

"My thanks." She took her pouch out of her kirtle and got a couple of pennies to give him. "If you hear more, tell my page. Darro, that is, the red-headed lad."

"My thanks to you, my lady." He clutched the coppers tight in his fist. "I will indeed."

As she turned away, she saw Merryc making his way through the crowd. She waited for him to join her.

"Did the prince plan this whole thing?" she said.

"He didn't. He can think on his feet, Gwardon can." Merryc grinned at her. "And parry with the best of us."

"Parry? More like a thrust. That's a huge fine the priest levied. Standyc's going to want that land he and Father are fighting about even more."

Merryc winced. "I hadn't thought of that. Dovva—may I call you Dovva?"

"By all means, Merro."

"I'm thanking the god who brought you to me."

"Actually it was our mothers."

He laughed, and in a quick moment she did as well. You're weakening, she told herself, but oh, well, I suppose I'll simply have to marry one day anyway. It might as well be him. Her fine indifference was spoiled when he grinned at her. A stab of warmth—she felt as if the ice around her heart had melted.

⊛

"Ye gods!" Cavan said. "How greedy are those priests? That's a huge fine. You could buy the best warhorses for fifty men with a pound of pure gold. And their battle gear, too. And maybe have enough left over for oats and hay."

"Where's Standyc going to get it?" Alyssa said.

"I have no idea. His guildsmen don't have that kind of coin. His people can't afford more taxes. They're poor enough already. A Westfolk moneylender, maybe."

"That'll make things even nastier on the border, won't it?"

"Much worse."

The news of the law-speaking priest's decision had spread fast in the streets as well as to the embassy grounds—and soon would, Alyssa was sure, to every noble lord within miles. When they met later in the day, Dovina confirmed the latter.

"Father's gloating, I'm afraid," she said, "but the other gwerbretion are furious. A whole pound of gold! The pages and the servants tell me that everywhere they go, they hear talk of the huge fine— inns, taverns, public fountains. Standyc's been shamed as well as driven into poverty."

"That's not good."

"I know. I feel bad for his lady and children. He's the only one liable for the fine, but they'll bear the burden just the same. Huh, I wonder what the other lords will think?"

"They should see that the priests have too much power. Do you think they will?"

"I don't. But I can hope. I—what is it?"

Darro had come bustling into the chamber. "News, my lady," he said. "Malyc Penvardd is here in Cerrmor. He arrived this morning by ship, and he's staying at the Bardic Guild's town house."

"More tinder for the fire," Alyssa said.

"Ever a ray of sunshine, that's you!" Dovina said. "But you're right. Darro, take a message to my betrothed's mother. We don't dare meet with Malyc here, where everyone can see him arrive and wonder what we're talking about. But I'll wager that Amara will let us get together with him at her town house."

Amara, of course, was pleased to do so. That very night the Penvardd was the honored guest at a small dinner, served in her town house suite rather than the noisy great hall. While they ate an excellent fish course followed by grilled beef rosettes, each with all the proper accompaniments, Dovina and Alyssa informed Malyc of the various recent events in Cerrmor. Merryc mostly listened, but with the course of tiny sweet cakes, he weighed in.

"I'm going riding with the Prince Regent on the morrow," Merryc said. "If you have your guild apply for a formal audience with him, I'll do my best to see that you get it."

"Most excellent!" Malyc said. "I'll be endlessly grateful."

"Merro, let me know what the prince says as soon as you return," Amara said. "Then I'll send pages with messages to our guests. I think we'd best forgo written messages."

Before Malyc left, he and Alyssa retired to a small chamber off the foyer to talk in private.

"If you would like to give a tribute to Cradoc," Malyc said, "I was thinking you might speak at the justiciar hearing."

"It would gladden my heart to do that. I'm still sorry that I had to sneak off and miss hearing your gorchan."

"I wondered where you'd got to. I was quite surprised when Lady Tay told me what had been happening behind my back. I probably should deliver some sort of stern rebuke, but in truth, I'm very proud of you all."

Alyssa felt her face burn with a blush. She managed to stammer a quiet "my thanks."

"Now, I've got a hidden dagger in my boot," Malyc continued. "We may be able to claim that the Fox clan has no legitimate right to rule."

"Honored one, do you mean Maelaber, the Westfolk herald?"

Malyc gaped, speechless for a long moment. Alyssa started to apologize, but he waved one hand for silence and laughed.

"I do, at that!" he said once he'd recovered. "How do you know?"

"A woman at Haen Marn told me the tale, and then she arranged for me to meet him. I had a letter asking him to help us. Alas, he wants naught to do with our suit. He told me Ladoic's support is too important to the Westfolk. They're not going to anger him over a claim that has little legal basis."

"I see." Malyc thought in silence for a long moment. "Well, so much for my mighty threat, my hidden dagger of truth. This should teach me summat, but I'm not quite sure what the lesson is. One thing it does mean, however, is this. Our words are now the only weapon we have. What we may say in any hearing matters twice as much."

Alyssa's first impulse was to back down, to say that she couldn't possibly risk speaking and perhaps ruining everything. She pushed the fear away.

"Then I'll work twice as hard on my words, honored one."

"Excellent! Well, none of these legal affairs will matter unless the regent agrees to hear us. Let us hope he will."

"Just so. It's a good thing we have Clan Daiver's support."

"It is. We'll see what Lord Merryc can do for us. Not a word till then. One never knows when royalty will find insult where others would find opportunity."

Prince Gwardon was willing to receive Aberwyn's chief bard, and not merely to do a favor to a friend, as he told Merryc.

"The more information I can glean about the situation in the west, the better. This bard's going to have his own reasons for seeing me, but we can sort that out later." Gwardon paused to gesture to his councillor. "What about tomorrow morning early? Are we free?"

"We are, Your Highness."

"Excellent! Bring him along to the villa some while after break-fast, Merro, if you'd not mind."

"It would gladden my heart to fetch him, Your Highness, and my thanks."

Malyc, in turn, was more than glad to be fetched, no matter what the time of day. In honor of his position as a Penvardd, Merryc bor-rowed his mother's open carriage, a groom to drive it, and one of her footmen as well, just for the show of the thing. When they arrived at the prince's country estate, servants rushed out to assist.

It stood in the midst of gardens with a stable and barracks complex off to one side, hidden behind a row of poplar trees. Merryc handed the carriage over to the grooms, tipped them a couple of pennies, and escorted Malyc to the door. Behind a low ornamental wall, the villa itself spread out around a central courtyard. In the middle of the courtyard stood a tall, slender tower with a flat roof and a precarious flight of stairs wound around it. Merryc noticed Malyc watching everything with a slight smile. Gwardon's councillor, Bedyl, waited at the door to usher them inside—an honor that brought a broader smile from the Penvardd.

"The Prince Regent is most interested in meeting you," Bedyl remarked.

"And I him," Malyc said. "One hopes things will be agreeable all round."

Gwardon received them in a private reception chamber, where the walls were painted in the Westfolk manner with views of imaginary gardens, thick with red roses. Councillor Bedyl stayed with them as well. As they entered, Malyc paused to view the nearest panel.

"Those roses never stop blooming," Gwardon said with a grin. "But of course, they have no scent. Nothing's perfect in this life."

"True spoken, my liege." Malyc bowed, then began to kneel to the prince.

"No need, good bard," Gwardon said. "I'm not the king himself, you know. Do sit down."

"My humble thanks, Your Highness," Malyc said.

Everyone sat in the chairs by a small round table. A maidservant brought a glass pitcher of white Bardek wine and small glasses. Although Malyc accepted one, Merryc noticed that he drank no more than the first polite sip.

"So," Gwardon said. "Lord Merryc here tells me you have a suit to lay before me."

"A suit concerning a suit, Your Highness. I'm quite sure you're aware of the recent trouble in Aberwyn over the death of one of our guild members."

"I am."

"The guild wishes to receive some compensation for Cradoc's

death or, at the least, a recognition that a grave wrong occurred. We doubt if we can obtain this in the usual gwerbretal courts."

Gwardon's mouth twitched in an abbreviated smile.

"So," Malyc continued, "we found ourselves thinking about the Justiciar of the Northern Border, a post your royal ancestors founded. We are, of course, much too far away to fall under his jurisdiction."

"I see. It would be most convenient if such a justiciar existed on the western border?"

"Your Highness has spotted the thrust of this argument."

"Allow me to parry. The gwerbretion of the western border won't react well if the throne establishes an independent court."

"Quite the opposite of well, Your Highness. We do understand that."

"Good."

"We've put some serious thought into the matter, Your Highness, concerning the difficulties. The arguments are far too long and complex to lay out in an informal meeting such as this. We'd never presume to trouble Your Highness privately with them. But since you're in Cerrmor to hear other legal proceedings, we were wondering if you could spare a little time to hear our request in some detail."

Gwardon glanced at Bedyl, who nodded.

"Quite possibly we can," Gwardon said. "Do these arguments include more information about the situation in Aberwyn?"

"Of course, Your Highness. It's all most relevant."

"One last question. What makes you think you've got any chance of winning the case even with a justiciar to try it? My understanding is that Cradoc voluntarily agreed to starve at the gates."

"He did, Your Highness, but the laws against bringing death to a bard are very clear and very . . . well, very fierce. Consider the old days! There's an important precedent in the case of Lord Maroic and Gweran the bard, if Your Highness might have studied that as a student."

"We did, truly."

"Well, then, Your Highness! If a man so much as threatened to harm a bard, the bard's lord had the right to seize and hang him." Malyc slapped his hands together with a loud pop. "Just like that. Done!"

"Here! I'm certainly not going to hang a gwerbret!"

"Of course not, Your Highness. Never would I even think such a thing! I was merely emphasizing how grim the situation is. It's bad enough that I do believe we're due a public apology, at the very least. But of course, that would be for an impartial court to decide."

Gwardon turned his glass around and around in his fingers while he considered. Finally he looked up. "Very well, then. We'll have the formal proceeding. The mayor gave me permission to use the public Justice Hall for judging the feud, so I'm assuming we can use it for your matter, too. My councillor will arrange everything. He'll send you a message about the time and place. Once that's done, we can meet again in private, and you can tell me more about the situation in the west."

Malyc stood up and bowed very deeply indeed. "You have our humble thanks, Your Highness. The guild will be most grateful."

Merryc got up as well and bowed, but Gwardon raised a quick hand. "Come back later when you can."

"Of course, Your Highness."

After Merryc returned the Penvardd to his inn and his mother's carriage to her stables, he fetched his own horse and rode back to the villa. Gwardon was still sitting in the rose garden room, but on the table sat a heap of pieces of pabrus, not wine. Bedyl was explaining some fine point about harbor taxes on the pier allowed for royal use. Gwardon listened with his usual deep attention. Merryc bowed, sat down, and waited until they'd finished. Bedyl swept up the pabrus, nodded Merryc's way, and left the chamber.

Gwardon stayed silent for some moments. His facial expression revealed nothing, but Merryc knew the prince's moods well.

"My liege?" Merryc said. "What's so troubling?"

"About the Penvardd. I'm just wondering if this proceeding's going to be an utter waste of time. It's going to rile up the western lords over nothing, as far as I can see. A justiciar on the western border would be a fine thing, but I can't just ram it down their throats. There has to be some sort of reason, more than just the Cerrgonney precedent. That really was a historical oddity."

"Not exactly nothing." Merryc allowed himself to smile. "I swore I'd keep the details to myself, my liege, but I'll wager I can tell you this much. They have a decent basis for their suit."

"Oh, do they?" Gwardon returned the smile. "Maybe it'll be interesting, after all."

"Very interesting, since one of their chief speakers is going to be a lass."

"You're jesting!"

"I'm not."

"Not your betrothed?"

"One of her close friends, another scholar from Aberwyn."

"Well and good, then. The petition's going to be worth hearing for that alone."

"Tell me summat, Cavvo," Alyssa said. "You don't feel humiliated, do you, that your wife went and got you out of a bit of trouble? I mean, a lot of men would."

Because he loved her, Cavan thought about an answer rather than simply growling "of course not" and changing the subject. They were alone in their little guest cottage at the embassy, sitting side by side with the remains of a cold supper on the table in front of them. He picked up his table dagger and poked at a bit of roast fowl, then laid the dagger down again.

"A bit of trouble?" he said. "You pulled my neck out of a noose. More than a bit, I'd call it. I'll always be grateful for that."

"But that's what's troubling me. I don't want you to feel grateful forever and ever. I'd hate to feel that way, and for a man it must be much worse."

Cavan had to laugh with a shake of his head. "It is," he said. "How did you learn so much about men?"

"I had three brothers, didn't I? And we grew up in the same house, not kept apart like you noble lords do with your children."

"Right you are! Well and good, then. Not humiliated, but a bit queasy, wondering what other men will think of me."

"I can see why. But I promise that I won't hold it over you one fine day."

"And I promise I won't do anything that would make me deserve that. Done, then?"

"Done!"

He leaned over and kissed her. He would have taken another, but a servant knocked on the door.

"Visitors!" she called out.

"Show them in!" Alyssa called back.

The door opened with a flourish. Bryn and Merryc came in, both of them grinning. Cavan got up and met them by the door. He realized with a flash of anger that he was close to weeping with gratitude at seeing them again.

"What by the hells are you doing here?" he said. "Consorting with a cursed silver dagger?"

"Lowering ourselves to the gutter, obviously," Bryn said. "Ah, come on, Cavvo! You never should have been exiled, and the whole cursed kingdom knows it."

"Even the bastard who got you exiled," Merryc said. "That's why he had to weasel around and lie."

"Here!" Alyssa got up from her chair. "Who was that?"

"My dearest younger brother," Cavan said. "Careg, of course. He said I drew first, and our father took the chance to believe him. Here, my love, I'll tell you the tale later."

"Of course. No need to remember all that now." She smiled at the three of them. "I believe that your friends are here to take you out drinking."

"Just that." Merryc clapped a hand on his shoulder. "Let's go put your troubles aside."

The troubles, however, appeared again once they reached Merryc's chosen tavern, a clean and decent place, or so Merryc said, near the public guesthouse. At the door the tavernman looked Cavan up and down and spoke only to Merryc. "No silver daggers in my inn, milord, begging your pardon and all that."

"Oh, come now!" Merryc said. "His person's been declared sacrosanct, and I'm here to stand surety for him, and this is Tieryn Bryn of Dun Cengarn."

The tavernman shifted his weight from one foot to the other and looked this way and that. Offend the lords, or let in scum? Cavan could practically hear him thinking the words.

"Cavvo," Bryn said, "put the dagger inside your shirt. No one will see it and think ill of our host that way."

Cavan followed orders. With a sigh, the tavernman relented.

"Not a lot of custom tonight, not yet, anyway," he said. "Come in, milords, come in."

Only a few patrons sat scattered in the clean and carpeted public room, nicely lit with fresh candles in polished lanterns. In the curve of the wall stood a small table with chairs instead of benches. The tavernman seated them there and bustled off to bring dark beer— the newest vintage, or so he promised them.

"I hope you like the taste of hops," Merryc said.

"When didn't I, as well you know!" Cavan said. "Can beer have a vintage?"

"In a place like this it can," Bryn said. "You do yourselves well in Cerrmor, Merro."

"We try, truly."

The tavernman returned with the beer, which all three of them tasted and pronounced fine. The taverner took Merryc's coin and bustled off again to greet six newcomers. For a few moments the three friends drank in silence.

"No wonder the prince keeps a villa here." Bryn turned to Cavan. "Gwardon's in residence. Did you know?"

"I do. I did see the entry, or a bit of it. I was up on the roof of the embassy with some of their lads."

"Ah," Bryn said. "He made an impressive show of it, I thought."

"He did that. He still has that blue dragon on his banner."

"Why would he take it off?" Merryc said.

"Not what I'm getting at. I saw a dragon just like that one, you see, at Haen Marn. A flesh and blood dragon, I mean, not someone's device. I wondered if maybe he'd seen it too at some time or other."

Bryn and Merryc both hooted and saluted him with their tankards.

"Tell us another, Cavvo," Bryn said.

"It's the solemn truth, I swear it. There are dragons out on the western border. Ask Lyss if you don't believe me. She doesn't lie."

"You're marrying a woman who doesn't lie?" Bryn grinned at him. "Sounds reckless to me."

"She's the reckless one," Merryc said.

"I can't believe my luck," Cavan snapped. "If that's what you mean."

"My apologies. She's splendid, truly, is all I meant."

Cavan shrugged and downed more beer.

"More about this dragon, if you please," Bryn said. "Let me wager a guess. You'd been drinking and saw a lizard crawling on the wall."

"Naught of the sort." Cavan forced out a smile. "It flew in at sunset one night, and its wings made a sound like the biggest drum in the world."

"I'd imagine they would," Merryc said. "If such actually existed."

Cavan recovered himself. "If you'd seen it, Merro, those fine breeches would have needed a good wash. The cursed thing was huge."

"One of those books they read to us at collegium mentioned dragons," Bryn said. "I've forgotten the name of it."

"I'm surprised you remember anything we learned there," Merryc said. "The way you drank."

"I'm surprised you can remember I was there, since you could drink me under the table."

They all laughed.

"But never mind the dragons," Merryc said, "I want to know about summat fair different. This charge that got you the silver dagger. I was up in Dun Deverry, and the gossip! Ye gods, some said you drew first on some commoner, some said you went mad and killed dozens of noblemen. I knew you would never draw first, so I—"

"Careg lied! Of course I didn't! The fellow had a sword every bit as good as mine, and he drew on me. But the little weasel turd came forward and insisted he'd seen me do it, all mealy-mouthed and ever so sorry to say. I would have strangled him gladly if we hadn't been in malover."

"So! I was right about that. But most of the gossip mongers hadn't the slightest idea why your father was so happy to send you off. He could have paid the man's blood price and gotten it out of you one way or the other later."

Cavan hesitated, but both men's faces showed nothing but concern.

"I'd cost him a good bit of money," he said. "It's a complicated sort of tale. You know about the taxes he takes in from the smelters, right?"

"Of course."

"Right."

"So the other side of that coin is, he has obligations. There was this accident, a ghastly thing, where the merchant had used cheap materials to build the furnace—know what those are? These little brick towers. You get the charcoal going, then pour ore on top. The metal drips down at the bottom. And the wall of one of them broke just as an apprentice was taking out the bloom. Hot slag and burning charcoal poured out. He died thanks to the outflow. Burns that wouldn't heal. He lost flesh down to the bones in his leg."

Bryn muttered an obscenity and had a long swallow of beer. Merryc turned stone still, as abnormally calm as he always became before a fight or duel.

"The merchant tried to blame the men. I looked into it and found the truth. My father was responsible for half the blood price, and you know what he's like when it comes to his precious coin."

For some minutes they drank in silence.

"There'd been a few other things before that," Cavan said at last. "Words I'd spoken when we'd had one of our quarrels."

"Ah," Bryn said. "I wondered about that. Your temper, Cavvo—"

"I can't deny it. So Careg saw his chance to step up and lie. My father's always favored him."

The tavern was a popular one, and now and then other men had come in to find a table and drink. This time, when the door opened, Merryc glanced at it and swore.

"They always say," Merryc said, "that if you name the Lord of Hell, he'll send one of his minions to trouble you. There he is now."

Cavan slewed around in his chair and saw Careg crossing the room, flanked by two friends. *We've got even odds for a fight,* he thought—then cursed himself. He could feel his temper turning into a longing to grab his brother by his skinny neck and slit his throat with the silver dagger. *Stop it!* he told himself. *What would Rommardda think?* Somehow he knew that she would hear about it if he gave in to the rage.

"Well, good taverner," Careg said, and he spoke loudly enough for the room to hear, "I'm surprised at you, letting in a scum of a silver dagger."

The room fell abruptly silent. Bryn, who outranked Careg and his friends, rose from his chair, but he kept his arms crossed over his chest and his hands, therefore, away from his sword.

"I'm surprised," Bryn said, "that he'd let in a liar like you. Giving false witness in a court of law."

Careg flushed scarlet. One of his friends laid his hand on his sword hilt. With a terrified whimper, the landlord came trotting over. "Milords, please!" Careg ignored him and turned to look straight at Cavan.

"What do you have to say for yourself?" Careg said. "Silver dagger."

"Naught that you haven't heard already," Cavan said. "By the by, silver daggers only fight for coin. We don't waste ourselves in cheap tavern brawls."

Careg stared, started to speak, hesitated, then glanced at his friends. They appeared as puzzled as he did. Cavan was more sure than ever that his brother had been planning on a good fight. Thwarting him, he realized, was almost as pleasurable as slapping the little weasel's face and starting one would have been.

"Oh, come on, Carro!" Cavan said. "Everyone knows why you lied. It's our uncle's rhan, innit? I would have inherited when he died, but now it'll come to you, a nice bit of Cerrgonney land."

"How very convenient for you." Merryc stood up at that point and turned to look Careg's way. "To have him exiled, eh?"

Careg snarled and tried another insult. "He's a coward! Why doesn't he stand up and face me himself?"

The landlord whimpered again. Cavan nearly did get up, but he forced himself to stay sitting and silent.

"Because he's smarter than that," Merryc said. "As a son of Clan Daiver, let me remind you that this city is under our protection. We don't like trouble here." He glanced at the tavernman. "Call for the night watch."

The tavernman rushed to the door and began to yell.

"You're not going to get your fight, Careg," Bryn said. "Why don't you and your friends just leave?"

"And the night watch will make sure you don't hover around outside and wait for us," Merryc said. "Go drink somewhere else."

Careg hesitated, then cleared his throat and spat right on the expensive carpet. With a wave to his friends, he turned and strode out of the door. Cavan heard voices—the night watch, the tavernman, and Careg himself, snarling away. Bryn and Merryc sat down and grinned at him.

"My thanks," Cavan said.

"You're the one who deserves the thanks," Bryn said. "I was sure as sure you were going to draw and go for the little bastard."

"Wouldn't have blamed you if you had," Merryc said, "but it gladdens my heart that you didn't."

The tavernman had returned. He brought over another pitcher of the dark beer and began to refill their tankards. When Merryc started to get out another coin, he shook his head no.

"This one's on me, milords," he said. "And the next one as well."

Alyssa rose early the next morning and left Cavan asleep and snoring. When he woke, he'd doubtless be sick, she figured, after his late night, and she preferred to be gone rather than join him when she saw him heave. She dressed fast against the chill from a heavy fog and left without disturbing him. With Gurra for her guard, she went up to the public guesthouse.

Mavva and Dovina were just waking for the day. Dovina sent her page off for fancy breads and boiled milk. Over breakfast they settled in to plan.

"We need to let the Advocates Guild see the book," Dovina said.

"True spoken," Alyssa said. "I want to ask Master Daen how we should present it in the court hearing."

"Once Darro's eaten, I'll send him off with messages. I need to ask Merro—I mean, Lord Merryc—"

"Oh, get along with you!" Mavva said and grinned. "We all know you're getting sweet on him."

"Well, so I am, and it's a cursed good thing, innit, since I have to marry him."

Mavva wiped the grin away.

"Be that as it may," Dovina continued, "I'll ask him to escort us to the guild again, and then I'll send a message to Master Daen, asking him if he'll receive us. Or hold! It should be the other way around."

"Truly," Alyssa said, "because if your betrothed drank as much as my husband did last night, he's not even awake."

Alyssa's prediction turned out to be true. Darro returned with the news that Master Daen would receive them after the noon meal and Lord Merryc's page would give him the message when the lord got out of bed.

"Naught to do but wait," Dovina said. "Darro, I'll send you back in a bit to see if he's up yet."

"My lady." The page bowed, then sat down on the floor near her feet.

"If he's not," Mavva said, "maybe your father will lend us a couple of men from his escort."

"It gladdens my heart, Mavva, that you're the practical sort. We'll do that."

"I've got news of a sort," Alyssa said. "We should chew on this in the meantime. When Cavan was exiled? It was Lord Careg's lies to their father that tipped the balance in the hearing. His own brother!"

"Oh, was it now? What a nasty little weasel!"

"My lady?" Darro turned to look up at her. "May I speak?"

"By all means."

"When she was still here, y'know? Lord Careg was seen talking with Lady Rhonalla. A lot. One of the pages told me they were sneaking around on her husband, but I don't think so. They always talked right out in the open, is why. In the great hall here, in the gardens, that kind of place."

"Hah!" Dovina said. "I bet you're right. They were up to a very different kind of trouble."

"So I thought, my lady. But now a lot of people think that's why she got sent back to Abernaudd."

"Do they? A nice stain on her honor, such as it is." Dovina smiled and batted her eyelashes. "Poor dear Rhonalla!"

"Indeed," Mavva said. "But ye gods, the people here gossip worse than washerwomen! Especially the noble-born."

"They have the time to spend, that's why," Dovina said. "Besides, that's what a free city's for, innit? A place where everyone can talk freely, so the men in power can know what's being said about them. And in Cerrmor, it's rarely anything good."

When noon came without a response from Merryc, Dovina sent

her page off to her father. Darro returned with four men to help
Gurra guard the women on their walk, a sign, as Dovina remarked,
that Ladoic was worried about possible trouble.

"No one's going to call us names with them along," Alyssa said.
"I'm very glad of it, too."

"We're taking the book, you know," Mavva said. "I'm more worried about it than I am about my tender ears."

"Good thing we'll be guarded then. My page brought me a message earlier. Malyc Penvardd's going to be there."

"Splendid!" Alyssa said. "Then we can show him the book."

"And scheme." Dovina grinned in an evil manner. "It's a good
thing we're good at that."

Late in the afternoon, Merryc joined his uncle in the gwerbret's
suite to hear what their priest of Bel, Argyn, had to tell them.
He'd stopped by on his way back to the farm.

"I'm glad I'm going home, too," Argyn said. "Visiting the Cerrmor temple was a bit tiring."

"Huh, I'll wager," Verrc said. "You can have things your own way
back at our shrine."

"Just so, Your Grace, just so. Peace and quiet. A man gets used to
it, he does."

Argyn accepted a glass of dark beer and toasted the noble-born
with it before he drank.

"Can you tell me," Merryc said, "what the priesthood thinks
about Standyc's fine? Or have you been told to hold your tongue?"

"Quite the opposite. It was implied—not stated outright mind,
but implied—that the town might need to know that not everyone
agrees with the harshness of that judgment."

"Not every Lawspeaker, eh?"

"Not only the Lawspeakers. Here, the entire city's flooded by gossip. Some of it's washed up on the temple steps and brought plenty of
flotsam with it. His Most Exalted Holiness spent a year scraping
mud off the temple's name. He's furious that he's got a new lot to deal
with now."

"Can't they just set the fine aside?" Merryc said.

"Not since it was pronounced in an open hearing with the gold sword to bear it witness and all of that. Once a Lawspeaker announces the law, the law is the law." Argyn set his empty tankard down on a nearby table. "I'd best not have more, my thanks. Bending the vows is one thing, breaking them another."

Was there a second meaning in that remark? Merryc wondered.

"The temple, Your Grace," Argyn continued, "is officially of divided opinions. Unofficially, I'd say it resembles a round of hurling, though no one has a hurley, and a good thing too, or there'd be some cracked skulls."

"What matters, I'd say, is what your head priest thinks."

"Just so." Argyn folded his hands across his comfortable stomach and smiled. "Odd about that. Just the other day His Exalted Holiness received a request from another temple that needs an experienced Lawspeaker. The fellow who assessed the fine's gotten the post, not that he could have turned it down."

"Where is it?" Merryc said.

"Cerrgonney. Up in the northern plains, just beyond Gwyngedd."

Verrc snorted with laughter. "The place they call the Desolation, innit?"

"I've heard it called just that," Argyn said. "And I gather it deserves the name."

"So we'll have a new Lawspeaker for the next hearing?"

"You will indeed. Now, there's a number of things you may not know, young Merryc, about the priests and the laws and the like. Let me tell you in case you're minded to pass them along to that Aberwyn bard and his assistants."

"My thanks," Merryc said. "I'm sure they'll be very grateful for any help you can give them."

It was late in the day when Lord Merryc's page came to Dovina with a long roll of pabrus, sealed on one edge with a couple of blobs of red wax. Mavva unrolled it and held it flat to allow Dovina to study it through her reading-glass.

"Useful, oh so very useful!" Dovina said. "Let me read you some of this."

The others listened as carefully as they did to a book being read aloud at the collegium. When she finished, Mavva rolled the scroll up again with a triumphant rustle.

"In summary," Dovina said, "we can't take on both the priests and the lords and hope to win. We have to throw the priests a bone."

"More like an entire joint of meat," Alyssa said.

"True spoken," Mavva said. "But you'll need to grant them their position early on. Fortunately, Dwvoryc says that these drwidion were the keepers of the laws. So that joint's already roasted for us."

"Excellent!" Dovina said.

"If we only had more time!" Alyssa said. "I could comb this book and pull out a great many lice to vex the heads of the gwerbretion!"

"Oh, ych!" Mavva snapped. "You could find a better figure for it, too."

"I have to agree," Dovina said, "about the figure and the tenor as well. It's a cursed thick book, innit? But look, we've got part of the day left plus the whole night. Darro can ferret out extra candles. We can take turns. Stand watches, as it were, one of us reading and one making notes while the third is sleeping. Lyss, you've got to do the presenting tomorrow, so you should get the most sleep. Mavva, will you do the precis?"

"I will. And I brought summat with me, too. Rhys gave it to me on the sly, like. It's a cheat thing that the students at Wmm's use for their studies of the written laws. It's buried in my clothing chest."

"Splendid!" Dovina said. "I'll take notes on that. We'll need some precedents."

"I'll start on my speeches," Alyssa said. "I've got ideas of what I want to say, and so I can just leave room, like, for tipping in the precedents when we find them. But I do want to read that bit about the electing over again myself."

"As soon as you're ready," Mavva said, "I'll hand the book over to you. I've read a fair bit of it already. I discovered a nice little thing, too. Lyss, your name? It comes ultimately from Alesia, the place where Vercingetorix made his stand against the Rhwmanes."

"Truly?" Alyssa said. "That's splendid! We shall make our stand here."

"With, let's hope," Dovina put in, "a better outcome."

Although Cavan had wanted to accompany Alyssa up to the guesthouse, some odd quirk in his mind prompted him to stay away. He found out why that evening, when he dined with Markella and Hwlio. After the lavish meal, Hwlio left the room for a quick word with one of his legal councillors. While the servants cleared the table, Cavan and his hostess retired to a window seat out of their way.

"I've heard from the Rommardda," Markella said. "She has left the matter up to others. If there's an omen, you may study. If not, not."

Cavan's heart pounded. He caught his breath before he spoke. "May I ask what the omen could be?"

"If you and Alyssa settle somewhere on the western border, one of the Westfolk teachers will take you on. If you never go back to Aberwyn, there's an end to the matter."

"Well and good, then. That gives me hope, and that's all I can ask for."

"Valandario might well be interested in an apprentice. You've met her, or so Alyssa mentioned."

"I have. I can't tell you how grateful I am for your help."

"Put yourself into position to profit by the help before you thank me. Ah, here's Hwlio back." With a sigh she heaved her pregnant self up from the cushions. "Who knows what the gods have in store for any of us, hmm?"

"Indeed." He joined her. "And whether I ever see Aberwyn again is definitely a question in the laps of the gods."

chapter 12

THE MORNING CAME UPON the three conspirators far too quickly for Alyssa's liking. After a few hours' sleep on Mavva's bed, she woke to find the others already up and dressed.

"We saved you some breakfast," Mavva said. "Polla's bringing you wash water."

"My thanks. You could have woken me—"

"We figured that you needed sleep."

After she washed and dressed, Alyssa gobbled a hasty breakfast while they rehearsed their plan for the hearing one last time.

"I had a thought," Dovina said. "Even if we lose, it won't matter in a way. The fox will be out of the trap. The ideas—that's what counts. The gossip will spread them, and people will know that the gwerbretion didn't always rule like little kings."

"It will give the priesthood of Wmm a wedge, like," Mavva said, "to drive into the crack."

"Maybe so," Alyssa said, "but I want to win right now."

When they were getting ready to leave the guesthouse an escort of four men from the Aberwyn warband appeared at the door. Ladoic had sent them to "help the Bardekian," his note said. "We don't want anyone getting in your way in the streets."

"I wonder if he's heard things," Dovina said. "Hints of trouble?"

"It could be. Let's go. We're safe enough with his men along."

When they reached the Justice Hall, they found it already half-full of the curious as well as the concerned. They took good seats near the front and watched as the hall filled with onlookers. Outside the town criers began clanging their bells to announce that the hearing was beginning.

"Here we go," Alyssa said. "Courage!"

"If that fails," Dovina said with a grin, "we'll have spite to fall back on."

Alyssa laughed, and laughing she became preternaturally calm. *I'm ready for battle*, she thought. *It's like my whole life has led to this day.*

With a great clanging of bells, the door at the rear of the platform opened. As the prince and his retinue came through onto the platform, Alyssa noticed the new Lawspeaker immediately. Their shaven heads and archaic costumes tended to make Bel's priests hard to tell apart, but this one had dark eyes instead of blue, he was a fair bit taller than the previous speaker, and some years younger as well. They settled themselves at the table. Eddel followed with the gold Sword of Justice.

"I declare this hearing open." Eddel laid the sword on the table. "Let's get on with it." He sat down and nodded at the prince.

"I understand," the prince said, "that this matter before us hangs upon certain actions of Ladoic, Gwerbret Aberwyn. Your Grace, please come forward."

At the command, Ladoic came up the stairs and bowed to the prince and the Lawspeaker, but when Eddel held up the golden sword, Ladoic ignored it.

"Your Highness," he said, "I'm not a man who can twist words like a bard. I want my councillor at law to speak for me."

"It may be possible," the prince said. "Answer me a question first. They say you let Cradoc the bard starve to death at your gates. Is this true?"

Ladoic's expression turned grim. "It is." He spat the words out.

"My thanks." The prince turned to the Lawspeaker. "Shall we allow his request?"

"For the nonce, Your Highness. I reserve my right to ask questions later."

"Done, then. Send your councillor to us."

Ladoic bowed again and retreated. As Nallyc came forward, Alyssa noticed how pale his face was. His hands clutched one another, half-hidden by the full sleeves of his black robe. Before he mounted the steps, he paused to clear his throat several times. He went up, knelt, and kissed the offered sword.

"Very well," Gwardon said. "Malyc, the Penvardd of your city, has asked that the gwerbret himself not judge what happened at his gates. Do you agree?"

"I do not, Your Highness."

"Why?"

"Because the bard himself decided to sit before those gates and starve. The gwerbret's response was a decision allowable under the ancient traditions of our laws. What he chose to do was right and proper therefore. Thus there should be no question of a suit against His Grace."

Gwardon glanced at the Lawspeaker.

"An allowable decision in some circumstances," the priest said, "is not necessarily allowable in others. When a man dies, say the laws, a reason must be established and a degree of culpability defined if indeed culpability exists."

"I see. Malyc Penvardd, come forward!"

Malyc strode up to the dais, climbed the steps with a toss of his cloak, a plaid of green, blue, and white that harked back to the Maelwaedd clan, his remote ancestors. At one shoulder a gold brooch in the shape of a harp pinned the cloak. He kissed the sword, but he stood, not knelt, as a sign of the special place of bards under the laws.

"My thanks." His voice boomed out over the crowded Justice Hall. "I come to lay a complaint against Ladoic, Gwerbret Aberwyn, that he let Cradoc of Dun Gwerbyn, a bard of sacred person, starve to death before his gates."

"Very well," Gwardon said. "Did the bard choose to sit and starve of his own will?"

"He did."

The Lawspeaker leaned forward. "What then is your charge,

Penvardd? If he chose to take up that position, the gwerbret has the ancient right, does he not, to refuse to hear him?"

"I most humbly suggest, Your Holiness, that he has that right in matters of grave import."

"True spoken. That he does."

"But this matter was a small thing, Your Holiness, at least in the opinion of the Bardic Collegium. I beg you to rule upon our opinion."

"Tell me, and I will."

Malyc bowed to him, then paused. Alyssa felt her heart pounding. Here was the moment of greatest risk.

"Your Holiness," Malyc said. "Cradoc wished only this, that the gwerbret would hold a public hearing upon certain matters. We did not ask for a decision to be handed down, only that he would hear us. Is a bard not the voice of the people? Is there not a tradition that he may not be silenced when he speaks for them?"

In a rustle and whispers, the gwerbretion in attendance leaned forward, waiting. The Lawspeaker glanced at the prince and the mayor, then cleared his throat.

"Under the laws, specifically, The Edicts of King Bran, the person of a bard receives many a special consideration. Several times indeed it is stated that the bard is the voice of the people. Therefore, the Edicts continue, let him speak." He paused again, briefly. "I agree with the Penvardd. The matter should have received a hearing. Cradoc's death was unnecessary."

Ladoic forgot himself enough to bark out an obscenity. He immediately stood and bowed to the dais. "Forgive me," he said. "I am at fault, and I apologize."

"Accepted," the prince said. "Malyc Penvardd, what do you want from this court?"

Ladoic sat down fast.

"I want, Your Highness, two things. First, the opportunity to ask for redress for Cradoc's death. Second, that this opportunity come not in Aberwyn's court, but some impartial place distant but not too distant from the gwerbret's rhan."

"Does such a place exist?"

"Not to our knowledge, Your Highness, unless you rule that we come to Dun Deverry itself. Such a journey would be a great inconvenience for all concerned. No doubt you, as well, in your position as regent, have more pressing matters to deal with. What we would hope for, Your Highness, is that you would establish a justiciar for the western border, like unto the one your wise ancestor established in Cerrgonney all those years ago."

"This is a grave thing you're asking," the prince said. "Do you have more reasons you can lay before me?"

Some of the gwerbretion began to speak, but Gwardon glared them into silence.

"Your Highness, Your Holiness, honored mayor," Malyc said. "You have granted the request of Gwerbret Ladoic, that someone else may speak before you. I make the same request now. I have a witness to the events, one who also has a thing of great import to lay before you. May she speak?"

At the pronoun the audience rustled with whispers. Eddel knocked the pommel of the sword on the table and silenced them.

"She may," Gwardon said. "If she has knowledge we need to hear."

"She does, Your Highness. I stand surety for that." He rose and turned to the audience. "Alyssa vairc Sirra of Aberwyn! Come forward."

Alyssa took a deep breath and rose, smoothing her skirts. She mounted the platform, kissed the sword, and started to kneel. Mayor Eddel waved her up with a flick of his hand.

"You'll need to stand if you've got a speech to make," Eddel said.

"My thanks, honored sir." She rose, then curtsied to the prince and the Lawspeaker. "Your Highness. Your Holiness." She turned and curtsied to the gwerbretion in the audience. "Your Graces. My lords." She turned back to the regent. "We have heard about ancient laws today. We all know the unwritten laws, the customs, the beliefs that go back hundreds of years. Yet no one seems to have mentioned the oldest customs of all, those of our ancestors, they who fled the homeland to escape the Roman yoke. Ah, the wisdom and the daring of King Bran and our vergobretes! Trusting in their gods, and in Great Bel above all, they took ship on strange seas to bring their beloved people and their beloved traditions to this new land. Here they could live free as their ancestors lived, not as slaves to some foreign race."

Many in the audience were listening to, or at least, staring at this phenomenon, a lass in a law court—enough for now, Alyssa thought. Others were fiddling with bits of clothing, picking at the dirt under their nails, or gazing round the chamber. She did her best to ignore them.

"You have heard about the death of Cradoc of Aberwyn today. He was my teacher, my guide on the three paths of speaking well. I have come to pay tribute to his memory, but there is no better tribute to him than honoring our ancient ways. He is the one who taught me to look deep into the well of history. Does not a bard look into that well to see the truths of the past? Does not his Awen come to him and speak?"

The regent nodded his agreement. The priest showed no reaction at all. The prince is the one that counts, Alyssa reminded herself.

"Yet for those of us who are not true bards like Cradoc of Aberwyn, who will bring up the truth from the deep well of history? The dead cannot speak for themselves—or can they? In the past they have spoken, but can we hear them? So much time lies between us and the dead! Even on Samaen, when a scattering of them come to visit us, their descendants, we can only see them, not hear them speak. And yet, even so, we have some voices from the past. Some few of the dead still speak to us across the long years.

"How? What is this dwimmer that lets us hear words spoken hundreds and hundreds of years ago? No dwimmer at all, truly, but the written word. Books, Your Highness, my lords, books live on past the hands that wrote them. And the oldest of them tell us about our ancient traditions, those honorable ways of living that we still follow today."

She paused to the silent count of five, just as Cradoc had taught her. The regent leaned forward a little in his chair.

"Or do we follow them, Your Highness, my lords?" Alyssa continued. "Do we remember in our law courts and in our lives the paths that our ancestors marked out for us to follow? One of the oldest voices, in one of our oldest books, tells us otherwise."

The regent quirked both eyebrows. Dovina rose from her chair and hurried forward with Annals of the Dawntime, opened to the correct page. Alyssa took it and with a flourish laid it down in front of Prince Gwardon and his councillor, who immediately leaned over to inspect it. Alyssa took the letter from her kirtle and laid it down in front of the priest.

"From Haen Marn, Your Holiness," she said, "stating that this book is true and truly ancient."

The priest muttered a few purifying words over the page to erase her female touch, then picked it up to read. Alyssa turned back to the audience.

"This ancient book speaks of the ancient traditions of our people. Then as now, it informs us, the priests of Great Bel, the drwidion, guided our laws and spoke them in the courts." She turned and curtsied to the Lawspeaker before she faced the audience again. "But what of the magistrates themselves? The book tells of the days when the vergobretes, our magistrates, the ancestors of the gwerbretion, were not born to their task but elected. They were acclaimed by assemblies of the people. Their sons did not inherit their courts. They did not receive land and fees for their services to their people. Do we live that way today? Do we—"

Except for Ladoic, the gwerbretion in the chamber all stood up and began to yell. Curses, demands for Alyssa's silence, demands to speak—Prince Gwardon stood up and out-yelled them all.

"I will have silence in this chamber! This is a court of law, not a riot in a marketplace!"

"Impiety!" Caddalan called out. "Raw stinking impiety!"

"It's not!" The Lawspeaker rose from his seat and flapped the Haen Marn letter in their direction. "Let the lass finish!"

Alyssa was so shocked that their sops to priestly power had brought him over to her side that she nearly forgot her words. She had some moments to recover while the regent and the Lawspeaker calmed the gwerbretion. It took both of them.

"And remember, Your Graces," Gwardon said, "that this lass is under the protection of the sanctuary laws. She should be treated with respect." He sat back down and nodded at Alyssa to continue.

"Times change, Your Grace." Alyssa looked straight at Caddalan. "No one here would ever suggest we return to those chaotic days of assemblies and torchlight acclamations. The kingdom is far too vast, our laws too complicated, as I'm sure His Holiness would agree. We would merely point out that the ancient traditions contradict the popular beliefs about the law courts themselves. They were, in the ancient days, left in the hands of those who had spent their holy lives studying the laws of our tribes, the priests of Belinos and Ogmios, as the gods were known then."

The priest nodded his approval. Caddalan laid a hand where his sword hilt should have been. The prince rose from his chair. Caddalan crossed his arms over his chest to keep his hands still. Gwardon sat down.

"One would hope," Gwardon said, "that everyone here honors the holy servants of the gods."

Gwerbret Ladoic made a sound suspiciously like a snort: hah! The nervous laughter that followed calmed the commoners in the audience. The gwerbretion, however, looked at one another, rose, and swept out of the Justice Hall—all except Ladoic. Through the open door, however, Alyssa could see that they hovered just outside to listen.

"Enough!" Gwardon said. "Alyssa vairc Sirra, you have my thanks for your words and for this book. You may join Lady Dovina."

While the audience murmured and shifted in their seats, Alyssa curtsied and followed his order, though she would rather have cursed him. *Have we lost? What about the rest of my speech?* When she sat down next to Dovina, Dovina took her hand and squeezed it. The regent's councillor was reading the open page. In a moment he leaned over and whispered something to the prince. Gwardon rose and picked up the Sword of Justice.

"The evidence our learned ladies have brought before me," Gwardon said, "has made me consider Malyc Penvardd's request in a new light. I hereby announce that I shall establish, furnish, and appoint the office of a justiciar for the lands of the kingdom on the western border."

Dovina clasped her free hand over her mouth to stifle a shriek. Alyssa felt too stunned to respond, too disbelieving that they had won their point. Dovina risked a whisper: "You carried the day."

The prince gave her a stern look and laid a finger over his mouth for silence. Dovina nodded and rustled her skirts in lieu of a curtsy.

"The Penvardd," the prince continued, "has made an excellent point about the complexity of this process. I shall consult the Lawspeakers and my own legal council to decide which cases shall come under whose jurisdiction."

A few foul words and curses drifted through the open door. The prince knocked the pommel of the sword on the table. The noises outside stopped.

"This hearing is now over," Gwardon said. "The town criers will announce when it's to resume should I so decide."

As the audience stood up to leave, Lord Merryc made his way through the crowd. He had his two bodyguards with him.

"These lads will escort you for the rest of the day," Merryc said to Alyssa. "I think it's wise. Gurra, you're a good man with your sword, but there's only one of you."

"Just so, milord," Gurra said.

"I agree," Dovina said. "You have my thanks, Merro."

"Welcome. Alyssa, you were splendid."

She felt her face burn with a blush and curtsied for want of anything to say.

"Dovva," Merryc continued, "I'll wait here to escort you when you're done, but your father wants a private word with you."

"Gods!" Dovina rolled her eyes. "I'll just wager he does."

Ladoic was waiting outside the chamber by the staircase. As she joined him, Dovina was relieved to see that the other gwerbretion and their men had taken their weapons and left.

"I don't know whether to congratulate you," Ladoic said, "or disown you."

"The former, Father, by all means. It gladdens my heart that you didn't storm out with your peers."

"It didn't gladden theirs, I assure you. Dovva, I'm afraid that trouble's going to come out of this."

"No doubt they're more determined than ever to keep the courts in their greedy little paws."

"Greed has naught to do with it!"

Dovina rolled her eyes toward the heavens. "Father, truly! Do you think I'd believe that?"

She was expecting a furious outburst.

"You have a point," he said instead. "Young Bryn, and he's the poorest of all of us, suggested that we all give Standyc some coin, enough to pay for at least some of that cursed fine. Don't faint, now, but I actually agreed I could part with a little myself."

"After the way you smirked at the hearing?"

"Now and then men do have second thoughts. I've been thinking a fair bit lately. Besides, it would have turned your delicate stomach, my daughter dear, to see how fast Caddalan weaseled out of it. He's got enough coin to make a bed out of it, him and the iron trade!"

"I'm not surprised."

"Well, no more was I. Besides all that, though, the Penvardd has a point about that cursed justiciar. I'm tired of taking grief from my peers about the Westfolk. They resent my taking the Westfolk side when there's a legal wrangle to sort out. I keep telling them I'm bound by treaties. They keep refusing to listen."

"But if the justiciar were doing the judging, they could say naught to you about it."

"Just that. Humph, it's an ill-omened flood that doesn't leave fish behind, eh?" He sighed with a shake of his head. "I can live with the wretched decision."

It took Dovina a moment to recover her powers of speech. "That gladdens my heart, Father," she said. "Besides, Standyc and every gwerbret on the western border will have to live with it, too. There must be some comfort in that."

He grinned, then let the smile fade. "Let's hope they do decide to live with it. Dovva, I'm a bit worried. Naught's been said, yet, but."

"Rebellion?"

"The west's got summat of a tradition of that, doesn't it?" He hesitated for a long moment. "You might mention it to that betrothed of yours. If he thinks the matter's serious, he can drop a word into the right ears."

"Father! You won't be joining them, will you?"

"Would I be telling you about it if I were? Think, lass! Besides, naught's been decided yet. I just don't like the talk I hear. We need to take steps, Caddalan says, all puffed up like a toad. Steps! Hah!"

"Well and good, then. I'll do that."

Ladoic strode off without glancing back. Merryc had left the council chamber to wait off to one side. She hurried over and laid a hand on his shoulder. He smiled and slipped his arm around her waist to draw her close. She was surprised at how pleasant his touch felt. Besides, the courting couple gesture was useful.

"A message from my father," she said in a whisper. "The talk of rebellion's grown more urgent. He'd like you to warn the prince."

"Ye gods!" Merryc answered in the same low tone. "Here, my lady. You and your page go on downstairs ahead of me. Just for the look of the thing. I'll wait here."

"Right. I'll see you later at your mother's."

After some small while, the prince and his retinue came strolling out of the Justice Hall. Since the councillors were talking to Gwardon, Merryc waited until they reached him before he stepped forward and bowed. Gwardon stopped and acknowledged him with a raised hand.

"What brings you to me?" Gwardon said. "Must be summat important."

"Indeed, my liege. A private word?"

Gwardon led the way to the curve of the wall. Two men of his armed escort stood between them and eavesdroppers, but Merryc kept his voice low and soft.

"Bad news, my liege. My betrothed told me. That talk among the gwerbretion about rebellion? It's grown a cursed sight worse. Naught's fixed or sworn yet. She made that clear. But there's talk. Her father warned her, which means he'll hold for the king."

"Good for Ladoic! Talk is always the beginning of these things. Ah, curse them all! The western provinces can't muster as many men as Deverry proper, but it's a long march away."

"Lughcarn's a good bit closer."

"Just so. At least Gwaentaer hasn't joined them. Well. Not yet, anyway."

"True spoken. Caddalan may make some show of force right here for a start."

"And what good will that do them?"

"If they kill you, my liege, the kingdom falls apart, and the gwer-bretion may do as they please."

"You're right. I'd not thought of that."

"It's not a pleasant thought."

Gwardon stared down at the floor in silence for some short while.

"Very well, then," he said. "I'll give the matter some attention. A great deal of attention, actually. There's naught wrong with being prepared for trouble." He suddenly grinned. "Since it usually comes."

hanks to their bodyguard, Alyssa and Mavva reached the guesthouse without anyone troubling them. In the great hall they saw Amara, sitting in a quiet nook with her companion and pages beside her, but they hurried up to the suite to wait for Dovina in private. Long before she returned, her father caught up with them there.

"Goodwoman Mavva," he said. "If I may trouble you? I need a word with Alyssa alone. I promise you she'll be perfectly safe. I merely want to ask her a question."

"Of course, Your Grace." Mavva curtsied to him. "Lady Amara's waiting with her retinue down in the hall, and I'll go join her."

Alyssa had no idea of how to entertain a gwerbret, especially since the two maids were nowhere to be seen. When she offered him a chair, he shook his head no.

"This won't take but a few moments, lass. I've got a legal matter to lay before you."

"Your Grace, I'm only a raw apprentice at this."

"I know, but I like your spirit. I daren't go to the Advocates Guild, anyway. What if one of them wags his tongue, eh? Priests of Bel are worse, a lot of old women with naught to think about but gossip and rites. Dovina tells me you're absolutely trustworthy."

"I do my best to be, Your Grace."

"Promise me you won't say a word of this to anyone, not even Dovina."

That he'd drop the "lady" before Dovina's name when speaking to a commoner convinced Alyssa of his sincerity.

"I promise on my scholar's calling, Your Grace, and there's naught I hold higher than that."

He smiled, a crease of lip under his gray mustache. "Well and good, then. Is there any way under our laws that I can pass over Adonyc and make Dovina my heir to Aberwyn?"

Alyssa caught her breath with a gasp.

"Hah!" Ladoic's grin deepened. "That got you, eh?"

"Indeed it did, Your Grace! May I ask why?"

"Adonyc's a lackwit. She's not. I care more about Aberwyn and her folk than some think I do. The gods only know what'll happen to them if he's ruling."

"I see." Alyssa decided that agreeing with him about his son was too dangerous. She nodded in what she hoped was a sage's wise manner. "I understand now, Your Grace, why you didn't want to go to the guild." She thought for a few moments. "I'll have to think about this, Your Grace, and search some of the books in the guildhall. I'll tell them that I'm just looking things up in case I need to give another speech."

"Well and good, then. When you know, tell my page you want to speak to me about that bounty on your husband's head."

"I shall beg for your mercy, Your Grace."

"You just might get it. His father—but that's neither here nor there." He turned toward the door. "A good day to you, fair scholar!"

"And to you, Your Grace. I promise that I'll give the matter my best thought and attention."

With a last smile the gwerbret let himself out and shut the chamber door quietly behind him. Alyssa sank into a chair in something like shock. In but a moment, though, she turned to the legal problem at hand. Her education in the laws had been minimal, only the overall structures that bards were expected to know in order to compose flyting songs and the like. Yet she could think of a historical precedent here, a chance remark there, that might relate to the gwerbret's question. Better yet, Rhys's packet of notes still lay on the table before her. She got her writing chest from the bedchamber and sat down to see what she could find.

She was hard at work when Dovina returned, sweeping in with her page. Alyssa picked up her written notes and folded them as if she were only tidying them away.

"You were splendid!" Dovina said.

"My thanks, but without you and Mavva, I would have been an abject failure."

"Such modesty! I was thinking of ordering a small supper here. Or do you want to go back to the embassy?"

"I'd best leave. Cavvo's probably pacing around and wondering where I am. He was afraid to come to the court today."

"Why? It can't be because of the bounty."

"It wasn't. Because his father and brother were going to be there."

"What a charming clan they are!" Dovina rolled her eyes. "Do you need an escort?"

"Gurra's waiting in the servants' hall. Darro, if you could fetch him for me?"

The page bowed and trotted off on the errand.

"**W**here's Lord Merryc?" Mavva said.

"Gone off with the Prince Regent at his invitation," Dovina said. "Would you like more of this roast partridge?"

"My thanks," Mavva said. "I'll carve it, Darro. You eat your dinner."

"Merryc is dining with Prince Gwardon," Lady Amara said. "Which is very exciting. I'm hoping he'll tell us more about what the prince has in mind."

"I'll be meeting him in the great hall later," Dovina said. "We'll see if he can share what Gwardon says. He may want it kept secret."

"Let's hope not," Mavva said. "In those papers Rhys gave me? I found another precedent for some kind of independent court. One of the ancient laws allows for an 'appointed learned man' to hear cases of justice if the gwerbret's off at war."

"I hadn't known that," Dovina said. "These days everyone just has to wait."

"I wrote a note to the prince's councillor about it. I gave it to him at the hearing. As it was breaking up, I mean."

"Smart!" Amara said. "Listening to you lasses, I truly wish I'd been able to go to a collegium, but my father wouldn't hear of it."

It was late in the afternoon when Dovina went down to the guest-house's great hall with only Darro for an escort. Lady Amara had returned to her town house, and Mavva stayed in the suite to continue studying Rhys's papers. Dovina and the page wandered through the crowded hall but saw no sign of Merryc.

"We should go back to the suite, my lady," Darro said. "It's not fitting for you to be here if his lordship isn't."

"I'm too tired to climb that cursed staircase. My friends and I didn't get enough sleep last night."

Eventually they found a corner quieter than most and sat, Dovina in a chair beside a little table crowded with empty candlesticks and Darro on the floor at her feet. They'd barely gotten settled when a gaggle of young lords, all of them carrying goblets of some sort of drink, strolled by. The only man she recognized was Lord Careg, the youngest son of Caddalan of Lughcarn. One of the lordlings with him bowed, somewhat unsteadily, to Dovina. She acknowledged him with a nod.

"Best watch that," another young man said. "That's Lord Merryc's betrothed."

"No offense taken, I hope?" the fellow said to Dovina.

"None," Dovina said. "Merryc will be here soon."

He nodded pleasantly and strolled off to join the others, who had settled around a table some feet away. Dovina was just deciding that Darro was right, that she really should go back upstairs, when she heard Careg laugh like the bray of a mule.

"One of those lady scholars, is she?" Careg paused for a smirk. "I'll wager they do their studying on their backs."

The gaggle of men around him laughed. Darro bristled and started to scramble up, but Dovina pushed him back down. She was just reaching for a bronze candlestick to use as a club when she saw Merryc striding over to the lordlings. Apparently he'd overheard the remark because he'd gone white around the mouth with rage. The young lords fell silent as soon as they recognized him. Careg looked up, the smirk gone from his thin lips.

"You're speaking of my betrothed," Merryc said.

"Indeed? Well, at least you'll be marrying a lass who's well-trained."

Merryc swung backhanded and slapped him across the face. Blood ran from the lordling's nose. At Dovina's feet Darro let out a squeak of delight. Dovina let the candlestick remain on the table.

"You're too drunk to fight at the moment," Merryc said. "My second will come to you with the time and place. I suggest you find a second of your own, unless you don't have the guts for a duel."

None of the lordlings spoke or moved. Careg covered his bleeding nose with both hands and stared up, terrified. Merryc crossed his arms over his chest and waited. At last Careg lowered his hands and spoke in a reasonably steady voice.

"So be it. Our seconds will arrange terms."

Merryc made him a short, curt bow. He glanced around, saw Dovina, and hurried over to her.

"May I escort you, my lady?"

"Please," Dovina said. "I need a bit of fresh air."

As they left, arm in arm, the chamber behind them broke out in talk, as loud and sudden as a summer cloudburst. Darro trailed after them, a respectful distance behind. They hurried out to the silent garden, where the scent of some sweet flower drifted on the warm air.

"So much for my belittling of the honor code," Merryc said. "I'm afraid I acted on sheer instinct, not rational principles."

"In these circumstances I'll forgive you."

"My thanks." He bowed to her. "I wonder about Careg. He was probably just drunk, but that was coarse even for him. I'd think he wanted to provoke trouble, but when he got it, he looked less than pleased."

"Maybe he was just trying to smear my name. My father's not in good standing with the other gwerbretion at the moment. I'll bet they're trying to get back at him."

"Very likely, then. What would you like to do now? I'll escort you to your suite if you'd like."

"I would. I certainly don't want to go back to the great hall."

After Merryc left, Dovina sent Darró with a note for Ladoic. When he returned, the gwerbret came with him.

"What's all this?" Ladoic waved the note in her direction. "What kind of trouble?"

"It happened in the great hall just now. Lord Careg insulted me. It's that old lie, that women scholars are all just whores for the men."

"Indeed?" Ladoic's face turned a dangerous shade of red. "What did he say?"

"He implied that I was a common prostitute."

"The filthy swine!" Ladoic laid his hand on his sword hilt. "Where is he?"

"Merryc's already challenged him to a duel."

"I don't want to challenge him honorably. I want to cut him to pieces like the hog he is."

"Father, please don't! I know the clan's honor is at stake, but—"

"Not the clan's, you dimwit! Yours! How dare he speak that way about my daughter!"

"Father, please." Dovina laid a hand on his arm and did her best to look like a delicate, frightened female. "I couldn't bear it if they hanged you for killing him without a challenge. And Merryc's already had his challenge delivered."

Ladoic chewed on the ends of his mustache while he considered.

"Besides, Father, what would it do to Mother if—"

"Well, true enough." He let out an angry breath in a snort. "For her sake, then. And yours, I suppose."

"For the rhan's as well. Is Donno truly ready to rule Aberwyn?"

Ladoic snorted again, even more loudly. "Very well. Let me go see if this betrothed of yours needs a second."

Ladoic strode out and slammed the door behind him. Mavva, somewhat more pale than usual, came out of the inner chamber.

"Did you hear all that?" Dovina said.

"I did. I was afraid he was going to rush off and kill Lord Careg on sight. Your father truly does honor you."

"So he does. Well! Whoever would have thought it?"

Later that night Darro brought them the news. The duel would take place on the morrow morning. Lord Careg had named a second, but Merryc had yet to do so.

"It'll take place in the guesthouse," Darro said. "I mean, outside of course. That courtyard at the back, the one you can see from the upstairs common room."

"I've never been in that room," Dovina said. "But if there's a balcony, Mavva and I can watch from there. And Alyssa, if she'd like to come. Here, Darro, I'll write a note. You can take it to the embassy."

⑤

"Cavvo?" Alyssa waved the note in his direction. "I think you'd better read this."

Cavan took the invitation and frowned while he read it. They were sitting on the only chairs in the tiny reception room of their guesthouse. Dovina's page sat on the floor, waiting for an answer.

"How like my little brother," Cavan said when he'd finished reading. "If there's a way to offend someone, he'll find it."

"He makes a habit of saying things like this?"

"I'm afraid so. Usually his sword will get him out of the trouble his tongue's caused."

"You don't think Lord Merryc will lose, do you?"

"I doubt it. Careg is very good, mind, but Merro happens to be the best swordsman in the entire kingdom. Finesword, saber, old-fashioned broadsword—doesn't matter which. It's uncanny, how good he is. But, and this is the crux, you never know what's going to happen in a duel. Someone's foot can slip. Accidents like that happen."

"If there's going to be bloodshed, I really don't want to go and see it. Ych!"

"Right. You're not noble-born. Noblewomen are trained from childhood to deal with the blood their men spill."

The young page was listening to this exchange all wide-eyed and open-mouthed.

"You'll learn, Darro," Cavan said. "My wife will have an answer for your lady in a moment or two."

Alyssa took the note, got out her writing-case, and wrote on the back of the pabrus.

"Our Penvardd has kindly offered to escort me while I research a legal question in the bookhoard down at the Advocates Guild. It wouldn't be courteous for me to change our plans now. So please forgive me for not coming. I hope and pray your betrothed suffers no harm. I'll come see you the moment I'm free."

She sprinkled sand on the message, let it dry, then shook it clean and rolled it up.

"Don't let anyone see this, Darro. Here's a penny for you, too."

The lad bowed to her and left.

"I just hope Careg holds his tongue from now on," Cavan said. "If he starts spewing filth about you, I'll have to challenge him myself."

"Why would he do that?"

"Because from everything I heard, it's your speech that finally made Gwardon come over to the Bardic Guild's side of the case."

"Oh, here! It helped, I'm sure, but it wasn't the only thing."

"You don't understand, Lyss. When you're speaking in full voice, you're like a warrior. Your words cut like a blade."

She laughed and blushed with a little wave of her hand.

"I mean it," Cavan continued. "It's like you're swinging a sword of fire. Or truly, you are the sword of fire."

"Then my thanks, my love. I just wish I could get a real apprenticeship in the Advocates Guild. They don't give those to lasses, you know."

"Their loss. At least they're going to let you read in their book-hoard."

"And I'm grateful for that. It's an important question I'm trying to answer."

Alyssa was hoping that Dovina would assume the question concerned justiciars. It was likely she would never think of the truth, because the idea of passing over a son for a daughter in her position sounded like a bard's tale. Certainly women had ruled as lords at times, but always when no son existed to claim a holding that a clan wished to keep. She vaguely remembered one case where a woman in Eldidd had even ruled as a tieryn. But a gwerbret? The highest rank of all possible nobles? Back in the Dawntime, most likely, since Dwvoryc's book stated that women had fought as warriors and claimed high rank, even rulership of some of the tiny kingdoms of those times. Things had changed in Deverry over the long years. Her studies had made that amply clear.

Could they change again? Alyssa remembered the mysterious Hild and her talk of rivers cutting new beds and winds that blew where they wished. Maybe changes were on their way. Maybe. She could only hope and watch for the omens of their coming.

Because they were such a popular sport among the nobility, Dovina had seen a good many mock combats in her life. She'd also witnessed several duels meant to draw blood, and she was assuming that this one, like those, would be stopped at the first small cut. In the bright morning light she and Mavva sat together on the little balcony overlooking the combat ground where they could see everything but be safely out of the way of any thoughtless actions. At her order Darro placed their chairs as close together as he could.

"You look a bit pale," Dovina said to Mavva. "Do I?"

"Truly, you do. I hope naught horrible happens."

"I'm of two minds. I don't want Merryc hurt, but Lord Careg would be no great loss to the kingdom. But don't worry, these things never amount to much."

Mavva shuddered and drew her shawl tightly around her shoulders.

The Cerrmor heralds serving at the duel had marked out a big square of lawn with red ribbons for a combat ground. They took up their positions, staves at the ready, one at either side. A town crier stood in readiness. At a nod from a herald he rang his bell three times.

"The ground is prepared! The combatants may now enter."

To a few cheers but more catcalls Lord Careg and his second strode out of the guesthouse and marched over to one corner. The crowd fell silent for a few moments, only to return to frantic whispering with a sound like ocean waves on a gravel beach. Dovina leaned forward and peered. Lord Merryc was taking the field with his second beside him.

"What?" Dovina said to Mavva. "I can't see, curse it! Why is everyone so startled?"

"I don't know. I—oh, by the Goddess! The second!"

When the pair came closer, Dovina could at last identify Merryc's companion. With his pale doeskin breeches and linen shirt, he wore a cloth-of-gold waistcoat. The sleeves of his shirt were embroidered with wyverns, and pinned to the waistcoat glittered an enormous gold ring brooch.

"It's the regent himself," Mavva whispered.

"It is indeed. This isn't only about the slight to my honor. Not any longer." Dovina felt a warm flush of admiration for the man. "He does know how to make a grand gesture, doesn't he?"

The seconds remained in their corners when Careg and Merryc walked onto the ground. The heralds came forward, inspected their weapons, and proclaimed them equal—an elven finesword each in the right hand. The heralds withdrew. The two men faced each other, some ten feet apart.

"Proceed!" the heralds called out

They circled, slowly, stepped in, drew back. Blades met, clashed, withdrew. Dovina watched their footwork for a few moments. Careg knew what he was doing, she decided, but Merryc outshone him in confidence and balance. Another flurry, another parry, a clash of blades, but still no touch on either man, or so she thought.

As they drew back, Merryc lowered his guard so far that the tip of his sword hovered just above the trampled grass. Was he wounded? Dovina leaned forward but could see no trace of blood. In the bright sunlight she had a good view of Careg's face and saw him laugh as he stepped confidently forward. Merryc held his ground and waited. Careg lunged, striking hard, but Merryc flipped up his sword from below, caught the other's blade, and parried as he in turn stepped to close. With his free hand he grabbed Careg's arm in a gesture oddly like an intended embrace and twisted as he grappled. Careg swore. His blade went flying. The arm snapped with a sound like a butcher cracking a joint of meat.

Careg fell hard and nearly brought Merryc down on top of him. Merryc just managed to restore his balance and stepped free, then swung down with his sword. The point stopped just above Careg's throat.

"I believe," Merryc said, "that you owe Lady Dovina an apology. Now would be an opportune time to tender it."

Panting, sweating, his face dead-white from pain, Careg stared up at him while Merryc waited—unsmiling, but not scowling, not fierce, merely patient. At last Careg panted and choked.

"I shall beg her pardon." Careg could barely force each word out between his gasps for breath.

"Splendid! She's in attendance here."

Careg sat up and yelped in pain. With his good hand he caught the wrist of the broken arm and steadied it. His second stepped forward, but Merryc drove him back with a glance.

"There's naught wrong with your friend's legs."

With a great deal of effort Careg got to his knees. His head lolled back, and great drops of sweat rolled down his pasty cheeks. Merryc relented. He flicked his sword at the second to give him permission to come help. With someone to lean upon Careg got to his feet and staggered toward the balcony. Dovina started to speak to Mavva, but her friend looked as if she were about to be sick. Dovina rose from her chair. She had the awful feeling that she was grinning like a witch with delight and arranged her face into what she hoped was a suitably haughty and distant expression. Careg stopped just below the balcony's railing and gasped again. The second slipped his arm around his friend's waist to steady him.

"My lady," Careg said. "I humbly apologize for the foul things I said about you."

"You insulted more than me, my lord."

He winced. "True spoken. My apologies to all your fellows at the collegium."

Dovina started to answer, but he fainted and fell to his knees beyond the second's power to keep him standing. Over in Merryc's corner of the ground, Gwerbret Ladoic broke out laughing, and most of the men present joined in.

"Gods help!" Mavva said. "I'm glad you're marrying him, Dovva, not me."

It was some while later that Dovina had the chance to speak with Merryc, out in the gardens away from prying ears. They sat down on a bench, and Merryc turned to her.

"What would you have done if I'd killed the stinking little bastard? Would you have been pleased?"

"I doubt it. I probably would have fainted dead away, and Mavva with me." Dovina smiled at him. "If I'd gloated over his corpse, what would you have thought of me?"

"I would have honored you for it but, I'll admit, I would have had second thoughts about marrying someone that fierce."

They both laughed, hesitantly at first, then deeply when they saw that the other was laughing, too.

"You've made an enemy, though," Dovina said.

"He hated me already. Nothing truly lost there." He smiled at her. "One other thing, Dovva. After that public display, we may assume we're betrothed."

"Most assuredly we are. If your mother cares to discuss the settlement with my father?"

"I'll tell her straightaway."

Arm in arm they strolled back to the great hall. *You know*, Dovina thought, *this could do quite well, this marriage. I must send Mother a letter as soon as ever I can, thanking her.*

"Well and good, then," Merryc said. "Soon we'll be married. I take it you'd like to finish your studies in Aberwyn."

"I would indeed. We could have a long, formal betrothal to allow it."

He looked so disappointed that she realized he had grown fond of her.

"Or," she said, "I have land in my name nearby with a manse that might suit us while I finish. There's plenty of pasturage for horses."

"And a chamber for books?"

"Most definitely a chamber for books! No doubt my lord can find things to amuse himself with while I'm at the collegium."

"I've always wanted to follow Prince Mael's example and write a treatise on honor and its meaning—and its dangers. Struggling with the words would keep me occupied, I should think. I'm not sure how to start."

"What about notes in a commentary on Mael's writings? Like the one he wrote on Ristolyn?"

"You know, that would do splendidly, wouldn't it? My thanks! Duels are all very well, but they're a costly way of settling an argument."

"As Lord Careg found out? Summat I've meant to ask you—that trick, holding your sword point low, where did you learn that?"

"I'm not sure. It just came to me, once when I was practicing with a swordmaster." He frowned as he thought about his answer. "It was odd, but it seemed like a thing I'd always known."

The news of Lord Merryc's victory reached the Advocates Guild in the person of an overexcited apprentice, who rushed into the bookhoard and started babbling. Lord Daen listened to the end, Alyssa noticed, before he told the lad to hush and get back to work.

"It sounds to me," Daen said, "that your friend has found a kindred spirit for a husband."

"Doesn't it?" Alyssa said. "I'm so pleased for her! Those arranged marriages can be very difficult for the woman."

"Just so. It also sounds to me like Lord Merryc is capable of taking over at least some of a gwerbret's duties. The warlike ones."

With Daen's help, Alyssa had discovered that a daughter's husband might take over a rhan if he were willing to be adopted into the new clan—and if the Council of Electors agreed.

"Ladoic will have some arm-twisting to do," Daen said, "but one knows he'll be able to have his way in the end. He's that sort of man."

"True spoken. Besides, no one thinks much of Adonyc. Of course, Merryc will have to agree, too."

Daen snorted. "He'll jump at the chance."

"What man wouldn't, I suppose? My thanks for your help, good sir!"

"Is there aught else you need?"

"May I ask you a question? The woman who wanted to meet me the other day, Hild. Who is she?"

"A woman of great power in mysterious things. A healer, for one. She spends most of her time on the road, she tells me, helping those who need her herbs, seeing what she can see around the kingdom. I suppose you'll think me daft, but I swear! At times I'm sure she has dwimmer."

"I don't think you're daft. I rather thought the same thing."

Alyssa wrote out a clean copy of their findings, then with her Bardekian bodyguard, Gurra, went up to the guesthouse to deliver it. They met in Ladoic's private suite with no one else present, and Gurra stood outside the door to ensure things remained that way.

Ladoic read the report over twice before he commented. "I'd rather she held the right to rule."

"For the first few years, Your Grace, she'll be the real ruler. She knows Aberwyn far better than Merryc ever will. We all hope Your Grace will live for a very long time yet, of course."

"Of course. No need for flattery, lass, though I'll admit to hoping so myself. You're right, though, that the Electors would probably refuse to acknowledge her. I don't want to plunge the rhan into civil war. That's one reason why I'm doing this. Adonyc's about as diplomatic as that Careg fellow."

"In a few years, Your Grace, Merryc could always cede Dovina the rule in a formal court."

"Like in front of that cursed justiciar, eh? He might be good for summat after all." Ladoic tapped the rolled pabrus on the palm of one broad hand while he thought something through. "My thanks. About that no-good husband of yours? I'll withdraw the offer of bounty once we're back in Aberwyn. My councillor tells me we have to do it there. The decree of his sanscrosanct person will hold until then."

"My thanks, Your Grace! My most humble—"

"Enough! You may leave us. Dovva's expecting you to come for lunch. She probably wants to natter about her betrothed." He shook his head. "Ye gods! The kind of men you lasses choose! Oh, well, better than some mincing scribe."

Alyssa forced out a polite smile while he chuckled to himself. She curtsied twice and left.

CHAPTER 13

PRINCE GWARDON RETURNED TO his villa in order to let his councillor study the laws concerning the Justiciar of the Northern Border for precedents. After hearing the man's report, he returned to Cerrmor to release a proclamation. After much consultation on the part of his councillor with the Advocates Guild, he told the court, he had settled the question of who might attend the legal court of the new western justiciar. All suits involving only commoners would come to the local gwerbretion unless both commoners agreed otherwise, the gwerbret released them, and the justiciar agreed to take them on. Matters involving two noble lords would as well, but any suit in which a commoner and a member of the nobility were involved would have to come before the justiciar. Any legal matters involving two gwerbretion would continue to come before royalty, as was the case presently.

"A cursed compromise!" Dovina snarled. "I don't like this. A rich commoner will still be able to bribe and bend justice against a poor one."

"Indeed," Alyssa said. "I don't like it either."

"Nor do I," Mavva said. "But it's a start. Don't forget that the Wmmglaedd priests want changes. They'll be in a better position than we are to bring them about."

"Now that's true spoken!" Dovina said. "One battle does not a war make. I need to remember that."

"Just so," Mavva continued. "We've got a long, long war ahead of us. Lyss, you look so sour!"

"I want to win right now, is why, but I know you're right. It's going to take years before there are justiciars in all the rhans."

"If ever," Dovina put in. "Our next big campaign is getting a proper written law code like they have in Bardek. Once the laws are written down, they won't bend as easily as they do now. And then rich and poor can stand on level ground."

"Until the noble lords find some way around it, anyway," Mavva said. "But there's naught we can do about that now."

Gwerbret Ladoic's opinion of the compromise was higher than that of his daughter, though for reasons only indirectly related to the law itself.

"There had to be some kind of compromise, Dovva," he told her. "For the poor gwerbretion, it's a matter of revenue. For the rich, it's a matter of their high opinion of themselves. Those of us in the middle can shrug and see how things go. What I'm hoping is, this will quiet the mutterings about open rebellion. None of us needs a war with Dun Deverry."

"Well, that's certainly true. We don't all need to be cursed by the priests of Bel, either."

"Especially not now, not with the happy occasion, eh?"

"What happy occasion?"

Ladoic looked heavenward in disgust. "Your marriage, you dolt! It's time for me to hire this guesthouse for one of those wretched afternoon fêtes. We'll have a proper traditional feast when we get home. We'll celebrate your betrothal in grand style then. But Amara's already put on one fête here, so this one's my responsibility."

"My thanks, Father." Dovina dropped him a curtsy. "But shouldn't you wait till the dowry and settlement are finished? What if his clan asks for too much?"

"Don't vex yourself. Amara's told me that the land you have will be more than dowry enough, and in fact she'll return half of it to you once the marriage itself is celebrated as a marriage portion."

"That's splendid!"

"I thought so, too. Much better than coin, land. Own land and you've got a solid thing. Coin? Huh, it dribbles away fast enough."

Dovina laughed. "Truly," she said, "I can see why the bards say the noble-born are all farmers at heart."

"For a change, they're right enough."

Once her father left, Dovina wrote a note to Alyssa, inviting her and Cavan for a small private dinner in her suite that evening. She sent Darro off with it, and he returned promptly with the answer that it would gladden their hearts to come.

"Cavan must be going daft, shut up in the embassy like that," Dovina remarked.

"He said as much, my lady."

"I see. Here's another note for you to deliver. It's for Lord Merryc. I'm hoping that he and his mother will join us."

The maids at the Bardekian embassy had done their best to clean and repair it, but none of Alyssa's much-used clothing would do for an event like a betrothal fête. Fortunately Dovina had brought an entire chest of clothing, including dresses fitted through the bodice in the latest style as well as the more traditional flowing cut. She laid a rainbow of silks out on the bed in her suite for Alyssa and Mavva to consider.

"I'd better wear these old-fashioned ones," Dovina said. "Father prefers them, and this fête is costing him deep in purse, so I suppose I can condescend to do what he'll like. You and Mavva can choose from the rest. Merryc says to tell you that he's got a fancy shirt and breeches that should fit Cavan well enough."

"No one's going to be looking at us, anyway," Alyssa said. "All eyes will be on the happy pair."

In that spirit she chose a modest costume in pale blue and left the deep red for Mavva. Before Alyssa and Cavan left, Polla made a tidy bundle of the blue dress and white underdress. Lady Amara sent them back to the embassy in her little open carriage, along with a footman on the back as well as Gurra, who sat facing Cavan and Alyssa, to ensure that any street thieves and beggars left them alone.

One of Cerrmor's main streets, wide enough for two full coaches to pass each other, ran from the guesthouse down to the harbor. To reach the Bardekian embassy, however, the carriage had to leave that street for a narrow lane, dimly lit by a single oil lamp hanging high above, between the backs of two stone buildings—warehouses, Alyssa assumed. The coachman had just negotiated the turn when shadows stepped out of a doorway and grabbed at the horses' bridles. The coachman shouted. The horses threw up their heads in confusion and danced in harness, making the carriage slew first to Alyssa's side, then to Cavan's.

Cavan, Gurra, the footman—they swore and struggled to get their weapons drawn as the carriage swung this way and that. The footman jumped clear, but the other two men were trapped. Alyssa grabbed the handhold inside the door with one hand. With the other she hitched up her tunic to get to the hilt of her elven knife.

"Help!" the coachman yelled. "Thieves! Murder!" He began lashing about with his whip at the men who'd stopped the carriage—a mistake, because in the uncertain light he clipped the horses as well. They kicked out, tried to rear, and made the carriage buck and slam into the wall of the nearest warehouse. As it slewed back again, Cavan finally managed to jump free. He stumbled, righted himself, and drew his finesword as he did so. Alyssa hung on and swore like a silver dagger herself. Gurra got free at last and drew his blade.

"Help the coachman!" Cavan shouted to him.

Gurra began yelling in Bardekian as he tried to slither past the carriage without getting crushed. Men were running down the alley behind them. Alyssa heard shouts, steel clashing on steel. She got a quick look back over one shoulder to see Cavan and the footman fighting men in dark clothing, a whirl of shadows in the dim light slashed now and then by a glitter of steel blades.

"Get the lass!" a voice shouted. "Curse you, get the stinking cunt of a lass!"

Gurra had reached the horses at last. At the sight of his sword the two men fled, and the carriage steadied. Alyssa drew her knife just as a burly fellow reached the door on her side. He wrenched it open and made a grab at her with the wide-open arms of a man who thinks he's in no danger. She stabbed with all her strength. He screamed in surprise as much as pain and grabbed with both hands as the blade sank into the flabby flesh below his ribs. She pulled the long blade out and back and, just as Joh had taught her, sliced up. His scream turned to a bubbling spray of something warm and sticky. She'd missed her target, but the dwimmerknife had plunged itself into his throat. He fell back against the wall, then slid to the ground and folded over like a half-empty sack of flour.

Other men were running, shouting, but these called out "Daiver! Daiver!" Alyssa heard scuffling, more cursing, more shouts of pain and surprise. She could neither move nor think, merely stared at her knife blade, wet and dark in the lamplight.

"Ye gods!" Lord Merryc's voice cut through the fog in her mind. "Cavvo's been cut!"

Alyssa shoved the wet knife back into its sheath. The trembling carriage lay too close to the wall on the one side for her to open that door. She forced herself to open the other and scrambled the two steps down even though she reached ground directly next to the dead thing lying there. She ignored it and rushed around the back end of the carriage, but she could see nothing. Men crowded round, some holding lanterns, most holding drawn blades.

"Cavvo!" she called out. "Where is he?"

"It's his wife," Merryc said. "Let her through!"

Cavan was lying with his head pillowed on the dead body of the footman. A man Alyssa didn't recognize knelt beside him, pressing hard on a wad of cloth—Lord Merryc's waistcoat—shoved into Cavan's side. Alyssa started to kneel, but Merryc stopped her.

"You'll get trampled, down on the ground like that," he said. "We'll save him yet."

Up at the carriage, voices were calling back and forth. "I'm a physician!" "Let him through, curse you dogs!" "Move move move!" The carriage abruptly jerked a few feet forward as two men shoved their way back through the crowd, Gurra and an older man holding a leather case. Alyssa let Merryc lead her a few feet back out of the way.

"Ye gods!" Merryc said. "Blood! You're hurt!"

"I'm not." Alyssa jerked her thumb in the direction of the dead man against the wall. "I killed him. It's his blood."

Everyone within earshot turned and stared. Alyssa drew the sticky knife and held it up. "A wise woman gave me this. An even wiser one said to carry it always. So I did."

On the ground the physician called for a second lantern. "Bleeding's eased!" he said. "Let's get him into the carriage, get him into the embassy. Got to get him warmed up and fast."

Alyssa began to tremble, but for Cavan's sake, not her danger now past. *Dear Goddess, she was thinking, don't let him die! Please please please don't let him die!* Over and over she repeated it, while all around her cursing men dragged corpses out of the way and did what they could for Cavan and a wounded man she didn't know. The world shrank to her silent prayer. The noise, the sight of the world in front of her, even the touch of Merryc's hand on her shoulder as he guided her out of the way— they seemed to be happening not to her but to some stranger, as if she listened to a marketplace storyteller describe it rather than lived the moment.

When the carriage took Cavan back to the embassy, Alyssa walked behind simply because no one thought to let her ride. By then she felt too numb, too disconnected, to even pray. Merryc walked with her.

"One of the maids overheard a couple of men whispering about an attack on you," he said. "She'd taken the leavings from the dinner back to the guesthouse kitchen, you see, and was taking the small scraps outside for the dogs. She heard more than barking. So she ran back upstairs with the news. Took me more time than I wanted to rouse a few men and get us down here."

"My thanks." It was all that Alyssa could manage to say.

They'd reached the embassy before she realized that she was still holding the knife. She wiped it off on her skirt, then sheathed it.

Hwlio was waiting at the embassy gates. Servants carrying lanterns hovered nearby.

"Get in fast!" His dark voice shook with rage. "How dare they! Just how—embassy protection—practically at our door—how dare they!"

"They'll pay," Merryc said. "We know who's behind this, good sir, and they'll pay."

ovina, Mavva, and Lady Amara stayed in the suite to wait
for news. Polla and Minna started to leave for the servants'
quarters, but Dovina called them back.

"It might not be safe," she said, "if someone realizes you were the
one who gave the alarm."

"Truly," Amara said. "Minna, that was very brave of you to come
tell us."

"Well, my lady, I've not been treated this well before in my whole
life, and the hells may take me if I should let great ladies like these
come to harm!"

"You have my thanks," Dovina said. "My humble thanks, even. I
just hope to every god that Merro reaches Lyss and her husband before those scumbag bastards do."

They waited. After what seemed like half the night, but what was
probably a bare half of one watch, Dovina sent Darro off to find out
what he could, with Amara's second footman along for a guard.

"Be careful!" she said. "Stay on the lighted streets!"

"We will, my lady," the footman said. "Have no doubt about that."

After another interminable wait, they returned with the news that
Alyssa was safe but Cavan gravely wounded. Two attackers dead,
one merely wounded, and, worst of all, the other Daiver footman
dead as well.

"He died defending the guests and the carriage, my lady."

"Ah, ye gods! I'm so sorry!" Amara rose from her chair and laid a
kind hand on his arm. "I know he was a good friend to you."

The footman nodded, his lips pressed tight together.

"Go wait in the servants' hall," Amara said and released him to
his grief.

More waiting. Mavva finally could stay awake no longer, but she
curled up on top of her bed fully dressed. The two maids huddled
together on the floor in a corner and slept. Amara dozed in a cushioned chair. Dovina managed to do the same, only to wake to
Merryc's familiar pattern of knocks on the door. She got up and
rushed to open it to find the corridor full of armed men, her father
among them.

"Come in, come in," Dovina said. "How does Cavan fare?"

"Badly," Merryc said. "But I've not given up hope yet."

The men, all from Aberwyn's warband, stayed out in the corridor when Ladoic and Merryc entered. Amara woke, Mavva hurried in from her chamber, and the two maids scrambled to their feet to curtsy.

"Your carriage is outside, Mother," Merryc said. "My two men and two more of Aberwyn's will escort you home."

"After I hear your news, Merro." Amara turned to Ladoic. "Well, this is a fine turn of events!"

"A grave one, my lady," Ladoic said. "There's one of your men dead, first off. And then there's been an attack on persons the laws declared sacrosanct, and that wretched priest backed me up, even."

Dovina shuddered in a brief chill. "I'd forgotten about that."

"I haven't! The Lord of Hell's going to demand a bit of tribute for this, say I."

"As soon as it's light," Merryc said, "we'll be sending messages to the mayor and to the prince."

"I'll take the messages to the prince myself," Ladoic said. "Attacking a woman, and her but a lass, truly!"

"Who did this?" Mavva said. "Do you have any idea, my lords?"

"Plenty of ideas," Ladoic snapped. "Little evidence as of yet."

"As far as I can tell," Merryc said, "the fellow that Alyssa killed belonged to Gwerbret Caddalan's warband." He glanced at Minna. "Would you recognize him, do you think?"

"He was standing in the light from the kitchen window, my lord, so I will. The other fellow, he was in the shadows, like, but I did hear him say Caddalan's name. Caddalan's going to be pleased with us, he said, for this night's work. He sounded like a lord to me, my lord, not one of the riders or suchlike. And he was holding one arm all strange, like, crooked and wrapped in a scarf or suchlike. That's all I heard, because I threw the scraps to the dogs and ran up here."

"More than enough," Ladoic said. "Hah!"

"It is." Merryc smiled, a slow, grim smile without a shred of humor in it. "Well and good, then. I'll go to the mayor, Your Grace, if you go to the prince."

"Done. I—"

"Wait just a moment here!" Dovina held up one hand flat. "Did you say Alyssa killed a man?"

"I did. Just luck, she says, and a Westfolk knife with dwimmer on it, but she cursed well did." Merryc laughed in one short bark. "The dolt thought she was an easy target. Huh. Well, he can think about his mistake in the Otherlands."

At the Bardekian compound, they'd taken Cavan and the other wounded man into the main building. The physician's apprentice bound up the wounded attacker, but Edry himself tended Cavan. In a room usually reserved for dining they put him on a long table with candelabra massed on the sideboard so Edry could see to work. To wait, Alyssa sat in a little side room with Hwlio's wife, Markella. She, Hwlio, and the physician had all been dining at the embassy when a guard had rushed in to say Gurra was yelling for help nearby.

Maids and other servants kept offering to escort her to the cottage so she could change her blood-stained clothes, but she refused to go. She did let Gurra have the knife to clean it and the sheath before the blood dried and stuck them together. Now and then she would think, I killed a man, but the thought seemed utterly meaningless. Again, it seemed to refer to some incident in a story she'd heard.

Alyssa was drowsing on the edge of numb sleep when she heard a door open. Two servants carried buckets of red water out of the improvised surgery. In a short while they returned with buckets of clean water and carried those inside. A third servant followed with a blanket.

"He's going to die," Alyssa whispered. "I know it in my heart."

"Nah nah nah!" Markella said. "He's a strong man and a warrior, and he has you to live for."

Markella was proven right shortly after. Edry, his fine clothing all streaked and stained with blood, came out to say that Cavan was out of danger. In sheer relief Alyssa wept even as she laughed in a choked little mutter. Edry turned to Markella. "I want him to rest before we try to move him."

Alyssa managed to speak at last. "Can I see him?"

"You may, but only for a little while. I'll come in with you."

As she walked into the room, she nearly stumbled over a heap of his blood-stained clothes, sliced and shredded where the physician had cut them off in his hurry. Wrapped in the blanket Cavan still lay on the table. His face had gone dead-pale, his lips bloodless, his eyes half-open on the edge of consciousness. Yet he managed to smile at her, briefly but a smile, when she walked up to him. She stroked his sweat-soaked hair back from his face, so cold under her fingers.

"My love, my heart!" she said. "Please don't die."

"I won't," he said. "Sewn up like a rag doll."

He smiled again and fell asleep.

Not long after dawn, Merryc arrived at the civic broch tower to find the mayor of Cerrmor there ahead of him. In the Justice Hall Eddel and five men of the night watch were sitting around the table on the dais and sharing a couple of loaves of bread and butter. Eddel stood up and called to Merryc.

"Come up, my lord! I was just thinking of sending you a message."

"My thanks! I take it you've heard about the trouble in the streets last night?"

"I have, and we'll be holding a hearing this afternoon. I've sent a message to the Prince Regent. He may want to attend. I've also sent some of the lads round to the embassy to collect the wounded man, one of the ones who did the attacking, that is, not the fellow who was trying to defend the lass."

"Then my thanks again."

Merryc sat down and accepted a chunk of bread. He'd just finished it when a servant came running to say that the wounded fellow had arrived.

"We've put him in the little room," the servant said. "The one with the bars in the door."

Everyone got up and trooped down into the cellar of the broch, where prisoners were kept before a trial or hearing.

"You can talk to him first, my lord," Eddel said. "He might listen to you better'n me, like."

Barlo, his name was, a big burly man with thinning red hair and a slack mouth, at the moment, from the pain of his slashed ribcage. He was foolishly still wearing the blood-soaked shirt embroidered with Lughcarn's device, though he had turned it inside out, that marked him as a member of Caddalan's warband. Apparently he had decided he wasn't going to hang alone. As soon as Merryc came up to the barred window in the door to confront him, he blurted out the truth.

"It was Careg, my lord, the gwerbret's cursed son, who came up with the cursed plan, and may the Lord of Hell take him for it, too."

"And what did he hope to gain from it?"

Barlo hesitated.

"Out with it!" Merryc said.

"He wanted us to take your betrothed, for revenge, like, but Seddo—he's dead now, and he won't mind me telling you—he was our captain, so we had to take his cursed orders—so Seddo says to him, she's a gwerbret's daughter and are you out of your mind, my lord? Then we'll get her cursed slut of a friend, Lord Careg said, that's almost as good, them and their—well, he went on a bit about it."

Merryc felt himself turn very cold and very still. You had to humiliate him, didn't you? he was thinking. It wasn't enough to just win the cursed duel! You had to go and humiliate him, and now there's men dead over this. And if they'd taken the lass? His face must have revealed his flare of rage, because Barlo took a step back and stared at him with the hopeless terror of a rat cornered by a ferret.

"I see," Merryc said. "You have my thanks, for what that's worth."

With a grunt Barlo left the window. He staggered to a cot and lowered himself carefully onto it. Merryc turned away. Eddel and the guards were waiting by the stairs.

"I heard all that, my lord," the mayor said.

"Indeed? You'd best start mustering your archers and spearmen."

Eddel's pale eyebrows shot up.

"Well?" Merryc said. "Do you think Gwerbret Caddalan's going to turn his favorite son over to you, all nice and peaceful, like?"

"Good point, my lord. Huh. If I ask for the prince's aid, think he'll give it?"

"More than likely, but he'll be the one to decide."

As a victim and witness, Alyssa was required to attend the legal proceedings. After a flurry of messages, she left the embassy with Gurra and a second embassy guard to escort her. Just outside

Dovina and Mavva waited along with ten men of the Aberwyn warband and Ladoic himself.

"No chance of trouble this time," Ladoic said.

"My thanks, Your Grace." Alyssa curtsied to him.

"We can't expect you to kill them all for us, eh? But that was a nice bit of work, lass. My congratulations."

Alyssa curtsied again and forced out a smile. She'd spent the night having painful dreams that always ended with the sight of the dead man crumpling over like a half-filled sack of flour. Dovina caught her hand and squeezed it.

"Don't mind Father. He's an old warrior. He can't help being bloodthirsty."

Alyssa nodded, but a second smile was beyond her. Mavva took her other hand. She clung to both of them the entire way up to the city broch. And yet, as they made their slow way through the crowded, busy streets, she realized that rather than feeling shamed and sick over what had happened, she was very glad to be alive, just as much as she was glad that Cavan still lived. The fog was peeling back from a blue summer sky. Gulls wheeled and called overhead. Now and then she caught a glimpse of someone's little garden, or a woman passed carrying a baby, all of them beautiful each in their own way.

Better him than me, she thought. *Far better him than me!*

Prince Gwardon attended the hearing, but he stood in the back of the crowded Justice Hall with three of his men. As the sole concession to royalty, the four of them were allowed to keep their weapons. Merryc, who had surrendered his finesword, stood with them and watched Eddel run the hearing. On the dais with the mayor sat a Lawspeaker priest and two men from the Advocates Guild.

Once the Sword of Justice lay on the table, Merryc studied the small crowd of witnesses, guards, and the merely curious. Alyssa, with her enormous Bardekian guard beside her, sat near the front. The two Aberwyn maids sat just behind with Dovina, Mavva, and Gwerbret Ladoic. A surprise arrived when Hwlio of House Elaeno, the Bardekian ambassador in Cerrmor, strode in and took the last vacant chair near the front. There was no sign of Caddalan or Careg, but just as the guards were shutting the door, Caddalan's noble-born councillor, Lord Vupyl, rushed in. A local man surrendered his seat to allow the lord to sit as far from the Aberwyn contingent as possible. With him came a scribe who scribbled notes all through the proceedings, as Mavva did as well.

"We have before us," Eddel said, "a lot of things to sort out. First, attacking people in the night streets. Worse yet, killing one of 'em and cursed near killing a couple of others. Second, two of these people were under strict protection of our ancient traditions."

He paused and glanced at the priest, who nodded. Hwlio rose from his chair.

"What is it?" Eddel said.

"They were also, honored sir, under the protection of the Bardekian embassy."

The priest winced.

"My thanks," Eddel said. "We'll add that right in."

Hwlio sat down again.

"There are smaller matters," Eddel continued, "like the damage to the carriage, but we'll let those go for now. There are a couple of persons charged with these offenses, but two of 'em are dead. We've got a third one in custody. There must be at least two others, judging from the reports I've heard of the incident. Witnesses tell me that all of these men rode in Gwerbret Caddalan of Lughcarn's warband."

Lord Vupyl hesitated on the edge of his chair. Eddel waited, but the lord shook his head no and settled back again.

"What counts is who came up with this idea in the first place," Eddel said. "We have witnesses accusing Lord Careg of Lughcarn."

Vupyl jumped to his feet.

"Honored mayor! I demand—"

"You'll hear 'em, my lord, and right now."

One after the other, the witnesses spoke: Minna, Alyssa herself, and Barlo, carried up from the cellar by two burly guards. He had repeated what he'd told Merryc in front of so many listeners that it was far too late for him to lie in court. Once he'd been carried down again, the mayor called Merryc. Merryc went up to the dais, kissed the Sword of Justice, and knelt before the table. The priest leaned forward to listen.

"I was having dinner with my betrothed and my mother when the maid told us what she'd heard. I gathered my two men. As we were leaving the guesthouse, we saw two men of Aberwyn's warband. I commandeered them, too. So we ran down toward the embassy. I knew the carriage was on its way there, you see. We could hear the noise of the fighting easily enough, anyway, when we got closer.

"By then a couple of your men from the night watch had joined us. As we ran up, we heard someone yelling 'Lughcarn! Lughcarn!' So I yelled 'Daiver' right back, and we joined the scrap."

Merryc glanced over his shoulder and saw Lord Vupyl sitting slumped in obvious defeat. Servant witnesses could be bullied. The nephew of Gwerbret Daiver could not.

"Well and good, then," Eddel said. "I think we've got enough to get on with. Lord Merryc, you may rise and go."

Merryc decided against returning to the prince's side. He took a vacant spot on a bench at the back instead. A shabby woman who smelled of fish moved over to give him room.

"I'm going to call for a formal malover for this afternoon," Eddel said. "If of course our Lawspeaker agrees. Your Holiness?"

The priest got up and addressed his remarks to Lord Vupyl.

"These are grave charges laid against the son of your lord," he said. "I would suggest that you advise him to appear before this court as soon as it reconvenes in malover. The honored mayor of Cerrmor has rightly called for a continuing investigation into this matter. I shall be in attendance. It would behoove both the gwerbret and his son to be so as well. I hereby declare the charge. Lord Careg of Lughcarn appears to be red-tongued as per the third instance as listed under King Bran's laws of abetting murder. He has urged others to kill innocent victims."

The chamber fell so silent that Merryc could hear Vupyl's small gasp for breath. The lord rose, and the scrape of his chair on the wood floor as he did so sounded as loud as a trumpet call.

"I shall inform him, Your Holiness. I cannot answer for what he will do."

"Of course. If he refuses, will you return with news of his decision?"

"If he allows. I'll urge him to attend in any case."

"Good." The priest turned to Eddel. "Honored mayor?"

Eddel rose and picked up the Sword of Justice. "Come back when the sun's moved on about two hours. Until then, the hearing's over." He rapped the pommel of the sword on the table three times.

Although Merryc considered meeting up with Dovina and her women friends, he decided that as a principal witness he'd best avoid any appearance of collusion. He got himself a chunk of pork and bread from a street vendor and drifted to a quiet spot to eat it. After more aimless walking, he at last heard the town criers calling to reconvene the hearing. He hurried back to the Justice Hall in time to get a seat on a bench. After the usual noise and confusion of a swarm of people looking for seats, the court quieted, and Eddel reopened the matter at hand.

The first to speak was Lord Vupyl, who looked less than happy about it.

"Gwerbret Caddalan has told me to inform you that he, his men, and the offending son will leave Cerrmor as soon as possible. In that way Lord Careg will not remain as an affront to Cerrmor laws. His father will try him for the offense in his own court."

Several of the common-born onlookers hooted in scorn. Merryc heard a market woman mutter, "Fat lot o'good that'll be." Lord Vupyl turned and gave her a murderous look.

"Silence in the chamber, if you please," Eddel said. "Your lordship, I fear me you'll have to forgive our doubts about this."

Vupyl crossed his arms over his chest and glared at the mayor. The Lawspeaker rose from his chair.

"It's a grave matter to ban one of the great clans from the sacrifices. I will warn you that such could be the outcome of this affair."

Vupyl clutched himself a little more tightly. "I shall warn the gwerbret, but I'm merely his messenger, Your Holiness."

"Think well on the message you'll be bringing him. His son's charged with committing sacrilege by violating the law of sanctuary. He may also have committed a grave insult to important friends of both the High King and Cerrmor by offending the Bardekian ambassador."

"I understand, Your Holiness."

The real question, Merryc figured, was whether Caddalan would understand—or care.

"The laws of King Bran assess fines for these offenses. Should this case be declared proven, such fines will be assigned then."

"Very well, Your Holiness."

"Sacrilege can bring a curse upon the entire kingdom," the priest continued. "I hereby declare this a matter legitimate for royal concern." He paused to look over the crowd. "Will the Marked Prince answer me?"

Prince Gwardon stepped forward. "I accept the charge, Your Holiness. My men and I will endeavor to return the fugitive to Cerrmor. But my understanding is that I can't act until he actually leaves the free territory of the city."

"Your understanding is correct." The Lawspeaker turned to Eddel. "Unless you wish to take action in this matter yourself?"

"I can't, Your Holiness. We granted Gwerbret Caddalan and his son the safety of the city when he first got here."

And that's what Careg's been counting on, Merryc thought. *A bastard, but a clever one.*

Eddel paused malover at that point. Continuing meant nothing without Caddalan's answer. Lord Vupyl left immediately on his errand. Although most of the onlookers drifted away, Merryc waited along with the prince and his guards.

"What will you wager?" Gwardon said. "I'll offer good odds that Caddalan's holed up nearby, waiting to hear what happened."

"I'd never bet against that, Your Highness."

Vupyl's quick return proved them right. Merryc doubted if anyone in the chamber was surprised when the lord delivered his message: Caddalan was refusing to turn his son over to the free city's law court.

"He says to tell you," Vupyl continued, "that he will quit the city as soon as he can muster his men and allies. Thus any divine wrath at the sacrilege will fall upon him alone and not upon the city of Cerrmor. He asks you to remember that thanks to the outcome of a recent duel of honor, Lord Careg cannot defend himself."

"Well and good, then." Eddel picked up the Sword of Justice. "Your Highness, I hereby turn this matter over to you."

He knocked the pommel three times on the table. The rebellion had officially begun.

At the prince's request, Merryc waited with him until the chamber had cleared. Lord Vupyl left first, rushing away as if he feared arrest. The witnesses, including the Aberwyn contingent, followed more slowly. Ladoic did pause to bow to the prince, a good omen of sorts, but he said nothing. Up on the dais, the Lawspeaker and Eddel were conferring in whispers while a city official returned the sword to its cabinet.

"How many men can we raise, Your Highness?" Merryc said.

"I've got my fifty here. Plus two hundred waiting upriver."

Merryc frankly gaped, then covered it with a small laugh.

"I do pay attention to your warnings," Gwardon said with a grin. "I sent messengers as soon as you gave me the first one. Eddel told me yesterday that he'd already mustered the archers."

"I should have known you'd have an extra dagger hidden somewhere about the royal person."

"Always. Look, I know you can't raise more men of your own. I'd like you and the two you have to join me as part of my personal guards. My own men are ready. We'll ride out as sly as foxes and be waiting when Caddalan and his allies ride our way."

"Done then, Your Highness. And speaking of foxes, isn't that Ladoic waiting down at the foot of the staircase? I wonder if he wants a word with me. Is there time?"

"There is. I need to have a few words with our good mayor."

Merryc hurried downstairs. Ladoic nodded his way and jerked his thumb in the direction of the doors, but he said nothing until they'd walked outside and gotten a little distance away from the crowded public area around the civic broch. The sun already hung near noon in the sky—no time for delicate fencing, Merryc decided.

"I was wondering, Your Grace, if you were going to stand with the prince."

"How can I?" Ladoic made a vulgar snorting noise. "It would lose me every alliance I have."

Merryc winced. He'd expected no less, but hearing it hurt. He started to reply, but Ladoic held up one hand for silence.

"What a pity my warband has no horses!" Ladoic said. "Forced to leave them at home, you see, because Aberwyn only owns one ship large enough to carry stock or passengers. That means I can't ride with the rebels, either."

Merryc suppressed a smile.

"It'd be cursed unfair of me, wouldn't it?" Ladoic continued. "If I asked my allies for some of their stock. None of them came with a string of warhorses to spare, did they? And of course, if Gwerbret Daiver asks the Cerrmor council to keep my ship in harbor, I can't rush back to Aberwyn and bring the horses here. A pity, eh?"

The smile broke out before Merryc could stop it. Ladoic laughed, one sharp bellow.

"But here! Even without me and my twenty-five, he and his cursed friends have well over a hundred men between them. He's counting on the numbers to keep the prince at bay. Don't let the prince do anything rash, like charging right into a battle he can't win. They're hoping to kill him. Who's next in line, eh? A twelve-year-old lad. With one of them as regent, or so they hope."

Merryc hesitated, but trust in his new father-in-law only went so far. "I'll do my best to avoid that disaster, Your Grace."

"Good. As for you, lad, fight well but keep yourself in one piece. After all the work her mother's put into finding a suitor for Dovva, it would be a shame to lose you."

"I'll do my best, Your Grace. If you'll excuse me, I'd best make my farewells to your daughter." He turned away and saw a small group of people standing some distance away. "There she is with her women!"

"She just might be waiting for you, lad." Ladoic winked at him.

Merryc felt his face turn as hot with a blush as a child's. He made a sketchy bow to the gwerbret and fled.

Since Ladoic had promised to send Merryc to her, Dovina had lingered with Alyssa and Mavva in the shelter of the wall at the Advocate's Guild. Gurra and four of Aberwyn's men stood nearby on guard. As Merryc ran up, the other two women drifted a discreet distance away to leave them alone. Two of the guards joined them; the other two turned their backs on Dovina and Merryc and pretended to not be listening.

Dovina was shocked at how badly she took the news that Merryc would ride with the prince on his errand of justice. A rush and gulp of fear made her tremble.

"You could be hurt or killed! Do you have to go?"

"I do, truly. The prince has asked me to accompany him—"

"Curse him!"

"Stop and listen! Which means I'll be riding in some reasonably safe place with His Highness. He's too canny to risk himself over a stupid affair like this. Besides, we'll have fifty Cerrmor archers with us."

"Oh." Dovina collected herself with a deep breath. "My apologies. I was just frightened at the thought of losing you."

"Truly?" Merryc gave her the most beautiful smile she'd ever seen on a man's face.

"Truly. I don't want to have to go through all this betrothal business again."

"That's all, eh?"

"What else would it be?"

He broke out laughing, and in a moment she joined him.

"Oh, very well," she said. "You may kiss me."

He did. Twice. Then he bowed and ran off to collect his men.

A lyssa and Mavva hurried back to Dovina's side with their guards. For a moment they shared a few smiles and giggles, then got back to the matter at hand.

"I don't understand why Caddalan won't turn Careg over," Alyssa said. "They're not going to hang him or suchlike. It's just a fine for being red-tongued. I saw it in Rhys's notes. A Deverry regal for each degree."

"The Lawspeaker said three degrees," Mavva said. "That adds up to an entire boatload of luxury goods from Bardek. One of their biggest ships."

"It's not the coin," Dovina said. "Caddalan's rich as rich can get. It's the honor of the thing."

Three men and six horses, and one of the men was Merryc himself—not much of a warband, but all he had. They rode armed and battle-ready, sabers instead of fineswords, with an extra servant along to bring the extra mounts. Merryc rode his battle-trained chestnut and let his page lead the golden Western Hunter. Following the prince's orders, they left the city by the west gate. A mile on, they caught up with the contingent of archers and the prince's men, all of them riding armed and battle-ready, including the prince himself.

"My scouts have come in," Gwardon said. "Arrogance has its good side, when it's your enemy who's the one infected with it. Caddalan's not left the city yet. I've sent a courier to bring the army to meet us. Let's hope they get here before the rebels do."

Merryc felt his stomach churn.

"Perhaps, Your Highness, we'd best ride fast to meet them."

"The archers aren't mounted. They have to walk."

Merryc had no answer to that.

"Ye gods, Merro," Gwardon said. "I swear you've gone white in the face!"

"Ladoic tells me that the plan is to kill you and turn young Merro into the Marked Prince. With a new regent."

Gwardon blinked four rapid times, then smiled. "My thanks to Aberwyn, should I live to see him again." He laughed in a long berserk peal before he spoke again. "Well and good, then. I'll keep away from them if I can."

Merryc allowed himself a short sigh of relief. Thanks to the prince's love of the grand gesture, he'd been expecting an argument. There remained, however, the wretched truth: the archers could only walk so fast, and the mounted men would have to keep pace and guard them. Merryc was also expecting to argue with the free men of the Red Arrow company, but their captain, a stout fellow named Delber, understood more about war than he'd given the man credit for.

"We can double-march in short bursts, like, my lord. Let us set the pace. Fast when we can, then slower when we must. As soon as we see the dust ahead of us that means the prince's army, we peel off and begin setting our stakes and readying our bows." He chuckled under his breath. "Well, let's hope it's the prince's army and not the other lot."

"Splendid plan! I'm going to make sure the prince takes up a position well behind yours."

Delber smiled and patted the quiver at his hip. "We'll build him a wall, sure enough."

Whether it was luck or the will of the gods, they met the prince's reserve before Caddalan arrived, not that they had much time to congratulate themselves. The royal cavalry, two hundred men on good horses, disposed themselves in a crescent formation across the road and into the adjoining fields. The Red Arrow company picked a position at the west end of the crescent and set up in three lines of staggered rows. The archers had barely finished pounding in their wooden stakes, and the prince was still sitting on his horse in the middle of the road, when Merryc saw the dust cloud to the south that meant Caddalan's forces were on their way.

"Your Highness! Time to take up our position!"

"So it is!" Gwardon called back. "All right, men! No attack until I sound the horn. I'm hoping our heralds will get them to see reason."

Not much chance of that, Merryc thought. He was just about to scream at Gwardon to get to safety when the prince turned his horse and headed around the archers at a leisurely pace. He fetched up next to Merryc and grinned at him.

"Here I am, and with plenty of time, too."

"Plenty!" Merryc drew his saber. "Here they are."

Some hundred yards away Caddalan was yelling at his forces to halt. Silver horns rang out as the riders milled around in the road and fields as they tried to get into some sort of battle order. Had the prince wanted mayhem he could have sent a rain of arrows their way and followed it up with a charge that would have killed most of them—and of course, plunged the kingdom into an ongoing war. Instead, he took his signal horn in one hand and held it high into the air. Sunlight glinted and winked on the silver to make his message clear: hold your lines.

The royal herald hoisted his beribboned staff and urged his horse out into the road. He'd gone maybe twenty yards when Caddalan's herald rode out to meet him. Merryc tried to catch a few words of what they were saying, but restless horses stamped and shook their heads to make their bridles ring, and restless men shifted their weight in the saddle or leaned forward to make the leather creak and the horses stamp again. Finally the heralds turned their horses and rode back to their respective contingents.

"Your Highness," the royal herald said, "they respectfully ask you to have your men clear the road. That's all their herald was empowered to say. Not one word about Lord Careg could I get out of him."

"Very well," Gwardon said, "then tell them we'll gladly clear the road once we have the lord in custody."

Back and forth the heralds went to no avail. Eventually Caddalan's herald returned to his gwerbret while the royal herald waited out in the road. Merryc could see Caddalan gesturing and tossing his head like one of the horses while he talked to the lords accompanying him. Careg was riding back in the pack of warbands, safely surrounded by armed men. With a broken sword arm, he never could have fought, but still, Merryc despised him all over again.

"What is wrong with them?" Gwardon said. "Can't they count?"

"Apparently not, Your Highness, if they think they have a candle's chance in hell."

Out in the road the royal herald shrugged, called out a few words, and got no answer, apparently, because he turned his horse and rode back to the prince.

"It's hopeless, Your Highness," the herald said. "They refuse to hand over the lord, and they think you're too honorable to attack them since it would be a slaughter, and you're not known for slaughtering those below you in rank."

"Are all the lords holding firm? Or could you tell?"

"None of them looked anything but furious, Your Highness, but I'll wager it was at Caddalan, judging from the looks they gave him. Except for Standyc. He'd drawn his sword and, ye gods, he looks like death. But the herald, truly, he said that Caddalan would never yield. It's the honor of the thing."

"Honor must be satisfied. I suppose Caddalan has some." Gwardon rolled his eyes heavenward. "I could challenge him to single combat, I suppose." He grinned. "And then choose Merro here as—"

He stopped in mid-sentence. Out in the road, Caddalan's cobbled-together warband was sliding into chaos. Horns blew long cascades.

Lords shouted and bellowed with all their strength. The same message sounded over and over: retreat. Caddalan himself was riding back and forth, yelling, talking, waving his saber in the air as he entreated the others to stay. No one seemed to be listening. The warbands of riders were trying to follow their lords' orders in the narrow spaces available twixt the road and the ditches that lined the fields to either side. Nervous horses tried to buck as the men tried to back or turn them. Others bit or kicked the horses to either side of them, spreading the panic.

The Prince Regent's well-drilled men controlled their mounts, then sat in silence. They grinned at each other and pointed at the erstwhile enemies, but beyond that said not a word. The free city archers, however, began to laugh, softly at first, then louder, until they howled with laughter, or yelled insults and foul jests at the nobility they despised. Merryc felt a ripple of shock at just how much they despised them. He'd always known the common folk resented the privilege of the noble-born, but this was hatred far beyond resentment.

"Hold your tongues!" the prince screamed. "By the Lord of Hell's scaly balls, stop your gobs! Danger!"

Delber joined him in shouting the orders. At their leader's voice, most did, but out in the road the bitter slights to their honor had reached noble ears. Some of the lords tried to rally their riders, who were yelling insults right back at the Cerrmor men. Others kept on trying to get clear of the road and retreat. In but a few moments what had been an army became a screeching, swirling mob of men on horseback. The prince's men drew weapons just as a battle cry broke out in the opposing force.

"Bear! The Bear! For Standyc! Get the archers!"

Dust rose and plumed across the road. A futile charge formed itself out of the mob and rushed forward, as sudden as rain breaking from a swirl of dark cloud. At its head rode Standyc himself. The Cerrmor archers nocked, raised, and loosed. The arrows flew. The shadow of death darkened the road as the volley curved down into the charging riders. Standyc himself died fast and first, pitching over his horse's neck. The arrows came again and again. Out in the road the retreats became routs. Caddalan's other allies and their men peeled off as fast as they could and fled. Some scattered into the fields with their lords in pursuit. Others turned and galloped back toward Cerrmor.

"Enough!" Prince Gwardon was screaming at the archers, the silver horn forgotten in his hand. "Stop! Curse you all! Stop!"

Merryc grabbed the royal bridle just in time to keep the prince from riding right into the archers' line of flight. Delber had a horn of his own, and he alternately blew and yelled orders. The rain of arrows stopped.

Out in the road Caddalan's warband had dwindled to his own escort. They clustered around their gwerbret, sabers drawn, ready to defend him or die with him, even though they all must have known the outcome would be disastrous. Between the two lines lay dead men, dying men, dying horses, dead horses. No one could have survived that steel-sharp rain. The dust and the shouting both settled and died as well, leaving naught but blood behind, staining the corpses and the road.

Prince Gwardon let the silence hold for some moments. He urged his nervous horse a little forward and called out.

"Caddalan! For the love of every god, look what your cursed miserliness has caused! Send your stupid arse of a son over now, and I'll stand surety for some of the blood prices on these dead men. Otherwise . . ." He stopped and waited.

Caddalan must have heard, because he turned to Careg and began talking, his words too low to hear. Careg shook his head and talked right back. Finally Caddalan yelled out an order to his men. His captain grabbed the reins out of Careg's hand and tugged. Careg's horse followed him, ignoring the squawling, complaining lord on his back, as the captain led them around the edge of the welter of blood and mayhem in the road.

Caddalan followed them for a few paces. "Gwardon!" he screamed. "Forget your cursed surety! I'll pay the lot myself. And may your balls freeze in the hells a thousand years for every coin!"

Gwardon responded with a long peal of berserk laughter. His men stayed on alert, sabers in hand, as the captain led his captive up to the group around the prince. Merryc rode a few paces forward and caught the reins when the captain tossed them over. Careg started to speak, then merely glowered, sitting slumped in his saddle, and stared at his horse's neck.

"Enough murder, milord," the captain said. "Ye gods."

"My thanks," Merryc said. "Not murder. Suicide. The temples will have to lay aside their dream of that pound of gold. I'm bitterly sorry that he took his men with him."

"So am I, milord. I'll pass that remark on to His Grace, if I may."

"Please do."

The captain made half-bows from the saddle to the prince and Merryc both, then turned his horse and rode back to Caddalan and the warband. Without so much as a glance at his son, Caddalan gathered his men around him and led them away, heading east toward home.

Once they were out of sight, the archers hurried forward to loot the dead. At a signal from Gwardon, his personal escort walked their horses forward to protect the Cerrmor men in case of some trick on the part of the enemies. The archers held the right to loot by charter. They worked silently and fast—out of respect for the dead, or so Merryc preferred to assume.

The captain of the contingent from Dun Deverry detailed men to pull the dead free and arrange them decently in the road. They needed an armed guard against a different sort of scavenger. Already ravens were gathering overhead. Out in the fields, farmers and their families had come out of hiding and stood watching from a long distance. Gwardon turned to his herald.

"Tell them they can have the horsemeat when we're finished."

"Done, Your Highness. Shall I send a messenger to the supply train? I'm assuming, at least, that the reinforcements have one."

"Do that, and messengers to Cerrmor. Have one pair go to the mayor, another to the Bardekian ambassador. The mayor can round up carts or river boats to take these men back for burial."

The herald rode off. For a little while more Gwardon and Merryc sat on horseback and watched the grim work out in the road. Finally Gwardon shuddered with a toss of his head.

"Suicide indeed," the prince said. "I'll be having a word with the Dun Deverry temple about this affair. We'll see what His Most Exalted and Supreme Holiness has to say about it and their cursed pound of gold."

"If the gods are as great as they all say, he won't be pleased about it."

"If." Gwardon glanced at Careg. "Let's take this rat back to the cage ready for it. If its kin want it back, they can pay the fines and ransom it out."

Alyssa and Cavan heard the news of the battle back at the embassy guesthouse. With the long cuts on his ribs and shoulder still fresh, he was bandaged so tightly and dosed with so many herbs that he could do little but lie still unless he was desperate for a chamber pot. That afternoon, he was awake and more alert than he'd been the day before—a good sign, Edry told her.

Alyssa was sitting at Cavan's bedside and reading to him from her legal notes for want of anything more entertaining when Hwlio himself came in. He repeated what the messengers had told him and shook his head over the slaughter in the road.

"A ghastly sort of battle," Hwlio said.

"Don't dignify it by that name, sir," Cavan said. "Ye gods, more men dead because of my wretched brother! Red-tongued, indeed."

"Lord Merryc called it suicide. And it does sound to me like Standyc was determined to spare his family the weight of that fine." Hwlio glanced at Alyssa. "What do you think?"

"I agree with you. Gods, what a horrible choice!"

With one last sad shake of his head, Hwlio left to attend to embassy business. Alyssa rearranged Cavan's pillows and helped him settle himself. As he shifted his weight, he winced, his face paled, and he bit his lower lip to squelch the pain.

"You called me a sword of fire once," she said, "but we forgot one thing. Wielding a sword of fire is a cursed good way to get burned."

"So it was." He managed a smile. "Wound does ache a bit."

"Do you want a sip of this stuff Edry left?" She held up the bottle of cordial, a sticky dark wine-like liquid.

"I don't. It makes me sleep. Here, Lyss. This morning I heard summat I'd missed before. You killed a man that night. Do you regret it?"

"Not half as much as I'd regret being raped and murdered. A year ago I'd have been all tears and moans and apologies, but it's an odd thing, this journey we've been on. I'm not the same lass, and truly, I don't regret it."

"I do love you." He smiled again, more easily this time. "I'd ask for a kiss, but the way I ache, it might not be such a fine idea."

"I can manage it if I lean over just so—oh, curse it! What is it?"

A maidservant had appeared in the doorway. She curtsied before she spoke.

"Lord Merryc, my lady. Should I let him in?"

"By all means," Cavan said.

Merryc strode in, bowed to Alyssa, then stood by Cavan's bed and considered him.

"They tell me you're going to live," Merryc said at last. "Good."

"My thanks. It gladdens my heart, too."

Merryc turned to Alyssa. "Is he well enough to talk for a bit?"

"Edry said so this morning."

"Good." Merryc turned back to Cavan. "I spoke with the Prince Regent. He wonders if you know why your father's so dead-set against a justiciar in the west. It's several hundred miles from Lughcarn."

"I don't know for certain," Cavan said. "Except maybe he's afraid of the legal precedent." He paused for a smile. "My wife's been educating me about things like that."

"I suppose that's reason enough, then."

"He—my father—hated the Cerrgonney justiciar. I do know that. The court there had ruled against our clan over some matter. I was but a lad at the time." Cavan paused, thinking. "We need to remember that the iron ore comes from Cerrgonney. Any change in the way things are run could look like a threat."

"Of course." Yet Merryc sounded doubtful. "I suppose he'd be concerned with what happens up there."

"No doubt we'll all find out soon enough," Alyssa said. "And we'll be sorry we know."

Merryc winced and nodded. "True spoken."

Cavan sighed and leaned back into the pillows.

"I'd best let you rest," Merryc continued. "But I had another reason to come see you. My father-in-law's giving me coin to maintain ten riders. I'm going to need a captain for my new warband. I can't think of a better man for the job than you."

Cavan's eyes filled with tears. "You're jesting," he whispered.

"I'm not." Merryc turned to Alyssa. "Ladoic says he told you that he'll renounce the charge against Cavvo as soon as he gets back to

Aberwyn. So you both can go back when your man's fit to travel."
He grinned. "I thought I'd best figure out some way to keep him out
of trouble. Who knows what he'd get up to if I didn't?"

"You have my thanks, my lord, my most humble thanks," Alyssa
said. "I'm most truly grateful."

"But I can't—" Cavan began.

"Of course you can," Merryc said. "Don't be a dolt, Cavvo. Everyone knows now that your brother's a lying little bastard. Why should
they hold the silver dagger against you? Besides, there are precedents,
and right in Eldidd, too. Mavva looked it up and told me so."

Cavan wiped his eyes with a shaking hand. "Done, then. And my
thanks."

"I should warn you that we'll be stuck in this little town on the
edge of the kingdom called Cannobaen. Probably alone there for
months while our wives finish up their scholar's badges. It's right on
the border with the Westfolk. They've got that town out there.
Mandra."

Cavan opened his mouth to speak, but no words came to him.
Alyssa reached out and grabbed his hand.

"What's wrong, my love?"

"Naught wrong." He took a deep breath. "Good tidings. An
omen." He gave her a grin. "A very good omen indeed."

Alyssa assumed he was merely speaking generally, but later, after
Merryc had left, Cavan explained.

"I've been given the chance to study summat I've longed for my
whole life," he began. "Lyss, I hope to every god this won't offend you,
but while you're off in your collegium, I'm going to study dwimmer."

"Dwimmer?"

"Just that. With the Westfolk master we met, though mostly I'll
be in Cannobaen."

"I'm not offended. I'll admit to being well and truly surprised."

"Are you?" He grinned at her. "Good. I was afraid you'd tell me
you'd known it all along."

For the first time in years, Alyssa found herself without a thing to
say. He laughed in delight, not mockery, and in a moment, she
joined him.

"So we're going home after all," she said. "Here I was afraid I'd
never see Aberwyn again."

"You'll be able to see your family."

"True. I—oh, ye gods, what am I going to say to my mother? About you, I mean. I don't even know where to start!"

"Hah! I never thought I'd see a time when you couldn't think of summat to say. This is a grand day indeed."

They laughed again and shared a few kisses before Cavan's wound forced him to rest. For the remainder of that afternoon, Alyssa sat by the window and looked idly out at the trees bobbing and bowing in a rising wind. *The wind's at our backs indeed,* she thought, *but who knows what it's bringing with it?*

THE HONOR OF THE THING

DEVERRY AND PYRDON
1423

A couple of years ago I wrote this short story. If you're curious about Rommardda, Cathvar, and Benoic, read on!

"If that's the sort of book you're looking for, my lady," the priest said, "you need to go to Haen Marn, but it's a long ride from here."

"Quite so," I said.

He laid one hand on the blazon on his shirt, the orange pelican of the god Wmm, while he considered the problem. We were sitting on plain wooden chairs in the small, bare reception chamber of the temple of Wmm in Dun Trebyc, a town known for its book dealers. Sooner or later, any book copied for sale anywhere in the far-flung kingdom of Deverry would turn up here, or so I'd always been told. Unfortunately, the volume I was looking for, a medical treatise on healing burns and other such blacksmithing injuries, had decided to arrive later.

"Truly," he said, "I can think of nowhere but Haen Marn."

"The road there runs through some dangerous territory," I said. "I've heard much about it."

"True spoken, alas." He paused for a glance at the leopard who lay by my feet like a dog. "Now, your friend there could doubtless fend off one thief, but not a band of them."

Cathvar raised his head and yawned to expose his fangs. I could feel his amusement at the skinny little man's burst of fear.

"Indeed," I said. "I have my page, but he's only a lad."

"Just so, my lady." He paused again, one eyebrow raised. "Is your clan nearby?"

"It's not, but up in Gwingedd. My name is Rommardda, but no need to call me 'my lady.' I'm not noble-born."

"Ah, I see." He smiled and nodded.

He knows not what that name means. Cathvar spoke in mind speech, the only way that he could speak, and of course, only I could hear him.

It doesn't matter, I answered. I don't need to trumpet who I am.

Cathvar thwacked his tail once against the wood floor in agreement. The priest flinched at the sound.

"Now, Haen Marn has an immense library," the priest continued. "They allow anyone who wants to hire a scribe to make copies of most of the books. There are a few so old that they keep them in glass boxes and won't let anyone touch them."

"The sort of book I'm looking for should be reasonably new. I'm a healer, you see, for the Blacksmiths Guild. I gather none of the canals run by Haen Marn."

"They don't, and the mail coaches don't travel that particular route, either. Too much wild country, they tell me, ruled by lords who don't care to stand the coin to keep the coaches in fresh horses. Very old-fashioned men." He shook his head. "Things are changing all over the kingdom, but there's plenty of the noble-born who are trying to turn the wind around by huffing and puffing in its face."

"That's true, and a nuisance as well."

"What I'd recommend is you hire yourself a silver dagger or two. They have a sort of guildhall here in town." He shrugged and smiled. "Very much of sorts. A tavern, but what else would you expect from men like that?"

"Naught, truly. We see a fair many silver daggers back home. Now, your guildsmen here, are they reliable?"

"Very. They've nothing left but their reputation, after all, and their band treats anyone who soils that reputation very harshly." He drew a finger across his throat. "The Prancing Ram, down by the river. I'd suggest you send your page to inquire rather than going yourself."

"Doubtless that's good advice. Well, my thanks, Your Holiness. I've very much appreciated your help. May I make a small donation to the god to thank you further?"

"Never would I slight one who wishes to honor our god."

I took three silver coins from the leather pouch at my belt and laid them into his outstretched hand. He smiled and bowed. I curtsied and left with Cathvar, a hundred and some pounds of wariness, padding along next to me—on the same side as I wore the pouch. Thanks to him, no thief had ever tried to rob me, not once in all my travels. Bandits were a different matter. If we were going to travel through the wild country of southern Pyrdon, we would need some sort of guard.

My lad, young Waryn, was waiting back at the inn, where he was keeping watch over our goods and horses. I called him my page to distinguish him from an ordinary servant, but in truth he was common-born, a lad I'd rescued from a brutal father when he was but three years old. I'd rescued Cathvar as a cub as well, in his case from a sleazy gerthddyn who kept the poor creature in a wooden cage on a cart. Both of them had talent, each in their own peculiar way, for the craft that was my true calling, the dweomer.

If you've never seen a leopard, and they are very rare in the kingdom of Deverry, they're a species of large cat. Cathvar has the usual coat of his tribe, a honey-gold dotted with black rosettes, and wide gold eyes brimming with intelligence. My human lad has hair of an auburn red, typical of a Cerrgonney person, and the usual freckles and green eyes to go with it. Even though I'd been feeding Waryn well, at that time he had the skinny, rangy look of a lad who's going to turn into a very tall man one day.

Despite the priest's well meant advice, I decided to go look for those silver daggers in person. I did, however, collect Waryn first. We were staying at Dun Trebyc's best inn, the Red Rose, a two-story affair with whitewashed walls and a newly thatched roof. The three of us shared two good-sized rooms with windows that looked out over the stableyard. The town as a whole was remarkably clean, at least in the neighborhood where the temples and bookshops stood. Its folk took pride in their tidy houses and well-tended kitchen gardens.

As we wandered down Dun Trebyc's winding main street, Waryn did the asking and soon found out that the Prancing Ram stood down by the river road. The twisted narrow streets in that district soon turned into alleys, scattered here and there with rubbish and garbage, more typical of most cities and towns. The tavern itself leaned a few feet from the vertical. Smoke-stained thatch covered the roof, and none of the windows held glass.

"Mistress?" Waryn said. "Do you really think you should go in there?"

"From what the priest told me, I'd say it's safe enough. I doubt me if the silver daggers are going to ruin their reputation and their livelihood by robbing an old woman."

And risking a good bite or three, Cathvar said.

Although the tavern room looked battered, with stained, chipped walls and tables and benches that leaned in various directions, it was surprisingly clean, with fresh straw on the floor and an innkeep dressed in unstained clothes and leather apron. He came bustling over to greet us at the door.

"Er, ah," he said, "I'm not sure if you—"

"I wish to hire a pair of silver daggers," I said. "I need guards for a journey."

He smiled. "Well, then, you are indeed in the right place."

Over by the hearth stood a table that looked sturdier than most. At its head in an actual chair sat a man with scant gray hair, a gray beard, and only one ear. Where the other should have been he had a thick clot of scar tissue. Two young men sat on the benches, one to his left, one to his right. As I approached, the graybeard got up and bowed. When the others didn't move, he snarled a few words at them. They rose and bowed.

"Good morrow," I said. "I need to travel to Haen Marn down in Pyrdon. I'm told I'd best hire an escort if I'm to get there safely."

"Quite so." Gray Beard pulled out his chair and offered it to me. "I'd say you'd best hire two guards, and I'm not merely saying that for the coin."

"The priest of Wmm told me the same thing, good sir."

We all sat down, Waryn and Cathvar on the floor. The innkeep came over with a small glass stoup of pale Bardek wine, a gift, which I accepted. While I had a sip, I considered the two silver daggers at the table. The older fellow introduced them. Ddary, a pale, skinny young man with gray eyes set too close together and a sharp nose, had a couple of fingers missing from his left hand. Benoic, tall and dark-haired, would have been a good-looking man if it weren't for the barely suppressed simmer of rage in his dark eyes. His posture, so tense and watchful, reminded me of Cathvar when he was about to spring on prey. When I used a bit of the Sight, I saw red streaks and glimmers dancing in both of their auras. Benoic's had a core of gold, as well, something of a surprise in the aura of a dishonored man.

"Both are good men in a scrap," Gray Beard said. "I've fought with them, and I can attest that."

"I'm hoping that having them along will mean there won't be any scraps," I said. "But that may be too much to hope for."

"True spoken, alas. Now, since you're heading west, this time of year a good many merchants head out to trade with the Westfolk. If you can find a caravan over in Cennyn, I suggest you join up with them. Since you'll have your own guards, you'll be doubly safe that way."

"That's sound advice."

"When do you want to leave?"

"Tomorrow morning. I've done what I can do here."

Since I wanted to hide how much gold I was carrying, I made a great show of haggling over the price. We finally settled for a silver piece a week with provisioning at my expense. Benoic owned a pack-horse as well as a mount. I handed him a silver piece to load it up with oats for all the horses in our little caravan, then returned to the Red Rose.

Just at dawn, our two silver daggers showed up with their riding mounts and laden packhorse. It took some time for me to work the dweomer—Pyr's spell, it's called—that calmed the horses and convinced them that Cathvar would do them no harm but, in the end, each horse touched noses with the leopard, snorted once or twice, and took little notice of him from then on. The silver daggers watched, amazed.

"I don't suppose," Benoic said, "that you'd tell me how you did that."

"Would you tell me why you came to ride the long road?"

He laughed and made me a half-bow. "I understand, good dame. No more questions from me, I assure you."

He had decent manners, Benoic, not courtly, mind, nothing that would have marked him as noble-born, but he must have come from a good family, a well-off merchant clan, perhaps. Ddary, on the other hand—he was never downright rude, but things like a bow or a pleasantry lay beyond him.

They were further amazed when they saw that Cathvar had his own horse. Strong as the leopard was, he could never have traveled a steady fifteen miles a day on his own four paws. Old Dee, as we called him, a black with a white star on his forehead, came from broad-backed plowhorse stock. Rather than an ordinary saddle, he carried a contraption of leather and thick quilted wool pads, shaped rather like a gravy boat, that allowed Cathvar to ride securely without his claws digging into Old Dee's back.

For several days we traveled southwest on the decent road that brought us to Cennyn. The little town sat behind walls on the crest of a low hill. At the foot of the hill a ramshackle village spread out along the road to cater to the merchant caravans that camped there before the trip west. Beyond Cennyn lay a range of higher hills that marked the border of the central province of Deverry with the western province of Pyrdon. The road and a decent pass ran through them and down to Dun Drw.

Once we rode within sight of the town, we saw horses and mules grazing in meadows to either side of the road, a sign of at least two caravans. Both had set up tents, odd, considering that they normally stayed no more than a day or two in Cennyn. We found out the reason when we arrived at the only inn in the village at the foot of the hill.

"Bandits," the innkeep told us. "Harrying travelers in the pass, they were. Our Lord Avy's gone after them with his warband. No one wants to travel through until he does summat about them."

I groaned aloud. Sitting around Cennyn with a pair of silver daggers for company struck me as a tedious prospect. Cathvar growled under his breath, and Waryn sighed.

"Howsomever," the innkeep continued, "one of the merchants, he's an impatient man. He told me he's going to lead his men out on the morrow to turn south and head over Eldidd way. I'll introduce you, if you'd like."

"I would." I handed over a couple of coppers. "That'll be the pass at Bryn Tamig, I suppose."

"Right you are." He pocketed the coins.

I felt rather than saw Benoic stiffen. Cathvar turned his head to consider him.

Fear, Cathvar told me. I can smell it on him.

"Benno!" Ddary snapped. "You can't spend the rest of your cursed life avoiding the place. This hire's a good one, and you can't desert the lady, anyway."

Benoic scowled at him but said nothing. Ddary walked some distance away, and Benoic followed him. They stood arguing in a corner of the innyard while I haggled with the innkeep for a night's shelter. They returned to carry our gear upstairs.

"Is somewhat wrong?" I said to Benoic.

"There's not." He spat the words out. "If we go south, we go south."

"Well and good, then." I could guess that Bryn Tamig had something to do with the dishonor that had earned him the silver dagger. "Now, Waryn will share a chamber with you lads, but Cathvar will come with me."

The moment smoothed out, but for the rest of that day, Benoic said barely two words to anyone.

The innkeep earned his coppers at the evening meal by introducing me to Graun, a short, barrel-chested merchant from Arcodd province. He was more than willing to let us travel with his caravan.

"Now, Lord Avy's a good man," Graun said. "I've no doubt he'll put an end to these bandits once he finds them. It's the finding that could take half the summer. I can't afford to sit here and miss the big horse fair near Haen Marn."

"You're going all the way to Haen Marn? So am I!"

"Splendid! You'll be welcome, good dame, and your silver daggers, too." He paused to look Cathvar over. "Er, I take it he's tame?"

"Very. Most well-mannered."

"Good, good. Then all should be well."

In the morning, however, it took me a fair while to introduce Cathvar to Graun's long line of mules and horses. My silver daggers grinned as Graun and his muleteers watched, amazed and a little frightened. After that, the muleteers made the sign of warding against witchcraft every time I passed by them.

For our long ride down to Bryn Tamig, the weather held mostly warm and pleasant, marred now and then by a brief spring shower. Cathvar grumbled mightily about the rain. Just like a house cat, he hated being wet. Fortunately, I was the only person who could hear his constant whining and snarling every time the sky dripped on him. Most of the men ignored the weather, thanks to the general good cheer among them. They'd been spared a dangerous journey through an area known for murderous thieves.

The only exception was Benoic. The closer we got to the town, the darker his mood became. On our last evening before we reached it, young Waryn had a chance to speak with me alone while the silver daggers were tending our horses and Cathvar was off hunting his dinner in the hedgerows and coppices.

"Mistress," Waryn said, "the muleteers told me that the Bryn Tamig pass is haunted."

"I wouldn't be surprised. A long time ago there were slavers taking travelers on the roads around there, but the local gwerbret caught and slaughtered them all. That's why it's called 'tamig.' But don't you worry. They can't hurt us now. They're dead."

"Well and good, then. But do you think Benoic's afraid of the ghosts?"

"Because of the way he's brooding? I think he's dreading seeing some real flesh and blood person, someone who knows of his dishonor."

"Oh. It's a hard thing, being a silver dagger. I forgot about that."

"Benoic can never forget it. So don't blame him for his black moods."

Of course, nattering old woman that I am, by then I was thoroughly curious about the reason he was riding the long road. Unfortunately, I found out in a way that caused the lad a great deal of pain.

Round noon on the morrow our caravan reached the walls of the town of Bryn Tamig, nestled between two foothills on the eastern side of the pass. Graun the caravanmaster paid over some taxes to the town guards for the right to camp on a broad common just inside the east gate. Since big white clouds were sailing in from the north, the muleteers unloaded their stock and stacked up the packs under rough canvas shelters. I'd had quite enough of sleeping on damp ground and told my silver daggers that I was going to find an inn.

"You're quite welcome to come with me at my expense," I said. "We need to buy provisions, too."

"If it's all the same to you," Benoic began.

"Oh, by the black hairy—" Ddary caught himself with a sideways glance my way. "Umph, well, don't tell me you're going to hide out here like a rabbit!"

Benoic's face turned bright red, and his eyes narrowed with rage. Ddary set his hands on his hips and looked at him, his mouth twisted with disgust. Young men! Benoic couldn't take the charge of cowardice, I suppose.

"Oh, very well," Benoic said. "Lead on, good dame!"

So we rode into town and found an inn that was respectable enough, just barely, two stories built around a circular courtyard humans on one side, horses on the other. I hired two reasonably clean chambers, and the men stowed our gear. I'd planned on letting Ddary and Benoic go down to the stables to bargain for oats from the stableman, but Cathvar stopped me.

I smell danger, he said. But not to you or me or our lad.

Had I best go down with them?

You should, and I will, too.

So we all trooped down together and found the stableman more than willing to sell us oats at a reasonable price. I'd expected to haggle. Perhaps it was the way Cathvar glared at him the entire time that made him so generous.

"Well, lads," I said to my silver daggers, "I can give you some of your wages if you'd like to have a tankard. I see that this inn sports a tavern room."

Ddary grinned and held out his hand, but Benoic stood silently, his thumbs hooked over his sword belt. He was looking across the innyard, I realized, at a man who was just dismounting from a blood-bay Western Hunter. He was a tall young man, dressed in the tartan knee breeches, leather vest, and embroidered linen shirt of the noble-born. At his side he carried an elven finesword in a scabbard of pale Bardek leather. His boots were of the same and set with silver buckles on the side. He threw the reins of his horse to the stableman, turned, and saw Benoic. He sneered and spat on the ground. Benoic stiffened and laid a hand on his sword hilt.

The lordling strolled over. "I'm surprised you've got the gall to ride into this town," he said.

Cathvar growled and took a step toward him. The lordling yelped, then flushed with embarrassment.

"What's this?" he snapped. "Can't be a dog."

I took the chance to intervene. "He's a leopard from the eastern lands. A species of large cat."

"Ah." The lordling recovered his composure and made a half-bow my way. "Are you the one who's hired this silver dagger? If so, good dame, watch your coin. He's been caught thieving once."

Ddary moved so fast that it took me a moment to realize why. He grabbed Benoic's sword arm and hauled him back before Benoic could draw his blade.

"I'm in no mood to see you hang," Ddary muttered. "Let it pass, Benno!"

Benoic took a deep breath. "That's a false charge, my lord Aeryn," he said. "If it had been true, I'd have only one hand."

"Huh! You mean, if they'd been able to prove it."

Ddary grabbed Benoic a second time and pulled him a couple of steps farther away. I stepped in front of the lordling and sent a line of etheric force to his aura. "My dear sir," I said. "Perhaps if your lordship could be so kind as to let the matter drop?" I curtsied to him while I gave his aura a good spin.

"Of course, good dame." Aeryn shook his head and yawned. "My apologies. Unpleasantness. Must mind courtesies in front of a lady." He staggered off to the tavern room as unsteadily as if he'd already drunk his fill.

Ddary nearly ruined everything by laughing aloud, but luckily Aeryn didn't notice. "You *are* a handy sort of woman to know," Ddary remarked. "Come along, Benno. You go upstairs to our chamber. I'll buy a flagon and bring it up."

"Splendid idea!" I said. "You all go up. See if they have Bardek wine, Ddary. I wouldn't mind a wee drop of summat myself."

Ddary, Benoic, and Waryn all followed my orders. Cathvar and I walked over to the stableman, who'd been watching all this while clinging to the reins of Lord Aeryn's horse.

"Do you know aught about this matter?" I said to him. "I could have sworn that Aeryn was hoping Benoic would draw on him."

"So could I, good dame. It chilled my blood, it did. Don't want no bloodshed in my innyard! All I know is that young Benoic there got turned out of our local lord's warband last summer. That be Lord Marc, not that young popinjay you just met. Lord Aeryn's betrothed to Marc's daughter, but he comes here for one of the tavern lasses, you see, who doesn't mind earning a bit of coin on her back."

"Indeed?" I fished in my pouch and brought out some coppers. "That's very interesting."

He paused to glance around and make sure he couldn't be over-heard. "There was ever so much gossip about the affair at the time. Benoic was accused of stealing from the lord's daughter, but no one believed it."

"Didn't they now?" I handed over the coin. "Did they have some-one else in mind?"

"Well, who else would have been in her chamber but her be-trothed? I—" He broke off and bowed to me. "My thanks, good dame. I'll have oats sacked and ready for your men on the mor-row morn."

I turned round to take my leave of him and saw Lord Aeryn and a blowsy blonde lass just leaving the tavern room. She was giggling because he had his hand on her buttocks. When he saw me, he had the decency to blush. I nodded, Cathvar flicked his tail, and we hur-ried upstairs.

The pair of chambers joined with an open doorway. In theirs, Ddary and Benoic were arguing, or rather, Benoic was snarling at his fellow while Ddary tried to calm him down. Waryn hovered nearby, watching open-mouthed.

"Why in the names of the gods did you think I wanted to stay away from here?" Benoic was saying. "One of these days I'll kill that stinking little bastard. I dream about it, spitting him like a chicken."

"And they'll hang you if you do," Ddary said.

"I don't care. It's the honor of the thing!"

"Silver daggers don't have any honor, you dolt!"

"It'd still be worth it just to watch him bleed."

"Now, now," I said. "You wouldn't think so when they were put-ting the rope around your neck."

Benoic crossed his arms over his chest and glared at me, but he stayed silent.

"You can go down to the tavern now, Ddary," I said. "Lord Aeryn's taken his doxy off to the hayloft. Waryn, our things are in the other chamber. Find our drinking cups. I'm afraid I can't re-member where I packed them."

In your saddlebags, Cathvar said.

I know. Hush.

Ddary and Waryn left on their errands. Benoic sat down on the floor with a sigh and ran his hands through his hair. I perched on a rickety wooden chest that stood by the unglazed window.

"My apologies," he mumbled.

"For what? That piss-poor excuse for nobility threw some nasty taunts. I'm not surprised you took them to heart."

He looked up with a twisted little smile. "He wanted me to draw on him. If I hanged, he'd never have to deal with me again. I'm just cursed glad Ddary stopped me."

"So am I. My apologies for choosing this inn."

"It's the only decent one in town. I should never have let Ddary shame me into coming with you."

"True. But here we are. I suggest you stay indoors till it's time to rejoin the caravan."

He nodded his agreement and returned to staring at the floor, as intently as if he were counting the straws on it.

"I assume," I said, "that Aeryn must be visiting at Lord Marc's dun."

"No doubt. Visiting his betrothed."

He reeks of hurt, Cathvar remarked. Females!

Indeed. "Let me guess," I said aloud. "He had reason to be jealous of you."

Benoic raised his head and stared at me, his mouth working.

"What went missing?" I continued. "But here, I should hold my tongue and not pry! Forgive a nosy old woman!"

"Huh." He managed a smile. "A nosy old woman who happens to know a lot of powerful lore, I'd say. The thing was a piece of the daughter's jewelry, a little silver brooch. I'd saved my wages to buy it for her at the spring fair."

"That's an odd thing for you to have stolen."

"True spoken, and that's what saved my hand from the execution-er's axe. Lord Marc's a fair-minded man. When they found the brooch in my saddlebag, he said that if I'd bought it, I had the right to take it back, because Yvva had gotten betrothed to another man."

"Who found it? Lord Aeryn?"

"You've got sharp wits, good dame."

"And I'll wager he had no idea you'd given it to her. He must have been bitterly disappointed."

"He made a great show of wondering how I'd gotten hold of it. Threatened to break off the betrothal if another man had been in her chamber."

"So Marc kicked you out to save the match?"

"Just so."

"Not as fair-minded as all that. I pity your Yvva, married off to a stoat."

"She could have turned him down."

Could she? I doubted it. The match must have brought her father some advantages, if he'd been willing to shame one of his loyal men for so little reason. No doubt he'd given her no choice. For the hundredth time in my life, I thanked the Goddess that I wasn't noble-born. Benoic might have told me more, but Waryn returned with the cups, and Ddary with two flagons, a big one of dark ale and a small one of Bardek wine.

"The innkeep's lad is bringing up fresh bread," Ddary announced, "and a rack of mutton for us, and a leg for Cathvar. Raw, I told them, for the leg."

"Excellent!" I said.

Splendid! Cathvar said. This fellow has some good qualities after all.

More than a few, mayhap, despite the rough way about him.

That evening, when the men and Waryn slept, and Cathvar drowsed at the foot of my bed in our chamber, I lay awake considering Benoic's story and the fate of Lady Yvva. I wondered if she approved of her arranged marriage. The nosy old woman that I am would have liked to get a look at her, but on the morrow the caravan would ride on westward and take us with it. Unless somehow or other we met the lady and her father on the road—not likely, unless I put some effort into creating a coincidence.

It's possible, if you know the ways of the dweomer lore, to make certain things attract each other as if they were a lodestone and a bit of iron. It's a matter of astral currents, of directing their flow here and there. Now, if I had no right to meddle, the dweomer would fail.

If I did have the right, I'd get to meet the lady some way or another, if not on this trip, then when I passed through Bryn Tamig on my way home.

The rain came down hard in the night. The day, however, dawned clear and warm. We rejoined our caravan and headed west for the pass. About a mile out, Graun the caravanmaster rode up next to me. He pointed uphill to our right.

"Lord Marc's dun," he said.

Well-built stone walls surrounded what appeared to be a large complex. Over the walls I could see the tops of several tall stone towers clustering around an even taller central broch.

"Very impressive," I said.

"It is, but the tavern gossip told me that he's heavily in debt."

"Indeed? And is his daughter betrothed to a wealthy man?"

"So the townsfolk I met told me."

"Gossip about the noble-born is always splendid entertainment. Especially for the folk in these small towns."

"As good as bard song, truly." Graun grinned at me. "Marc's so poor that he's sold off half the dun's furnishings, they told me. Aeryn has a rich vein of silver on his clan's lands up in the hills. He's leased it out to some of the Mountain Folk. They pay him a goodly fee every year."

"I see. How did Marc end up in poverty?"

"Most lords out here are always short up for coin. But in his case, his second son ran up huge gambling debts, and the lord felt honor-bound to pay them off after he sent the lad into exile."

"Ah, so the marriage is important to his lordship, then."

Like an omen a silver horn rang out. The heavy wooden gates to the dun began to creak open. Graun turned his horse into the open road and began to call for a halt. Through the opening in the dun gates I could just make out a group of riders.

"Get the mules to one side, lads," Graun yelled. "The noble-born will want the road!"

In a swirling confusion of mud and brays and oaths the caravan got itself moved over just as the gates held steady. The horn sang out again as the riders walked their horses through the gates and out onto the hillside path that led down our way. A hawking party, it turned out to be, and sure enough, a lovely dark-haired lass in a white, gray, and blue tartan riding habit rode sidesaddle among them. I cackled in glee like a hag.

Before they joined the main road, the noble-born paused their horses off to one side in order to allow the muleteers to settle their stock. Lord Aeryn and a stout older man sat on horseback at the head of their party. Since the older fellow wore brigga in the white, gray, and blue tartan, he was noble-born and most likely the lady's father, Lord Marc. Lady Yvva rode next to him. Behind them came three pages, carrying hooded hawks, a groom, a couple of servants riding mules, and a cager struggling along behind. I could see that Aeryn was talking, not that I could hear him. Lady Yvva smiled and nodded at intervals as she idly surveyed our caravan. All at once her face flushed, then turned pale. She'd seen Benoic. I turned in the saddle and saw that the silver dagger had gone tense and still. He might have been carved out of wood, like a rider-figure in a temple of Epona.

Lord Aeryn had seen him, too. He spurred his horse and headed straight for us at a trot.

Time for a jest, Cathvar said.

Before I could say him nay, the leopard rose up in his peculiar saddle and growled. Aeryn's horse bucked straight up. His lordship went flying into the rain-filled ditch beside the road. Freed, the horse kicked out, then leapt the ditch and raced across the meadow with the groom chasing after. Cathvar lay back down again and began to lick a paw as if nothing had happened. The servants hesitated, just briefly, but they did hesitate before dismounting and running over to help Aeryn out of the ditch. Not a popular fellow, though an extremely muddy one, he yelled and blustered as he scrambled back to the road. I looked for Lady Yvva and saw that she'd clasped a hand over her mouth. I could just see enough of her aura to know that she was honestly distressed for his sake. So! She liked the marriage well enough—or the wealth it would bring her.

"You!" Aeryn pulled his sword and pointed it at Benoic. "You did that on purpose."

The muleteers all broke out laughing, partly at the very thought, and partly because duckweed festooned Aeryn's beautiful sword. Lord Marc was grinning and trying not to laugh as he rode over to join Aeryn. Apparently he enjoyed seeing his pompous son-in-law taught a little lesson. I urged my horse out of line and joined them.

"I hardly think we can blame anyone but that cat beast," Marc said. "Good dame, is it yours?"

"He is, your lordship," I said. "I'm afraid he was startled by a stranger's fast approach. He's perfectly tame. I'm sure all the men on the caravan will vouch for that."

"They wouldn't be traveling with him if he wasn't, truly." Marc leaned down to speak to Aeryn. "Mount up behind me, and we'll go back to the dun. You could use a bit of a wash."

Aeryn shook his head no. He pulled the duckweed off his sword and threw it on the ground. "I want that animal killed! I've been dishonored, and I demand—I—ah, curse it!" He was trying to sheathe the sword, but mud or suchlike had clogged the scabbard.

"Now, here," Marc said. "It's a rare beast and doubtless valuable. The caravan's moving on and taking it away."

"Besides," I said, "you're the one who frightened him. He's my guard, and you were riding straight for me."

"I wasn't riding for you, but that cursed silver dagger!"

Lord Marc swung his head around and for the first time noticed Benoic. No matter what his daughter felt, Marc winced so painfully that I knew he regretted sending Benoic away.

"Why?" I spoke to Aeryn. "To admit, perhaps, that you're the one who stole that brooch and put it into his gear?"

Caught utterly off-guard, Aeryn froze. He stared up at me wide-eyed but said not a word. I turned to the older lord and smiled in an apologetic way.

"I've heard the tale from Benoic," I said. "I'd be curious to hear what you think of it."

"Now, here!" Marc snapped. "I don't discuss such things on the open road."

"Not in front of a pack of commoners? Would his lordship prefer to hold a hearing in his chamber of justice?"

"Hold your tongue, you old crone!" Aeryn set his hands on his hips in a gesture meant to be defiant, but his soaked clothing made a squelching sound and spoiled the effect. A gobbet of mud slid from his hair down his cheek. He swore and wiped it away.

Marc scowled first at him, then at me. "I've no reason to doubt Lord Aeryn's word that he found the brooch in Benoic's saddlebag."

"Oh, I don't doubt it, either. Especially if his lordship put it there."

Aeryn squalled.

"Whatever makes you think that?" Marc said, and he sounded so surly that I figured he'd had doubts all along. "Admittedly, someone else might have done so, a servant or suchlike. There's no reason to suspect Lord Aeryn."

"Oh, but there is! My dear Lord Marc, who else would have had access to your daughter's chamber? Would her maid have dared touch her box of trinkets?"

From behind me I heard Ddary whoop in delight. Marc looked at me, then looked at Aeryn. "Well?" Marc said. "I can't believe that a noble-born man like you would lie about this. Could she be right?"

Aeryn snarled under his breath, a nastier little sound than ever Cathvar's growl could be. "I was sick to my guts of seeing that— that—commoner staring at my betrothed."

"Indeed?" I said. "Or did she have a habit of returning those stares?"

Aeryn's face flushed scarlet. "None of your affair, you old crone! What matters is, I wanted him gone!"

"You might have challenged him honorably," I said. "Or is he a better swordsman than you?"

Aeryn spun around and stalked off down the road in the direction of Lady Yvva and the pages, who all still waited where they'd halted. Lord Marc gave me a twisted grin.

"Benoic could have beaten him in a trice," Lord Marc said with a sigh. "I fear me I've been a fool."

I arranged my best sad smile. "Or too honorable, my lord, to see dishonor in another noble-born man."

"A nice balm for my wound, good dame, but naught more. My thanks. May I have a word with your silver dagger?"

"By all means."

When I motioned to Benoic, he rode up next to us. He made a half-bow from the saddle to the man whom he'd once sworn to serve.

"I owe you an apology," Marc said. "Yvva will be going to her husband's dun in three days' time. Will you return to mine and your old position, Captain?"

Benoic squeezed his eyes shut for a few brief moments, then shook his head no. He looked the lord full in the face. "I've been a dishonored man and a silver dagger. Nothing will ever take that away, my lord." He smiled, a tight cold gesture of pure rage that belied his next words. "I'd only shame you if I rode with your warband again."

"I'd not see it that way."

"I would," Benoic said. "My thanks, but I'll ride the road the gods have given me." With that he clucked to his horse, turned it around, and trotted back to the end of the line.

Marc started to speak, then merely shrugged. He nodded my way, then called out to the caravanmaster, "You may have the road. We're returning to the dun."

Yet the lord's party waited while the caravan got itself moving again, all except for Aeryn. The groom had retrieved the lordling's horse, and Aeryn was already riding up the hill to the dun. Once the caravan began filing past, Lady Yvva urged her horse up close to our line of march.

"Benno!" she called out. "Benno, forgive me!"

Benoic said not one word, nor did he turn in the saddle to look her way. She raised a gloved hand to her eyes and wept.

For the rest of that day, and when we camped at night, Benoic spoke to no one but Cathvar. Even then, all he said was, "my thanks." I hoped that he might unburden himself to me, but he never brought the matter up, not once during our long ride to Haen Marn.

At the ferry to the island we parted. I paid the lads their hire, and they rode off on their long road. Some months ago, that was, and I'm still at Haen Marn, though the gods only know where the lads are now. At times, when I take a moment's rest from copying out the book I found, the one about healing injuries from fire, I think of Benoic and hope that he fares well.